ALSO BY C

CHRISTMAS WITH A CRANK

A LOVE STORY

COURTNEY WALSH

Sweethaven
Press

CHAPTER 1

OLIVE

*W*hen I agreed to participate in the Pine Creek Tree Farm's Ugly Christmas Sweater Contest, I forgot my mother had such a competitive streak.

The woman is so determined to win that she went out and bought the most hideous sweaters she could find.

There were eight.

She handed them out last night after Thanksgiving dinner, an expectant look on her face.

I think my favorite was the one with Nicolas Cage's face on it.

Merry Cage-Mas it read, in knitted, slightly off-center block letters.

It's not the one I was given, however.

Horrified (and amused) expressions pinballed around the living room, from me to my brother Benji, to my best friend Phoebe, to my dad, before finally settling on my mom.

She looked positively perky.

"Aren't they absolutely perfect?" she'd asked, holding her own sweater, which, once I looked more closely, was more of a poncho with stripes of actual tinsel and ornaments attached to it. She gave the sweater a shake, and it jingled.

"We're going to win this year," she said like a Bond villain, a conspiratorial glint in her eye.

Looking at the array of machine-woven assaults to our eyes and the color wheel, I couldn't argue. I knew that there was absolutely no way anyone in their right mind would don sweaters as offensive as these.

Now, standing outside the Christmas tree farm, I tug my coat around my torso a little tighter. I have no delusions of escaping this fiasco, and I know the rules. In order to win, the entire team has to remain in their sweaters for the duration of the party.

Whoever came up with this contest is a sadist.

Phoebe emerges from inside the car after reapplying very red lipstick to her very full lips. I frown at her. "Lipstick?" Phoebe is perpetually dating, always looking for the right guy but running into all the wrong ones.

She gives me an exasperated look. "I'm just putting out the vibe."

"Do you actually think you're going to meet a guy at this party?" I give her a once-over. "In that sweater?"

Hers was the one with the dachshund in the oversized sunglasses. The dachshund was *also* wearing a sweater. That lit up.

She shrugs. "It could happen."

"Nobody is going to look twice at us when we're dressed like this."

"Oh, they'll look twice," she smirks, opening her coat and clicking the small battery pack on the inside of her sweater.

The glow from alternating green and red LED's dance on my face, which isn't amused.

"See, that's your problem, Olive. You're too cynical." She takes me by the shoulders and shakes me. "There are opportunities *everywhere.*" She whispers that last word for dramatic effect.

"I'm taking a break from men, remember?" I say because Phoebe isn't the only one who's endured a string of bad first dates, and the last one, who actually stuck his finger in my coffee, was the last straw.

"That would imply that you, at one time, feasted on them," Phoebe cracks.

She and I both know that's not the case. Taking a break from men for me is like taking a break from deep sea diving.

Which is to say that I haven't dove headfirst in like, ever.

She continues her ribbing. "Are you sure you want to fast men during the holidays?"

I resist the urge to whine. After enduring another solo Thanksgiving dinner yesterday, for the third year running, I really don't need any more humiliation. "Yes. I'm sure. I can't keep doing the dating app thing. It's unnatural. And weird, frankly. The guys say the grossest things. I've had horrible luck."

Phoebe frowns. "That's because you go into every date thinking he might be Mr. Forever. Think of him as, you know, Mr. Right Now," she glances over at me, "or at least Mr. Keep Me Occupied For The Next Hour or So While I Eat This Salad."

I sigh. It's just not how I'm built. I don't want Mr. Right Now. "I think I'm going to focus on myself for a while." Lord knows I have a lot of work to do.

"Well, that's depressing."

I shoot her a look.

She changes her face. "I mean, it's *great!* How modern of you—self-care and all that." She reaches inside her collar, clicks another button, and the knitted Christmas lights on her sweater light up. "I'm here to party." She pumps her eyebrows.

"How many battery packs does that thing have?" I ask, still not amused.

She shimmies her shoulders, and I stifle a smile.

I'm not here to party. I'm itchy.

"Let's just get this over with," I grumble, knowing I need to fix my attitude.

"Oh, come on, you mud stick. It's going to be so fun!" She prances off, as I trail behind, thinking she meant to say *stick in the mud*, but mud stick is more apropos.

I really just want to be home in my knitted slippers working on the big chunky scarf I'm knitting my mom for Christmas.

The tree farm is a Pleasant Valley staple, and every year, on the day after Thanksgiving, the Williams-Fisher family hosts a Christmas Kick-Off celebration in their barn. I've always loved it out here. The smell of the pine trees alone makes it instantly feel like Christmas. Add in all the decor, the Christmas shop, the white twinkle lights . . . and it's next level. A tradition I, like so many others, have come to rely on.

And, with the exception of the abomination I'm currently hiding under my coat, I love Christmas and all its traditions.

Phoebe, who seems to be running on lipstick and delusion, leads us to the door of the barn, and when we walk inside, we quickly realize that we are among a very small minority of people who are actually competing in the Ugly Christmas Sweater contest.

I tense up, and Phoebe links her arm through mine. "The trick is to own it. My boobs will twinkle like the top of the Chrysler Building."

I frown at her. "Are we really doing this?"

"It'll make your mother so happy when we win."

True.

I'm comfortable in my skin, and secure in who I am—but even I can admit my confidence these past few years has been shaken.

Bad business decisions coupled with bad dating decisions all happening in a small town? Disaster.

I know I'm disappointing everyone. I know I was supposed

to do more with my life. I was on a certain path, and I took a nosedive . . . and now I'm working odd jobs to try to keep my head above water and wondering if I'll ever recover.

For someone who loves Christmas, I'm struggling to jingle.

"Girls! You're here!" My parents emerge from a small crowd standing off to the side, and when she sees me, my mother beams. "Olive, let's see it."

"We're for sure still doing this?" I ask, taking a cursory glance around the barn. "Nobody else is wearing an ugly sweater."

"Not true," my mom says. "The entire Jenkins family is decked out. And they have seven kids." Her eyes narrow. "That's big competition."

"Right, but their kids are all under the age of twelve." I see Josephine Williams-Fisher making her way through the crowd, and she's headed right for us.

The Fishers used to live next door to us, but when I was twelve, they moved here to run the farm. Jo said it was her duty to the town—and to the family—to keep it going, so she and Brant moved to Pine Creek and took it over. The tree farm is in the Loveland school district, so that meant their kids, Liam and Lacey, didn't go to school with Benji and me anymore.

The four of us were inseparable back then, and it was hard when they weren't right next door. But we had the kind of childhood that kids don't have anymore. Running around outside, riding bikes to the park, eating picnics on the grass.

When they moved, we sort of lost touch, the way you do when you're twelve and you aren't in control of your own transportation. Sure, we'd run into each other occasionally, and I'd hear bits of gossip about the Fisher kids over the years, but mostly—sadly—the close bond of friendship we were poised to have for life slowly disappeared.

I absently wonder if Liam or Lacey ever come home

anymore. If I had lived at Pine Creek, I don't think I would've ever left.

"Olive, look at you!" Jo says when she reaches us. She's older now, but you'd only know it by the gray in her brown hair. Her big, hospitable energy is still intact. "Your mother says she gave you the best sweater of the bunch."

Everyone laughs, including me. I try to get the attention off me by pointing to Benj. He whips open his coat and says, "Merry Cage-Mas!" Phoebe catches a giggle in her throat, giving me a shove.

"*That* will be hard to top." Jo turns to me. "Come on. Let's go. I absolutely *must* see yours." She squeezes my shoulder, and I notice we've now drawn the attention of a small crowd. People I see often—in town, at the coffee shop, at the post office, at the farmer's market.

These people will never look at me the same way again after I take off this coat.

And then, before I can make a move, a familiar—yet unfamiliar—face emerges from the crowd.

Liam. Fisher.

"Whoa," I hear Phoebe whisper beside me, echoing my exact thought.

I freeze. So I guess that answers my question.

He does come home for holidays.

Liam seems to be on a mission and doesn't notice me standing here. Given what I'm wearing, that's a good thing, but I also take it as an opportunity to stare at him.

And then, I'm five years old, roller skating down the sidewalk and I fall. My knee screams in pain as blood begins trailing down my leg. A younger version of the man standing in front of me, a six-year-old with a mop of dark curls and bright green eyes, is at my side. He holds my hand. He wipes my tears. He is so kind, even at that young age.

Liam has the same dark hair and bright green eyes, but he's

tall now, has the start of a beard, and is a little disheveled. I try—fail—to recall the things I've heard about him over the years.

Nobody ever mentioned he grew up to look like this.

"Mom, Grandma has questions about peppermint sticks?" Liam says, an edge in his voice.

"Oh! Yes! For the hot chocolate bar," Jo says. "Shoot. I forgot." She shakes her head, then to me she says, "Olive, Liam can take your coat." She looks at him with a knowing glance. "He's *supposed* to be working the coat check counter."

Now, he looks at me. I search his eyes for a hint of recognition, but he barely acknowledges me. "I just needed some air," he says.

I know how he feels. Because with him standing this close to me, I also need air. And possibly CPR.

Which is dumb because this is *Liam*. Boy next door Liam. The kid who thinks people getting hit in the head with a football is funny. The kid who hit lightning bugs with the big red Wiffle Ball bat to watch them light up as they arc to the ground.

Kind, yes, but also totally annoying.

And a perfect stranger to me now.

Jo must notice me staring, because her expression shifts and she says, "Oh, gosh, it's been ages since you two have seen each other, hasn't it?"

"Uh, yeah, uh, it's been, I mean, um. . ." I stutter.

"Sound it out. Use your words," Phoebe whispers, and not quietly.

"Liam, good grief, will you say hi?" Jo says.

He does that annoying chin lift thing guys do when they think they're being cool, and I straighten.

My mother, always ready to make awkward situations *more* awkward, steps forward. "Olive was just about to show off the sweater I bought her for the contest." Then to Liam, like a pirate captain not wanting to give up where he buried the treasure, "we really want to win this year."

My cheeks flame. My entire head is about to light on fire. And Liam, I notice, is wearing an unmistakable look of amusement, his brow quirked in expectation. Unlike me, he's dressed in jeans and a simple navy blue henley.

He looks good in it.

"Let's see it, Olive," Jo says. "Before my mother-in-law has a meltdown over peppermint sticks."

There's no way out of this. I'm going to have to unveil this hideous sweater.

But then I see my mother, watching me with quiet excitement, and I know Phoebe is right. She loves this stuff. Christmas isn't a single day for her, it's a whole season. Winning this trophy and first pick of the cut-your-own Christmas trees, silly as it may seem, means something to her.

So, I need to suck it up and force myself to be a good sport.

Even if it means looking like a complete fool in front of half the town.

And now, in front of Liam.

Slowly, I unzip my coat, and when I slip it off my shoulders, Mom lets out a squeal of what can only be described as glee.

"Oh, my goodness, Marcia, you weren't kidding," Jo says, surveying my sweater. "It's perfect! I wish I was judging this year"—she reaches over and squeezes my arm— "you'd take home first prize for sure."

I wince.

The sweater, in all its glory, is cream colored, with playful sparks of red, green, and gold peppering the front, sides, and arms. And, of course, what makes this sweater *super amazing* is the faux coconut bra knit over my chest, lovingly draped with holly.

And below the coconut bra is a facsimile of six pack abs because it's made to look like a man. As if one couldn't tell by the fake chest hair sticking out from behind the coconut bra.

In addition, this sweater would be perfect for someone who is, let's say, more buxom than me.

To finish off the look, right underneath the abs, are the words *Mele Kalikimaka.*

My face is officially on fire.

Even Phoebe is having a hard time controlling her giggles.

My brother is outright laughing, pointing his phone at me. "Oh my gosh, it's so much worse on!" Then, after a pause and what I'm guessing is a burst of photos, he adds, "I love it!"

I try to own it. "Feast your eyes, buddy. And don't forget that you've got Nicolas Cage on your stomach."

"Nic isn't *nearly* as offensive as that." He looks at our mom and cracks, "I thought you didn't want her to be single for the holidays."

"I don't," Mom says, eyes wide. "I think she looks adorable."

"She doesn't," Benji says, still chuckling.

Mom swats him across the arm, then looks at me. "You do, Olive. You look so festive."

My mom isn't old enough to think this sweater is festive. She *is* old enough, however, to lament the fact that I'm facing yet another solo holiday season. And Benji's right—she's not helping the cause. The threads of faux chest hair should've clued her in.

"Judging will be in about an hour," Jo says brightly. "Have fun until then!"

The small crowd disperses, but before they do, my eyes drift to Liam's. He gives me an amused smile, and before he walks away, he says, "Nice coconuts."

CHAPTER 2

LIAM

*C*oat station.

May as well be Shawshank.

I'm standing behind the counter, trying to calculate how long it's been since I was actually home for the Pine Creek Christmas Kick-Off.

The years away have stacked up so much that they blend together.

I look around the entrance, thick log walls and sparkly lights, thinking about how Pine Creek has been in our family for ages. My great-great-grandparents bought the land, built the old farmhouse, and each generation has added to the property.

Generational fingerprints.

Now, there are multiple barns, stables, out buildings, the café, and acres and acres of trees.

I should feel at peace here, but I don't.

I should feel calm and relaxed out in nature, surrounded by the scent of pine and spruce, but I don't.

Maybe because I was given the keys to this forest kingdom— and I walked away.

My first adult decision, and I still don't think my dad has forgiven me for it.

I half-smile as I take a stack of coats from a family of four with two little girls in cream and velvety red dresses. As I hand them the return tickets, I see the glint of wonder and awe in their faces, the pointing and giggling, the vying for who gets to be first in line . . . it should make me feel something, shouldn't it?

But it doesn't.

It's like this whole place has lost its luster.

Not that it matters. I don't even live here anymore.

I have a whole life in Indianapolis. A whole world outside of this slice of rural land between Pleasant Valley and Loveland.

A world I need to get back to because it's basically falling apart.

My plan was simple. Come for Thanksgiving, make an appearance, then go back to Indy the next morning. I hadn't expected my parents to drop a bombshell the second the dessert plates had been cleared.

The last Pine Creek Christmas. Ever.

I know they didn't do that to get me to stay. I know everything isn't always about me. But seriously, how could I leave when it might be the last Christmas Kick-Off my family ever hosts?

Somewhere around the corner there's a big reaction with hearty laughter.

I sigh.

Where is Lacey? My sister swore she'd be here tonight, but so far, there's no sign of her. Unfortunately, the same can't be said for my grandmother who has been insisting I meet her best friend's granddaughter, Janine, because she's "just who I've been looking for in a wife."

How do I politely explain that I'm not looking for a wife? Or anyone?

I'm about to slip out from behind the counter when Olive appears on the opposite side of it, still wearing that goofy coconut sweater. My mind flicks back to vanilla ice cream and a sunlit treehouse.

And a fumbling first ki—.

"Hey," she says, thankfully interrupting my memory.

"Hey."

Her eyes dart up to mine, and she shifts, folding her arms across the coconuts. "I'm wearing it for my mom." Her misery is evident. "She *really* wants to win that competition."

I take her coat and hand her a ticket. "Sounds like her. She always was a bit competitive."

"A bit?" She holds in a laugh. "Do you remember the living museum we had to do in third grade?"

I do. Her mom dressed her in a full Abraham Lincoln outfit, and even rented drywall stilts to make her taller.

"She's nuts," she adds.

"Well, it's nice of you to make such a . . . uh . . ." I gesture to her outfit, "sacrifice."

"I look like a retired male hula dancer." She grumbles then closes her eyes and pinches the bridge of her nose. "This is more humiliating than Thanksgiving dinner."

I pull out a hanger and slide her coat onto it.

She opens her eyes, continuing her story as if I've asked her to go on. "My brother brought his new girlfriend, which would normally be totally fine, but he didn't tell anyone she was coming, so there weren't enough spots at the table. Since I was alone, they moved me to the kids' table."

"Sounds fun," I say, finding it odd that she's talking to me like we were mid-conversation and she came back to finish. People don't usually talk to me this much.

Maybe because I don't respond.

"Yeah, it really wasn't because my cousin's stupid son threw up on me." She frowns. "To quote her, 'Hey, it washes off!'" Her

face falls. "I'm sorry—I didn't mean to call him stupid. He's *fine*."
A pause. "Oh, good grief. I'm like, prattling on, and . . . you
probably don't want to hear all about . . . Yeah. It's just been how
long since . . .? And you haven't really been . . ."

So far, she's up to four sentences she's started and hasn't
finished.

So I wait.

"I'm so whiny! And you're probably like, 'give me your coat
and get out of here, you weirdo.'" Her face brightens, and I note
she still has the same trail of freckles across the bridge of her
nose.

I used to love those freckles.

When I don't respond, Olive starts fidgeting. I should speak
up. Ask her how she's been. Find out what she's been doing with
her life since her store closed.

But I don't. I can't figure out how to get past my desire to
not be here right now.

It dawns on me that the reason I don't know anything about
Olive's life is that to find out I'd actually have to answer my
mom's calls.

When I see her name pop up on my phone it feels . . . heavy
somehow. Like facing things I don't want to face. Or talking
about things I don't want to.

My mom walks up, and I see relief on Olive's face. I've never
been great at conversation.

That's not true. I used to be totally fine.

"Hi, kids," Mom says. "Olive, I wonder if you could come out
to the farm tomorrow. Do you have time for a chat?"

Olive frowns. "Uh, sure. Is everything okay?"

Mom's eyes jump to mine, then back to Olive. "Oh, yeah! No,
I just have a few things I'd like to run by you. Lacey's coming
home—you can come for dinner. It'll be fun!"

Olive's brow furrows in confusion. She glances at me and I
look away. "Okay."

My mom looks from Olive to me and back again. "I'm so glad you two are catching up. Liam, did you tell her about your latest video game?"

My stomach knots. It's the last thing I want to talk about.

"Oh, right! Video games! I was trying to remember what you do. That is such a cool job!"

Olive looks genuinely interested.

Usually, only video game people are genuinely interested. Overly interested once they find out where I work.

I stand there, aware they're both watching me, waiting for me to launch into some big story about how great the game is doing. The game I've worked tirelessly on—my chance to prove that I wasn't a one-hit wonder.

The game that got me sidelined for the foreseeable future.

"Uh, well, I mean, it's not that big of a deal." I feel myself squirming.

"Oh, come on, it's amazing! I'm sure Olive would love to hear—"

"I need to get some air. I'll be right . . . Sorry, 'scuse me," I push past Olive and through the crowd.

Just get me out of here.

Pine Creek has me in a choke hold.

I make it outside and draw in a deep breath, inhaling the crisp, brisk scent of trees and the unmistakable smell of earth. It's not frigid cold, not yet, but it's cold enough to chill your lungs when you breathe in. The party is mostly in the barn, but there are people out here. Down by the fire pit, on the chairs of the porch, walking through the rows of Christmas trees. They have no idea that tomorrow we'll officially open for our last Christmas season at Pine Creek.

My emotions are . . . mixed. And I don't know why. I'll finally be free of the guilt that this is my legacy. A legacy I never asked for and don't want.

I should be ecstatic. It's exactly what I've hoped for—a

chance to choose for myself without the pressure of "doing the right thing" for my family.

But I'm not ecstatic, and it doesn't make sense.

This place stole so much from me—shouldn't I walk away without a second thought?

I glance back to the main barn, and I see Olive through the large front window, backlit from the enormous Christmas tree in the main entrance.

And for some reason, walking away doesn't feel as easy as it should.

CHAPTER 3

LIAM

*T*he morning after the Kick-Off party, I'm up before the sun, mostly because the farm is too quiet. Silence does nothing to smooth out the anxious thoughts bouncing around in my head.

When I first moved to Indianapolis, I had a hard time getting used to the noise. It's not New York or Chicago, but it's a city. A clean one. One with a walkable downtown and art installations and neat lines—but it's still noisier than here.

I realize the bustle keeps me out of my head.

I pull on a sweatshirt and walk into the kitchen, where my mom is standing at the counter under the dim light of the oven hood, stirring something in a bowl.

I can smell the vanilla and cinnamon, and I'm instantly struck by a pang of nostalgia.

She looks up when she hears me and smiles. "Hey, sunshine. Lacey got in late, finally. She'll probably sleep 'til noon."

My younger sister is a self-proclaimed free spirit who has been traveling across the country for the last six months in an old van that she had outfitted into a living space. She works remotely, forages things if she needs them, and documents the entire experience on social media. She stops to interview people, and she's found this whole community just like her, living in refurbished vehicles and camping on beach fronts. Somehow, she's found a way to pay for this vagabond life.

To her credit, it's kind of brilliant. Go see the world while you're young and have nothing tying you down? Yes, please.

However, my parents think she's running from something. Home? Responsibility? Love? All of the above? I'm not sure, but given her personality, I'm guessing she won't stick around Pine Creek for long. She's created this off-the-grid life for herself where she doesn't have to think about the real world.

Must be nice.

"Did you tell her about—"

Mom shakes her head and cracks an egg into a bowl. "Not yet."

I make a face. The real world is coming for her. Because our parents are going to need her help. I've got a life and a condo and a job to figure out how to keep, and she's got a van.

"Let me guess—" I nod at the bowl— "chocolate chip pancakes?"

My mom smiles. "Everyone's favorite."

I pour myself a cup of coffee then sit down on the barstool across from her.

She cracks another egg. "Are you okay?" She looks at me. "You never came back in last night."

I know she thinks it was rude of me to walk out like I did, but I've got a lot on my mind. The farm. My sister. Work. It's a lot. But all I say is, "I'm fine."

"Good, because Olive is coming for dinner tonight, and I want you to be nice." She briefly looks up at me and then quickly back down at the bowl.

"Okay, I'm going to stop you right there."

She shrugs innocence. "What? I'm not doing anyth—"

"You're trying to play matchmaker," I say. "You need to give it up. I'm not interested."

She frowns. "Why not? She's adorable."

That's a fact. Olive *is* adorable. But I'm not the same kid I was all those years ago—the one who pined away for her like she lived on some balcony and I spoke in iambic pentameter.

"It's not about Olive," I say. "I'm not interested in dating anyone. I have more important things to worry about."

She frowns. "You do? Like what?"

I start to reply but stop. I feel stupid talking about it. It's too hard to explain anyway. I'll just figure it out myself.

I look up and see her watching me. "You're doing that thing where you don't talk."

I don't respond.

"Well, I'm not going to apologize for pushing you to be nice to an adorable girl," she says as she takes the bowl over to the stove. "And I'm not going to stop talking to you." She narrows her eyes at me.

I give in and smile. As much as I'm not a fan of gushing about feelings or even talking about what's bothering me, I do appreciate her not giving up on me.

I change the subject. "Selling this place is more important than finding me a date anyway. Getting it ready, fixing things, listing it so you can get the most money—all of that is way more important."

She waves me off. "I'd rather sell it to someone who's passionate about it."

"Well, that's not practical," I retort.

She sighs. "I know. There aren't many people who want to take on a Christmas tree farm." She looks up at me. "But that won't keep me from hoping."

I sigh. Everyone always romanticizes this place, when they should see it for what it is—a money-sucking business that can barely make ends meet. This isn't a rom-com. Nobody is going to swoop in and save this place.

"Besides," she adds, "I don't want to think about any of that until *after* Christmas."

"That's a mistake," I say, certain I'm right. "Potential buyers could come out and see how things run. They could see the crowds of people and—"

Mom grimaces.

"What?"

"It might be better if they *don't* see that." She cracks another egg in the bowl. "People aren't exactly busting down the doors here." She starts scrambling the eggs. "It's just not like it was when you were kids. People have artificial trees. They spend less quality time with their families. The shop does okay, but most of the year it just collects dust."

"So, this is a financial issue?" I ask, thinking about the times I tried to convince them to expand. The times my dad shot me down. The times I realized this *legacy* wasn't one I wanted—not like this. Still, I hear myself say, "Because you could adapt and build a few—"

She holds up the spoon to cut me off. "When your father agreed to move out here and take over the farm, he did that for me. Because this place was home to me. And because it was part of our family for so many years."

"He didn't want to move here?"

She leans against the counter. "This was never his dream."

I frown. If that's true, then why did he pitch it to me like it was? Why try to push it on me? To guilt me into taking it over? The day I switched my major from agriculture to game design was the first time I ever made a decision for myself, and I didn't tell my parents for an entire year.

If you want to get technical, I didn't tell him at all. He found out. Town gossip strikes again. Come to think of it, that probably hurt him in ways I didn't intend it to.

My parents aren't villains. I just don't like hard conversations. Some things never change.

Mom goes on. "And when you and Lacey moved away, well, it just became clear that maybe it's time to hand our legacy over to someone else. And to let your dad do what he wants to do."

"Which is what?"

She shrugs. "We're still figuring it out, but he has a friend who works for a baseball team in Colorado. They need a bookkeeper, and your dad is qualified, but we also want to travel. The money from the sale will allow us to do that, so . . ."

Colorado?

If they move to Colorado, there won't be any reason for me to come back here. Why isn't that thought more comforting?

I press. "But there's no guarantee that whoever buys it will keep your traditions going."

"No, there isn't."

"They could bulldoze the trees and build a—resort or something." I'm so confused. This was always my father's argument, or guilt trip, depending on which side of the conversation you found yourself on.

Has he forgotten? It doesn't make sense. Am I really supposed to believe he's done a complete one-eighty?

"And we'll have to make our peace with that." She picks up a knife, cuts into the butter, and drops a pat of it into the frying pan. She sounds resigned.

And the pang of guilt is back. I know that nothing would make my mother happier than for me, or Lacey, or both of us, to say we'd change our lives, move back here, take things over, just like they did. Just to keep this place going.

But I can't. I won't. There's no way.

Unlike most people, my feelings for Pine Creek aren't exactly warm with marshmallows on top.

Growing up, I noticed that most people came here for fun, or because it was an important part of their holiday traditions—

or they just wanted a live tree. To me, Pine Creek was an anchor. Or a straitjacket.

First, it took me away from the home and friends and school I loved, and soon after, it became a burden. A responsibility. A *have to*, never a *want to*.

I take a drink, trying to figure out why my feelings are so conflicted. This is good news. Pine Creek will finally be off my shoulders. No more farm. No more legacy. No more guilt.

So, what is nagging at me?

Mom pours batter onto the skillet in a practiced, perfected motion. "We aren't going to get into the sale of the farm stuff until after the New Year. We want to make this Christmas the best one we've ever had at Pine Creek. Really go out with a bang." She smiles, but I see sadness in her eyes. "That's why I'm meeting with Olive."

I frown. "Why?"

"Because she's brilliant and creative and I need her help," Mom says pointedly, as if it's obvious. "And you're going to be nice to her."

"I'm not *not* nice."

Mom shoots me a look. "You weren't nice last night."

Guilt nips at the realization.

But I don't *feel* like being nice. My mom thinks that because Olive and I have a shared history, ancient history at that, it makes her special somehow. It really doesn't. I'm sure she's a great person now, but she's just a girl I used to know when we were kids.

At least that's what I'm telling myself.

The image of a college-aged Olive enters my mind. It had been years since I'd seen her, but I recognized her the second she and her friends showed up at the farm for the party I'd thrown when my parents were gone for the weekend.

I was instantly drawn to her. I kept angling around the barn to keep her in my sightline. She almost made me forget that I was angry and had a giant chip on my shoulder.

Almost.

Being around her, even for a short time, made me forget that I'd turned down an internship because my dad needed me at home, working on the farm that summer.

It wasn't even a conversation between him and me—he just said, "Oh, that won't work. We're counting on you."

I was mad. Bitter. Frustrated. So I invited everyone I knew to come out to Pine Creek while they were out of town.

I didn't expect Olive.

I didn't expect preteen feelings for her to resurface so easily.

And I didn't expect her to walk right up to me like no time had passed. Like we were still two kids, communicating through our own made-up Morse code using flashlights shone into our respective bedrooms, spending summer days that lasted forever in the treehouse, sheltered from the rest of the world.

She was *exactly* the same.

It was like I'd been given a second chance with my first crush —a real chance, because we weren't kids anymore.

But things don't often work out the way they do in your juvenile fantasies. My only saving grace was that my friends and family never knew the truth of how I felt or of how that night went sideways.

"Liam?"

I glance up and realize the memory took me away for a minute. I missed whatever question my mom now expects me to answer. "Yeah?"

"I asked how long you're going to stay," she says. "Can you stay through the holidays?"

Everything's changed. My "quick weekend trip" turned into an open-ended stay the second my dad mentioned selling Pine Creek.

I might not love it here, but I'm not a total monster. I need to help if I can.

"Yeah, Ma," I nod. "I'll stay."

"You can get the time off?" she asks. "I don't want it to interfere with work."

I'd already emailed my boss who agreed to my paid time off. After that runs out, I'll work remotely until it's time to go back.

I could tell her the truth about what I'm up against, but she's got enough on her plate, so instead I say, "I'm good."

She smiles. "Yay! Oh, that makes me so happy! Maybe we can actually catch up. You can tell me about your life. I'd love to hear how things are going. You aren't great at keeping in touch." She tosses me a look.

I know where she's going with this. "Let's talk about something else."

She waves her spatula in the air. "There are things I'd like to know, you know. I am still your mother."

Before I can protest further, Lacey opens the back door and walks in, sweaty and out of breath.

She jogs in place for a few seconds, looking at her watch. "Hey, Bill."

She's the only one who calls me that. Apparently, she feels entitled to shorten William however she wants, so long as it's not predictable.

"Hey, Shoelace," I say.

She puts her hands on her hips and inhales a deep breath.

"You're up? And running? I thought you were still sleeping," Mom says, turning toward Lacey.

"I am. And . . . I am." My sister glances at her watch, checking her stats, I think.

"When did you take up running?" Mom asks. "And did you get any sleep? You came in so late, but you must've been gone before I was even out of bed."

Lacey walks over to the refrigerator and pulls out a bottle of

23

water. "I slept. I'm good. I love the sunrise. Makes me feel grounded."

I think Lacey was born in the wrong era. She's the closest thing to a hippie that I've ever seen. She always did march to her own beat, but unlike me, she was given permission, praise even, to do so.

Nobody ever expected Lacey to be the one to take over the farm. As a result, she romanticizes this place like everyone else. To her, Pine Creek is a treasure.

"You should be careful if you're running alone when it's still dark out," Mom says. "Do you carry pepper spray?"

Lacey looks at me, and I quirk a brow.

Instead of answering, my sister changes the subject, which is always the best course of action when our mom starts parenting us like we're still children. "What are you making?"

Mom pulls the skillet out of the cupboard and sets it on the counter, her back to us. "I'm making pancakes. You *do* still eat pancakes, right?"

Lacey looks at me, and in a show of solidarity I scrunch up my face.

"Yes, Mother." My sister does nothing to hide her annoyance. "I will eat a pancake."

"And I will eat a *stack*," I say. "So make a lot."

Mom spins around. "Okay, but save room because we have our Thanksgiving dinner tonight." She says this as our dad strolls in from outside.

"Another dinner?" He closes the door behind him. "I'm still full from the first one." He rubs a hand over his belly.

"Brant!" Mom says, half scolding. "It's for our kids."

"They didn't ask for more turkey," Dad says.

"I don't even eat turkey," Lacey says.

Mom sets down her spatula, her frown deepening. "Why not?"

Lacey shrugs. "Stopped eating anything with a face or a mother."

My mom freezes mid-pour.

I lean back and watch this familiar exchange. My sister dropping some new life choice like a grenade with the pin pulled, my mother reacting, clashing ideas ricocheting their way around the kitchen as my father ducks out of their way.

"Lacey! A face or a mother? Really?"

"What? It's a perfectly acceptable way to eat." Lacey's eyes are wide, defensive.

Ah, family.

It feels normal.

I've missed *normal*.

The thought surprises me.

This could be one of the last times we're all here, being "normal," and it's stirring up feelings I don't like.

CHAPTER 4

OLIVE

*W*hy did I agree to this?

I'm the type of person who needs to know what I'm walking into. Don't text and ask if you can call me. Tell me what we're talking about or I'm not answering.

I was so caught off guard last night when Jo asked me to come for dinner, and I blindly agreed.

I forgot to get details.

And now, I'm standing on their porch.

I'm standing on their porch, holding a pan of freshly baked pumpkin bars.

I'm standing on their porch, holding a pan of freshly baked pumpkin bars, and I'm having second thoughts.

I haven't spoken to Jo outside of the Christmas Kick-Off party for years. Despite our best intentions, I didn't stay in touch with Liam or Lacey—or their parents.

I did date one of Liam's good friends for a short while, but oddly, when we went out, even in groups, Liam was never there. Now I wonder if he just grew up to be a different kind of person than the kid I remember.

Maybe rude is his personality now.

I'm still processing this and pep-talking myself when the door opens.

Liam is staring at me. He doesn't say anything.

Yep. Rude.

"Hey!" I force myself to sound more cheerful than I feel. "I was just getting ready to ring the doorbell."

If it's possible to over-smile, I do.

He doesn't. "You've been standing out here for three minutes."

I raise a brow. "Were you watching me out the window or something, creeper?"

He looks flummoxed for a second. Point for me.

"Your nose is red," he says flatly.

"Well. As you know I've been standing here for *three whole minutes* and it's freezing." I watch him. "A polite person would invite me inside."

He gives me a quizzical look, probably wondering why I didn't ring the bell sooner, but I'm thankful he doesn't ask.

I hold up the dish. "I made pumpkin bars. Felt wrong to show up empty-handed, even though I have no idea why I'm here." I say that last part quietly under my breath.

He looks at me.

"I'm still outside, Liam."

"Oh! Yeah, sorry. . ."

He moves out of the doorway, and I step inside. I swipe my stocking cap off and hold it over my cold nose for a second, letting the hot air from my lungs warm it up then set the pumpkin bars down on the entryway table. When I shrug out of my coat, I give my simple green sweater and jeans a quick once-over, hoping they're appropriate, then slip my low boots off as Liam reaches for my coat. I turn but don't let go of it right away.

"I'm not going to steal it," he says dryly. "Pink isn't my color."

A slight joke. Maybe not as rude as I thought?

I let go, and he stuffs the stocking cap into the sleeve, then hangs the coat in the front closet.

"Olive!" Jo calls out as she walks into the small space by the front door, followed by a lumbering yellow lab. "You're here!"

The dog runs an excited circle around me, and I lean down to pet its head. Liam's family always had a dog, and my family never did. The thought makes me wonder why I haven't gotten one now that I'm an adult. I *feel* like a dog person.

"This is Hank," Jo says, and then switching to baby talk she adds, "he's such a good boy."

"He's so sweet." I kneel down and rub Hank's ears as he pushes his face into my chest. I laugh, but then I turn to Liam and see his deadpan face.

He probably doesn't like dogs either. What a sourpuss.

Thank God Jo is here. Someone other than Liam to talk to. I don't know what his problem is, but I suddenly don't feel bad that I didn't keep in touch with him. I can't believe Phoebe gushed the entire way home from the party last night about how hot he is now.

I didn't object. Maybe I should've. Sorry, but rude people are not attractive. Even when their face looks like Liam's.

"Why do you think they want you to come over?" Phoebe had asked. "Do you think Jo's trying to set you guys up?"

"By inviting me to a dinner at their house?" I'd asked. "No. It's got to be something else. Plus, he's not really my type."

"Please. How do you even know that?"

I shrugged. "Eh . . . gut feeling." I'd prefer to date someone who makes better conversation than a cadaver.

"Right, because your gut has *never* been wrong before."

I took her point because I do seem to have a knack for picking the wrong guys. That started all the way back in high school, and it seems I've just never gotten the hang of it.

"Thank you so much for having me, Mrs. Fisher." I reach

across Liam for the pan of pumpkin bars that I'd set on the table next to the coat closet.

"You're an adult, and we're practically family," she says. "Call me Jo."

Practically family is a stretch. Maybe before they moved, but now? Almost twenty years later? I'm an acquaintance at best. Though, I suppose there *is* something about the people who knew you when you were becoming who you are that makes them always feel like family.

I hold up the pan. "I made pumpkin bars."

"Oh, my goodness." Jo takes them. "Cream cheese frosting?"

I nod. "Is there any other kind?"

"Your mother's recipe?"

"My grandma's actually, but Mom always leaves that part out."

Jo laughs, then glances at Liam, and her smile falls away. "What is wrong with you? Why do you look so serious?"

His frown deepens, something I never thought possible. "I don't."

"He does, doesn't he, Olive?"

I meet his eyes. "Yep. Like a grumpy statue."

I clock the tiniest raise of his eyebrow, and then Jo loops her arm through mine and tugs me toward the kitchen. "Lacey will want to say hi." Then, over her shoulder, looking back at Liam, she adds, "She remembers how to smile."

I can practically *feel* him roll his eyes.

I walk into the kitchen as Hank plunks down in the doorway and see Lacey standing on the other side of a large island. When she sees me, her face brightens. "Olive! Hi!" She walks around the island and pulls me into a tight hug. "Oh my gosh, it's been forever!"

Lacey and her brother could not be more opposite. Unlike Liam, she's got a sunshiny demeanor, and I know this because I am one of her many—many—social media followers.

"I don't feel like it's been that long because I keep up with you on Instagram," I say. "I cannot believe your whole life is traveling the country in that van." I grin. "I saw it outside. Can I get a tour later?"

"Of course, you can!" Lacey goes back to chopping vegetables. "We'll totally go for a ride."

"Can I help?" I nod at the carrots, feeling slightly out of place. I need something to do with my hands.

"It's all ready," Jo says. "We kept it simple since we just did the big dinner thing."

I hear a loud noise from somewhere in the house, a mix of a groan and something being thrown.

Jo and Lacey roll their eyes. "The Bears game is on," Jo says.

"Apparently, they're supposed to be good this year." Lacey tucks the carrot sticks on the vegetable tray, then walks it over to a long counter covered with other dishes.

We exchange all the typical catching up, small talk pleasantries, and I really just want to ask what I'm doing there. At *their* family Thanksgiving.

But I chicken out, and before I know it, I'm sitting around a beautifully decorated table, passing dishes and trying to think of something—anything—to say.

There's an odd tension in the air, and I'm not sure why.

"So, Olive, tell us about your work," Jo says. "I know you had that cute, little shop downtown for a while. I was so sorry to hear what happened."

I turn briefly to see Liam looking at me. It's not hard to let myself believe he has no idea about my failed business, and I really would've loved to keep it that way. Everyone around here, it seems, associates me with bankruptcy and failure, even though I did *not* go bankrupt.

No such luck there. I simply lost the money my grandparents gave me, and now I'm still digging myself out of that debt.

I take a drink of water and clear my throat. "Yeah. That."

Lacey jumps in, a kind savior. "Oh, she doesn't have to talk about it if she doesn't want to."

I offer a weak, grateful smile, and say, "No, it's okay. I did have a shop for a couple of years." I swallow. Is it hot in here? "Still recovering from that, I suppose, but now, I, uh, work at the coffee shop. And do odd jobs." I scrunch my nose. "I'm figuring it out."

My face flames. I'm embarrassed. It's hard to admit that the girl voted "Most Likely to Succeed" by her senior class grew up to be a giant flakey disaster.

"But Olive, you're an *artist*," Lacey says, as if talking about dreams and utopia. "I follow you on social media too."

I absentmindedly push my mashed potatoes around on my plate. "Oh, it's not that big of a deal."

"You should totally share more of your work—your process, the design, the behind the scenes would be fascinating."

"Lacey, sweetheart," Jo says with a laugh. "Give her a break."

Lacey shrugs. "Sorry. She's really good. I think her account could be a lot bigger."

"Thanks for that." I smile at the compliment, trying to think of the last time I posted anything on social media. The last time I created. I come up empty. I haven't had time. I *don't* have time. I'm too busy working every odd job I can find to try and pay back the loan.

"You've always been so creative," Jo says. "I am sorry the shop didn't work out."

I shrug. "I tried, right?"

"Will you try again?" Brant asks.

I draw in a breath. "Uh, I don't know. Maybe? It was, you know . . . a lot."

That's putting it nicely. It was brutal. There's nothing quite as depressing as watching a dream die. And while I don't say so, I can't imagine trying again.

Liam looks vaguely interested. Or maybe that's his default setting now.

I happen to know—thanks to my mom—that he has been very successful professionally, so I'm guessing my failure seems pretty ridiculous to him. He's probably someone who actually understands things like numbers. Someone who probably would've been smart enough to listen to everyone who said not to rush into starting a business before he was ready.

Or to everyone who said not to pursue a degree in art in the first place.

Unlike me.

"Do you miss it at all?" Lacey asks.

I set my fork down, unsure why I am the topic of conversation and really wanting to go outside to get some air. "Sometimes? Kind of?" I would love to change the subject, but I'm not sure how. "Do you mind if I use the bathroom?"

Jo's eyes go wide. "No, of course not. It's right down the hall."

I push my chair away from the table and force myself to smile, despite the uneasy feeling rumbling in my chest.

As I walk down the hall, I hear Liam say, "Way to go."

"What?" That's Lacey.

"You're freaking her out," he says. "She obviously doesn't want to talk about that stuff."

"We're just making conversation," Jo says.

"Maybe we should just get to why she's here, then."

They go quiet, and my skin prickles at possibly being caught eavesdropping. I continue down the hall, slowing to look at the gallery of framed family photos neatly hung on the wall.

There's a picture of Liam and Lacey as kids, standing in the back of the trusty, old, red Ford pickup truck with the Pine Creek logo on the side. Another one of the entire family, posed in front of the Pleasant Valley Christmas tree, which they provide for the town tree lighting every year. I lean in closer to one of the collage frames and that's when I see it—a photo of me and Liam, standing in the treehouse our dads had built right along the property line between our houses.

All at once, I'm a younger version of myself, trying to sort out the big feelings only a twelve-year-old can have, about my best friend moving away and going to a new school. Pine Creek felt like the other side of the world at that age.

Liam wouldn't have the bedroom facing mine anymore. We wouldn't be able to shine flashlights into each other's windows just to say hi. He wouldn't be twenty-eight steps from my front door.

We counted.

He was going to be way further away than twenty-eight steps, and I didn't know how to process that.

I remember the way he and I hid in the treehouse the day the moving van showed up in their driveway. As if our parents might not be able to find us. As if the van might pull away without him. He reached out and swiped a tear from my cheek, and then, in the sweetest, most innocent way, he leaned in and kissed me.

My first kiss.

The kiss by which I measure all other kisses, even though neither of us had any idea what we were doing.

It wasn't about the kiss, which was tender and awkward and perfect, so much as the way it made me feel. Like I was something special to someone, something worth remembering. Like he was going to miss me as much as I was going to miss him.

I'd given him my most prized possession—a four leaf clover I'd found on one of our hunts. I'd been so shocked I'd finally found one, and he'd been a little jealous. But now, I wanted him to have it. I thought it would keep him from forgetting me.

If you'd asked me at twelve if there would ever come a day where he wasn't a part of my life, I would've answered with an emphatic "no way." Liam was one of the best people I knew. And just when my feelings for him began to shift, he was gone, and I never got a chance to find out what we could've been.

I mentally shake off the memories like cobwebs from your gloves when you're cleaning out the attic. It was silly. Kid's stuff. A childhood crush. And yet, staring at this photo, all those hazy memories come into focus, and it feels like it was something more.

"You okay?"

I startle and turn toward Liam's voice. Heat rushes to my cheeks. "Uh, yeah, sorry."

He looks down the hall, seeing that I haven't made it to the bathroom.

I shrug. "I didn't really have to go."

He nods, but doesn't say anything. At this moment, I actually don't mind it.

He takes a step toward me, glancing up at the photo collage. "Feels like forever ago."

I smile. "Right? Forever and a lifetime." So much had happened in the years since that photo was taken.

And in those years, the boy I knew had become a stranger.

Does he remember it all the same way I do?

"Listen, whatever she's about to ask you, just remember you can say no," he says abruptly. "They have a way of making it seem like you can't."

And then he walks away.

I frown. I follow him back into the dining room.

"Everything okay?" Jo asks.

"Yep," I say, taking my seat. "I just—I have to be honest. I'm not sure what I'm doing here."

Jo and Brant exchange a quick glance, and then she turns to me. "Olive, we're selling Pine Creek."

A chill runs down my spine.

Lacey straightens and Liam avoids my eyes.

"Wait. What?"

Jo reaches over and takes Brant's hand. "It's time."

My eyes pinball around the table. "Time?"

They smile at each other, almost looking resigned to the decision. "We think we might look at some opportunities elsewhere."

"You're moving? To where?"

Brant looks at his wife. "We're not sure. We're looking into a few things, but we know we want to travel more, while we're still young enough to enjoy it. We're ready for the next adventure."

"I'm not hungry." Lacey pushes her chair back from the table and storms out of the room.

"She's . . . adjusting to the idea," Jo says when Lacey's out of earshot.

There's an uncomfortable pause, and I glance at Liam. He's pushing food around on his plate like a child getting a stern talking to, and I want to ask if he's okay. This is a really big deal.

But more than that, I'm wondering— "How do I fit in?"

Jo's smile is warm. "Well, I want you to help us make this the very best Pine Creek Christmas ever. We want to go out on a high note." She looks at Brant who smiles. They're resolute.

They're really doing this.

"Okay," I say tentatively. "How can I help?"

There's a shift in the room, like after you acknowledge the elephant in the corner, you invite it over to sit with you for a spell. "I was at your store's grand opening, Olive. I know you know how to plan an event. You're creative and smart and artistic and Liam can help with the farm side of things."

At that, my mouth goes dry. She wants me to work with Liam on this?

"I'm not an event planner," I say. "I. . .I draw things." And I want to remind her that my business failed. Is she sure she wants to put this in my hands? It feels important.

"We were hoping you'd think about it," she says. "Brainstorm some ideas so we can come out in full force. We've already got our usual things happening at the farm—Santa's Village, the Christmas shop, and the hot chocolate shed—but we want more events. A packed calendar. More reasons for people to come out here."

"But it's two days after Thanksgiving," I say dumbly. Because really—it's two days after Thanksgiving—that doesn't give us a lot of time for getting the word out.

She winces. "It's short notice, I know. This is all happening rather quickly."

"It's crazy," Liam says, suddenly and a bit forcefully. "It's a crazy idea. We should just cut our losses and get it on the market. Packing the calendar full of a bunch of events isn't going to change anything. It's just going to drag everything out."

He's right, but he gets zero points for subtlety. I wonder if he's given the chip on his shoulder a pet name.

Jo looks at him, warmth in her expression. "Liam. This is how we want to say goodbye. We want the people of this town to have a chance to come out here and experience the magic of Pine Creek one more time."

I'm not looking at Liam, but I hear his sigh.

"What do you think, Olive? Do you want some seasonal work?" Jo asks.

"Wait. This is like, a job?" I ask out loud, really wishing someone would crack a joke to lighten the air in here.

Jo picks up her water. "Yes, of course! We wouldn't ask you to lend us your creativity and artistic talent for free."

I still have so many questions. "But, with the . . . it's not . . . can I just . . . why me?"

She gives me a slight shrug. "When I saw you at the Christmas Kick-Off, I remembered how much joy you always have coming here year after year. You understand Pine Creek like you're a part of the family. And I know you love this holiday as much as I do."

Well, that's all true. I do love Pine Creek and Christmas. Although I might've preferred not to deck the halls with the Hawaiian Christmas sweater.

It was nice of her to see that.

Liam stands and picks up his plate. Before leaving, he nods at mine. I look up and smile, nod back, and he takes my plate for me. He silently walks into the kitchen, and his dad follows suit, leaving Jo and me alone at the table.

I draw in a breath. "Okay—" But a wave of uncertainty washes over me. Yes, I'm creative, and yes, I'm an artist, but this is a lot of pressure given how important this place is to our community, to this family . . . to me.

They really think I'm the best person for this job?

"I sense hesitation," Jo says, with a half-smile.

My hands feel icy. I rub them together, but it doesn't help. "I just don't want to let you down. This is a big deal."

She scoots over one chair so she's right next to me. "I have a good feeling about this, Olive. I need fresh eyes on this place. Someone who knows how to highlight all the things that make Pine Creek special. Someone who's good with people, someone —honestly—a bit younger than me, and someone who can get buy-in from the community."

"And that's me?" I ask. "The community isn't about to jump on my bandwagon, not after my shop tanked."

She looks at me, kindness in her eyes. "You only fail if you don't learn from your mistakes."

Wise words that clearly come from experience.

"You have a lot to offer this town, Olive," Jo continues. "Maybe I'm selfish that I want to steal a little of it for Pine Creek."

Unfortunately, I'm still not sure I can pull this off.

Also unfortunately, my head is already spinning with ideas.

This venue is phenomenal, and I won't tell Jo this, but they could be doing so much more here. There are a million ways to expand, to bring people in.

"I just want people to have a chance to say a meaningful goodbye," she says, quietly. "And maybe if we get the word out, the perfect next owner will walk through our doors."

I study her, the bittersweet sadness clear in her expression. "Are you *sure* you want to sell?" I ask, because I can't not ask. "I mean, what about Liam and Lacey? Would they take it over like you guys did?"

Jo covers my hand with her own, and her expression shifts. "One thing I've learned, Olive," she says, "is that you can't make someone do something they don't want to do. Or love something they don't want to love. Especially your kids," she says with a rueful chuckle. "Not if you want to keep your relationship." She pats my hand. "What do you think? Are you up for this?"

I draw in a breath. I haven't created anything in months. Not since I closed the door on Wit and Whimsy over two years ago.

It feels daunting. And big.

But Pine Creek matters to me. This *family* matters to me. The magic they're talking about—I've felt that. Everyone who's been here has felt that.

Core memories are carved here.

I have to at least try. "Okay," I say, summoning my courage or my stupidity, depending on where you sit. "When do we start?"

CHAPTER 5

OLIVE

*A*pparently, we start immediately.

As in this exact moment. Jo is brimming with ideas and she wants me to jump in, but I do my best creative work when I'm alone. Which is why, after two pumpkin bars, I stand and say, "I'll take everything you guys said and work out some ideas that will engage the community and appeal to as many people as possible."

Jo pulls me into a tight hug. "I knew you'd be perfect at this."

I smile. "Thanks, Jo. I won't lie, your vote of confidence is appreciated."

I keep my chin up and stay positive and sunny, but when I get really honest with myself, it's been a long time since I believed I could do anything other than mess up.

Maybe that's why I've settled into low stakes jobs. If you mess up a coffee order, it's not a big deal. You punch the clock and you still get paid. Messing up a business? That's bigger than messing up a latte.

I feel stupid even now just thinking about it.

"Give me the morning to pull some ideas together." My head

spins with ideas, determined to make Jo proud. "I'll come back after lunch, if that's okay?"

"Even though it's Sunday?"

"I think we need to get started, don't you?" I ask. "We're on a tight timeline."

"Agreed," she says, handing me my coat. She pauses, sincere. "Thank you, Olive. This is a really special place, and I know you're going to add so much to this season."

I smile. "I hope so." I slip my coat on, pushing my hat out of the sleeve and pulling it on my head. Jo opens the front door, ushering me out into the crisp late-November weather.

"See you tomorrow," she says as she closes the door behind me.

I stand there for a moment, only the faint glow of a single bulb overhead lighting my path. I stare out into the darkness, inhaling the chilly, pine-tinged air.

"This is crazy, you know."

"What the—?" I gasp, hand to heart, and turn in the direction of the voice. Liam is sitting in a chair at the corner of the wrap-around porch, Hank at his feet. "You scared me to death, you psycho!"

He doesn't apologize. He doesn't even respond.

"Fine. I'll bite, Mr. Chatty," I say. "Why is this crazy?"

He ponders for a moment, and I think he isn't going to answer. But then he leans forward and spews, "She wants to cram a bunch of events into the next four weeks when she should just be enjoying what we have around here right now. Say goodbye quietly. Everything doesn't have to be a big production."

I pull my stocking cap down a bit further and walk over to the seating area. There's a handmade bench across from Liam's chair, and I sit facing him.

"Maybe she wants it to feel like it did back in the day," I say, knowing the tree farm must feel the pinch of commercialized

Christmas. It takes effort now to do anything in a traditional way, and I feel for parents who are desperate to pull kids out of the constant spin of flashy screens and loud toys.

Everything is bigger, but not necessarily better.

And nothing lasts anymore. It's like things are manufactured to break down, forcing people to buy things again.

Good grief, what's next? Yelling at people to get off my lawn?

I turn the thought around in my mind . . . *Christmas like it used to be . . . An old-fashioned Christmas . . .* there's an idea in there somewhere.

He shakes his head.

"Are you upset they're selling?" I ask.

"Nope."

He answered that quickly.

I study him. He clearly doesn't want to talk about it, which is why I should leave him alone, and also why I don't. He doesn't scare me.

I draw in a breath. "I'd be upset. It's such a special, magical place."

At that, he scoffs.

I frown. "What?"

"You sound just like them." He shifts in his chair.

"I don't understand," I say. "You lived here. It's like Winter Wonderland in a movie during the holidays. You must know how much it means to people. It doesn't mean ten times more to you?"

He stands and Hank lifts his head.

"Well? Doesn't it?" I repeat, standing.

"No," he says, flatly. "This place is a business. And if you let it, it'll bleed you dry."

I cross my arms and let out a slow breath. "So, to you, the farm is . . .?"

". . . Thankfully soon to be history." He crosses his arms, mirroring my stance.

"Wow. Okay. That's . . . sad." I study him. "You really have no idea how amazing it all is."

"I hate to tell you this, Liv, but it wasn't amazing for me."

I freeze. He called me "Liv." Just like when we were kids. It throws me. And maybe it throws him too because I get the sense that familiarity wasn't his intention.

Still, he's the only person who ever called me that.

He looks away.

I press my lips together and force his gaze. "Come on, there must be something about this place that you like."

He pushes a hand through his hair, turning toward the darkness beyond the porch. "I spent most of my time wrapping trees, weeding, planting, and mucking around through mud taking orders from. . ." He looks away, stopping from finishing the thought. "My experience was maybe different from everyone else's. It's just a farm."

"Just a farm?"

He frowns, annoyed.

I had no idea. I thought he saw this place like I saw this place.

Like everyone did. Like everyone still does.

And a thought shoots across my mind like Santa's sleigh across the sky.

"It's okay—" I say, grinning. "No, this is good."

He looks at me. "What?"

I grin.

"Your face looks weird," he says. "Stop looking at me like that."

I grin wider. "I'm going to show you."

He grimaces. "Show me what?"

I take a few steps back, shaking my finger at him like I've got a point to prove. "Liam Fisher, I'm going to make this the best, last Pine Creek Christmas you've ever had."

I step off the porch, propelled by delusion and pumpkin bars, suddenly certain that Jo is right.

I'm the perfect person for this job.

CHAPTER 6

LIAM

*A*fter Olive leaves, I find my sister in the kitchen, eating a slab of pumpkin bar.

When she meets my eyes, there is guilt in her expression. "What? It needed to be evened out," nodding at the pan, half gone now.

I chuckle to myself. Lacey eats like someone is going to take away her food.

"I think I'm in love with her," she says, mouth full. "These are *so good.*" She pushes the pan toward me. "You know you want more."

She's not wrong. Olive's pumpkin bars might be the best thing I've ever had, and I'm not sad she didn't take the leftovers with her. I get a plate and fork and cut myself an equally giant piece, then sit down next to Lacey.

"Great, now you've made it uneven again," she says, knifing another thin slice and scooping it onto her plate.

"You okay?" I ask between bites, because while I have strong negative feelings about this place, I know Lacey doesn't.

She slowly shakes her head no, still chewing. "No. I'm not."

Lacey and I don't see each other often, but when we do, the

instant connection comes back. We were siblings who grew up getting along. Maybe that's rare, but I consider my sister a friend. Though I realize in this moment, I have no idea what she's thinking or feeling, because Lacey romanticizes life at Pine Creek the same way Olive does. Same way my mom does.

"I guess . . ." She takes a drink from her water bottle, draws in a deep breath, then looks at me. "I just can't imagine not being here at Christmas." A pause. "Did they ask you to come back and run it?"

"Shockingly, no." I have to give them credit for that. Maybe they finally accepted my decision to do something completely different with my life. Or maybe this is all a power play to try and guilt me into doing exactly what they want. Reverse psychology or something. "You?"

She tilts her head at me and makes a face. "No one is delusional enough to think I could handle it."

There's something under the way she says it. Like people don't think she's capable.

"I'm sure they just don't think you'd have any interest. You travel, it's not like you want to be tied down. Especially not here. And maybe dealing with me showed them that shoving it down our throats is a bad idea."

"No, they just think I'm a mess," she muses, shoveling another bite into her mouth. "I gave up my scholarship, quit school, bought a van, and went on the road. They don't get my life."

"Lacey, nobody gets your life," I say.

"Mmm. Fair." She takes another bite, but it doesn't stop her from talking. "It's a little unconventional, I'll give you that. Mom always asks me when I'm going to settle down."

"What do you tell her?" I've wondered that myself. What is her plan—to drive around forever? And is she running away from something?

"I'm not sure." She takes another drink. "I mean, this is years and years—" she looks at me— "and *years* away, but I do want to have a family one day." She goes quiet. "And I always pictured them growing up here. Like we did."

I half-laugh. My experience with Pine Creek was vastly different than hers. She was free to pick and choose what she did or didn't do while Dad gave me work gloves and made me part of the crew. After we moved out here, it was a healthy dose of reality —it was clear I needed to do my part to keep this place afloat.

But I wasn't a part of it—not really. My ideas weren't welcome. My suggestions were met with "Ah, we tried that already," or flat dismissed.

I was just hired help.

Inwardly, I bristle. I should be over this. It's not like Dad and I haven't already had it out. More than once, in fact. When he and Mom found out I changed my major from agriculture to game design, he went through the roof.

"Ken Mariani told me his son is in a computer science class with you," he'd said. "I told him he must be mistaken, because Liam isn't in computer science. And Ken said it's required for the game design degree. I said maybe he had you confused with someone else, but he called his kid up right there and got the confirmation that it was Liam Fisher from Loveland High School. The one whose parents own the Christmas tree farm."

At that moment I wished I'd told him everything. I wished I'd spoken up and said exactly how I felt, exactly where I wanted to go, and exactly what I did—and didn't—want.

But I didn't.

"Liam, what have we been working toward all this time if you're going to throw it all away?" he'd asked. "This place, it's supposed to be yours. All you have to do is walk into it, and you'll have a great life." He scrubbed a hand down his face. "I can't believe you'd do this without talking to me about it first."

The look on my dad's face told me more than his tone of

voice or his body language ever could. He was enraged. Not only because I'd made this life-altering decision, but that he'd been blindsided by the news.

Hindsight, as they say, is 20/20.

"I guess I was just thinking—" Lacey sets her fork down and turns toward me. "What if we did take it over?"

"Lacey, we can't." I cut her off before she starts dreaming. "You can't do it alone, and I—"

"You what?"

"I don't want to." I push the plate away, thinking about the courage it took to finally tell my parents this wasn't the life I wanted. Because once they found out about my decision, there was a conversation, and they forced me to explain myself. It was hard and uncomfortable, and the truth is, I don't think my relationship with my dad has really recovered. But I felt better once it was over.

I'm not going back on that decision now.

"You really don't?" Lacey asks. "Even if we're in charge? I mean, we would make the decisions for this place. I know you had ideas—we would be the ones who got to choose what we did with it."

I glance at her.

"I know it's not the farm you resent."

And I hear what she isn't saying. I hear a truth I'm not willing to entertain.

She presses her lips together. "This place is our legacy, Bill. Shouldn't we at least try?"

"Lacey. It's a ton of work." I stand, needing some space from Lacey and her sentimentality. "And Mom and Dad need the money from the sale."

"Did they tell you that?"

"Not in so many words, but yeah. How else are they going to travel and start a new life somewhere else?" I look at her. "I think they've put everything they had into this place." I rinse my plate in the sink.

She raises her eyebrows. "Maybe they could draw a salary from the farm. Or we could buy it? We could take out a loan—"

"Lacey," I cut her off. "I have a job."

"Which you don't like."

I frown. "What? I like my job fine."

"Don't pretend you're okay with what they did to you," she says. "You could go out on your own. You don't need them, not really—"

If her words were fingers, they'd be pressing against a bruise.

I picture myself back in my cubicle, working through code, dying on the inside. I think about my boss, Aaron, and how unsupportive he's been of my most recent ideas. He wants five new pitches each week, and so far, he's yet to pick any of mine.

"Aren't you like, The Boy Wonder of video games?" he'd asked, irritated that my ideas weren't exciting him. "I'm not seeing it."

Then he stuck me and my team on a game with an impossible deadline. When I tried to explain this to him, he told me I was being difficult, then threw in a "Bring me solutions, Fisher, not problems," which I'm sure he read on the back cover of some business book.

Our team worked around the clock for a solid month, and we still had to cut corners. It looked horrible and the controls were clunky, so I wasn't remotely surprised when it tanked.

And to make it all worse, our team was completely disregarded and given another impossible deadline.

Lacey interrupts my spiraling thoughts. "We could keep the staff and hire a—"

"I can't," I cut her off. "I know how things work around here. It's not a part-time job. It's a lifestyle. I'm not a tree farmer. I'm a game developer." And even if things are rough right now, I have a good job. A dream job. A job people in my field would kill for at a company that's as exclusive and pedestaled as they get. I'd be crazy to give it up.

It wouldn't make sense to walk away.

Especially to take on this mess.

"We can do this, Liam." She sounds almost convincing. "We grew up here. We know what we're doing because it's in our blood."

But that's not a reason to uproot my life and plant it back here.

"Just think about it, okay?" Lacey asks.

I don't answer because I know my sister. This is the shiny new thing. The second she gets bored, she'll be back on the road, and I'd be stuck running this place by myself. Contrary to what most people think, a tree farm is a year-round operation.

But without a year-round income.

"Say you'll think about it," she says, her eyes pleading.

"I'm not going to lie to you," I say, softening.

"Liam." She levels my gaze. "This is our home. We can't let someone else take it over." Lacey stands and takes her plate to the sink. She rinses it, then turns back to me. "You know I'm right."

She walks out, leaving me standing in the dim kitchen, feeling guilty and a little like a jerk. Still, my sister is not a realist.

She lives in a van, for Pete's sake.

She has no clue what it would take to make a go of this farm. But I get why she's sentimental. I get why she wants to try.

As I fall asleep that night, my thoughts turn from Lacey's insistence to Olive's certainty. She sees something in Pine Creek that I don't. Or won't.

Either way, she's convinced she's going to convince me, which only proves how little she knows me now. Which only reminds me what an idiot I was for not figuring out a way to keep her in my life.

CHAPTER 7

LIAM

*O*h, how I love being summoned.

The following afternoon, I'm pulling up to the Pine Creek office located in one of the barns on the business side of the property.

Acres of trees separate this side from the side where the house and family barn are positioned, higher up the hill.

I park the red Pine Creek pickup truck next to a small powder blue VW bug that I'm certain belongs to Olive. If people could be cars, she would be a VW bug.

Hank trots over, mildly interested as I get out of the truck. I bend down to give him an appropriate amount of attention and also to prolong going to this meeting.

Maybe I should feel comforted that Olive is still as determined as she always was, but knowing she's turned her attention toward proving a point to me has me a little on edge.

I really don't want her to waste her time trying to convince me this tree farm is anything other than what it is—an overly romanticized money pit.

I rub Hank's ears, and he steps closer, burrowing his face between my knees. "I've got this, right, Hank?"

He pants and pulls back, lifting his front paws, hitting my forearms in what I can only assume is an effort to get me to pet him for the next eight hours. I give him one last rub, then stand.

Time to get this over with.

I walk into the barn and look around. This outbuilding is less barn and more office space. It's still wide open in the center, a bit barn-like, all high ceilings and rafters that creak when the wind blows too hard, but along the perimeter there are smaller offices and rooms, with one functioning as a conference room.

When my parents gather the entire staff, they assemble in the big open space, but smaller groups can meet around the handmade table in the conference room, which is where I find Olive sitting. Alone.

Before she looks up, I'm weirdly struck with a twinge of nerves and consider leaving. Why am I nervous?

She glances up. "Your mom had to take a call."

I nod and take a breath, making it semi-clear I'm not happy to be here. I sit down at the rough-edge table at the center of the room. My mom's version of a conference table—hewn wood from the farm and mismatched chairs. We aren't fancy people, that's for sure.

I think of the conference room at Arcadia, with embedded tilt up screens, all modern lines and white space. There's a single piece of abstract art on the wall behind the head of the table where Aaron sits. I've discovered that if you sit in the fourth chair on the right side, the art behind him makes it look like he has horns.

I try to sit there a lot.

The whole place is like that. Where you sit reveals the true nature of things.

It's all abstract and clean and modern and boring, and now that I think about it, not suited for creative work at all.

Olive is clutching a small stack in front of her—a notebook, a smaller notebook, her iPad, and a phone. She's not looking at me.

"What's all that?" I nod to her things.

Her eyes flick to mine. "My presentation."

I lean back in the chair. "You're giving a presentation?"

"Well," she says, "kind of. It's not formal or anything."

I nod, slowly.

Another pause.

"Liam, what is . . ." She stops and takes a breath.

I stare.

She looks right at me. "You don't like me, do you?" she blurts out, as if the words have been wanting to escape for a while now.

I wet my lips, then press them together. "I . . ." I shake my head, as if that's going to help me form words and actually speak. I say the one thing that is true, but hopefully not offensive.

"I guess I don't really know you anymore."

I do know that ever since I saw her in that coconut sweater, I've been replaying memories that I thought I buried a long time ago.

I also know that she has the potential to get in my head in ways other people can't.

She and I had something special. Or at least, I thought we did.

I've also spent an ungodly amount of time trying *not* to think about her bright blue eyes or how soft and smooth her skin appears. When I'm around her, sometimes I have to put my hands in my pockets just to make sure I don't do something stupid, like reach out and touch her.

She narrows her eyes, like she's putting me in the center of her crosshairs. "So, is this just your personality now?"

"Is what my personality?" I ask, emotionless.

"This sort of—" she waves a hand in my general direction—"salty, cranky thing you've got going on."

Since when does not having anything to say make you cranky? I think, wondering how she expected me to act around her. "I'm not cranky."

She scoffs, eyes wide as if to say, "Yeah, okay."

"Sorry about that!" My mother walks into the office, tucking her phone into her pocket. "Little crisis in the Christmas shop." She scans the room. "Where's Lacey?"

As if the question summons her, Lacey rushes in. "I'm here! I was filming content for social."

I frown. Filming content? For *social*?

Olive brightens. "Oh, good! I was going to ask about that. I noticed our social media presence is a little on the quiet side."

Our?

My mom loves when farm employees take ownership of their work, when they put themselves on the team. But is Olive serious? She knows this place most likely won't even exist in a month, right?

Mom smiles and pulls out a chair for Lacey. "Sit."

I glance at my sister as she takes a seat, hoping she's started to accept the fact that this is all happening—this is our last Christmas at Pine Creek, regardless of how we feel about it. Maybe our mom got her on board with this plan to cram the month full of things to get people out here one last time.

"Okay, Olive," my mom says. "The floor is yours. We can't wait to hear your ideas."

Olive fidgets with the corner of her iPad. "Right, okay—" She stares at the stack of things in front of her, and for a second I wonder if she's decided she doesn't want to pitch these ideas after all. She looks—conflicted.

And vulnerable.

It's a different side than the blunt, call-me-out-on-my-crap side she's been showing.

How can those two things coexist in a single person? It's a mystery. One I'd like to solve.

Olive looks up, courage summoned, and paints a bright smile on her face. It's the same smile she often had when we were kids. Like when she picked up that frog that somehow got stuck in the bird bath and tormented me with it all afternoon because she knew it grossed me out.

"I was thinking about what makes this place so special." She opens her iPad, flipping the cover around so it becomes a stand and sets it on the table facing us. "In addition to the ongoing activities you already have here—" She touches the iPad and an image pops up. A hand-drawn pink and red and green image that says *The Last, Best Pine Creek Christmas.*

Her eyes lock onto mine, and she straightens.

Bring on the convincing, I guess.

"I propose—" she pauses, staring straight at me— "the Last, Best Pine Creek Christmas." Her lips twitch into a slight smile and she looks away. "A full month of activities celebrating the holidays the Pine Creek way. We will put the emphasis on the joy of being together with family, at this place, during this very festive season." She swipes the iPad. "'Together at Christmas' would be the theme, and we would center all activities around making memories together, with friends, with family, with anyone we love."

My mom is eating this up. Lacey has her phone out, and when she starts typing on it, she lifts a finger and says, "I promise I'm not being rude, just getting some of these ideas down for social media."

I frown. The change in my sister is a little suspicious.

Olive goes on. "I was thinking we could share about what we already have going on here on all social media channels. Maybe focus on the hot chocolate shed and bring back the carriage rides because everyone loves those. And I think it would be fun to do featured treats every week in the café."

"On it," Lacey says, furiously typing ideas into her phone.

"Those are things we can do immediately, but some things will take longer to plan. Like—" Olive swipes to a new page on the iPad to reveal another image, clearly hand-drawn. At the center of it are the words "Pine Creek Christmas Market" layered over a hand-drawn image of an old red Ford truck with a vintage Pine Creek logo on the door—my truck. The one I drove all through high school. And when that one died, somehow, my parents found another identical one.

Not sure why I've been driving it while my Altima sits parked in my parents' garage, but I'm sure Olive would turn that into something sentimental when really, I just love a vintage truck.

"I thought the venue would be perfect for a makers' market." Olive looks away from the iPad.

"Olive. I *love* this idea," Mom says. "Unique, handmade Christmas gifts—"

"Locally made," Lacey says. "We lean into that and put 'shop local' on all our advertising."

Olive beams, and I start to see the ripple of excitement make its way around the table until it reaches me, the lone speed bump slowing it down.

"I know a lot of people in this community from doing so many markets myself," Olive says. "And if I pitch this to them, tell them we want the farm to go out with a bang, I think they'll come—"

"Even though it's such short notice?" I ask, skeptical.

"I have a call in to a friend who's planned them before," Olive continues, undeterred. "I'll get her to talk me through the details, but I think we can do it. I mean, we already have the venue, and that's usually the hardest part. We just need to figure out where on the property to set up and how to manage the flow of traffic."

"Oh, Liam can help with that," my mom says. "He knows this place better than anyone."

Olive seems unfazed. "Perfect." She grins at me, half *can you?* and half *gotcha.* I hear what she's not saying—this is a perfect way for her to try and brainwash me into changing my feelings about this place.

Sorry, Liv. It won't work.

"So you want to have an arts and crafts show," I deadpan. "Before Christmas."

Olive's shoulders drop.

"Good grief, Liam," Lacey says. "Why don't you just take her balloon and pop it right in front of her?"

I'm not trying to do that, I'm just—

She dismisses me before I can finish my thought, which is a good thing because I have no idea what I would've said.

"This is a great idea. You're obviously not the target audience for this." She looks at Olive. "He's not the target audience."

Her face is flushed, but she still manages to dig, "You mean cranky, unhelpful people?"

I take a deep breath and let it out slowly.

I'm not cranky.

"Is this going to be expensive?" I ask, because honestly, I have no idea. I only know my parents don't have extra money to throw at these whimsical ideas.

"Actually, we should *make* money . . . if we're smart about it. Vendors would pay to be a part of it, and I thought we could also set up a booth for all of the Pine Creek merchandise."

"But we don't have any. . ." Mom begins.

Olive swipes to the next page on the iPad. "I think we use your vintage logo—put it on shirts, mugs, things like that."

I shift in my seat. "Sounds expensive."

Lacey smacks me across the arm.

"The upfront costs are going to be high," I say. "Someone has to be the voice of reason, here."

"Yeah well, that *someone* doesn't have to be a buzzkill about it." Lacey rolls her eyes at me, then turns back to Olive as my mother shoots me a look of warning.

Olive clears her throat and continues, focusing on my mom. "I was also thinking you could host a wreath-making class. Remember those big, beautiful wreaths you used to make? People went crazy for them."

My mom's face lights up. "Really? You think people would like that?"

"Uh, yeah. They're amazing. I'm *sure* they would," Olive says. "And people are always looking for fun things to do with family during the Christmas season that aren't just shopping or fighting crowds." She smiles, and my mom smiles right back. "Something that you can make with your own hands, with your family, and have as a gift? It's a no-brainer."

Mom's smile takes up her whole face. "Well, then it's a done deal!"

"And also—I'm guessing the community will want to support you all." Olive says this so earnestly, even *I* believe her.

She taps the screen and reveals another image that says: *Pine Creek Kids.*

"We can have more fun activities for the kids, maybe tours around the property or hayrides?" She looks at me. "You could pull a trailer with your truck, right?"

I make a face. If I'm honest, it looks amazing. These ideas of hers, back in the day, would've partnered perfectly with what I suggested—

No. My dad shot those ideas down. And I hate that I'm now slipping into his role, sitting here at this table.

Seeing ways that this *won't* work.

Still, there's no way I'm not getting suckered into this. "Look, I'm not saying this can't work . . . but do you really think you can pull this all together before Christmas?" I watch her and see her confidence falter slightly.

"Liam," Lacey snaps.

I look away. I know she's right. *What is my problem?*

"Not by herself." My mom turns to Olive. "If there's one thing I've learned it's that people need people." She covers Olive's hand with her own. "And we've got plenty of those. *Lots* of volunteers are ready to get to work, and our staff is completely on board."

Olive nods. "I would focus the bigger events mostly on the weekends, and I think we can also open the lake for weeknight ice skating when it gets colder and bonfires—" her eyes are back on me— "and maybe bring back Family Day?"

A memory resurfaces.

Every year before we moved to Pine Creek, my parents and Olive's parents would pile us all into their minivans and drive us out here for Family Day, something my great-grandparents started ages ago.

Pine Creek closes for one peak season afternoon, and friends and family are invited to explore all it has to offer. Bonfires and hayrides and ice skating and hot chocolate—was all fair game. We had a big dinner in the main barn and a scavenger hunt that took you through the whole property.

Olive and Benji and Lacey and I were always a team, pitted against our parents who I'm pretty sure always let us win. Every time we'd come back, victorious, and we'd find them all sitting around a table on the patio, drinking wine and laughing.

We'd run all over the property, looking for clues that would lead us to the big prize—a giant chocolate Santa. We'd all get sick eating it, but it didn't matter.

We didn't live here then. We were visitors, and this place did hold a strange magic, like it was begging to be explored, like there were secrets waiting to be uncovered. It was a massive, secure, personal outdoor playground. As a kid I couldn't think of anything better.

But, like pretty much everything, that changed after we moved.

Olive and her family came that first year, but the following year, they were out of town, and then the drift happened. Her parents showed up a few more times, but Olive and Benji usually had other things going on.

"I was thinking it would be amazing to do a candlelight walk, maybe on Christmas Eve?" Olive is saying when I tune back into the conversation. "We could talk to one of the high schools or churches to see if we could get some carolers to come out and sing at specific spots along the path to fill the property with music."

Olive is so smitten with these ideas. I can see her passion for them bursting through. Every idea she pitches has a corresponding slide on her iPad, and at the end, she lands on a hand-drawn map of the property and a calendar of events.

My mother gasps. "You did all of this today?"

"Eh . . . last night." Olive fidgets. "I didn't really sleep."

"You're incredible." Lacey turns to me. "Isn't she incredible?"

Olive doesn't meet my eyes, but I can sense her wanting my approval. "It's . . . ambitious."

"You mean *awesome!*" Lacey grins. "Seriously, I'm going to promote *all* of this. Are you cool if I start a promo plan, Mom?"

My mother is visibly as confused as I am. Lacey seems to have made her peace with the sale of the farm overnight, and even seems excited to celebrate our last season here.

It's weird.

"Of course, Lacey, if you're sure," Mom says.

Lacey reaches over and squeezes Mom's hand. "I'm sure. I love all of these ideas." Then, to me, "What are you going to do to help? I mean, aside from scoping out spots for the market."

I bite back "Nothing" because I don't want to be a part of any of this, but instead I say, "Oh, I'm sure Dad will put me to work."

"No." Mom shakes her head. "He's covered. You're free to spend the holidays however you want."

"Great. So Liam, you can help Olive," Lacey says. "Be her point person. You're already giving her a tour, so just, you know, do whatever she says." I don't miss her conspiratorial wink at Olive or Olive's amused reaction.

I really don't have time for this.

"Good idea." Mom looks at me. "I'll also need you to hang the mistletoe." She walks over to a little table in the corner and returns with a tray of small bunches of greenery, tied with ribbons.

"Oh, and Liam, could you trim the big Christmas tree?" Lacey is smiling now.

Not missing a beat, Mom jumps right back in. "And Liam, if you could, maybe wash the windows outside?"

"And make me a ham sandwich?" Lacey is full on giggling now.

Olive presses her lips together, doing a terrible job of holding in a smile.

"Yeah, you three are a riot."

"Oh, sweetie. Just pretend you're having a good time, okay?" My mother slides the cardboard tray toward me. She insists on hanging mistletoe all over the property— "to open the door for romance." It's one of her many traditions, and this is where I'd be smart to shut my mouth and do as I'm told.

At least it'll give me some time alone.

But then Mom says, "Olive, do you mind helping him? It really is a two person job, and Liam, you can show Olive the grounds at the same time. Two birds . . ." She smiles sweetly, and I see right through her.

Olive doesn't seem to. Instead, she stands and smiles. "I'd love to!"

So much for alone time.

"Once you're done, come back here, and we'll get you all set up as a contractor so you can get paid." She opens her arms to Olive, who hesitates a moment before stepping into one of my mother's hugs. "Welcome to the family."

The words catch me off guard. They shouldn't, but they do.

Lacey gives me a pointed look. "Have fun, you two," she sing-songs.

I look at her, then at Olive and my mom, and then down at my hands.

I'm holding a sprig of mistletoe.

Great.

Before anyone else can make some kind of comment, I gather up the tray, give a sarcastic smile to Lacey, and make my way out of the room.

CHAPTER 8

OLIVE

I pack up my things, feeling uneasy about time alone with Liam. I'm trying to figure out if his problem is with me, with his family, or just the world at large when Lacey stands and smiles at me.

"You're so good at this, Olive," Lacey says, and the words land in a fragile space inside of me.

Jo gives me a nod, hand still on my shoulder from her hug. "I knew you would be." She squeezes one last time and then walks out, leaving me standing there with Lacey, who has had quite the turnaround since last night.

"You can leave your stuff in here if you want to," she says, nodding at the table. "Nobody will mess with it."

I glance down at my iPad, thinking that once upon a time, my whole life lived inside that device.

It felt good to dust it off and see if I remembered how to create.

It felt even better to discover that I did.

I set my things down on the table, and pull on my coat, but before I can leave the room, Lacey says, "So. Olive."

I smile at her and mimic her tone. "So. Lacey."

She straightens her shoulders as her face turns serious. "I need you to help me with something."

"Okay," I say. "With what?"

Her face turns sour. "With Liam."

I scoff. "I think you're asking the wrong person."

"Why? Because he's cranky?" she asks.

"Because that crankiness seems to be aimed at me," I say nonchalantly, like it's not bothering me one little bit, *thankyouverymuch.*

"Oh, it's not you. He's an equal opportunity grump. He just doesn't like being here." Lacey looks at me. "Eh. And maybe it's a little bit you."

My frown deepens. "Why? What did I ever do to him?"

Lacey's face goes blank. "You forgot about him." She says this like I should already know it.

"I—" I snap my jaw shut, processing, then say, "What? When?"

"After we moved," she says with a shrug. "I think he thought you guys would find a way for things to stay the way they were."

"That's crazy. We were . . . kids," I say, searching for logic behind why he would feel that way. "Not even teenagers."

"Liam doesn't have many people that he's close to. Shocking. I know," she adds dryly. "There was our grandpa, who had a heart attack and died *way* too young, a friend who totally stabbed him in the back, me, of course, because I'm awesome. And . . . you."

My frown holds because yes, Liam and I had a special friendship, the kind of friendship you only have when you're twelve, but everyone has friends when they're younger. Most of them you outgrow.

Right?

When she sees my face, Lacey shakes her head. "Actually, I don't know what I'm talking about. Liam says I'm a crazymaker. Sometimes I forget he doesn't think like me."

But the words still hang there, in the air, waiting for me to pay attention to them.

"Okay, so this favor—" Lacey takes a breath. "I need you to help me convince Liam to buy the farm with me."

"Uh, you just said he hates it here."

"I know, but you said you were going to make him love it." Lacey grins.

I frown. "How do you know that?"

Her smile holds. "I was eavesdropping."

I shake my head, realizing that *this* is why her mood shifted. She's not focused on the last, best Christmas. She's focused on convincing Liam to stay.

"This place is our legacy, Olive," Lacey says. "I don't want to lose it. It's. . .important."

She pauses, looking momentarily emotional.

"Maybe you don't get it, but it is."

"No, I do get it." I chew the inside of my cheek. "I guess I just didn't realize that was an option. You know, you and him taking it over."

She pulls a face. "It's not, really. I'm not sure I could do it without Liam. It was always supposed to be him taking it over, you know."

Whoa. "I didn't."

"Yeah. It was his if he wanted it. But he didn't. He took a different path."

That's the truth. I can't think of anything on the complete opposite spectrum from a tree farm than video game design. It's like a longshore fisherman's son going into theatre.

"And what, he won't even consider it?"

She shakes her head. "No. It's a sore spot. He and my dad have never seen eye-to-eye about it."

"Then you might want to leave it alone," I tell her, starting to get a clearer picture.

"I can't. And if they give me a chance, they'll see that I could be great at this too. I could be a legitimate asset. Liam knows everything about how this place works, and I know I could get more people out here, falling in love with it—" She goes quiet for a beat before going on.

"I get it, people think I'm some flighty, impulsive, *whatever,* but I know this place, too. Nobody showed me—I had to ask— but I know more than they think I know. And I love it here. I also firmly believe that I can figure out anything."

I'm in awe of that confidence.

"If I hang around with you, will some of your confidence rub off on me?" I half-joke.

"I would love it if you hung around! And listen—Liam and I *could* do this." An earnest pleading washes across her face. "We would be an amazing team."

"What about hashtag van life?" I ask honestly, because Lacey has turned her "hashtag van life" into a whole brand, a legitimate money maker and, by my calculation, that job feels like a dream. No boss. No time clock. No chance of failing.

She sighs. "I've seen so many amazing places and met so many amazing people." She talks with her hands, excited. "It's just . . ."

I stay quiet, giving her space to finish her thought.

"I think about roots sometimes." She looks at me, and I see a shift behind her eyes.

She shrugs. "Mine are here."

On some level, I understand, but I can't get in the middle of this. It's a family business, a family affair, and from what it sounds like, a family drama.

The last thing I need to do is stick my nose in it.

"I get it, Lacey. I do. But . . ." I hesitate

Her face falls. "I know he's being weird right now, but I think he's just processing all of this. If anyone can get through to him—it's you. He values your opinion."

"Oh, I'm not sure that's true." Not anymore, I think.

65

At that, I hear the barn door open and Liam call out, "Olive! Little help here?"

I side-eye Lacey, and she puts up her hands and shrugs.

"If he thinks that's the way to get my attention, he's got another thing coming," I say. I pull out a chair at the table and sit back down.

She laughs. "Atta girl."

A few seconds later, Liam is in the doorway, glaring at me. "What are you doing? Didn't you hear me?"

I quirk a brow. "Did I hear you *bellow* at me? Yes."

"Nobody says 'bellow.'"

"I just did."

"Are you coming or not?" he asks.

"That depends on whether or not you can be nice."

He glowers. "Are you serious?"

I raise my eyebrows. "Try me."

He huffs and storms back out. I look at Lacey, who gives me a knowing look. Seconds later, Liam is back in the doorway.

He pauses for a second, then steels himself and says, "Olive, are you ready for your tour?" He seems to be using every ounce of energy to speak calmly and politely, but he's speaking through clenched teeth. It's like Beast when he's asking Belle to dinner, Cogsworth and Lumiere reminding him to be a gentleman.

"Why, yes, Liam, I would *love* for you to show me around," I say, mock sweet, with a Southern twang. "It was so kind of you to wait for me to finish my conversation."

I stand.

He glares, unamused.

I zip my coat, and when I look up, he's gone again.

"See?" Lacey hisses, with a smirk. "He listens to you."

I shake my head. "We'll see how long this lasts, Lace." I walk past her, but turn back and see her brow knit in worry. "You said you know more than they realize."

She meets my eyes and nods. "Way more. I was always around. Manny used to let me help him after Liam went away to school and I'm naturally curious, so I asked a lot of questions."

"Prove to them you can handle it," I say. "Let your actions speak louder than your words."

She straightens, like she's just been zipped up in the back. And then, a slow smile spreads across her face. "You really are a genius, Olive."

I grin. "I know."

I leave the office, bolstered by the encouragement and reaction to my ideas, but the second I walk outside and see Liam's grim face?

Good feelings gone.

CHAPTER 9

LIAM

an, she is frustrating.
    I lift the tray of mistletoe into the back of my truck, next to a ladder. Despite what my mother said, this is not a two-person job. And does Olive *really* need a tour of this place? It's hardly changed since we were kids.

I'd say as much if she didn't look so excited to be out here.

Why the heck is she so excited to be out here?

She stands a few yards away from the truck, just looking around, like she's seeing it all for the first time. She draws in a slow, deep breath, then lets it out like she's in a yoga class and has been instructed to count to ten.

"There's something about nature, isn't there?" She smiles.

I squint into the sun, which is doing its best to warm the land on a blustery early December day.

"Oh, wait," she says, walking toward me. "You're a city boy now. Does that mean you've forgotten where you came from? Do you remember what dirt is?"

I quirk a brow and let her amuse herself.

"Seriously though, do you like living in the city?" She makes her way around to the passenger side of the truck.

"Yeah, actually."

"What do you like about it?" She asks genuinely. "Because it's so peaceful here."

"The city can be peaceful," I say. "Just in a different way." But the words feel surprisingly hollow.

I open the door and pull myself up into the truck, waiting for Olive to do the same.

When she does, she inhales another deep breath. "Smell that?"

Yeah. Trees. Same way it's smelled since I was a kid.

"It's like pine trees and nature and Christmas all rolled into one." Then, as if the idea has fallen out of the sky and landed in her brain, she says, "Do you guys sell candles?"

"No clue."

She pulls out her phone and starts typing. "Pine Creek needs a signature fragrance."

"It's dumb to put so much time and energy and money into this," I say, because nobody seemed to note my objections in that meeting. I don't understand why they can't see the logic.

I start the engine. "It's our last year here. Even worse, it's our last holiday season. We should keep things small, save as much as we can, and bow out gracefully."

"But then the rest of the community won't get to say good-bye." She looks at me. "That's what your mom really wants."

I roll my eyes.

She narrows hers. I can feel her trying to read me, trying to figure out what it's going to take to convince me that this is the *best place on earth.* I could save her time because the answer is—nothing. At this point, I just need to get back to my real job. To finish what I've been working on to redeem my last disaster and prove I wasn't a one-hit wonder.

The thought rumbles around inside of me, an unwelcome angst accompanying it.

I know it's not Olive's fault I came home to this huge mess, or that I really don't like being home. But somehow she's tied up in the crappy feelings I have for this place, and I don't know how to keep her separate.

Shouldn't it matter that when she was a part of the Pine Creek experience, I felt exactly the opposite?

This is why I come home as seldom as possible. I don't want to start unearthing ancient history.

"I looked you up online," she says, derailing my train of thought.

Inwardly, I groan. Outwardly, I choose silence.

"I knew you designed video games, but I'm not much of a gamer, so I never really paid attention. I can now say I've played one." She pulls out her phone, clicks around on it, then holds it up to show me. There, on the screen, is the logo for *Castle Crusade*. A passion project—not even an assignment—from my senior year at the University of Illinois. I'd been so obsessed with it, but I was never convinced it would be something unique and have a wide appeal.

I just did it because it was fun. And I wanted to see if I could.

Flash forward years later, almost every phone in America has downloaded it, and it's become one of the most widely played and replayed mobile games in the country.

And seeing that logo is a punch to the gut.

"I'm *terrible* at it," Olive continues, undeterred by my reaction. "Maybe you can give me some insider tips." She grins at me, and I'm twelve years old again, pining away for the girl next door.

We're a long way from twelve, Fisher.

"Oh, I also learned that you have, like, no social media presence." She cocks her head and looks at me. "Why is that? Just don't like it or . . .?"

"Waste of time," I grumble.

That's not true. Most of my upper-level classes in college covered how to market yourself as an indie game publisher by curating an online presence, editing videos to be snappy, funny, irreverent, and current, connecting yourself and your personality with your fans.

After what happened with *Castle Crusade*, though, it just didn't seem worth it.

"Hm." She considers this, like I've just said something she's never heard anyone say, then says, "I can see how it could be, but if you at least had Instagram, I'd know something about you. I only get the bits of gossip my mom hears when she's out walking in Corner Park." She tosses me a look as I pull into a parking space down by the front gates. "Which is actually quite a lot." She grins again. "Do you know you have a reputation?"

I shake my head and turn off the engine. "I didn't know that, no." I also don't care, but I don't say that out loud.

"Apparently, you're commitment phobic," she says. "A chronic first-dater. I think that one came from your Aunt Mary to her best friend Peg to Peg's niece Ashley, who happens to be a third grade teacher at PV Elementary." She stops for a brief second. "I'm not sure how it got from Ashley to my mom, but . . .?" A shrug. "So, are you?"

"Am I what?"

"Commitment phobic?"

"No."

She squints, like she's a human polygraph trying to determine if I'm telling the truth. "Last long term relationship?"

I frown. "Let's not do this."

"Let's not do what?" She's genuinely confused.

"Small talk," I say. "I hate it."

Her brow furrows. "It's not small talk if I'm genuinely interested in the answer. Small talk would be like, 'How's the weather?' or 'How about them Bears?'"

I shake my head. "It's uncanny."

"What is?" She's genuinely confused.

71

"You're exactly the same as you were when we were kids." I open the door and step out onto the gravel drive.

"Oh, so you *do* remember," she says, following my lead and getting out. She walks around to the back of the truck. "Is it a bad thing? If I'm the same?" There's an earnest *please like me* look in her eyes, and I soften at the sight of it.

"No." I look into her eyes. "It's not. It's . . . just an observation," I say.

Her eyes flicker, and I force myself not to linger there. When you grow up with someone, even if you lose touch, there's still a part of you that will always know them at their core.

I can see that trusty Olive-curiosity being piqued, and I remind myself to be careful.

"*You're* completely different." She walks over to the bed of the truck and slides the cardboard tray of mistletoe out.

"No, I'm not."

"Yes, you are."

"Not completely."

"I mean, your hair is still dark and your eyes are still green, but otherwise?" She stands there, holding the tray, and looks me over. "I hardly recognize you."

I grab the ladder with a scoff. "Why, because I grew up?"

"No, because the Liam I knew wasn't a Scrooge."

I pull the ladder out and grumble to myself before I realize I'm proving her right.

"You used to love Christmas," she says. "Don't you remember? You led the charge during Family Day. You were the one who *had* to win that scavenger hunt. You were the one who was so excited to show new people around this place. You were their best tour guide."

She goes still, suddenly more serious. "Liam," she says my name, and I don't hate the way it sounds. "What happened?"

I sigh.

I wish I was the type to just spill everything, to talk about how I'm feeling about stuff, to confide, but I'm just not.

I slip to my default, which is deciding not to burden others with all of my stuff, thinking that it's stupid to talk about, a shrug my only reply.

"Things change."

I know it's not what she wants to hear. I also know it's not all I want to say.

A part of me hopes she keeps asking. If anyone could wear me down, it's Olive.

I take one of the bunches of mistletoe and start toward the main barn, ladder under my arm. "Hey, um, can you grab the hammer and box of nails from behind my seat?"

"Yes, boss!"

I picture her saluting and hold back a smile.

She meets me at the entrance, and I set the ladder up underneath the roof of the wide porch. I hand over the bunch of mistletoe and start up the ladder. She puts a hand on the back of it, steadying it as I go.

"What are you doing tomorrow?" she asks.

I hold my hand out toward her, and she gives me the hammer and a small handful of nails, then holds up one of the sprigs of mistletoe and watches as I fix it to the roof right above the door.

I hand the hammer back and start down the ladder. "Nothing." Once I'm back on solid ground, she takes a step back, and I watch her. "Why?"

"I wondered if you might be able to help me cut my tree down," she says. "For my house."

For some reason I can't explain, this makes me want to know where she lives. I've been picturing her in her parents' house, in that same bedroom that faced mine, but of course she'd have her own place by now.

"I know what you're doing," I say, folding the ladder. "You told me your *show Liam how great Pine Creek is* plan."

She frowns. "That doesn't mean I don't actually need help."

"Who would help you if I wasn't here?" I use the ladder as a prop and watch her turn this over in her head.

"Probably my dad," she says. "But I don't usually cut my own. I usually get one of the small precut ones."

"So do that," I say, walking off the porch.

She follows. "No, that's like cheating. It's my last chance to cut down a *real* Pine Creek Christmas tree. I want the full experience!"

I shove the ladder into the back of the truck. "The full experience?"

She smiles. "Yep."

I tilt my head at her. "You know this isn't going to work, right? This whole plan, cramming everything in, last best whatever?"

"See, that's where you're wrong, Liam."

I lean against the truck.

"Am I?"

"Yes." She meets my eyes. "You know why it's going to work?"

I hold up both hands as if to say, *lay it on me.*

"Because I'm very persuasive."

My breath catches, because there's a part of me that I'm sure could be persuaded without any effort on her part at all.

I hold her gaze for a three-count that feels like an hour, then laugh, mostly to dispel the tension.

She mock gasps. "A laugh! Oh my gosh!" She starts shouting as if there's a crowd. "He laughed, everyone! He's human, after all!"

I shake my head, thankful for the levity. "Will you knock it off, you lunatic?"

She looks right at me. "I've never cut down my own tree

74

before. There are things I can't do, but you can. Please, Liam. I don't want to mess it up."

I look at her, all earnestness in her wide, pleading eyes, and I give in.

I take the hammer from her and walk around to the driver's side door. "Fine."

"Fine?"

"Fine," I repeat.

She clasps her hands together in front of her face, a tiny gasp escaping as she does. "For real? You'll help me?"

I don't respond. Instead, I toss her a *don't push it* look and move around to the side of the truck. I get in, then catch a glimpse of her smile in the rearview mirror.

I don't know what game she's playing . . . but I have a feeling she's winning.

CHAPTER 10

OLIVE

*H*e's going to help me.

A crack in the wall. A chink in the armor. A laugh that sent my senses reeling.

There's something wildly appealing about Liam, and it kept me a little on edge the entire time we hung mistletoe all over the property. While we walked around, I got the idea to create a sign for the front entrance telling people to "Watch Out for Mistletoe!" with a pair of lips underneath.

Most people probably don't look up enough to notice the little clusters of greenery, and it's such a fun tradition that I want to draw some attention to it. In fact, a whole *Mistletoe Walk* could be so charming . . . my brain spun with ideas I couldn't wait to flesh out.

Not then though, not while I was walking around with Oscar the Grouch.

Despite my many—many—failed attempts to spark a conversation, Liam remained quiet and stone-faced.

And maddening.

But I'm not deterred.

He always had a melancholy side. He's a creative like me, and we can be a finicky bunch. I learned early on that he has a tender heart and big feelings.

Other people didn't always know what to do with those, but I can speak Liam. Or at least I could back in the day. I remember his mom told me once I was the only one who seemed to know exactly what to say or do to cheer him up.

So, that's what I'm going to do.

Even if he really doesn't want me to.

Too bad, sucker.

I guess somewhere along the way, his melancholic mood became his whole personality. He needs some Christmas cheer. He needs some holly and some jolly. He needs a tinsel intervention.

A tinselvention?

Liam dropped me off at the main barn to get all my paperwork sorted, but before I got out of the car, I gave him the address of my little bungalow three blocks away from downtown and made him promise to pick me up to cut down my tree.

He grunted his first response, so I told him to use his words.

He sighed, exasperated, then said, "Fine." And now, I'm standing in front of the full-length mirror in my bedroom, trying to decide if the red turtleneck and jeans will be warm enough for a night outside.

I'm also replaying the tour of the Pine Creek property in my mind because I never did land on where to set up the market.

I spent the day working on the big event, and I've already gotten three confirmed vendors along with a long list of positive replies. I set the date with Jo, and I have a good feeling about the whole thing. A really good feeling. It's so euphoric, it makes me think, *who cares if we only have three weeks to pull it all together?*

Or, to quote Elle Woods: "What, like it's hard?"

I'm deep in thought when I hear the sound of a vehicle in the driveway.

Operation Last, Best Christmas is underway. And for me, it's about more than a tree farm. It's about Mr. Moody, who has clearly forgotten how to have fun.

I give myself one last once-over in the mirror, then head downstairs as I see a dark figure walk up onto my porch. I'm instantly nervous, which is stupid.

It's not like this is a date or anything.

According to the town gossip, i.e. my mom, he doesn't even do relationships. Which means he's all wrong for me anyway.

Not that I'm interested.

I pull the front door open before Liam rings the bell. He looks caught, and his eyes widen slightly as they take me in.

Weird.

"Hey," I say.

"Hey." He gives a nod, then looks away.

"I gotta grab my coat," I say, deciding it is definitely *not* warm enough for just a turtleneck, no matter how cozy it is. "Do you want to come in?"

He meets my eyes for a split second, then says, "I'll, uh, just wait for you in the truck."

I frown. "Okay, I'll—"

But he's already walking away.

"—hurry, I guess, just need my coat, won't be but a minute, nice talking to ya," I mumble to myself. I grab my things and walk outside, closing the door behind me. I feel like Liam missed the lesson on manners in middle school.

I get into the truck and force myself not to linger on the scent of it, the scent of him. Instead, I glare at the side of his face, willing him to look at me.

He doesn't.

It's actually kind of impressive. I mean, I wouldn't be able to do it. I'd start laughing or at least glance over or something.

He puts the truck in reverse and backs out of my driveway. He doesn't look at the house, at me, or at anything other than the road in front of him, and I decide two can play this game of silence.

I'm a rock.

I'm immoveable.

I will not lose this test of willpower.

Grr.

Fifty-three seconds later, I say, "I never really found a spot for the market," even though I know he's not interested. "I have three vendors already confirmed and paid."

"You do?" He glances over, and for a second, I think maybe he's impressed.

"Yes," I say. "It's a word of mouth kind of thing at the moment. If I had more time, there would be a website and online registration and swag, but since we're in a hurry, I'm relying on email and social media. I'm hoping we can get a lot more vendors to sign up. Big markets are so fun."

I don't expect him to reply, so I'm surprised when he asks, "Are you going to have a booth?"

"Oh! Um . . ." I frown. "I don't know. I hadn't thought about it." I haven't done a market in a long time. Not since before my business tanked. Wouldn't it just be a bitter reminder that I'm in a booth and not in the beautiful brick and mortar store that's since been turned into an insurance agency?

He stares at the road. "You should do it."

"Aww," I lay it on thick. "You think I should?"

He side-eyes me with the hint of a smirk. "Not anymore."

I chuckle.

It's a start.

That's all he says about it, but somehow it's enough.

The days are short now, and it's already getting dark even though it's barely 5:00 p.m. But as I dare a glance in his direction, I can still make out his features. The clenched jaw. The

79

hand, tightly wrapped around the steering wheel. The stony expression on his face.

A thought hits me.

"What do you do for fun?" I ask.

He frowns but doesn't look at me.

"I mean, do you chase kids away after you ask them your riddles three from under your bridge or . . .?" I crack a smile.

"Are you going to tell me again how cranky I am?" he asks.

"Nope," I say. "You won't be able to stay cranky with me around." I say this with far more confidence than I feel.

"Really?" he asks. "Is that a challenge?"

I shake my head. "Just spitting facts, Scrooge. I hope you're ready for some Christmas cheer!" I reach into my bag and pull out two Santa hats.

He tosses me a wary look. "Not a chance."

I narrow my eyes. "I think red is your color."

He doesn't respond.

I lean forward and flip the radio on to the station that plays Christmas music twenty-four hours a day. The unmistakable tune of "Sleigh Ride" by the Ronettes sounds through the speakers.

"Oh, I love this one!" I start singing along—badly—bouncing to the beat of the music. To his credit, Liam maintains his sulkiness, not showing even a hint of amusement.

When the song ends, I click the radio off. "Wow. You're good. That would've gotten at least third place at karaoke night." I say this like I'm diagnosing him, not as a person who just made a complete fool of herself.

After all, he saw my coconuts. We're well beyond humiliation here.

We're about to hit the bend in the road just before the main gates of Pine Creek when I remember the real reason we're doing this: to make Liam remember what it feels like to go tree hunting on his family's property.

The tree hunt isn't new to either of us. Our families used to go every year. We'd bundle up and pile into the cars and drive out together and make a whole night of it. Our fathers insisted there were only two perfect trees on the entire lot, and we had to find them. And we believed it.

And when one of us found it—the perfect enchanted tree—it was like we had unearthed a buried treasure.

Once Liam and his parents started working out here, which meant we'd go hunting without his family and if we were lucky, he might be the one to wrap and load our tree.

I'd see him for about five minutes, always working, busy with other families.

It's strange how adolescent awkwardness plus distance plus time apart can result in a weird *un*knowing. It didn't happen often, but the few times I ran into Liam after they moved were always the same. Forced and awkward. It felt wrong because we used to be so close.

Is it naive to think we could be again? Especially when neither of us is the same person we were? Is it silly to treat him like that time and distance were never an issue? Like we never lost touch?

Signs point to yes. He's just not the same.

"Do you want to take the back way in?" His question interrupts my nostalgia. "We can park by the house and go up into the back lots?"

"No." I pull my Santa hat on. "We're doing this like we used to."

I don't even have to look over to know he's shaking his head at me.

"Don't pretend you didn't have fun," I say.

"I never said I didn't have fun."

"Then what?"

He makes the turn into Pine Creek and parks the truck

outside the Christmas shop. "You can't just pretend everything is still like . . . that."

"Like what?"

"Like how it was." He turns the engine off and looks at me. "A lot has happened since we were twelve."

"Okay, so tell me," I say, genuinely curious.

He sits. I can tell he wants to say something—he just doesn't.

"Liam. It's me. You can tell m—"

"I can't talk to you when you're wearing that hat."

I slowly pick the other one up and hold it out in his direction. "You can if you put yours on," I whisper.

He laughs to himself and looks away. "I get what you're trying to do, Olive. And it's, you know, annoying . . . but nice. Your heart is in the right place. It's just . . ." he sighs. "Don't get your hopes up that a trip down memory lane is going to make any kind of difference." And then, he meets my eyes and adds, "You don't really know me anymore."

The words are true, of course, but they make me feel like I just slipped on ice. "Right, I know."

Because I do know.

He lets out a heavy sigh. I wonder if he notices that he does that all the time. I don't know why he's carrying the weight of the world on his shoulders. I only know that I'm going to take his mind off of whatever is bothering him, just like I used to.

"We'll start with hot chocolate," I say, intentionally brightening my voice. "How does adult Liam feel about marshmallows?" I open the door of the truck and step outside, inhaling the crisp air.

Fishing my gloves from the pockets of my coat, I pull them on as I walk to the back of the truck. Liam's door opens and he meets me in the parking lot. Maybe I'm supposed to feel put off by his crankiness, but it's only making me want to try harder.

"Personally, I don't think hot chocolate can have too many

marshmallows," I say, walking toward the hot chocolate shed that's a Pine Creek staple.

To my surprise, he actually follows. For a second, I thought he might refuse the same way he rejected the Santa hat.

We make our way over to the little shed where Lacey is filming one of the workers handing a cup out the window to a small child. The little boy beams as he takes a sip, and Lacey nods at his mom, who is standing off to the side.

Lacey spots us, and her smile widens. "Well, look at you two, out after hours."

Liam stuffs his hands in his pockets. I can't be sure, but I think he might've groaned.

"I suckered him into coming with me to cut down a tree," I say.

"Oh my gosh, it's been ages since we've done that." Lacey looks at me. "After we moved here, we were lucky if we ever had a tree of our own on Christmas morning."

I frown. "Really?"

She shrugs. "There really wasn't time. Everyone was so busy —" she stops abruptly. "Ooh. Cute old couple at ten o'clock. I need to film them going on a carriage ride. Have fun you guys!" She rushes off.

I meet Liam's eyes. "Are you ready?" He starts walking. "The best trees are in the back lot."

"Wait." I reach for his arm.

When he stops moving, he looks at me, concern on his face.

"I don't want to rush." I rub my hands together. "I'm here for the experience."

Liam closes his eyes and inhales, almost like he's trying for deep, calming breaths. "Seriously?"

I level with him. "Liam, come on. I'm not asking you to dance under the Christmas lights or sing a carol outside someone's door. I just want you to see this place the way I see it. Just

83

for a minute." I pat his arm. "I'm just asking you to be open to the idea of—" I pause for effect— "fun."

"Fun," he repeats dryly.

I grin.

He doesn't respond.

I raise my eyebrows. Then lower them, then raise them.

He shakes his head and tries to hide a smile.

I point at him. "Ah ha!"

He clears his throat. "Whatever."

I turn and start walking.

"Okay. Pretend you don't know anything about this place. You're coming here for the first time. You get out of your deliciously smelling truck and look around, your dear, sweet, delightful, old friend in tow—"

"You forgot annoying."

I shoot him a look. "Fine. I'll own that. Dear, sweet, delightful, *annoying* old friend in tow. You look around at this place, all lit up with white twinkle lights and Christmas spirit, and you start to feel it—" I put a little bounce in my shoulders.

He looks at me like I have an arm growing out of my forehead.

"Do you feel it, Liam?" I whisper.

I think I see a sliver of amusement behind the look of abject horror.

Maybe it's just wishful thinking.

I plow ahead like a runaway tractor tire rolling down a hill.

"It's *joy*." I drag the word out, like I'm a presenter on a game show. "Joy, Liam!" I move like something's taking hold of me. "It's there, just waiting for you." My grin widens, and my shimmy grows. "You feel that?"

Still no reaction, other than a slight twitch. I've seen that twitch before, in animals that are about pick flight over fight.

I've gone too far now, may as well keep going.

"You see this festive little shed advertising hot chocolate, and you think, 'My favorite person in the world, Olive Witherby, *loves* hot chocolate. We should get some before we head out to hunt for her perfect, enchanted tree.'" I hold his gaze.

He purses his lips . . . then finally breaks. He shakes his head and lets out a small laugh. "You're crazy, you know that?"

"Finally!" I mock that I'm out of breath, hands on knees. "Good grief, that took for*ever*!"

"Liv, seriously, you're—"

I hold up a finger at him, still feigning like I just ran a 400 meter Olympic trial, telling him, "You gotta let me get my bearings here, that was rough."

I glance up, panting, and he folds his arms across his chest, like one might do waiting for a toddler who's explaining that she wasn't the one who broke the vase.

"Oh, come on," I say, standing up straight and arching my back, stretching it out. "Admit it. This is what makes me so lovable."

He looks likes he's going to argue, then glances over to his left.

The hot chocolate line.

He bobs his head toward it, indicating that we should move over there.

"Yes!" I exclaim, thrusting my hands up in the air, but then he stops me with a finger of his own.

"Don't push it."

"Okay, okay."

But then, just for a second, I look at him and he looks at me, and for the tiniest of moments, we connect like we did as kids.

It's there. A flicker.

And then, just as quickly as it came, it disappears.

We step into the hot chocolate line. The girl working doesn't recognize him, and I watch as he says, "Two hot chocolates—" he tosses me a look and adds, "extra marshmallows on both." I turn away to conceal my smile.

Point for Olive.

I move next to him as he gives her cash, which is hilarious since his family owns this place. I know I've got a smug look on my face.

"Extra marshmallows don't mean anything," he says.

I press my lips together, but choose not to respond. Because it *does* mean something.

The girl hands us our drinks out, and as we walk away, I say, "Thanks, buddy."

"You're welcome, chief—" he answers, almost like muscle memory, but stops before he can finish. He looks at me and shakes his head.

It's something we used to do, as kids, going back and forth, thanking each other with more and more ridiculous names.

Thanks, friend into *No problem, boss,* then onto *My pleasure, doc,* to *You got it, mi amigo,* until we ran out of names and breath from laughing.

"We're not kids anymore," he says, voice flat.

"Well, thank goodness for that." I muse. "We both drive cars."

We walk in silence for a bit, and I realize that I might've been a bit much in the last ten minutes. I let the moment breathe, hoping that he's enjoying the atmosphere—and the company—as much as I am.

After a while, I gently ask, "Do you remember how much fun we had out here?" We angle in the direction of the carriage rides.

"Blocked it out," he says dryly.

"I don't believe you."

"I keep telling people this place wasn't magic for me." His tone is blunt. "It was a job. A prison camp, more like."

I scrunch up my face at him. "Don't you think that's a bit of an exaggeration?"

He glances over, a serious look in his eyes.

"No. Not for me."

I wish I knew the rest of the story behind those beautiful eyes.

We reach the line, and he looks at me. "We're not doing this."

I shrug. "Why not? We used to love it."

He squints off at something in the distance.

"You're not really into nostalgia, are you?" I tease. Then, because I really want to know, I ask, "Is there *anything* you like about being back?"

He waits for a moment before answering, pausing so long I don't think he's going to say anything at all.

"I like the parts that are away from all of this." He sighs, leaning against a wooden fence.

I go quiet.

I take another sip, considering how different his experience here was after they became the caretakers of Pine Creek.

"Can I ask you something?" I ask.

"As if I could stop you," he says quietly, but not unkindly.

I chuckle. "Fair. But in my defense, my back hurts from carrying both sides of this conversation."

He glowers.

"Did your parents ever think about expanding?"

He shakes his head and sharply says, "Nope," then takes a drink. I get the sense he's avoiding the question.

"I just think there's a lot of potential here. You know, for growth," I tell him. "When I was researching ideas, I looked up a ton of other tree farms, apple orchards, barn markets, and I noticed most of them do way more than just sell trees or apples or homemade jelly."

He looks uncomfortable. I'm not sure why.

"It got me thinking, I guess, about all the things you could do out here," I say. "It's such a big space, and so much of it isn't being used to its full potential." I look away.

"Yeah," he scoffs, "tell my dad that, see how *that* goes over." He doesn't look at me, but it's obvious there's more there. I want to press, but the carriage returns. I'm grateful because I wasn't sure what to say.

There's a young couple inside, hunkered together under a red plaid blanket. They're cozy, holding hands and smitten with each other. As the horses come to a stop, I pull out my phone and snap a quick photo just as they gaze at one another, all big eyes and glinty smiles.

Good for social media. Bad for me.

All this does is highlight what I don't have this holiday season, and maybe—I glance over at Liam—

No. Liam isn't the only chronic first-dater between us. I've had my fair share of first date horrors, so much so it'd fill a nice montage in a rom-com.

Never mind that for me it's unintentional. A lack of options. Poor choices.

I'm better off focusing on myself. Oh, and the whole getting out of debt thing.

The young couple steps down from the carriage, and as the older couple moves forward in the line, moving us closer to the front, I notice that Liam looks uncomfortable. He pushes a hand through his hair and looks like a cornered kid talking with the aunt with the mustache.

"Hey, uh, can we—" He looks at me.

"Yeah. Totally. Let's—" I pull him out of the line. "I wouldn't want someone else to get to the one perfect tree before I do." I also wouldn't want anyone—namely, me—to get the wrong impression about what this is.

A romantic carriage ride would be a very bad idea.

"Right," he says.

I force a smile. "Do you have an axe or a chainsaw or a trained beaver, or something?"

"In the barn." He starts walking, and I have no choice but to follow, and five minutes later, we're trudging into the barely lit field, in search of the perfect tree.

To me, there are a lot of perfect trees. Tall and full and beautiful. The kind most people would want.

I start to think we should've done this in daylight. I can't get a read on Liam if I can't see his face. Right now, he just feels like a man on a mission. It's less "enjoy the ride" and more "get this over with."

I worry my plan is failing.

We're at the back of the property when he veers away from the rows of trees. For a second, I assume he's lost his patience—we've been out here about fifteen minutes already—but then he turns back and says, "I want to show you something."

"You're holding an axe," I say. "Should I be worried?"

He doesn't stop moving, but I hear him laugh to himself. The sound of it cuts through the darkness, a small sliver of light.

We walk for a few more minutes, and it's dark enough now that I can't make out where we are. "These trees are too big," I say. "My house is really small."

He keeps walking.

"Seriously, this is not the typical Pine Creek experience." I say this to the back of his head because he's walking faster than me, and he's making no attempt to slow down.

He turns off the path. "Trust me."

I freeze, fishing for my phone so at least I'll have a little bit of light. "Liam, is this like a practical joke where you're going to jump out and scare me or someth—"

But I'm rendered mute when the area around me suddenly lights up.

I'm standing in a wide clearing, and all around us are trees, twinkling brightly in the darkness. The strands of lights are hung in swaths, connected from one side of the clearing to another, creating a ceiling of shimmering starlight over a pathway of grass.

"What is this place?" I ask in wonder, because in all my years of coming to the farm, I've never seen it.

"My mom calls it 'Christmas Tree Row,'" Liam says, then points down the path. "There's a separate entrance to the farm beyond that grouping of trees."

"It's amazing," I say, truly struck by it. "Has anyone ever had a wedding out here?" I spin in a circle, taking it all in, picturing rows of wooden chairs set up to face a small stage at the opposite end of the space with a wooden backdrop decorated with flowers. It would be perfect. Imagine the photos. They could book this place out for—

"I. . .uh. . ." He stops.

I wait.

And then, a glimpse of the boy I knew in the face of the man I see before me makes an appearance.

"I thought it might work for your market," Liam says, shyly shrugging, looking at the ground.

I watch him for several long seconds, willing him to turn my way, but he doesn't. Almost like something about this embarrasses him.

Finally, he glances at me, and I can't do a thing to conceal my smile.

He rolls his eyes. "Oh, great."

I open my mouth wide.

"Nope. Forget it, just forget it, forget I even said anything," he holds up his hands.

I point at him.

"Don't make a thing of it."

"You *were* listening to my presentation!"

"Like I had a choice."

"Admit it. You think it's a brilliant idea."

"I think you're all going to freeze, I think it's a ton of work, and I think it's not going to make a difference at all."

I put my hands on my hips. "Why don't you tell me how you really feel there, big guy."

He shakes his head and walks past me in the open space.

"Since nobody can speak *actual logic* to you, I figured you can line the booths on either side of the path—" He motions over to the other side, gesturing to make the idea clearer. "I don't know how many people you expect, and it might get crowded, but we can figure out a way to wind it around—" he points off in the direction of darkness— "back there."

"Liam. You've actually thought about this," I say. "Like, you spent time thinking about it."

"Like, five minutes."

"And you think it might get crowded!"

He groans.

"You like my idea, you sucker," I tease.

"I know you and Lacey are going to rope me into it, so I might as well make it easier on myself."

"Uh-huh," I say. "Whatever. Keep telling yourself that's what this is."

He levels my gaze. "Seriously. Will it work?"

I grin. "It'll work."

"Great." He walks back over toward a small shed and unceremoniously flips a switch.

The world, like Liam, goes dark all over again.

CHAPTER 11

LIAM

*S*he picked the ugliest tree on the lot.

She either did it on purpose or has zero taste.

Or she's the only one who can see its potential.

I'm sure she could tell by the look on my face that the choice confused me, but once she made up her mind, that was it.

Classic Olive.

She made me show her how to use the axe even though I'm pretty sure she could've snapped it right out of the ground with her bare hands, and a few minutes later, we were hauling it back to my truck. It's skinny and sparse, but Olive said it had character.

I'm starting to see that she grew up to be exactly who I expected her to be—quirky, creative, and determined. And talkative.

It was always obvious, even as kids, when Olive was on a mission to break me out of one of my moods. She had a natural brightness about her, but she'd kick it into high gear if she sensed I was having a bad day.

She's doing that now. It should annoy me but it doesn't.

I never realized how much I relied on that until I didn't have it anymore.

Even now, after my conversational absence, she's sitting in my truck, staring out the window, quietly humming a Christmas carol and still wearing that Santa hat. Just having her next to me calms something inside of me. It's familiar. I don't have to try, or perform or live up to anything.

She just is and I just am, and it's nice.

The angry part that resents everything about Pine Creek isn't as loud as it was before.

It's probably a coincidence.

"Oh, wait! Turn here." She points to a road up ahead, and I flip on my blinker, though I'm not sure why we're headed this way.

"I thought we were going back to your house."

"We are," she says. "By way of the old neighborhood."

I frown.

"Have you been back?" she asks as I come to a stop at a red light.

I shake my head and begin to accelerate as the light turns green, then make my way over to the once-familiar neighborhood where Olive and I grew up.

"My parents are in Green Bay," she says.

I grimace. "Your dad is a raging Packers fan. I forgot about that."

"He wears that cheese hat so proudly, you'd think it was a trophy." She shakes her head.

"You can park in their driveway."

Again, I do as I'm told, and once we're parked, I'm more aware than ever of the silence. I lean forward, looking out the front window.

"Wow. It hasn't changed much." I study the once-familiar scene in front of me—the backdrop of so many childhood memories. The pair of matching houses have both been updated, and both yards are as pristine as I remember.

"I thought our houses were bigger." I tap my thumb on the steering wheel.

She chuckles. "Everything feels bigger when you're ten, I guess."

Feelings included, I think.

"Did your parents get rid of the treehouse?"

She shakes her head. "No, my mom said they want to keep it for their grandkids." She laughs. "No pressure, right? Like I'm going to pop one out in the next nine months." She opens the truck door and gets out. "Come on!"

She immediately stops and whips back around. "That came out wrong. I didn't mean *come on* like we're going to make a baby . . ." She looks horrified.

I really try to stifle a laugh, but a snort escapes.

"Shoot. I didn't mean it . . . I meant . . . *argh*." She struggles to find words that make sense and ends up muttering, "Let's just go."

She slams the door, and I can hear her muffled self-scolding from inside the truck.

It's adorable. She might be infuriating, but I'm finding more things to like about her than I want to.

I get out and follow her down the driveway, stopping when she opens the garage and flips on the lights in the backyard. I look around. "So not *everything* is the same."

She does a half turn. "They built the three-season room after you guys moved."

"And got a hot tub," I say, pointing.

"Apparently for my dad's back, but honestly, I don't ask questions about that because I don't want to know."

I grimace. "Thanks for *that* visual."

"Yeah. I think they've gotten friskier as they've gotten older, if that's even possible." She shudders.

94

And it strikes me that while I was out there growing up, Olive was doing the same. She had a whole life here that I wasn't a part of. I'm hit with the sudden urge to find out more about that life, but I tamp it down and steer my thoughts in a different direction.

I turn to face the treehouse. "That looks the same."

She nods.

"Ooh! All that's missing is—" She spins around. "You go up, I'll be right back."

I watch as she walks toward the house, knowing exactly what she's going to get. The part of me that thinks this is ridiculous wrestles with the part of me that thinks it's exactly what I need.

I look at the old treehouse, back toward the house, and decide to go with it.

I hoist myself up. I remember it feeling more precarious and taking longer when I was younger—I would routinely scrape my stomach shimmying onto the platform. Now, though, it's not that difficult.

If only everything figured itself out so easily when you got older.

Olive returns a few minutes later, carrying two blankets. "This one's for *you*," handing it out sing-songy like a waitress bringing extra breadsticks.

I take one of the blankets and look at it, then at her.

"Well, come on, Cranky, spread it out."

It feels odd, familiar, and new at the same time. I spread it over my legs as she does the same. Once her blanket is in place, she reaches inside her coat and slowly, with mouth agape and visual fanfare, pulls out two foil-wrapped circles.

"Are you even ready?" She grins.

It's freezing out here, but that smile warms me.

"Listen. I don't know what's going on with you, I don't know what life's been like between the last time we were up here and

95

now, but I know for a fact that nobody can stay grumpy while eating one of my mom's homemade ice cream sandwiches."

The memory of the last time we were here flashes in my mind like a scene on a drive-in movie screen.

Before I can get lost in it, she hands one over. Two thick, soft chocolate chip cookies held together by a healthy portion of vanilla ice cream.

I take my gloves off.

"Before you say it, I know it's kind of a dumb thing to eat outside in December," she says. "Do you want to go inside?"

"I'm okay." I'm surprised to discover I'm telling the truth. I start to unwrap it. "I didn't realize until this second how much I missed these."

She's already got the foil off of hers, and as she takes a bite, she looks at me and smiles, and it's like no time has passed between us at all.

"Oh! I almost forgot." She reaches into her coat pockets again and pulls out two cans of Coke. "Do you still drink Coke?"

I motion for her to hand it over.

She gives me one, then cracks her can open and takes a drink, and it's like we're kids again, insulated from the world, from sadness, from complicated family relationships, from broken hearts.

Our treehouse, our oasis, our sanctuary.

"You didn't deny your reputation," she says between bites.

It takes me a second to remember what she's talking about.

"Is it true?" she asks as a chunk of the ice cream falls onto the floor of the small treehouse. "Darn it. I wanted that."

"You should take smaller bites."

She frowns and pulls the blanket tighter around her. "So? Chronic first-dater or . . .?"

I sigh. But I don't answer.

Her shoulders slump a bit, "Oh, it's . . . I didn't mean . . . If it's too personal, or whatever, it's fine, I—"

I'm not sure why, but I decide to talk. "I date."

Two words. Not bad. Probably a personal record when talking about this kind of stuff.

"Okay . . .?"

I take a bite. Wow, this is good, like rediscovering Pop Tarts as an adult.

I nod. "That's it. I date."

"Deep stuff there."

I shrug.

"How many second dates have you been on in the last year?"

I pretend to think about this for a second then say, "Ehh . . . let's talk about something else."

She cocks her head to the side and jokingly says, "Who broke your heart, Liam Fisher?" in an overdramatic tone.

I stop mid-bite and meet her eyes. "What makes you think someone broke my heart?"

She shrugs. "Lucky guess? I mean, we're thirty-one. We're both single. It stands to reason that someone, somewhere broke your heart."

"It's not as tragic as all that. There are other reasons relationships don't work out," I say.

"Like . . .?"

I shrug. "Like . . . it just runs its course? You discover you want different things? You realize you're not really compatible? You move away and . . ."

Shoot. I did not mean to say that.

I try to save it— ". . .like, meet new people, and you just don't click, you know, that kind of thing."

She takes a sip of Coke, then looks at me. "Can I say something without it seeming, I don't know, like weird?"

"That hasn't stopped you at all this whole night, why start now?" I quip.

"Oh, okay, pal. Calm yourself down."

It's getting easier to tease. She makes me feel comfortable enough to loosen up.

She looks straight ahead. "Do you believe you were my first kiss? Right here in this treehouse." She smiles, like it's a sweet, cherished memory. "Do you even remember?"

I go still.

I can't say that it's a conscious decision to say something, but "You tasted like vanilla ice cream" comes out of my mouth.

She freezes, holding her half-eaten ice cream sandwich in mid-air.

I tell myself not to look at her lips, but I fail.

There's a quick, quiet zap of electricity, and then I look away. "We should go." I eat the last bit of the ice cream, then shift toward the ladder and make my way down.

"Right." She follows me down.

I stand behind her as she climbs down, though it's obvious she doesn't need my help. And once both of her feet hit the ground, I start off in the direction of the truck.

I need space. Or distance. Or both? My head is swimming and my heart wants neither.

She was nothing more than a childhood crush.

Right?

As I get into the truck and start the engine, I realize something. Something I don't want to realize. Olive is the standard I've compared every other person I've dated to.

Which makes me wonder—is that why I haven't been on a second date?

CHAPTER 12

LIAM

I'm starting to think this whole night was a bad idea.

All I want to do is drop this tree off at her house and get back to the farm, away from complicated emotions and talking about them.

I park the truck in her narrow driveway, behind her VW Beetle, aware that my earlier plan to not look around at her house isn't going to be as easy to execute this time. I'll have to go inside her house. I'll have to look around the living room. I'll leave with the image of her on her couch, watching TV under whatever crazy blanket she's got draped over the back of the sofa because I know for an absolute fact she will have one.

She turns to face me, cheeks still flushed after being outside. Thankfully, she talks as if nothing happened, business as usual. She still has the same cheery tone.

How does she do that?

"Hey, thanks for your help tonight. And for finding the location for the market. I can't wait to draw a map once we have all the vendors! Maybe tomorrow we can measure the space? Break it all up into plots where the booths will go? That way I'll know how many we have room for, and I can start assigning people as they register. Numbering them, might make it way easier."

So much for keeping my distance.

"Yep." I open the door, motioning that I'll meet her in the front of the truck. I feel out of sorts, and everything I think to say sounds stupid in my head before I say it.

She pulls a face. "Shoot. I just remembered I need the tree stand. I'm not sure where that is." She looks around the yard, as if it might be out in the darkness somewhere. "Oh wait! I think it's in the garage."

I watch as she fishes keys from her pocket, then opens the door of the garage. I'm not sure if I'm supposed to follow her, but I figure an extra pair of eyes won't hurt, so after a few seconds I walk in behind her.

Most garages are reserved for lawn equipment and tools and maybe a deep freezer. Olive's seems to be reserved for— "What is all this stuff?"

She spins around, visibly surprised I'm there. "Oh! I didn't know you were—" Her shoulders drop. "It's leftover inventory. From my store." She looks away, a bit embarrassed.

There's sadness in her voice as she says this, and while I don't want to pry, I'm also curious to know more about her shop beyond the stories I heard when it closed. I didn't ask my mom many questions when she mentioned it, but I was disappointed it was the one subject she didn't linger on.

It sounds like it was a special place, and I want to know more, which is why I start looking around the garage for some clue of what it might've looked like.

I'm about to formulate some sort of question when Olive gives me a sad smile. "I don't come out here much."

Unlike me, Olive wears her heart on her sleeve. She doesn't mind telling anyone how she feels about anything. I can't imagine being that open. Especially with something as uncomfortable as my feelings.

But then again, I've always been the kind of person who smashes a lid on my emotions.

Haven't I?

"You must think I'm a total disaster." She doesn't look at me when she says this, but I can see the humiliation on her face. Her default is upbeat self-deprecation, so this is a switch.

"Why would I think that?" I ask.

She walks behind a workbench, as if it can protect her. She picks up a stack of cello-wrapped cards and studies them. "Everyone I knew and trusted said it was a huge mistake—" she looks up— "opening the store. Venturing out on my own. To be fair, everyone said majoring in art was a huge mistake too, so I don't have a very good track record when it comes to taking advice."

I can relate.

She sits on a stool, and I close the door of the garage to keep out the chilly breeze.

"I'm kind of stubborn." Her smile is weak.

"You? Really?" I say without smiling.

It's not well-lit in here, and I get the sense that she's shoved everything in this space so she doesn't have to look at or think about it.

We have more in common than I thought, only my garage is mental.

"I know we didn't really know each other in high school, but everyone had pretty high expectations for me," she says. "I'm not the person you would've expected to end up bouncing around from job to job."

I take a step closer, then sit down on a stool across from her. I don't like talking, but I like to listen to Olive.

She shuffles the wrapped products around on the table. "I started college with this grand plan to major in architecture. It was something artistic but professional. A practical choice, right? Architects get jobs."

I watch her, as I try—fail—not to draw similarities to my own story. I know a little bit about trying to manage everyone else's expectations with my own desires. "What happened?"

"I hated it!" Her eyes widen. "It was *so* wrong for me. I'm sure some people have figured out how to express themselves through architecture, but it just wasn't my style. So I changed my major to art, much to my parents' dismay, and here I am."

Huh. She changed her direction, too.

"A sometimes barista-slash-dog-walker-slash-failed-business-owner." She holds her arms out in a "ta-da!" motion and shakes her hands like it's the end of a tap number in a musical.

"And now tree farm savior," I add.

She laughs ruefully and shakes her head. "Yeah, we'll see. A leader who doesn't have anyone following her is just going for a walk."

If she thinks she's shocking me, she's wrong. She has just described so many of my own experiences it's uncanny. I should tell her how much I relate . . . explain that she's not the only one who feels like she tried to do something big and important and missed the mark.

She's not the only one still trying to redeem herself.

But I don't say anything. It feels like opening a door that I don't want to open.

She hands me a stack of cards, and I flip through them, noting her clever, quirky sense of humor is captured on each whimsical design.

A sketchy, hand-drawn dog wearing glasses, sitting behind a computer with the words *This could've been an email.* underneath it.

Two sets of hand-drawn feet sticking out from under a cover. This one reads *Pajamas>Plans.*

They're so . . . Olive.

"It's not exactly fine art." She looks away.

"Does it need to be?"

She shrugs. "I didn't think so. I never wanted to make the kind of art that would go on a gallery wall. I wanted to make art that made people think. Or laugh. Or both. I wanted to put joy into the world." She stills. "The world is dark enough already."

I turn one of the cards over in my hand. There's an avocado staring back at me with a speech bubble off to the side. Somehow, the avocado has a personality, and in the speech bubble, in Olive's artistic handwriting, is the word *Bravocado!*

The quality is good. It's obvious she's paid attention to every detail.

"Turns out nobody but me took me seriously." She looks away. "I mean, how could they? I draw fruits and vegetables and anthropomorphic animals and make greeting cards. It's hardly serious."

"What do you think of it?" I ask, turning around the bravocado so she can see it.

She looks at the cheerful avocado and smiles sadly. "Oh my gosh, I love that one."

"Then, what's the problem?"

She laughs ruefully. "You don't get it."

"I kind of do," I tell her.

She shoots me a look. "Please. Your castle game is huge. You must be, like, a gazillionaire by now. Meanwhile, I'm the person they call when the espresso machine breaks down."

"That's a critical skill," I say.

She laughs.

I don't bother correcting her mistaken assumptions about me. That would involve an admission of my own.

"My entire senior project was a series based on literature. I illustrated my favorite quotes from my favorite books. It wasn't edgy or thought-provoking. It was quirky and fun. Like, one was 'Multiple exclamation marks are a sure sign of a diseased mind.'" She looks at me, as if I'm supposed to get the joke. When

I clearly don't, she explains, "It's from a Terry Pratchett book," and waves me off.

She goes back to thinking. "My professors and the other students told me I should consider giving up on art and going to work for a greeting card company." She looks up. "They said it like it was an insult. Like I should be embarrassed or something." Her laugh is wry. "Little did *they* know, eh?"

She holds up a card with what looks like two cats in a car, and the car is in a traffic jam. The cat driving, paw on forehead, has a speech bubble that reads *You have cat to be kitten me right meow.*

"That belongs in a museum," I deadpan.

"Ha, ha." She turns it around, and chuckles at her own pun. "I just didn't fit there. I'm not sure where I fit, actually. I'm artistic, but not *high-brow* artistic." She slumps a bit on the stool.

I don't respond, partly because I don't know what to say and partly because I still don't want her to stop talking. I usually lose interest pretty quickly, or feel uncomfortable, which is part of the reason why I've earned a mom-labeled reputation as a chronic first-dater.

I haven't met anyone who makes me want to know more about them.

Until now.

Crazy since I thought I already knew her, but there's a whole section of her life I wasn't around for.

I suppose a part of me has always been fascinated with Olive. I just thought I would've outgrown it by now.

"I think the idea for the store came out of some misguided need to prove them all wrong," she says. "Like, I'll show you I can make a living!" A sigh. "I was so stupid."

"It's not stupid," I tell her. "I kind of know what that's like, actually."

Her eyes meet mine, and I don't look away.

Please don't ask me to explain.

Or do. I just might talk about it.

I don't think it's stupid to do something to make people happy. I think of tonight. Her plan to make me love Pine Creek again. I know it's not about the tree farm—it's about me. It's about her caring enough to remind me of something that used to be good.

Or maybe it was always something good, and I just didn't have eyes to see it.

"Well, in this case, it sort of was stupid, because my business failed," she continues, thankfully not asking me to expound on what I admitted. "I went into it without a real plan. I mean, I wrote a business plan—part of one anyway—I wasn't completely out of my depth. But boy, I found out real quick all that I didn't know about running my own business."

Designing your own game can be a solitary existence. I've taken classes that outline how to support yourself as an indie game designer. Most of what they teach is to create content online, so there's no brick and mortar store, and even that was time consuming and overwhelming. I can't imagine what it would be like with people and inventory and insurance and staff and bills.

"I had a very small online following," she goes on. It feels like she needs to talk about this—so I let her. I'm not terrible at listening.

"My grandparents had given me some money after I graduated," she says. "I put it all toward the store, but I still couldn't get a loan on my own." She half-laughs, as if remembering. "My parents co-signed." Now, when her eyes meet mine, I see pain behind her eyes.

"I, uh . . . I have a lot of debt." Her face falls. She looks up at me briefly, and then looks down again. "Like, a lot."

For the first time in a really long time, I empathize. I feel horrible for her, and my mind starts racing about how I can help. I don't know what that would look like, and I don't even know where to start, but in this moment, I really care about what happens to Olive Witherby.

"I really believed that if I worked hard enough, I could make my store a success," she admits. "And I *really* believed that people wanted to feel happy. What I didn't count on was how expensive it was going to be. Rent and inventory *and* utilities? I borrowed Wi-Fi from my neighbors. I picked which utility to pay each month based on how overdue it was. It's pathetic, mostly because everyone was right. It's a dumb way to try to make a living."

She takes one more look at the card she's holding and tosses it back into a cardboard box full of them.

"I think more than anything—more than proving people wrong—I wanted to be a part of something. A community." She shrugs. "I'm still trying to figure out where I fit in."

Immediately I picture her in my mind, behind the counter at Pine Creek, wearing that horrible Christmas sweater and a Santa hat, laughing and handing out hot chocolate.

She could fit right there.

The pointless thought hits me out of nowhere. Pine Creek isn't going to exist the way anyone knew it for much longer, and it feels cruel to bring it up.

So I don't.

Instead, I cross my arms over my chest and arch a brow. "You know borrowing Wi-Fi is actually stealing, right?"

She shoots me a look. "That's the part of my sob story you decide to zero in on, you psycho?"

I resist the urge to smile. Mostly, I want to know how it's possible that this failure hasn't broken her spirit.

And can she teach me to do the same?

"So, there you have it." She does a little curtsy. "I'm in debt up to my eyeballs, I've got a useless college degree, and I currently have no marketable skills. I know. It's shocking I'm still single."

She walks over to the corner and starts digging around in the bins on the ground.

"If I still had my lucky four-leaf clover, I bet my entire life would be different." She shoots me a look that seems like a challenge—like do I remember the day she gave it to me even though I know she was ridiculously excited to find it.

She holds up a card. On it there's a hand-drawn four-leaf clover in the style I now recognize as uniquely hers. "Just kidding, I made one for myself." She grins and goes back to rummaging around. I'm glad she doesn't seem to expect a response from me.

While she's occupied, I glance down and see a notepad with some of Olive's doodles on it. There's one—a little guy wearing a propeller hat—that I'm instantly drawn to. She's drawn him in a series across the top of the paper, like he's on the ground at the start and then takes flight.

Whirlybirds.

The word pops in my head, and I can see it. The hook my game has been missing. A character that makes its way through mazes and puzzles, propelled forward by his practical, magical hat. Not just hats though. What if he could put on other items of clothing that do various things? Spring shoes to get over higher objects? A coat that becomes an invisibility shield?

My mind starts spinning on a creative axis like it hasn't done in years.

X-ray glasses to see through obstacles. Muscle shirts to lift blocks to access hidden areas. Sweaty socks to wall climb. Combining outfits would stack abilities. Multiplayer. Competitive or cooperative. Race to the finish while punching your friends off the sides of ramps. Kids would flip out about it. Whimsical and fun and appealing to a younger audience.

I need to write this down.

"What about you?" she asks. "What was it like to be an

instant success straight out of college?" She continues rummaging through bins.

The question is there, waiting for me to do the polite thing and answer it.

"Ah. Well . . ."

Conversation only works if it's reciprocated, and yet, I can't bring myself to get into it. Even though she's just demonstrated that she might be the only person in the world who understands.

I search my mind for a way to change the subject, but I'm saved when I spot the Christmas tree stand on the bottom of a tall shelving unit. "Found it." I pick it up as she turns around. "Now we can unload the world's ugliest tree."

She smirks. "Oh, I'm not letting you off the hook that easily, my friend."

I'm surprised that a small part of me is thankful she's not.

CHAPTER 13

OLIVE

J'm doing that thing again.

That thing where I wake up super early to go to the bathroom, but then lay in my bed and try to fall back asleep but my brain plays embarrassing or idiotic things I do on repeat.

I overshare. I know I do. And now I'm wondering if it was a mistake to tell Liam so much about my life.

I fumble in the dark for my phone and tap it. It blinds me, and I squint at the time.

4:46 a.m.

Ugh.

You overshared. You blabbed. You were too honest, and he probably didn't even care.

Shut up, brain.

So what if I told him about my life? I want to know about his, too, but I didn't press. I can guess he doesn't like to be pushed into talking about things.

It's easy to fall into this pattern with Liam, because there's a sense of familiarity.

Platonic familiarity, for sure. He's made that clear. He darted out of here so fast last night he might as well have said so out loud.

Not that either of us is looking for anything else, him especially.

But there was a moment . . . I know I didn't imagine it.

And now my brain is telling me it was dumb of me to bring up the first kiss. *I didn't mean anything by it*, I talk back to the voice in my head, *I was just commenting on it*. But now, from his reaction—and the fact that he remembered it—what exactly did it mean to him?

What exactly did it mean to me?

We were twelve, for crying out loud. Just kids, right?

I sigh. I'm not falling back to sleep anytime soon.

On a more realistic note, I hope I'm succeeding at making him love the farm. He did find that amazing spot for the market, so that's something.

I try to sleep for a bit longer, but once I'm up, I'm *up*, so I give in and get out of bed. I pick up my phone, tap it to see the bright 5:12 a.m. shining at me and I tell my phone to shut its mouth and then toss it on the bed.

I shower and get dressed, and when I get downstairs, I take a minute to give my little tree the sideways glance it deserves. It's so strange-looking—tall and weird and skinny and sparse—but I love it. I loved it when I saw it at the farm, and I loved it when Liam set it up in my living room, and I love it now. I can already see how amazing the pink, red, and green ribbons and hand-made ornaments will look.

When I'm finished with it, it'll still look like a little weirdo, but it'll have way more personality than its taller, fuller, cookie-cutter cousins, and that's all I really care about.

As my coffee brews and my Pop Tarts toast, I start sending emails—people I know from living here all my life and from running my own business. People who will want to know that the Pine Creek legacy is going to change hands, one way or another. People who can help generate support for our Last, Best Pine Creek Christmas.

The Last, Best Christmas. I linger on the phrase. It's celebratory and nostalgic, with a hint of melancholy and tradition.

I attach the event calendar Jo approved, making sure everyone knows what's happening and when, in hopes that the word will spread . . . and even though it's only about 6:30 in the morning, I hit send.

I give a satisfied sigh and stand to grab my coffee when out of the corner of my eye I see a response push the rest of my emails down. Within seconds, more responses do the same. Do these people sleep?

The mayor wants to know if Pine Creek will still be supplying the town with its Christmas tree. Clark at the newspaper wants to come out and do a story. And the head of the Loveland/Pleasant Valley area chamber wants to know why "those Fisher kids" aren't taking it over.

"I wish I knew, Trish," I say out loud.

I open Instagram and see that Lacey has fully taken over the Pine Creek account. There are stories and videos and—a photo —I pinch my fingers on the screen to enlarge it. In the foreground is a little girl, holding her mother's gloved hand and wearing an adorably oversized stocking cap. But in the background, the area I'm enlarging, there's me, standing in the line for the carriage ride. I'm looking at the horse, and next to me is Liam—looking at me.

The photo is grainy and dark, but I've never seen this expression on his face. It's kind, almost admiring.

Opposite to the permanent scowl he's been wearing lately.

I'm trying so hard to figure him out, I'm probably projecting. I'm *sure* I'm reading into it. At the moment, Liam doesn't even seem to like me, let alone admire me.

Which means he's still a mystery.

After I eat, I grab a travel mug, fill it with coffee, and drive out to the farm. I don't know what time Liam will be available to help me measure the spaces for the market, but I work here now. Jo didn't give me a time to show up, and I don't punch a clock, but I still want to be here, in the mix of things. I want to be a part of it all. It's a shame it's only for the month because I think I would be pretty good at dreaming up fun events for the farm.

Last night, as I fell asleep, I found myself thinking of new ideas—ways to make Pine Creek a year-round destination. The property sits between two small, charming towns near one of the nation's largest cities. Surely it could attract enough business if marketed right.

I start thinking about it again, this time with clear eyes and fully caffeinated.

I know there have been weddings on the property, but I don't think Jo and Brant ever really leaned into that idea. It could be a full-fledged event center and wedding venue—off the beaten path, too, perfect for unique, memorable experiences for all walks of life, both corporate and personal. I wonder why they never pursued that. I can't think of a more beautiful place around here to get married.

This thought leads to another thought and then another and before I can stop it, my mind is whirring with new ideas. Cabins around the lake. Getaways for families or couples, each one with enough space to feel secluded. In the summer, we could play up a rustic, vintage glamping theme. We could do bonfires for all the guests or what about—honeymoon hot tubs in the woods?

That makes me think of my parents, and I shudder.

Maybe not honeymoon hot tubs in the woods.

The shop could become more seasonal, swapping out Christmas décor for other things—lake-inspired or camp-inspired and . . . what if the café became a full-fledged restaurant? The kind that garnered local and regional praise? What if

Pine Creek came out with a line of merchandise we could sell on the website and in the shop? Mugs and stocking caps and sweatshirts and cozy blankets . . .

Ideas start coming at me like a derailed freight train.

I pull over and grab my iPad from my bag. I start writing furiously, unable to keep up with all the "what if" ideas racing through my mind, not the least of which is—what if Lacey is right? What if she and Liam *are* supposed to buy the farm and turn it into something even more special than it already is?

Yeah, he doesn't want that.

But . . . she might. Is there any way that could work?

Once I've downloaded every creative idea in my brain, I pull back onto the road and drive toward Pine Creek. My heart is racing from the rush.

I've missed this feeling. The way creativity captures me, and I can't write fast enough to keep up with the ideas. Losing the shop closed that door for me. It didn't seem worth it to try to be creative when my creativity failed in such a monumental way.

But now, palms sweaty and mind reeling from a metric ton of ideas, I make a decision.

I don't want to sit back and watch life happen around me anymore. I want to be a part of something *great*. Could Pine Creek be that thing?

But as I pull into the Pine Creek lot and park in the space right next to Liam's truck, reality does its thing. He's made it clear he has no interest in running the farm, no matter how much Lacey wishes he would. It would be wrong to try and convince him otherwise.

Plus, logically and geographically, it wouldn't make sense for him. He hasn't said much about his job—or about any subject, for that matter—but with his prior mobile game success I'm guessing he's got a pretty sweet deal in Indy.

This realization doesn't stop me from thinking of T-shirt designs and branded scented candles and local wintertime soup mixes and a line of hand-drawn Pine Creek Christmas cards—but the sight of Liam standing near the office barn with his mom does.

They're talking to a man I don't recognize. He's wearing a suit and a long gray dress coat. He looks out of place next to Liam in his jeans, work boots, Carhartt jacket, and baseball cap.

I linger for a split second.

Okay, fine, a split three and a half minutes.

I watch. There's something about this guy I immediately don't like. I can't hear or even see what they're saying, but his body language screams smarm, and Liam looks like he's clenching his fists in his pockets to stop himself from decking him.

Liam is endearingly handsome when he doesn't talk.

That thought makes me laugh to myself. *Great guy, good-looking, but a total jerk when he opens his mouth.*

The kind, soft, tender side of Liam has to be in there somewhere, right?

What happened to you? Where's my friend? His name is Liam, have you seen him?

I tuck my iPad into my bag, grab my coffee, and get out of the car, and when I do, I hear Jo call my name.

I wave and trudge toward them as the man in the suit turns toward me. I stop moving.

Travis.

You've got to be kidding me.

"Olive, come here! We were just talking about you!" Jo's smile is so bright, it can only mean she has no idea Travis and I used to be a couple.

More than that.

He was the one who broke my heart.

My eyes drift to Liam, who refuses to hold my gaze.

Great. He probably knows the whole story. He and Travis were friends. Heck, they still could be for all I know.

So, Liam probably knows everything. I wish I did.

When Travis ended our relationship, out of nowhere and seemingly on a whim, I was the last person to find out. And once I did, he didn't even have the courtesy to call me. He sent me a "sorry it's not going to work out" text and called it good.

After a year of being together . . . who does that?

This walking tool bag, that's who.

That alone should've been reason enough to prove he wasn't worth my time, but he was my first real boyfriend. And when I'm in something, I'm all in. I wouldn't have been with him if I didn't think it could potentially last.

After it ended, I just felt dumb. Dumb for believing a single word he said. Dumb for wasting my time. Dumb for falling. Dumb for loving.

Does Liam know what a jerk his friend is?

Jo rushes toward me, loops her arm through mine and pulls me toward the men, where I'm met with familiar cold silence from Liam and an overly charming smile from Travis. The same smile that won me over all those years ago.

"I'm so glad you're here," Jo gushes. "I was just telling Travis about some of your amazing ideas. You two probably don't know each other, but Travis is an old friend of Liam's. They went to high school together."

"Actually," *blech, gag, I can't stand the way he talks*, "Olive and I have a history." Travis's eyes brighten, like the pleasure sensors in his brain have just sparked. He extends a hand in my direction. "Olive . . . is the one who got away."

I look at his hand, still outstretched, and notice that Liam looks like he's chewing glass.

"Oh!" Jo gasps, eyes wide. "Oh? Oh . . . I didn't know that! How—" She glances at me, then at Liam, and finally—finally—Travis realizes I'm not shaking his hand and tucks it into his coat pocket. His smile holds.

Jo shifts into full make-the-best-of-it mode, a carnival

barker in front of the burning big top because the elephant stampeded. "How . . .er. . . coincidental! And wonderful!"

"It is," Travis says. "Or it was." He looks at Jo and pastes on a pout. "I really messed it all up." He gives me a once-over. "Huge mistake letting her go."

"Letting me go?" I laugh, unamused. I feel heat start to rise on the back of my neck. "That's a funny way to put it."

Liam looks at me, but I ignore him.

"Water under the bridge, though, right?" Travis's smile hasn't faltered once. Twenty-one-year old Olive couldn't see what I see now. The way Travis chameleons depending on who he's with. The way he uses his good looks and his charm to get people to do what he wants.

He also made me believe he was someone worth loving.

Oh, buddy. Do I know better now.

"What are you doing here?" I use a purposely light tone, hoping my faking it covers the daggers my eyes are shooting.

"I came out to get a tour of the property," he says. "I was just telling Jo and Liam that I might have a buyer." He looks at Jo. "Should be able to get you quite a nice sum for this place. It has tons of untapped potential."

With that, a knot in my stomach tightens, and I bristle at his thoughtlessness. I glance at Liam again, and he finally meets my eyes.

He's ticked.

Internally, I'm screaming, *Say something!* Because honestly, is this what he wants? For the farm to fall into the hands of anyone Travis brings our way?

"I didn't know you'd already listed it," I say to Jo.

"We haven't," she says. "If this buyer isn't interested, then Travis is going to take care of getting it on the market. He's one of the *top* real estate agents in Chicago." She says this last part like a proud parent.

Sounds like exaggerated Corner Park gossip started by his

mother, but I don't say so. I steal a glance at Travis, certain he's aware I'm looking at him. His suit is expensive. His coat is expensive. Even the watch he's wearing is expensive.

Travis has done well for himself.

If only his hairline had stuck around.

"We think it would be smart to have it listed as soon as possible," he says. "Best to get moving quickly."

Ah. Now I see why she no longer wants to wait until after the holidays. Travis twisted her arm.

He looks at me. "Jo says you're quite the event planner, Olive."

Jo smiles sweetly at me. "Yes, if we'd hired her years ago, maybe there would be *less* untapped potential."

Liam looks away, the corner of his mouth lifting ever so slightly. I don't know if I've ever seen Jo's snarky side, but it's doing a number on Liam.

Travis is currently standing at the corner of Someone Else's Job and Oblivious.

"Well, I am enjoying it," I say, realizing that the flurry of ideas that just downloaded into my brain on my way out here doesn't matter.

The farm is being sold.

And unless the new owner wants to hire an event planner— and keep everything else exactly the same—there's no point to any of it.

Travis's phone rings, and he pulls it out of his pocket. "Sorry, I'll just be a minute."

Jo nods at him as he steps away, then turns to me. "Olive, I'm so sorry. I had no idea."

"It's fine, Jo," I say. "It was a long time ago."

But it doesn't feel that long ago. And I hate that it doesn't.

"Are you sure? If it's too awkward, I can—"

"List it with someone else." Liam's tone has a finality to it.

Jo frowns. "What? You're friends! I can't do that."

"Yes, you can."

The lines in her forehead deepen. "It's why I reached out to him in the first place, because you two knew each other. I hoped he'd help us find a buyer who understands how special this place is."

"He doesn't speak that language, Ma." Liam drags his hand down his face, and I notice his beard is a little fuller today. "And we aren't friends. I haven't talked to him since college."

"What? Surely not," Jo says, matching my surprise. "You boys played baseball together. He was always around."

"Yeah. Until he wasn't." Liam doesn't look at me, but if he did, he'd see a big, fat question mark over my head.

Jo leans in, as if there's a danger of Travis overhearing. He's in sales mode, slathering on the charm like he's got a mint condition Buick Skylark, low miles, one owner, non-smoker, he can't wait to see you in. "What happened?"

My eyes drill down on Liam's, but he's glaring at Jo.

"We should just get someone else," he snarls, then storms off.

Jo watches him go, and then looks at me, warily. "We already signed a contract. I think . . . I think it's exclusive too." There's a tight line of worry in her brow. "I didn't talk to Liam about it because I thought he didn't want anything to do with this place." She looks at me, a sigh crinkling the corners of her eyes. "And I really thought they were friends."

"I thought so too," I say sincerely.

Her lips go straight, in a tight line. "I'm so sorry. Was it a bad break up? You and—" She nods toward Travis. "Because at the very least we can keep him away from you."

I shake my head, not wanting to dramatize my heartbreak. "Let's just say life took us in different directions. He decided one day to . . . um . . .go in a different direction. He was playing baseball for a farm team, he moved away . . ." I glance at Travis. "Just timing."

It's the abbreviated, watered-down version of the story, but it's one I feel comfortable sharing. I leave out the part about how utterly devastated I was. And the part about how it took me months to recover. And the part about how I found out later he'd been stringing me along for weeks before he moved away.

Me and a few other girls.

Even the thought of it now churns up anger.

There's nothing quite as devastating as finding out someone you trust has betrayed you in such a basic, horrible, humiliating way. The fact that I let myself believe I was to blame wasn't his fault though. That was mine. And it took a lot of Phoebe time to start to believe there was nothing wrong with me.

Some days, I'm still not sure it's sunk in.

She squeezes my arm. "So, you're okay?"

I smile. "More than okay. Promise."

Travis hangs up his call and walks back over to where we're standing. "Sorry about that."

Jo smiles warmly. "Travis, I'm so sorry you chose today to drop in. Brant took Lacey to breakfast in Loveland, and Liam, uh, had some other things to attend to, so we will have to postpone the tour after all." She clears her throat. "I have to go into town. I'm getting a few supplies for my wreath-making class." She glances my way. "Lord knows I need to practice."

Travis looks at me. "I just need to get a feel for the place and take a few photos. Maybe Olive could show me around?"

Like heck I will.

I frown. "Yeah, no. I just had my tour yesterday. I'm hardly an expert."

"Like you don't know this place like the back of your hand." He scoffs. "I still remember how excited you got every time we came here."

"We came here once." I have to work to keep my face neutral.

He points at me, his salesman grin firmly in place. "But you were excited! Eh?"

I look at Jo, who is doing her best to make it clear I don't have to do this, but I work here now. I'm part of the team. And if someone needs to show our real estate agent around the property, why shouldn't it be me?

I also need to prove to myself that he can't get under my skin.

"Fine."

"Great!" He grins. "If Brant can send over those numbers, we should be good to go. I'll pull some comps and get the appraisal going, and we'll find a time for my potential buyer to come out and take a look if that's okay."

"Of course," Jo says. "And Olive, please come back to the office when you're finished. Liam says you two found a good spot for the market. I shouldn't be in town long, so we can go over everything when I get back."

"He found the spot," I say. "And it's *perfect*."

The spark of excitement is back, right there below my surface. As soon as I scrub off this icky Travis layer, I can spend some time with it.

Because I have to make this market a success. Partly to prove that Jo wasn't wrong to believe in me, partly to prove to myself that I can do creative things again.

But mostly because I'm really, *really* excited about it.

Jo walks away, and I look at Travis.

He grins. "Olive Witherby."

I raise my eyebrows, but don't respond.

"So, you work here now?" His smile is so dangerous, I have to look away.

"It's temporary," I say. "Seasonal."

"We met here, remember?" He looks off, as if trying to access some memory in his rodent brain.

"Oh, I remember." With Jo gone, I allow some of my true feelings to creep in.

A party Liam threw right before our senior year of college. Phoebe found out about it last minute, and we decided to go, along with every person our age in the tri-state area. I remember standing by the bonfire with Phoebe when he walked up.

Liam was different then. On his way to becoming the person he is now, I suppose. He seemed shy, a bit quiet, but funny in an observational way and a little nervous.

It had been years since I'd seen him, and then only in passing. But then he started talking about school, about this idea he had for a video game. I knew Liam spent a lot of time locked in his own imagination, but this conversation proved it.

There was so much more to him than anyone knew. I would've told him that, but in the middle of the conversation, Travis walked up.

I might be misremembering, but I think he slithered up.

He was flirty and charming and more handsome than anyone that age had the right to be. The kind of guy who oozed confidence and charm well beyond his age or experience, and he spent the rest of the party talking to me. I never did figure out why. Guys like Travis usually gravitated to Phoebe. Or . . . anyone else.

Before we left, I found Liam and said a quick goodbye, thinking it was odd he'd disappeared so quickly when our conversation had been going so well. It was nice to catch up with him, rediscovering why our friendship was special when we were younger, but then he was gone, and I don't know why he stopped talking to me.

I didn't question it that night—I was too shocked that someone like Travis seemed to like me. It was new. And fun. And exciting.

He and I dated for a year. Travis was my first real boyfriend. I'd dated in high school, sure, but those relationships consisted of standing on opposite sides of the gym at Sadie Hawkins. They felt so juvenile compared to my relationship with Travis.

I fell hard. Immediately.

He was so outgoing. So confident. So easy to talk to. Even though we went to different schools, we made it work. And then one day, with no warning and no reason—he stopped calling or picking up my calls. I'd text him and get no response.

I found out on social media that he'd started playing baseball for a farm team in Michigan.

In that moment, I realized our relationship meant a lot more to me than it did to him.

A couple weeks later, I got his brush-off text. It took me a solid week, a pallet of Kleenex, and a thousand pints of Ben and Jerry's Cherry Garcia to finally accept it.

We were done.

It was a terrible way to end a relationship, and standing here now, I'm not sure I ever really got over it. Maybe a piece of me didn't quite accept Phoebe's explanation that it was all him. That there was nothing wrong with me.

Because looking at his dumb face, reliving all those memories, I feel a lot like I did when I closed my shop for the last time.

Like a failure.

He reaches over and tugs on the sleeve of my coat. "You look good, Olive."

"I know," I say, feigning confidence. I cross my arms over my chest and meet his gaze. He watches me, and dang it—he's as handsome as he always was. I straighten. "What's up with you and Liam?"

Travis takes a step back and glances toward the barn. "Nothing's up. We haven't kept in touch is all. Now that he's back, maybe we'll go out for a beer and get caught up."

Good luck with that, I think.

After a pause he asks, "What's up with *you* and Liam?"

I frown. "We're friends." *Sort of.*

"Just friends?"

"Why do you care?"

A shrug. "I was thinking about asking you out."

122

I laugh, but it comes off like a scoff, which is also appropriate.

"Seriously, Olive, we were good together, weren't we?"

The absolute nerve. "Are you serious?"

"We were!" He watches me, and I wish I was the kind of person to act on instinct, because I feel the need to introduce Travis' face to my fist.

"You had a funny way of showing it." I glare at him through narrowed eyes.

He shakes his head. "Biggest mistake of my life."

I toss him a look that I hope communicates *whatever*.

"Seriously," he says, almost sincere. "I was an idiot. And a coward. I knew I was going to be gone that whole summer, and I needed to take my shot—concentrate on baseball."

"And you didn't think you should at least call and tell me?" I shake my head.

"I should've," he says. "It was dumb, and I'm really, really sorry."

I press my lips together and glance over at the barn, as if anyone in there is going to come save me.

Travis holds out his hand. "Let me make it up to you. We'll go to dinner—you pick the place. Catch up, like two old friends."

"We aren't friends," I say, arms crossed.

"We could be." Arms out wide, shrugging, grinning, Cheshire Cat-like. "We could be more than that, if you want to."

If he got caught on camera cheating on his wife in their own bedroom, he'd be the one to say, "Naw, babe, that ain't me. It's a deep fake, you know I only have eyes for you."

I shake my head and walk off in the direction of my car.

Travis follows. "Come on, Olive, give me a chance. I'm not the same guy I was when I was twenty-two. I'll prove it."

I stop beside my car. I slowly turn and level his gaze.

His smile hasn't dropped once. Neither have his arms.

"I'll drive," I say.

He gives my car a once-over, then glances over his shoulder at the big, fancy Escalade parked beside it. "For . . . the tour? Are you sure? I can—"

I open the car door. "I'm giving the tour, so it makes more sense if I drive." I get in and start the engine. I watch him hesitate, then finally fold his tall body into my tiny VW Beetle. He looks at me, and I don't even try not to smirk at him.

"Comfy?" I ask.

He shoots me a thumbs-up.

"Good." I pull out of the parking place and peel down the gravel driveway as he lunges for his seatbelt.

"Yeah, you'll probably need that," I mutter, making a hard left, enough to pitch his face into the window. "Careful, these roads are a bit rough." I smile at him.

He gives a weak nod and clips his seatbelt.

As I adjust my rearview mirror, I see Liam step outside the office, watching as I drive off with Travis.

I can't be certain, but through the dust kicked up by my cartoonish peel out, I thought I saw him turn around, go back inside, and slam the door.

CHAPTER 14

LIAM

*T*his has to be a joke.

Travis? Really?

I'm seething, pacing, and mentally trying to envision the consequences if I take a chainsaw to the hood of his car.

The way he showed up here like nothing happened? Like we were just two old friends?

Un-freaking-believable.

I storm out of the barn after storming *into* the barn after watching him drive off with Olive.

My fists are tight at my sides, my vision red, and my anger flaring.

It's just like that night.

The bonfire. The party. The conversation, the catching up, and him swooping in like he had some right to claim her. Stepping aside instead of stepping up.

Why didn't I step up then? Why can't I step up now?

Why can't I just say what I want? Tell people how I feel?

I get into my truck and slam my fist against the steering wheel, mad at myself more than anything.

Another missed opportunity, another chance to get things right. The farm, my job, Olive—it doesn't matter.

I keep going around the same mountain.

I start the engine and pull away, gravel dust following me like a cloud as I peel away.

I drive down to the main barn and park behind the equipment garage in the employee lot, waiting until I get a glimpse of Manny through the open overhead door. I see him walk across the garage toward one of the tractors.

Manny has been the Pine Creek farm manager for as long as I can remember. His dad had the job before him, and he slid right into the position when his dad retired just like everyone expected me to do when my dad retires.

But he's more than a guy who works here. No one knows how he's helped me. No one knows the years of crap I dumped on him—and he took it, listened, and told me exactly what I needed to hear.

He was a steady and calming voice in my life. For years, when my dad wouldn't listen—Manny would. And he never steered me wrong.

I walk into the garage and see him hunched over a tractor, working on the engine. When he sees me, he stops moving, stands upright, and wipes the wrench down with a rag from his back pocket. "Well, lookie here." He squints at me. "You look— like you want to throw something."

Travis's face comes to mind.

Manny tosses an old spin-on oil filter to me.

I catch it, and he says, "Here, chuck that against that wall. I've done it at least fifty times."

Without hesitation, I rear back, channel my baseball days, and whip the filter at the corrugated wall, throwing all my anger behind it. It cracks against the metal with a satisfying *p-TANG*, splitting in half sending the pieces spinning in opposite directions.

"Woo-eee, that was a good one! Feel better?"

I grit my teeth. "Yeah, a little."

"Women don't understand that. Every once in a while, a guy's just gotta throw something." He laughs.

I look at him, and his humor-filled face gets to me. I immediately start calming down with a laugh of my own.

"You good?"

I marvel at how perceptive Manny is, even after all these years.

"Better now."

Manny leans back toward the motor. "You want to talk about it?"

I scoff. "Do I ever want to talk about it?"

Without looking up he points a wrench at me. "Yeah, I wondered if maybe you've evolved past the grunts."

I grunt a reply.

"Guess not." He smirks at me, then walks around to the other side of the tractor and leans on it in front of me. "How've you been?"

I shrug and look away, blowing out a frustrated breath. "Being back here, man."

He folds his arms, nods, and says, "Yep."

Unlike everyone else in my life, Manny doesn't ask me to explain. It's like that's all I need to say for him to get it.

"Let's go for a ride," he says.

I follow him to the back of the barn where the ATVs are parked. He nods to the helmets. I grab two, handing him one.

"Keys are in 'em. All gassed up." He swings a leg over one, and I do the same on the one beside it.

We each start an engine, and without a word, both flip down the visors on our helmets, almost in unison the way we've done so many times before.

As we head off into the fields, the scene whisks me back years in an instant. Rows and rows of familiar trees pass by, and

I start to think about the countless hours I spent out here, planting, harvesting, weeding. Whatever the season, there was always something to do.

It was grueling sometimes, and sweaty and physical. And I don't miss it at all.

My current job in Indianapolis isn't perfect, but at least it was my choice to take it.

Manny speeds ahead, and I'm surprised the old guy still drives these as fast as he always did.

"No way, buddy. You're not beating me this time," I say to myself inside the helmet, and gun the engine harder.

I draw in a deep breath, the cool air coating my lungs, and I'm surprised when, on the exhale, something inside me loosens.

Something that's been there since I got home. The only other time it goes away is when I'm with Olive.

Huh.

I shake my head to clear the mental picture of her face. I try to think about nothing. Stare at the fields. The grass. The trees. But all of it makes me think of Olive. She's out here, exploring this place she loves so much . . . with Travis.

The part of me that loosened tightens again. I pop the clutch and drop into a faster gear, winding through rows and doing my best to keep up.

Maybe nostalgia will kick in and rekindle whatever they had all those years ago.

Something I never got over was the fact that if I hadn't had that stupid party, they never would've met.

I was twenty-one. Rebellious. Angry. My parents weren't on board with my career plans, and my dad did not understand how I could walk away from Pine Creek—it had always been the plan that I would run it.

Now it seems my plans will ruin it.

With or without Lacey, Pine Creek was *my* legacy.

I hate that word. *Legacy*. Why don't they just call it what it is? Responsibility. Duty.

Obligation.

Maybe I should've been grateful. Once upon a time, I'd loved it here even more than Olive. I'd loved coming out to see my grandparents. I'd loved the way my grandpa would show me how everything worked, the way the house always smelled like cinnamon, the way people would smile just walking around the property.

I understood that Pine Creek was special. But, while the farm gave other people joy, that's exactly what it stole from me.

Everything changed when my grandpa died and we moved here. Because it was our *legacy*. And from the jump, it was clear that my participation in the daily operations was non-negotiable. I was expected to be in the fields, doing the work. Nobody asked if that was what I wanted. They started saying things like, "one day, when this place is yours—" like it was a given.

My future was locked and loaded, and I didn't have a say in it at all.

I grumble at the thought of it, mad at myself for not saying something. I tell myself I'm over it now, the same way I'm over Travis and Olive, but I know I'm lying.

Manny knows it too. I don't even have to say anything for him to zero in on the problem. Same way he always used to.

Granted, the problem was usually my dad. Not listening. Barking orders. Taking his stress out on me. But this is different.

Manny slows near a row of trees on the extreme backlot of the property, and we park.

He pulls off his helmet, and says to me, "You've gotten slow."

I chuckle and shake my head, then glance up and find him watching me.

"Is it your dad?"

"No." I get off the ATV. "I've hardly seen him since I've been home."

Manny nods. "So, it's about the girl."

I don't respond. Of course he knows. He probably always knows I'm working really hard *not* to think or feel anything about "the girl."

"Yeah," he nods. "It's about the girl."

Manny gets off and walks around the back of the ATV and picks up a small trimmer. "Trim."

That's all he says to me. It's all he needs to say. Because I've done this a thousand times. I've done every job on the farm a thousand times. That was part of the deal—my dad wanted to make sure I understood how it all worked. And as I walk off toward a row of trees, I'm not all that surprised to realize I still do.

It's like muscle memory kicks in the second the trimmer is in my hand.

We have a fair number of people who want to cut their own Christmas trees, but there are also plenty who want to buy a precut one. And trimming them up so they look showroom ready is the best way to move them off the lot.

I get to work, thankful for the sunshine, even though the air is cool. As I work, Manny starts cutting down the trimmed trees down. We fall into a familiar rhythm, and eventually, I forget to be mad. I forget about everything except the task in front of me.

I let go of the conflicting emotions pinballing around in my head. I let go of trying to figure it all out.

This—trimming the trees—I can do.

I can clean them up and make them look good. I can make sure that when customers show up wanting the perfect tree, they find it.

I work in silence as a few other guys show up to haul the trees to the precut area and set them up for shoppers. I finish the row, then go behind Manny to help load the trees onto the trailer.

It's hard, physical work, the kind of work I hated all through high school and college.

But now I kind of enjoy it. It's not for a specific purpose. It's not for a deadline, and it's sure as heck not because my dad is barking at me to finish the checklist before he gets back.

I'm just . . . existing. And cleaning up some trees for people who may appreciate it later.

When we're done and packing up, I notice I don't feel exhausted. And I don't feel angry.

I feel good. Accomplished. Productive.

And I couldn't have predicted that. I let out a long, satisfied sigh.

Leaning on his ATV, Manny up-nods me. "There's something about it, right?"

I pull my gloves off, rubbing my hands in the cool air. "About what?"

"Working with your hands." He inhales a long breath. "Outside in nature. Not at your cushy desk job."

At the mention of it, I feel an uncomfortable twinge. Knowing how hard Manny and his guys work, I don't have any business complaining about my situation. And being here with him, after a hard morning's work, I have to wonder how it is that he seems more content with his work than I do with mine.

"Do you miss it?" he asks. "The toll it takes on your body? The way your muscles ache at the end of the night? The way your face is drawn up toward the sun every time you walk through these fields? The smell of it . . .?" He trails off, like he's lost in a pleasant thought.

I take in the green of the trees, the smell of cut pine, aware that my normal knee-jerk reply doesn't ring true.

"Is Lacey coming out today?" Manny swings a leg over his ATV.

131

I hop on mine and frown at him. "Lacey? Out here?"

"We've missed her too."

"In the fields?"

"Next to you, she's my best worker." Manny grins.

"Shut up."

"Actually, she might be better than you. She's a tree whisperer." He says this last part wiggling his fingers at me, voodoo style.

I chuckle. "Now I've heard everything."

"Don't believe me?" He glances at me briefly, then starts his engine. "She's got the magic touch out here," he yells at me.

I frown as I start my ATV. She never said anything to me about working anywhere on the farm other than in the shop or the hot chocolate shed. Once she tried driving the carriages and led the horses off the path straight into the lake, so she doesn't get free rein of this place anymore. "Since when?"

He shrugs. "After you left, I guess. Always felt like she had something to prove."

I think about that, about how my father never even considered Lacey to take over when they retired. How I never considered her either. And then I think about how she pleaded with me to do this with her.

I thought she was just being sentimental, but what if it was more than that?

The ride back isn't as fast. And I notice that my head is as clear as the air out here. It takes us a good ten minutes to make it back to the equipment barn where we started.

"Why do you stay here, Manny?" I ask, after we park behind the garage and I remove my helmet. "Don't you ever want to do something else?"

He frowns, almost like the thought has never occurred to him. "What would I do? Work in an office, like you?" He cackles. "Nah—the dirtier I am at the end of the day, the better I feel."

I laugh. "How's Brenda feel about that?"

"She tolerates it," he says. "But she knows she'd end up murdering me if I were stuck inside all day."

"I still don't understand what that woman sees in you." I laugh, and Manny grabs the trimmer off the back of the ATV.

"You and me both, buddy."

He makes his way into the barn, and I follow.

I don't want to know the answer to this question, but I ask it anyway. "What will you do after they sell?"

He shrugs. "Your dad is going to try to negotiate a way for most of the staff to stay on, so we're just waiting."

"You know there's no guarantee whoever buys it is going to keep it running," I say, because seriously—had my parents not told the staff this? There was no telling what would happen to Pine Creek.

"I know," Manny says. "Don't worry about me. I've got options."

"Any farm would be lucky to have you," I say honestly. "Heck, any company." Because really, where would we be without Manny and his family? We wouldn't have gotten our footing here, I'm sure of it.

He grins. "Don't go getting sentimental on me now."

"Have I ever been sentimental?"

He hoots and wraps an arm around me, which is, I'm sure he knows, the most physical touch I can stand at times. He gives me a paternal squeeze. "It's good to have you back, kid."

"I'm not back," I say. "Just home through the holidays. Promised Mom I'd help get things sorted, but I'm not really sure what I'm supposed to be doing. Mostly, I just feel like I'm in the way."

Also, I'm on Olive duty. Which could be worse.

Manny takes a step back and shakes his head. "You really don't know how lucky you have it, do you?"

The question nags, but I don't respond because my thoughts are sidetracked when Olive's car whips into the parking lot and skids to a stop right in front of the main barn where the shop and café are housed, a cloud of gravel dust kicked up in the car's wake. I watch as Travis gets out immediately and puts a hand on the car to steady himself.

I watch as she gets out, neat as a pin, and confidently walks into the shop without waiting for him. His shoulders and head sag, as if gathering strength, and he slowly walks to follow her.

Okay. My spirit rebounds at the sight. Maybe they won't rekindle what they had all those years ago.

They don't see me, standing here watching, the same way I did the night of that stupid party. Watching this guy who was supposed to be my friend move in on Olive, knowing exactly how I felt about her—it burned me up. It still burns me up.

Mostly because I did nothing to try and stop it. What would Olive have said if I'd stuck around instead of disappearing for the rest of the night?

I'm irritated that I can conjure that memory so easily. It was a long time ago. And Olive and I are barely friends now, let alone anything else. I have no claim, and I can't pretend I do, no matter how jealous I feel.

Beside me, Manny shifts, breaking the spell, and giving me a reason to look away. He watches me, amusement behind his dark eyes.

"See?" He nudges me. "It *is* about the girl."

CHAPTER 15

OLIVE

I keep telling myself—it's for the business. It's for Jo. It's for the farm.

But then I look over and still see Travis standing there and I think—*I want to punch him.*

After I show him most of the farm, including the exterior of the house, he asks to see the shop and the café. I managed to mostly keep him focused on the property, but I did catch him trying to take a photo of me at one point.

Oddly, the more time I spend around him, the less hurt I feel by everything that happened. I see him now for who he is—and it's clear that he is not the guy for me.

"Let's get some coffee," he says, walking toward the café counter.

"I'm supposed to head back," I say.

He stops and faces me. "You're only working here, like, three more weeks. What are they going to do, fire you?"

"I'm not getting coffee with you, Travis," I say simply, because Brené Brown says, "Clear is kind," and while I don't care much about being kind, I do want to be very clear.

"But I feel really awful about the guy I used to be." He takes a step toward me. "I was stupid and selfish. I'd like to hear what you've been up to, you know, as friends."

Even if I wanted to be friends with Travis, I wouldn't talk about what I've been up to. It's not exactly impressive.

At my hesitation, Travis leans a little closer. "We can stick to impersonal topics. You can tell me about the farm. What should I say to convince my buyer it's a good investment? I could argue that's part of your job."

"You could argue it, but you'd be wrong." I cross my arms over my chest as he takes a couple of steps backwards, moving toward the counter.

I sigh. Because *should* I tell him how amazing this place is? I don't want anyone else to buy Pine Creek, but ultimately, that's what Liam and his parents want. Which is why my sense of duty gets the best of me.

Still, as I order a latte and move to the end of the counter, I feel like sharing my thoughts about what makes it more appealing for a buyer is a betrayal of sorts. This place is semi-sacred to me, and even considering selling it feels wrong.

"Who's this buyer anyway?" I ask. "Do you just happen to know bored, rich people who are in the habit of purchasing and running Christmas tree farms?"

An amused expression skitters across his face. "Olive, they won't keep the farm. They want the land."

I frown. Of course.

At some level I knew this was an option, but I didn't think it would be the first option. I assumed Jo hired Travis because he'd be sympathetic to the generational aspect of this whole thing.

Shouldn't they at least try and find someone who will keep it going?

"What will they do with the land?" I ask, a sick feeling rolling through my stomach.

He shrugs. "Well, it's a development company, so they'll come out, take a look, and if they like what they see, they'll run

136

some numbers to see what the best thing would be. Residential or maybe vacation homes. It's a nice property, secluded and—"

"The best thing is to keep Pine Creek as it is," I say. "Didn't Jo tell you that?"

His smile is condescending. "Olive, the goal here is to sell Pine Creek. What they do with it after doesn't matter."

As the girl behind the counter hands us our drinks, she shoots me a look that tells me she heard everything he said. Which means the rest of the staff will soon know that nobody buying this place will be fighting to keep the tree farm—or their jobs.

I give her an "I'm so sorry" look and turn away.

"So," he oozes, as we take our drinks over to a table in the corner. "You're an event planner? That's a surprise. I thought you were going to do something, you know, artsy." He says this like the idea is ludicrous, like I was foolish to ever think I could make it.

Or maybe I'm projecting.

Or maybe he's exactly who I think he is.

"A lot of what I've done so far has been *artistic*," I say, leaning on the word that's more appropriate, in my opinion. I tell him about the branding I've done, the logos, the hand-drawn maps. I pull my iPad out of my bag to show him, as if I need to prove that I *am* doing what I said I would do, just not in the way I thought.

That idea stops me. I hadn't thought of it exactly in that way before. I'm using every creative bone in my body right now, but I couldn't have predicted the joy this kind of work would bring me.

I pause, my Apple Pencil hovering above my iPad, ruminating on this thought when Travis slides the tablet toward him. "Okay, okay, yeah. I get it now," he says, scrolling down the list I'd brainstormed earlier. "You're the . . . idea person." He says it like it's a made-up job title.

I reach over and snatch my iPad away. "Let's talk about something else."

"Okay . . ." He pauses. "Are you seeing anyone?"

I'm mid-drink when he says this, but I manage to laugh. "You're ridiculous."

He smirks. "I'm captivated by your eyes, what can I say?"

I gently set my cup down. I'm waiting for anger and belligerence to rise, but what rises instead is amusement. Watching him do this act is the equivalent of Will Farrell and Chris Kattan neck bobbing at a bar while *What is Love* blares in the background.

I smile, surprisingly at ease. "Does this actually work for you? It does, doesn't it? Women *actually* buy this." I shake my head. "Unbelievable."

He shrugs, as if to say *I can't help it if they love me.*

I give him a pitying look. "I should've seen it sooner. What a terrible match we were." *And what a horrible person you still are*, I think but don't say.

"Opposites attract?" He says this like it's a question.

"No, Travis. Opposites repel." But at the mention of opposites, my mind conjures an image of Liam. He and I are definitely opposites. Do we repel each other too, or is my argument faulty?

The thought is derailed when I glance up and find Travis watching me.

Apart from his painfully obvious receding hairline, he's handsome. And he thinks he is too.

"So, Liam never made a move, huh?" he asks, setting his cup back down.

I frown. "I already told you—"

He waves me off. "Friends, yeah, yeah, I know. I just always assumed you two would get together after you and I broke up."

"Why would you assume that?" My frown deepens, but my interest is piqued. "We knew each other when we were kids.

The night you and I met was the first time I'd had a real conversation with him in years. And another thing, we didn't break up. You left. Plus, you didn't even have the common courtesy to tell me to my face." I lean in. "*You sent a text*, Travis. A text."

"I was young and stupid, but I'm different now," he tries to play it off.

"Yeah," I quip. "You're not young."

His gaze settles, and his lips twitch. "And you're still beautiful, Olive."

I scoff, and don't acknowledge the comment.

"Come on," he croons. "One dinner. Would it kill you to have one meal with me?"

"You honestly think I'd do this—" I flick my hand between us — "at all? Ever?"

He shrugs. "We're adults now. Plus, when we were good, we were really good."

I lean back in my chair and study him. "If I look at your phone, how many dating apps am I going to find?"

His eyes flick over to his phone, turned upside down on the table.

"If I scroll through your text messages, how many girls did you cut and paste the same, 'Hey babe, you up?' message to in the past week?"

He slumps back in his chair, folds his arms, and looks a bit annoyed.

Good.

I speak slowly. "Let me be *crystal* clear. You and I do not want the same things."

He starts to speak but I hold up a hand before he can say anything.

"Actually, no. I'm done saying what I need to say." I pause. "But I'm thankful for the apology."

He reaches across the table and takes my hand. "I think you're making a mistake."

I try to pull away, but he holds it tighter.

"Let go of my hand."

"I think we owe it to ourselves to get to know each other, as adults," he says this so earnestly, putting his other hand over mine.

I owe him nothing, and I'm about to say so when the door to the shop opens and Liam walks in. His eyes zero in on me, then drift to the table where Travis is still holding my hand.

The "chewing glass" look returns to his face, and he looks away for a second before making a beeline toward our table.

I tug on my hand and Travis doesn't let go, so I yank it away.

Liam's expression is grave, and he looks genuinely pained to be standing here. I glance at Travis, who's smirking up at him. "Hey Fisher! Olive and I were just making dinner plans. Wanna join?"

I whip my head at Travis in disbelief, starting to say, "What are you talking about?" but I get as far as the "Wha—" when I look back and see Liam's face.

It looks . . . enraged? Hurt? I'm not sure. But he's glaring at Travis.

Something unspoken passes between them, and after a pause, Liam looks at me. "My mom asked me to find you and let you know she's back. I guess she texted—"

"Oh, right." I pull my phone out of my bag. "Totally missed that." I sling the bag over my shoulder and stand. Liam steps out of my way, and I expect him to come with me, but he doesn't. Instead, he slowly sits, eyes locked on Travis.

I glance at him, then at Travis, then back to Liam, but neither of them is looking at me now. "Does one of you want to tell me what this is about?"

"No," they say in unison, without glancing in my direction.

I shake my head and turn to go. "Fine. I'm leaving."

"I'll be in touch about dinner, *Liv*," Travis says.

I stop, spin around on my heel and glare at him.

Liam's eyes flick to mine, and for the first time since I pulled up and saw Travis standing near the office, I start to wonder if this thing between them—whatever it is—is about me. Because Liam is the only person I know who's ever called me "Liv." And given the emphasis Travis put on it, I think he knows that.

Travis leans back nonchalantly, in his chair and smiles at me. "It really was nice catching up."

Liam glares at him, but his face gives nothing away.

I will him to look at me, to tell me what he's thinking, but he doesn't.

Finally, I walk away, thinking that maybe it's more foolish of me to hope to reconnect to Liam than it would be to consider Travis's offer.

LIAM

"*What.* Do you *think.* You are *doing?*" I say this through clenched teeth, wondering if Travis has the guts to respond to a question I already know the answer to.

He takes a drink of his coffee, a smug expression on his face. Then, he smiles. "All these years and you still haven't done anything about that—" he glances toward the door just as Olive walks out.

"*Liv?*" I spit the nickname as an accusation.

His expression is faux innocent even though he and I both know better. Travis knew how I felt about Olive. He saw the way I reacted when she showed up at the party. If she was single, I reasoned, this could be my shot with her.

Years before, I'd gone to see a play at her high school for extra credit in English class. I had no idea she was starring in it until she walked out onto the stage.

I couldn't take my eyes off her that night. The childhood crush was back, like it never went away, and this time around, it had intensified.

But the timing was off. She was with her friends afterward, I didn't get a chance to talk to her.

Then a year later, our two high schools played each other in football, and I went to the game with my friends, Travis included. She was there, three rows in front of me, laughing and talking and cheering, and I was hardly paying attention to the game.

The timing wasn't right then either. I didn't say anything to her.

I told myself if I saw her again, I'd at least ask her to go out for coffee or something, to see if these really were stupid feelings just residually left over from childhood.

Or if maybe they were real.

Or could be real.

Flash forward to summer before our senior year in college and the party.

I found her by the bonfire with her friend Phoebe, and I swear there was a spark from the second she met my eyes. She threw her arms around me and hugged me, almost like she needed the comfort of familiarity as much as I did.

We picked up right where we left off, thick as thieves, finishing each other's stories—treehouse friends.

We were talking. Reconnecting. Reminiscing. She was laughing at my jokes. Her eyes were sparkling in the firelight.

And for the first time ever, the timing felt right.

It wasn't awkward to see this girl I'd grown up with but didn't really know anymore.

We'd outgrown that stage and had moved into pleasant adult conversation, the kind that might be nice to have in my life since I'd just changed my major and nobody knew yet. Somehow, it seemed like she'd get it. Might even support it. We'd skipped straight over the small talk, and it was the easiest, most laid-back conversation I'd ever had, maybe with anyone.

I was working up to the next step, asking her to go to coffee, when Travis walked up. He had a way of commanding attention. Almost like he could snap his fingers, and everyone's eyes would be on him.

Olive wasn't immune. I read the room. So I stepped aside.

I'd missed my chance again.

Travis always had a knack for zeroing in on what other people wanted and taking it for himself. To him, getting Olive to like him was winning the game. I just didn't realize it until it was too late.

I can tell by his posture that the game hasn't changed. "I know what you're doing," I say.

Travis laughs. "You're being dramatic."

You're being dramatic. The words hit like a punch to the gut. It's what he'd said that night, when I asked him, "What the heck, man?"

He figured out how I felt by my reaction to Olive, and he didn't care.

"Stay away from her," I say. "Pretty sure you had your chance."

He smirks, and I want to rearrange his face with my fist. "Pretty sure you had your chance, too, buddy."

"Yeah, and we both know who screwed that up," I say.

He shakes his head. "You're still not over that? Geez, man." He says it like I'm pathetic, and I have to look away.

Because there is truth in his accusation. It was a long time ago.

And yet, the fact remains that I'll always care about Olive. I'll always want the best for her.

And Travis Richmond is not it.

"Just stay away from her," I warn him again as I stand. "She's too good for you."

"I'll tell you what—if you stand there and tell me you're going to go for it, I'll back off," he says, like he's confident I won't.

He might be right.

I never say what I want. Especially, it seems, when it comes to Olive.

I don't look at him. I don't say anything. Instead, I just walk away.

My last thought as I shut the door to the café is, *she's too good for me, too.*

CHAPTER 16

OLIVE

"*P*ick a hand."

Liam looks at my fists with unmistakable skepticism. "What?"

"It's the thing! Remember the thing?"

He frowns.

"Come on, choose your adventure," I say brightly.

I haven't seen Liam since yesterday, and frankly, a part of me doesn't feel chipper and happy after the fated reunion with Travis.

But after a full day of working on the events we've lined up —getting the word out to surrounding communities, chatting with vendors, sending poster designs to be printed, and even making a few videos with Lacey, I feel energized enough to keep my promise to help Liam remember why he loves Pine Creek.

I'm convinced that deep down, he does.

Travis called the office to "clarify some numbers," which led to him asking again about dinner. "Or coffee. Whatever you're comfortable with. I want this to be about you."

Sorry. Nope. Not going to happen. And for the love, can he please take the hint?

So now, here I am. Standing on Liam's parents' porch.

Fists out, smile on, wondering if yesterday erased all the positive progress I've made with soothing the grumpy side of Liam—and if we've taken three steps back.

Travis' persistence isn't going to work with me. I wonder if my persistence will work with Liam.

Different motivations, for sure.

He takes a slow breath but doesn't respond, and I shake my hands at him, reminding him how this game is played.

His lip twitches. Involuntarily, I decide, given his stoic expression hasn't changed. "I was working."

"Oh!" I drop my hands to my sides. "What are you working on?"

"A video game." He says this with a shrug, a bit downplayed and slightly embarrassed.

"Can I see?"

"No."

"What's it about?"

His hand is still on the door, like at any second he could slam it in my face. "You wouldn't get it."

My eyes go wide. "Why not? Because I'm a girl? Girls do play video games, you know?"

He glares at me.

"Come on! I'll be such a great cheerleader. Or wait! I could be your crash test dummy. Like, if I can figure it out, anyone can."

"No."

I frown. "You're *such* a—"

"Crank, I know."

I cross my arms over my chest and glare back at him.

He pauses, like he's trying to muster up the courage to talk about it. "It's just . . . not ready yet. To be tested," he says. "It's just concepts at this point."

"That's so cool," I say honestly. "I would love to see your ideas if you ever want to show me."

"Noted."

I hold my fists back out, and he sighs. I grin. "We're going on a Pine Creek adventure." I shake my hands. "Pick one."

"Ice skating?"

My eyes drop to my left hand, then quickly back to him. "No."

"You're not going to go away, are you?" he asks.

I shake my head.

He taps my right hand, and I turn it over to reveal an acorn. He frowns. "I don't want to go hunt for acorns."

"It's symbolic, you dork." I turn him around and push him into the house. "Go get your snow clothes on."

"It's not snowing."

"I mean your winter clothes."

"Winter clothes?"

I'm exasperated now. "You know what I mean! Just do it!"

"You're awfully bossy." He walks over to the closet, opens it, and pulls out his coat. He steps into a pair of boots and produces gloves from his pocket. "What was in your other hand?"

"Hat," I bark like an exhausted mom, and he pulls one out of his pocket without responding. I take it, go up on my tiptoes, and stick it on his head.

"It was another acorn, wasn't it?" he asks dryly.

I quickly pocket the second acorn.

"Are you ready?" I ask, pretending he didn't see me pocket the second acorn.

"Do I have a choice?" he asks.

I pretend to think about it, then say, "Nope."

Ten minutes later, we're in the woods, still on the private side of Pine Creek, me with two acorns in my pocket, and Liam with a blank expression on his face.

I stop moving and look around the clearing, as if I wasn't out here a few hours ago on my lunch break, planning for this exact moment. "This is perfect. We'll stop here."

"We aren't camping, are we?" he asks. "Because you wouldn't last an hour."

I shoot him a look and stick my hands on my hips. "I'm tougher than you think."

One eyebrow lifts, but just barely. And then he smirks. "Are you?"

"I am." I hold his gaze, and I can't help it—I smile. Because Liam is smiling. It's like we have an inside joke or something, and I love it. Even if I *am* the butt of that joke.

I don't do a victory lap or anything, but I still count it as progress. I want to get sappy and tell him he should smile more —it's such a nice smile and *blah, blah, blah*—but I'm afraid acknowledging it is the fastest way to make it disappear.

I pull an acorn out and toss it to him. He catches it without even looking at it, holding eye contact the entire time.

"Show off."

"You wanna tell me what we're doing out here?" he asks.

"For today's Pine Creek adventure, we are taking it way, way back—" I walk over to the edge of the clearing and pull a picnic basket from underneath the brush.

His eyes widen. "Just happened upon a picnic basket, did you?"

I give a playful shrug and smile. Then, like he's a winner on a game show I announce, "We're building the best Pine Creek tree fort that has ever existed and eating dinner under the stars."

He watches me, but if any of this makes him feel nostalgic, he doesn't let on.

"Don't you remember the tree forts?" I ask, hands dropping to my sides. "They were amazing! You and Benji would never let Lacey or me help, so we built our own *girls only* forts, and they were *so much* better than yours." I laugh.

"That's how you remember it?" he asks.

"Until someone proves me wrong, that is the official story."

He shakes his head, and he looks like he's trying not to smile.

"It was fun, right?" Sometimes, Liam's mom would bring Benji and me out to the farm to play with Lacey and Liam when his grandparents still lived here. We had no trouble dreaming up ways to pass the time. This place kickstarts the imagination like nowhere else I've ever been.

One of those ways was to build forts. In the early winter months, there usually wasn't snow on the ground, so those forts were constructed with tree branches and sticks and fallen leaves. Sometimes they were barely big enough for one person to sit in, and other times, all four of us squeezed together inside.

The forts were never sturdy or warm and did nothing to shield us from the weather, but it kept us occupied, and it was fun. Some of my best memories were made here—it's strange to me that Liam doesn't feel the same.

I look at him, half expecting him to grunt and walk back to the house. But then, he turns away, walking in a slow circle, surveying the area, and I instantly know he's scouting the perfect spot.

We're going to build a tree fort.

Aw, yeah.

"Here." He's standing in front of a group of trees, naturally forming an arch with their branches. "It's practically got a roof already." He glances my way and finds me doing a Snoopy dance because I took a gamble and it paid off.

"Don't make it weird," he says.

I stop immediately, give him a stern salute, and mimic his expression, then head off to gather branches. When I return, Liam is coming back into the clearing with his own armful.

We get to work, tucking branches to form the sides of the fort. As we work, questions float in and out of my mind. *Why aren't you and Travis friends anymore? Why did he ask if you'd made a move? Do you really want to give up this place? Do you envision a world where you aren't a crabby old man trapped in the body of a hot guy?*

But I don't ask any of them. Liam seems to prefer silence, and honestly, I'm afraid of his answers. What if, despite all my cheer-spreading and market-planning and trying to convince Liam that I know what's best for the farm, I still fail?

What if it's not the last, best Christmas ever and he really does want to let it go and walk away?

And what if, after his parents move, I never see him again?

That's a lot of what ifs.

What ifs take up about seventy-eight percent of my brain capacity most days.

None of those questions should matter anyway. We haven't been in each other's lives for a long time. If I never see him again, it'll be just like the last several years, and I'll be fine.

Only . . . now that all these memories have been jogged, I can't imagine it. The friend I knew has to be in there somewhere, right? I just need to figure out how to draw him out.

I kind of miss him.

"So, you and Travis?" Liam says this without looking at me. He's stuffing greenery into the side of the fort, using fallen branches from the nearby Balsam firs.

"What about me and Travis?" I ask, sort of shocked he is the one initiating this conversation.

"Dinner?" Still working. Still not looking at me.

I pick up a stick and weave it into the makeshift wall on my side of the fort. I cock my head. "Did anyone ever teach you to use your words?"

He glares at me, then spits out, "Are you and Travis going to dinner?"

I narrow my eyes. "Does it matter?"

"Yes."

"Why? What is going on with you two?"

He looks at me, and I meet his gaze. There's something strange happening right now, and I'm not sure what to make of it. What isn't he telling me?

He goes back to working, and while I don't want to spend this time talking about Travis, I do want to keep Liam talking. It's as rare as seeing the northern lights, I can't shut it down.

"We aren't going to dinner." I glance at him, trying to catch a hint of what he's thinking from his expression, but he remains stone-faced as always.

"He said you were making dinner plans," he says, stepping back from the fort.

"He talks more and says less than anyone I know."

Liam's laugh is so subtle I almost miss it. He sticks his hands on his hips and surveys the job we've done so far. If I'm being objective, his side looks like Bear Grylls crafted it with the care and consideration of an expert.

Mine, on the other hand, looks like it was made by a chimp under a strict one-minute time limit.

He glances at me. "That's terrible."

I laugh. "It's the experience that matters, not the outcome."

He looks away, eyes wide with an *oookay* face.

"And shut up, I have a plan."

He shakes his head, then moves into the space beside me, picking up branches from the pile on the ground and working quietly, the way he always used to.

"Why do you ask? About Travis."

He shrugs.

"Liam."

He turns to me, looking like he's deciding on the right words. "Just don't think he's a good guy."

"Aww, so, you're watching out for me?" I keep my tone playful, lingering on the "aww."

But my teasing is met with an even more serious expression, so I shift.

"Sorry. Thank you," I say. "But don't worry about me. I learned my lesson about Travis."

"What happened with you two?" he asks.

"Oh, you know, girl meets boy. Girl falls for boy." I pick up a stick. "Boy falls for *lots* of girls. Boy doesn't tell original girl about lots of girls, nor does he tell her about moving away or breaking up." I throw the stick a ways away. "*Classic* rom-com stuff."

Liam stops moving and looks over at me. "Olive, I need to tell you something."

"Something about Travis?" I ask. "Because it's old news."

A pained expression washes over him and he sits back on his heels. "Something about me."

I stop moving and frown. "Okay." The look on his face is so troubled, my stomach drops.

He inhales a slow, deep breath, almost like he's working up the courage to say whatever he has to say. "The boy falls for . . . lots of girls part?" He meets my eyes. "I knew about that."

I look away. "Oh."

He knew and didn't tell me?

Because I found out the hard way.

"I should've told you," he admits. "I mean, I wasn't sure at first. I thought maybe he'd realize how lucky he was to be with you. I mean, even back then, you were so funny and easy to talk to, and—" He stops, catching himself.

I don't know what to say. I didn't know he thought any of those things.

"I thought maybe things would be different, but he just wasn't, and—"

"It's okay." I sigh, brushing it off like it's nothing because I desperately want it to be nothing.

He looks conflicted but goes back to working on the fort.

I sit there dumbly, for a long moment, wishing my feelings were easier to decipher. Or that they felt like I think they're supposed to feel. Because yes, it was a long time ago, but the more I think about it, the more bothered I am.

"But . . . why *didn't* you tell me?" I ask. "I mean if you knew, you could've warned me, and—" I think back on the weeks of agony Travis put me through. The empty pints of ice cream and the garbage bags full of Kleenex. The stalking of his social media accounts. I was wrecked because this guy I thought I might've loved just walked out of my life and couldn't even be bothered with a goodbye.

The last thing I want to do is dredge it all back up, but I can't help myself. My brain has a tendency to fill in the blanks.

I continue to press. "Did you just feel more loyal to him or something?" I ask, because now I'm kind of annoyed. I mean, he could've saved me so much grief. "I didn't find out about his cheating until we'd been over for a while."

His face falls.

"The whole time we were together, he was—" I look away. "And you *knew*? And you didn't tell me . . ." I try to process how I feel about this realization.

I didn't come here to relive this. I came here to make Liam fall in love with building forts at Pine Creek like we did when we were kids, and now I feel like I've gone off the rails, careening into the ravine.

His shoulders slump. "Olive, I'm sorry. I really am. I should've said something. And no, I didn't feel loyal to Travis."

The words hit me in a way I don't expect. "Okay, so if you weren't protecting your friend, then why not tell me? It would've been easier to know instead of—" I look away.

The worst part was feeling like I'd been played. I'd been so humiliated by the betrayal, and since Travis had just walked out, I never got the closure I needed.

Those feelings, though from the past, feel incredibly present right now.

"I didn't say anything because—" He looks away— "I didn't want to be the one to break your heart."

I watch him incredulously. I think he means for it to sound heroic and kind, but to me I can only see it through the lens of how hurt I feel right now.

It feels selfish.

"You didn't want to be the one to break my heart," I repeat, standing.

He stands and faces me. "No. I couldn't do that to you."

"So, you let a text from Travis do it. Which is *so* much better," my words bite.

He clenches his fists at his sides. "I know that now," he says. "And I'm sorry."

I scoff and walk back toward my sad fort. What a metaphor. "Why are we even talking about this?" I'm flustered now. And frustrated. I hate feeling this way.

"I know it's in the past and everything, but—" he takes a step toward me. "It's always bothered me. I guess I just figured you could take care of yourself."

I steel my jaw. "I can."

"I know." He nods.

"But you still should've told me."

"I know."

I look away. I don't want to go back down this road. Stupid Travis. Stupid cheating Travis. I cross my arms, fighting the urge to run away, knowing that every bit of pain I'm reliving in my mind right now is showing on my face. Because Liam's silly little betrayal, easy to understand and explain away, feels worse to me than finding out about Travis.

That likely has to do with the way I feel about Liam. He said I'd romanticized Pine Creek, but I'm starting to wonder if that's not all I romanticized. I obviously have a knack for thinking my relationships mean more than they do.

"I'm sorry," he apologizes again. "You deserved so much better."

The words hover in the air overhead, but I don't let myself process them. "Why aren't you and Travis friends anymore?"

Liam pulls his stocking cap off and messes up his dark, wavy hair.

He starts to speak but stops.

I swear, if he doesn't talk right now . . .

"*Liam?*"

"Because I don't want to be friends with someone who treats people the way he does," he says sharply. "That night at the bonfire—" He sighs, gaze falling to the ground. He clenches his jaw and goes quiet.

I cross my arms over my chest, silently willing him to go on.

"I just have some regrets about that night. That's all."

I study him for a few long seconds, suddenly desperate to know what those regrets might be, but he's not giving anything away.

I don't know why but I say, "You want to know something crazy? I actually thought *you* were going to ask me out that night."

His eyes jump to mine.

And I think, *Oh. My gosh. I cannot believe I said that out loud.*

I laugh, suddenly embarrassed because *what am I saying right now?* "Dumb, right? It was just—" I'm tripping over my own words— "we were talking and laughing and—"

Liam stares at me, brow knit together in a single, serious line.

"Sorry, that's . . . it's . . ." I wave my hands, like that might erase my embarrassment. "Forget I said that." *Please! Forget all of it!*

I walk over to the picnic basket. "I'm not really hungry anymore, but it's stuff from the café. All your favorites from what I remember. I'm going to head back."

I turn and start to walk away.

"Liv."

I stop.

"What would you have said?"

I close my eyes, still not facing him.

I hear the soft crunch of his feet as he walks toward me, and then I feel a hand on my shoulder.

I turn around and see an intent expression on his face. "If I had asked," he says, "what would you have said?"

I stare at him from across the small space, the weight of this conversation suddenly too heavy, the air too thick, so I do the only thing I know how to do at this moment.

I act like Liam.

I don't say anything, I look at him, and weakly shrug.

Because I know there would be no going back if I told him the truth.

CHAPTER 17

OLIVE

"*I* cannot believe he asked you out."

Phoebe's disgusted expression is expected, warranted even, because she was there, years ago, picking up the pieces Travis left behind. She was there when I found out the truth about his *extracurricular activities*.

And she's been there when every single relationship I've had since has gone south—fast.

She doesn't say this often, but I know she blames my commitment issues on Travis, too.

It's pretty hard to trust anyone after what he did.

Yeah, more fish, other options, not everyone's the same and all of that.

Still.

I don't want my experience with Travis to have that kind of hold on me.

I'm over all of this. Or at least I was. Then Travis sleazed back into my orbit, reconstituting all the things I'd burned years ago.

Now new tree fort revelations make it all feel so much worse.

157

Phoebe and I are walking around downtown Pleasant Valley, hanging up posters for the Christmas Market, which will be held two Saturdays before Christmas. Yesterday, the newspaper printed a small article about Jo and Brant's intention to sell Pine Creek. The hope is that this will lead to more foot traffic at the farm than usual, that everyone who loves Pine Creek will, as Jo said, come out to say goodbye.

"Honestly, Travis is the same as always. No surprise there. He's actually trying to sell Pine Creek to some big developer." I roll my eyes and motion for her to hand me a piece of tape. "I think I'm more upset about Liam. I mean, I know we weren't really friends in college, but shouldn't he have told me? Warned me? Told me what kind of guy his friend was when Travis asked for my number?"

Phoebe hands me the tape, squinting at me like she has a thought. But if she does, she doesn't say it. Instead, she looks away, focusing on the stores across the street. "Let's go into The Beanery and hang one on the community board. It's warm in there."

"And they have coffee."

"*Ooh.* Yes. Some of that, please."

We cross the street, and Phoebe opens the door of Pleasant Valley's local coffee shop, where I happen to be a part-time employee. Thankfully, once I told my boss, Baker, about Pine Creek, he was gracious enough to give me time off to help them over the holidays.

"But you're coming back, right?" he'd asked. "You're my best barista."

"Of course, I'm coming back," I'd said. "Where else would I go?"

We walk inside, instantly struck by the sound of "Winter Wonderland" playing on the speakers, the cozy warmth of The Beanery, and the quiet hum of conversation.

I spot Baker behind the counter, wearing a black Beanery T-shirt and a baseball cap. He waves at me, and I notice that his eyes quickly drift to Phoebe who doesn't seem to notice. "Baker, you've already got the Christmas music playing," I call out. "I'm impressed."

He grins. "Your Christmas spirit is infectious," he says and goes back to steaming milk.

It's barely December, but it feels like Christmas. I look at Phoebe. "You hang, I'll order?" I hold out the posters, which she takes with a firm nod before heading off in the direction of the bulletin board near the back.

I walk up to the counter and find Jackson, the barista who may or may not graduate high school this spring, grinning at me. "Olive! You're alive!"

"Alive and well."

"When are you coming back? We miss you." He leans across the counter toward me. Jackson is a shameless flirt, which would be flattering if he wasn't thirteen years younger than me. "*I* miss you."

"Okay, okay, calm down, Casanova. Are you going to take my order or what?" It's our dynamic, him flirtatiously teasing, me smacking his hand like it's in the cookie jar. He's harmless. Clueless, but harmless.

"Oh, I already know what my lady wants. White chocolate mocha. Extra whip." He taps his temple. "I keep space up here for all things Olive."

I shake my head. "You should find someone your own age to make brain space for."

"Nah, I'm good. I need a woman, not a girl."

"Good grief, Jackson."

"I've got a whole mental catalog," he says, not stopping to listen to what I'm saying. "It's how I know that sunflowers are your favorite flower, Christmas is your favorite holiday, you always smell like you just baked a fresh batch of cookies, and . . . you've secretly got a thing for younger men."

I groan, just as Phoebe returns from the back of the coffee shop.

"Jackson, leave my friend alone and get us our coffee." Phoebe gives him a good-natured eye roll.

He raises his hands in surrender. "Can't I just appreciate a woman's beauty?"

"Well, this woman is too old for you," I say.

He winks at me. "Age is just a number, O. W."

I shake my head. "You are *such* a cheeseball."

Phoebe laughs. "Caramel macchiato. Hot. Big. Double caffeine." She makes a shooing motion, and Jackson finally relents and punches our order into the register.

While Phoebe razzes him, my eyes drift to the back of the coffee shop where I see Lacey working at one of the tables. I pull my credit card out of my bag and hand it to Jackson. "Pheebs, I'll be right back."

I walk toward Lacey, who is so engrossed in whatever she's doing that she doesn't see me walk up.

"Hey," I say.

"Holy heck, Olive, you scared me to death." She slams the laptop shut, shakes her head slightly, and then her whole demeanor shifts. "Hey! I saw the posters. They look amazing. And Manny said he thinks the lake will be ready for ice skating next week." Her smile is sweet. Too sweet.

I narrow my eyes. "What are you doing?"

"Nothing," she says, but her eyes are too wide to be innocent.

I raise my eyebrows.

She sighs. "It's dumb."

I sit down across from her as she opens her laptop and spins it around to face me. I scan the screen, trying to make sense of what I'm seeing, but it's a little like walking into the middle of a conversation that's already in progress. "What is it?"

"It's a letter to the bank," she says, shaking her head like she's in over it. "I'm trying to get a loan."

"Oh. For the farm." Understanding washes over me.

"Yeah."

Phoebe slips into the seat next to me and hands me my drink. "Are we all friends now?"

Lacey laughs. "I would've killed to be friends with you guys when I was in middle school."

"Well, that makes me feel old." She takes a drink. "What are we talking about?"

"Nothing," Lacey says. "It's dumb."

"It's not dumb," I say. "And Phoebe is a whiz with numbers. Maybe she can help."

Lacey's eyes widen in surprise. "You are?"

"I know I don't look the part, but yes." Phoebe points at herself. "Accountant."

"Seriously?" Lacey doesn't hide her surprise.

I'd be surprised too if I didn't already know that my best friend is a mathematical genius. She never liked being grouped with all the smart kids, though, almost like she was embarrassed by her brain. Which is why she's done everything she can to craft a persona that's the exact opposite of what people would expect.

Today she's wearing a tight black button down, top two buttons unbuttoned, with a cropped black leather jacket and jeans. The red heels match her red lipstick, and the words "I don't look the part" are the biggest understatement of the century.

"So, you want to ask for a loan to buy the farm." Phoebe scans Lacey's document.

"Yes," she says. "I have some money saved—"

Phoebe's eyes go wide. "Uh, yeah you do. Why the heck do you want to run a farm when you're making this kind of money?"

Lacey shrugs. "It's my home," she explains. "When I'm out on the road, Pine Creek is the place I think about. It's the place I'm going to go to rest and recharge. When I'm there, it's like, instant peace—" She brushes her hands in a downward motion, like she's wiping away the stress.

"I get that," I say. "I wish I had money, I'd invest in it too."

"Wait," Phoebe says. "That's it."

"What's it?" I ask, turning my coffee cup around in my hands.

"You might not have money to invest—" she looks at Lacey— "but other people might. You could form like a sort of . . ." she searches the air until she plucks the word "collective" right out of it.

"A collective," I repeat.

"Yes," Phoebe says. "Like the Packers. It's not one guy who owns the team, fans can own a piece of the franchise as well. It's a non-profit, and like five hundred thousand people own the Packers." She stops and thinks. "I mean, it's a publicly traded company, so not *exactly* the same structure, but the same concept. Lots of people invest. It'd be a group of people who don't want Pine Creek to go to some big developer. People who care about it like you do."

"You think my parents will sell it to a big developer?" Lacey's brow is knit with concern.

Phoebe's eyes dart to me, and I sigh. "I think that's what the Realtor has in mind."

A worry line deepens across Lacey's forehead. "So . . . the community owns the farm."

"I think you could structure it so you own the majority. For instance, if you own fifty-one percent, and four other people each own ten percent and one person owns nine percent, or whatever, then the majority is still yours."

"Could I do that?" Hope washes over Lacey's face.

"Definitely worth looking into." Phoebe narrows her eyes.

"But couldn't you bypass all of this and just tell your parents you want the farm? You wouldn't need a loan if you bought it from them. You could set up the payment structure so—"

"No," Lacey says. "Liam said they need the money from the sale." Her face falls. "They sunk everything they had into the farm, and they haven't come right out and said it to me, but I think it's been struggling."

The thought weighs heavy—on Lacey, of course—but on me too.

"Besides, if they thought I could handle it, they would've asked me." She gives a soft shrug. "I want to prove to them I'm not a flake." A pause. "I also got to have a great life because of what my parents sacrificed. I have what I have because of them. It makes sense to pass it on so they can have the retirement they deserve."

That makes Lacey's plan even more appealing. She wants to help her parents—it's a noble cause.

"And Liam?" Phoebe asks. "Are you sure he doesn't want to do this with you?"

I huff out a breath at the mention of his name. Phoebe shoots me a look and Lacey frowns. "Sorry."

Lacey shakes her head. "I don't think any amount of convincing is going to be enough to rope Liam into this. I've tried."

I hate to say it, but I think she's right.

"He could at least take a look at your plan," I offer. "Before you make it public?"

She shakes her head. "No way. If I'm going to do this, I need to be strategic about how and when I pitch the whole idea to my family." She levels my gaze. "I don't want Liam to know, Olive. Promise you won't say anything."

My adrenaline spikes at that. Because while I'm annoyed with Liam at the moment, I don't like keeping secrets.

At my hesitation Lacey says, "I'll put a whole proposal

together with graphics and charts and graphs, and when I'm finished, they'll realize I'm totally capable—more than capable."

It feels like she's trying to convince herself.

Phoebe takes a drink, then says, "The beauty of a plan like this is that if you get enough people, anyone who invests could still keep their job. They could be silent partners. You hire out most of the labor already, right?" Phoebe asks.

"We do, yeah," Lacey says.

"So you could keep most of them on staff." Phoebe has shifted into business mode.

"Right." Lacey picks up her mug and takes a drink. "But I wouldn't want to just keep doing what we've always done. I'd want to, you know, expand."

My Spidey senses tingle, and, as if drawn by an invisible force, my hand moves over to the bag in my lap. My iPad is tucked inside, but I hesitate. Maybe this isn't the time to pull it out and dump a ton of ideas on Lacey.

"Listening," Phoebe says. She frowns at me, and I try to neutralize the expression on my face.

"A long time ago, Liam and I had this whole pitch that we gave to our parents about expanding the farm. I think we suggested things like a petting zoo and an arts and crafts barn." She gets lost in the memory for a moment. "We were kids. We had no idea what we were talking about or what things might cost. They were decent ideas, but now that I'm older, I think I can do better." She looks at me. "Plus, our dad shot them all down, so—" She chews on the inside of her lip for a second. "I think that's when they lost Liam. For the farm, I mean. I sometimes wonder if he just wanted his ideas to be heard."

Even though I'm committed to holding this grudge against Liam, the comment softens something inside of me. He is so smart—a unique combination of creative and practical. It's easy to imagine him coming up with clever ways to be more efficient.

Is Lacey right? Did he simply want someone to realize it? And when they didn't, did he just channel it into something else?

"Well," Phoebe says, drawing the conversation back to the present, "let's concentrate on buying it first, then we can talk about expanding."

Good idea, I think. Because expansion is going to be a whole different beast.

"Okay, so what should I do?" Lacey asks.

"Do you know anyone who might want to get in on this with you?" Phoebe asks. "You can make sure everyone knows they'd be a silent partner. The last thing you need is ten people trying to tell you how to run the place."

Lacey thinks for a minute. "What if I go to the next city council meeting? Would you help me work up a presentation? Help me make my case. I bet we could get people on board."

"I'm game," Phoebe says.

"And it's the perfect place to present it to my parents and Liam too." Lacey starts cleaning up her space, almost like she's been giving marching orders and now it's time to march.

"I'm not sure that's a good idea," I say.

"Why?" Lacey stops moving.

"You realize they could sell tomorrow, right? I think you need to tell them, like, yesterday."

Lacey thinks on it for a three count, then shakes her head. "No. It's better if they find out at the meeting. I'll get on the schedule and you guys will help me put a presentation together." She grins. "And nobody will tell my family." She holds up a finger, as if she needs to emphasize the stern reminder. "Right?"

Phoebe and I exchange a look. "Right," we say in unison. A knot twists in my stomach.

"Great!" Lacey stuffs her laptop into her bag and slings it over her shoulder, but before she walks away, she stops and looks at me. "It is a bummer about Liam though. I mean, I know

I can do this without him. I just don't want to." She gives me a sad smile and walks away.

Strangely, I feel the same way.

Sure, I could go on with life without Liam.

I just don't think I want to.

CHAPTER 18

OLIVE

*P*hoebe slides into Lacey's seat across from me.

"Do you really think she can come up with fifty-one percent of what she needs to buy that place?" I ask. "Even if she does find people to go in on it with her, that's going to be so much money."

"She's a sneaky little genius, that Lacey," Phoebe says. "She has zero expenses, no overhead, and a ton of social media followers, which has led to some seriously lucrative brand deals. Her YouTube channel is huge. Looking at what she just showed me, yeah. I think she might actually be able to pull this off." A pause. "I do think she should tell her family though."

I shrug. "She has something to prove. I suppose she feels like this is the only way to do that." I agree with Phoebe, but I understand where Lacey's coming from. It's especially hard to change the opinion of someone who's known you your whole life.

"I'm so jealous." And sad, but I don't say so. "I really love working out there, and I would love to be a part of saving it." I meet her eyes. "The job is amazing, Pheebs. I'm still being creative, just in a different way." I don't bother explaining that this job has got me rethinking things. Like, my life's work. Or that Lacey's business plan, if you can call it that, could've worked for me too, instead of trying to have a physical store. I'm not as great at making videos or as spunky on camera as she is, but I probably could've started online with no overhead and no risk.

Why didn't I listen to literally everyone who told me not to be so impatient?

"Yeah," Phoebe says. "It's a great fit for you."

"Too bad it's only for a month." I look away.

"Unless Lacey's plan works. If it does, I'm *sure* she will offer you a job."

I hadn't considered this. It's enough of a reason to calm my worries about keeping her secret, even though I feel a little bit like a traitor. I have to help her.

Phoebe takes another drink. "You seem happy, Olive. Like your old self."

"My old self?"

"Your *pre-shop* self, back before life knocked the wind out of you."

I absently wonder what it would be like to be as free as Phoebe. I mean, I'm outgoing, but Phoebe is a different kind of extrovert. She does not care what anyone thinks of her. It's a foreign concept, and for a fleeting moment, I wish it wasn't.

"It's good to see you being creative again," she says. "And I think you should have your own booth at the market."

I frown. "Oh, no. No, ma'am. I can't."

She ignores me. "You could take some of the cards in your garage and see if Jo will sell them in the shop at Pine Creek. There's that whole Christmas line, remember? The pink and blue one?"

"Oh, I remember. I'm not doing that."

"Why not?" She's giving off "Professional Phoebe" vibes now, and I'm bracing myself for it.

But is she onto something?

Something Jo said the other day about people needing people stuck with me. Maybe that was my first mistake with the store—thinking I could do it alone. Phoebe was living in Chicago at the time, but she would've helped me if I would've asked.

I never asked.

She would've happily looked at my books, helped me streamline, been there to support me however she could—if only I'd let her.

She's earned the right to say whatever she wants. So, when she reaches across the table and covers my hand with hers and says, "You're really gifted, Olive," I'm caught off-guard.

"What happened with the shop was a *setback*," she continues, "but it's not the end. You've still got so much to offer."

It's not at all the stern talking to that I'd expected. Which is probably why there's a lump in my throat and tears pooling in my eyes.

"Phoebe! Knock it off! You're going to make me cry."

"Look, I know you think everyone has this terrible opinion of you because your shop closed, that you're this big failure, or whatever, but it's not true," she continues. "*None* of that is true. You're the only one who thinks that." She squeezes my hand and leans back in her chair. "And it's nice to see some of your spark has returned. Is that because you're being creative or because Liam's back?"

I gasp. "What are you talking about?"

She shoots me a look that seems to say *Don't pretend with me.* "What's going on with you two?"

"Nothing." I hear the defensiveness in my own voice.

There's that look again.

"Seriously," I say. "Nothing. Right now, I'm just, you know, giving him space."

"Giving yourself space so you can be mad," she says, in a correcting tone.

"No," I say.

"No, you're not mad? Because outside, it sounded like you were mad. In here, it sounded like you were mad. " She shifts back against her seat, confident she's right.

And she is. Darn it.

"I'm not . . . *mad*," I say, knowing the second the words leave my lips that there is no good way to justify any of these petty feelings. "I'm just frustrated."

"With Liam." I know she's about to call me out. Because that's what friends like Phoebe do. They make sure you know they love you so they can tell you when you're being an idiot. "You said you're upset Liam didn't tell you about Travis."

"Ye-es," I say, not liking where this is going. "Maybe I am."

"Let's unpack that." I half expect her to tell me to lay down on the couch at the back of the coffee shop while she pulls out a notebook to write down her assessments.

"We don't need to unpack," I say. "Things can stay packed, thank you very much. I'm fine. In a few weeks, he'll be gone anyway." I take a drink. "I want a muffin. Do you want a muffin?"

I stand.

"Sit."

I sit.

"Look, I know you and Liam have a history," she says. "First crush, first kiss, all the things. And I know it's easy to think that was just kid stuff, and it doesn't mean anything."

"It *was* kid stuff," I say. "And it *doesn't* mean anything. Liam and I aren't even friends anymore. He's just a guy I used to know."

She cocks her head to the side and glares at me. "That might work when you're saying it to yourself in the mirror, but this is me you're talking to."

I sigh.

She's right.

"So, what, you don't think I have a right to be upset with him?"

She presses her red lips together and thinks for a moment. "How would you have reacted if he'd come to you back then and told you the guy you were so smitten with was a cheating jerk? Would you have been grateful that he was dropping a grenade in the middle of your life? You were so into that guy, you wouldn't have believed Liam, and honestly, Travis would've found a way to spin it to make Liam look jealous or something."

I scoff. "Why would Liam be jealous?"

She shrugs. "Because he knew you first? Because Travis practically derailed any shot he had with you that night? Because first kiss, first crush? Olive, he was your first *everything.*"

I sit with that for a brief second.

He was.

I raise a hand to cut her off, not realizing she's already stopped talking. "Wait. Back up. What did you say about that night?"

Phoebe widens her eyes. "Come *on.* Liam was totally into you that night."

I frown. "We were just catching up." But her words are confirmation of something I thought only I had noticed. Something I've been trying to ignore since I walked away from Liam's unanswered question yesterday.

"He spent the entire night talking to you," she says. "As soon as he saw you he stopped mid-conversation with the person he was with and practically ran over. You two have always had a thing." At my confusion, she adds, "You know, chemistry."

"When we were twelve years old? In a treehouse?" I roll my eyes, unwilling to believe her. "Or further back, when we rode bikes in our neighborhood at the tender age of eight?"

"You know what I mean," she says. "Even I was jealous of you and Liam. You talked about him like he was the best friend you'd ever had—how do I compete with that?"

I laugh, thinking about how ridiculous that is now. "I don't think you have to worry."

"Look, Olive, I know you don't go on a lot of dates—"

I shoot her a look.

She holds her hands up, as if to say *I mean no harm.* "—But I do. And I can tell when a guy is into me and when he isn't. Liam was *into* you. Just like he was every time he wrapped one of your family's Christmas trees. Or like that time he came to your play in the eleventh grade. He stood there, looking all dopey and smitten, but you were dating that guy, the drooly kisser . . .?"

"Tim."

"Yes! Tim Torino!" She shudders.

I laugh. "I think you're seriously losing it. Liam and I have never been anything but friends."

"Tell me . . . on the night you met Travis," she says, "that you didn't feel something."

I'm quiet for a long moment. Now that it's out there, there's no way for me to pretend, especially not with Phoebe.

I pull a face and sigh.

"Yeah," she says, putting a period on her point.

"Fine, yes. I did. That night. Something was different, you know? And then I felt so stupid when his friend asked me out. Isn't there some sort of guy code or something that says if Liam was really into me, his friend would've known, and his friend wouldn't have swooped in and gotten my number?"

"Yeah, Travis seems like just the kind of person to honor 'guy code.'"

I push my hands through my hair and let out a frustrated groan. "It doesn't even matter what either of us felt all those years ago because he's definitely not into me now."

Phoebe raises her eyebrows again, and takes a drink.

"Phoebe."

She just looks at me.

"*Phoebe.* He's not."

He's not. Right?

In my mind, I see the look on his face as he waited for what my answer would've been if he'd asked me out all those years ago. I'd chosen anger over introspection on this subject, but now that Phoebe's brought it up, I can't figure out how to keep pretending there wasn't a spark there.

Or maybe he was just curious.

She levels my gaze. "To answer your previous question, no. I don't think you should hold it against Liam. He was put in a horrible situation. He thought he was doing the right thing, and you need to quit being mad."

The words stop me.

And for the eighteenth time in the last five minutes, I realize she's right.

And I need to make it right with Liam.

CHAPTER 19

LIAM

I haven't been sleeping the greatest.

It's been two days since the fated tree fort project and three days since I've said more than a passing hello to Olive.

The way her face fell with understanding, that simple "Oh," escaping her lips, has been haunting me. During the day, instead of working on my assigned projects, I'm daydreaming about this new game, inspired by Olive's propeller hat kid, and when I get stumped on ideas there, I've been out in the fields with Manny.

He's always given me space to work out my frustrations. I don't have to talk. I can just think.

In the stillness, surrounded by nature, I can let my mind wander. I don't have to have the answers lined up—I can just muddle through the questions.

Why didn't I ask Olive out that night all those years ago?

What was the real reason I didn't warn her about Travis?

Does any of it really matter now when, in a few weeks, I'll go back to having little to no relationship with her at all?

I'm starting to remember the good things about Pine Creek, things I thought I had successfully pushed from my mind ages ago. But now, I notice the air is clearer. My nerves are calmer. I feel less pressure.

I think about a normal workday in what I thought was my dream job. Caffeine-fueled mornings, long hours of coding, cramped in a cubicle—I very rarely do anything creative anymore.

Troubleshooting, applying digital Band-Aids, and fixing other people's mistakes are now the norm.

I'm aware of my discontent. It feels like a Velcro undershirt. Part of me thinks that if I can get this new game concept finished and pitch it to Aaron, then maybe, *maybe* I'll get the greenlight to do something that excites me again.

Something fun.

But even as the thought enters my mind, I know it's a long shot.

Aaron hired me so he could acquire *Castle Crusade*. I couldn't see it then, but boy do I see it now. It was the game, not me, that was the draw.

Trying to chase that same lightning in a bottle but stuck in a creative black hole of an office, my three follow-up games underperformed.

I'm sitting on the porch at the side of the house, listening to the sounds of morning, drinking coffee, and contemplating all of it. It would probably be good to talk to someone.

I just wish it was easier to turn my thoughts into words.

The door swings open and my dad walks out of the house, Hank padding at his side. Dad's holding a steaming cup of coffee, wearing the same golden work coat and worn out baseball cap he's had since I was thirteen.

"You mind?" He nods toward the empty chair next to me.

I shake my head.

He sits in the rocking chair, and the dog flops in a pile at his feet.

I've been home over a week now, and I haven't had a single

solo conversation with my dad. I'd thought about finding him after they told me the news about the farm, but I never figured out what to say.

To be fair, he hadn't sought me out either.

We just don't have that kind of relationship. We aren't men who talk.

He's probably seething with disappointment that I've stood firm in my decision, and I brace myself for the guilt trip.

"So," he says.

I glance over. "So."

"You and Olive."

I frown at him, but he's not looking at me. He takes a slow drink of his steaming coffee and swallows, clearly not in a hurry to explain. "You gonna do something about that?"

"About what?"

He gives me a look, like he knows a secret.

"There's no 'me and Olive.'" I'm annoyed at the assumption.

He grunts. It's a familiar *I don't believe you* kind of grunt.

"I don't live here." I go back to staring at the trees. Are we really going to talk about girls for the first time in my life? At thirty-one?

"Hey, I've been around long enough to recognize a good thing," he says. "She's good for you."

"Can we not talk about this?" The last thing I need is someone putting more thoughts of Olive into my head.

He lifts a hand, surrendering.

"Besides," I say under my breath, "even if that were true, it doesn't mean I'm good for her."

Moody. Sullen. Withdrawn. Yeah, just what every woman wants.

He grunts softly as he shifts in his seat, but I think I can safely consider the topic dropped.

I take another drink, and we sit there, uneasily, for several minutes.

In the silence, I'm wondering where it all went sideways with him.

Unmet expectations and undiscussed assumptions are plentiful.

One would think that a simple conversation would help. Not so easy when you've got a non-communicative father sitting next to his non-communicative son.

He clears his throat.

Then, without looking at me, he says, "I owe you an apology."

The air goes still, and I wonder if I've heard him right.

"Time gives you perspective." He props an ankle on the opposite knee. "And I . . . I got some perspective."

I turn and look at him.

"I wish I'd handled things differently."

Yeah, I definitely don't think I heard him right.

"Mom put you up to this?" I ask.

"No." He chuckles. "I've never been great at—" he pulls a face — "sharing my feelings."

Now I chuckle. Understatement of the year. "Me neither."

"But you're my son, so I need you to hear a few things." He inhales, like he's bracing himself. The simple action tells a story —talking doesn't come any easier to him than it does to me.

"It never occurred to me you wouldn't want this life. I always assumed I was just a caretaker 'til you were ready. I'd never seen you happier than when you were working with Manny. So dirty and covered in sap your mom wouldn't let you touch anything. I'm surprised she didn't install an outdoor shower." He chuckles.

I smile at the lost memory. It means more having seen it through his eyes.

"You had so many ideas for this place—" he says.

"Ideas you shot down." The words are a reflex.

He looks at me, lips pursed.

"I'm sorry, Dad, it's just . . . you did."

"I honestly thought we'd get there,.." He looks away. "You know, eventually. You and me. Become partners or something. You could work on expanding and I could keep the day to day going."

He glances back, and I have to look away.

"I wanted you to learn it all. The business side. The farming side. The staff management side. I thought that when you came home from college, you'd already have life experience to match that degree, and you'd be ready to come on board. We'd phase me out." He inhales. "I didn't realize that what I was doing was making you hate this place. I had no idea I was driving you away."

My shoulders drop. "You never said—"

"I'm not good at talking," he says.

I shoot him a knowing look, because it's a trait I inherited from him.

When I switched my major, I didn't tell anyone. I didn't explain why. I didn't use it as an opportunity to share how I felt about the farm or about my lack of choices. I didn't say anything. I just did it. And when my parents found out, I didn't bother explaining then either. I was proud and frustrated and determined to live my own life.

A more evolved man, a less childish man, would've had a conversation. I was young and stupid and rebellious, and I made a lot of mistakes.

"It's funny, you got the idea for that video game working in the fields," he says. "I remember the day you came in, talking about it. I think you were fifteen?"

I'd forgotten that. A lot of my creative ideas came to me when I was doing the most mundane things. Trimming trees. Pulling weeds. Fixing fences.

"And then you actually went out and made it. Something I could never do, that's for sure." There's pride in his voice that catches me off guard. "I thought this place made you so happy."

He pauses. "I had no idea it was making you miserable. If I'd realized, I never would've—" His voice breaks, and I go still.

My dad isn't an emotional guy. He doesn't cry. Ever. And neither do I, which is why the lump in my throat is a surprise.

Now he looks at me. "I'm sorry, son."

I draw in a deep breath, turning so many thoughts over in my head. As I look at him, I hold back the emotion, and slowly nod. "Thanks."

He gives me a firm nod and goes back to whatever morning ritual this seems to be for him—sitting on the porch drinking coffee with Hank at his feet, soaking up the peace and quiet.

I take a drink, still trying to make sense of this unexpected turn. Without looking at him, I say, "Wait. Is this your way of trying to change my mind?" I keep the question light, but I have to ask. This is a version of my dad I haven't seen before. In all my thirty-one years, he's never once apologized to me—to anyone, if I had to guess—but especially not to me.

He's not unkind or angry. He's not bad or mean. He's a good guy. Hard-working. Loves our mom. But he's not reachable.

Emotionally unavailable, my last short-lived relationship called me. Something else I inherited from him.

He laughs softly and takes another drink of his coffee. "Did it work?"

I chuckle. "Jury's still out."

"Nah, I know you don't want to stay here. This is my way of telling you I wish I'd asked you what *you* wanted instead of assuming I knew. I hate to think your memories are tarnished because of me."

I set my mug down on the arm of my chair and think on this. "They're not all tarnished."

"No?" He brightens a bit. "Found some good times out there, did ya?"

I'm liking this conversation—it feels easier, somehow, like we're on common ground.

179

"A few."

"Care to share?"

I shake my head, smiling. "Eh, I'm guessing some of them might get me in trouble."

He leans back and looks up, "Oh, there wasn't much that I didn't hear about. The ramp you built for the ATVs, the rock through the window, the party you threw when we were gone—"

No way.

"You knew about all that stuff?"

He leans forward, smirking. "Hard to hide the ash of an all-night bonfire."

I sit back in my chair, stunned. He hadn't said anything, and I didn't get in trouble for throwing a party. I glance at him, and he's wearing the smile of a father who let his kid think he'd gotten away with something he absolutely had not gotten away with.

He chuckles and says, "I did the same thing when I was a kid."

I'm floored. We've just connected more in the last ten minutes than in the last ten years. As I look out at the trees and the land and the sky, my thoughts settle, and I think about the true beauty of this place.

Which makes me think of Olive.

About how she was so shocked to learn that Pine Creek and I had parted ways. About how she insisted she could make me love it here again.

There's a quiet lull before my dad says, "Do you think you can try and enjoy these last few weeks? I'd love for you to have good feelings about Pine Creek when we close on the sale. Maybe it'd make you less—" he gives me a side-eye— "cranky?"

"Come on. You too?" I shake my head to convey my annoyance.

"You're kind of unbearable," he says. "Misery just looking for company, and you're not going to find it here because you're surrounded by people who love Christmas." He laughs. "If Jo cut herself, I'm pretty sure she'd bleed tinsel. And Manny, that guy has more Christmas spirit than anyone I know. Did you know he's been playing the title role in our Santa's Village for the last five years?"

Now I laugh. "No, he failed to mention that."

"That man is a different breed."

I go still. "What happens to him after you sell?"

Dad sighs. "Depends on the buyer. If we do find someone who wants to keep all this going, I'll try to get them to keep our staff. It's their home too." He leans back in his chair. "There's a lot to love."

I wonder if he knows how unlikely it is that anyone Travis brings through here is going to want this place for anything other than the land.

I follow his gaze out across the yard and decide not to bring it up. At the tree line, there's a giant oak that looks out of place among so many spruces and fir trees. The tire swing is still hanging around its sturdy branches, and I'm filled with some of my oldest—fondest—memories.

Grandpa pushing me on that swing, and it felt way too high —giving the kind of rush to a kid that only comes on the edge of perceived danger. Grandma baking our favorite chocolate chip cookies, me begging to lick the bowl. Mom and Dad, relaxing on the porch while Lacey and I ran around, screaming and playing and laughing—barefoot and sun-kissed and dirty and, by the end of the night, exhausted.

I'd forgotten about all of it.

And now that I'm losing Pine Creek, I think it might be too painful to let myself remember.

CHAPTER 20

OLIVE

*N*ormally I wake up with that ridiculous Rebecca Black song on repeat in my brain, but this Friday I wake up nervous.

It's the day before our first weekend of new events hits. Tomorrow evening, we'll open Santa's Village, preview new specialty items on the café's menu, have carriage rides and hayrides around the property, and debut a fun new addition just for the hopeless romantics—a Mistletoe Walk.

I designed a sort of scavenger hunt with clues that will lead couples around the farm in hopes of locating all the little bunches of mistletoe Liam and I hung around the property.

In the morning, Jo will host her first wreath-making class—and it filled up so quickly she had to add another two sessions. I knew people would love it. And then Sunday, in the late afternoon, Pine Creek will close early for Family Day.

It's been a lot getting everything ready, but people are more willing to handle last minute events considering it's their last chance to enjoy Pine Creek.

In spite of my nerves, I'm excited as I make the turn into Pine Creek. At least I am until I catch a glimpse of Liam over by the equipment barn, chatting with the guys who will wrap and haul trees for customers throughout the day.

The nerves turn into what some people call a flutter.

I tell my body to stop it right now.

I think about what Phoebe said, about how I shouldn't be angry with him and realize I'm not angry—but it would be easier if I were.

The real feelings that have started to form when I think about Liam are going to be far more difficult to navigate than anger.

I park and pop the trunk, then exit the car. I feel Liam's gaze, but I don't turn to confirm it. I do the thing people do when they know someone is watching them but they don't want to acknowledge it—pretend to be super involved with the task at hand. I open the trunk and find the yard signs I designed and had printed to post around the farm.

It was one of my midnight ideas, to create branded signage to lead people around the farm. And because I apparently no longer sleep, I also created others with hand-lettered Christmas movie quotes like *She's a beaut, Clark!*, "Photo op" spots, and arrows with faces and arms directing people to the mistletoe.

In my head, it's an easy way to add a bit of festive cheer to the farm, but also to create a unified look for all printed materials. I'd be lying if I said I'm not proud of it.

I sling my bag over my shoulder and start pulling the signs from the trunk. I'm gingerly stacking them in a haphazard pile, one hand underneath and a foot on the bumper, when they teeter and fall to the ground.

As I kneel to pick them up, a man's voice calls out, "Let me help."

I glance up, hoping to see Liam striding toward me, but it's Travis. My heart sinks. And I'm not sure if I'm disappointed because it's Travis or because it *isn't* Liam.

Yeah. It's both.

I sigh. Liam's still standing in a group of guys near the barn, but now I can confirm his gaze is trained on me.

Me. And now Travis.

"I'm fine." I lift a hand, hoping to signal that I don't need Travis's help.

He doesn't stop helping.

Travis is the kind of guy who thinks he knows better. So much so that you might as well not speak at all. He's not going to listen.

"They're awkward to carry. Where are you going with these?" He leans the signs up against my car, then slides his arm under the metal base like it was the obvious way to transport such awkward cargo. "Will you just let me help?"

I draw in a breath, and on an exhale, I ask, "What are you doing here?"

"I'm the real estate agent," he says. "I had questions."

I frown. "My grandparents sold their house before they moved to Arizona. I think they saw their Realtor like, twice."

He holds his hands out, "What can I say, I'm a hands-on kind of guy."

Good grief. Does everything he says have to be dripping with innuendo?

I don't acknowledge him. Instead, I slip an arm under the yard signs, take them from him, then tromp toward the equipment barn, disappointed to see that Liam is no longer outside.

"Have you thought any more about dinner?" Travis calls out, trailing behind me.

"No," I say over my shoulder, barely looking back. I trudge my way down the gravel road, and when I reach the barn, I lean the signs against the side of it and walk inside.

I know I'm out of place here, but if I wasn't aware, the complete silence that follows my entrance would've clued me in.

I wait a second, thankful Travis appears to have given up. For now, anyway.

"Hey." I lift a hand and wave at two of the young guys standing near a workbench next to an oversized door. They half-heartedly wave back, then glance off toward the back of the large building. I take the cue and start walking in that direction when I find Manny and Liam standing next to a tractor.

Manny turns toward me, his face brightening. It's been a while since I've seen him, but years of coming to the farm revealed that we have something in common—we both love Christmas.

"Finally! I was wondering when you were going to come see me!" He walks over and pulls me into a paternal hug. "I heard you started working here." He leans in. "Wish you'd come sooner—things might be different."

I pull back and shake my head. "Aw, thanks." I force myself not to look at Liam, but I see him turn away. I don't blame him if he's upset with me. He apologized for something I'm not even sure he needed to apologize for, and I practically said, *apology not accepted.*

I'm the worst.

I turn my attention back to Manny.

"I heard about your ugly Christmas sweater," he says.

I wince. "You did?"

He laughs. "They're hanging a photo in the main barn."

My eyes go wide. "They better not be!"

"Your family won! You get a place of honor on the wall of winners." His eyes drift over to Liam, and I see a tiny shift in his expression. Amusement at the memory of the coconut sweater, maybe?

"I hear you're reprising your big role this weekend, Santa." I give my shoulders a little shimmy.

"It's the most wonderful time of the year," Manny sings. "What can I do for you? Did you bring me your Christmas list?"

"Uh, no, I was hoping I could borrow an ATV."

Liam turns toward me. "No way."

Manny frowns. I frown.

"Why not?" I ask.

"One, they're dangerous," he says. "Two, you don't know how to operate them. Especially around here."

"I think I can handle it," I say, though his reaction makes me unsure. "It'll be quicker getting around the back parts of the farm. I have signs to put up before tomorrow."

"If you're concerned, Liam, why don't you take her?" Manny says. "Probably go quicker, and you can keep her out of the way of the field trip."

"There's a field trip?" Liam groans. "I didn't think we did those anymore."

"Oh. Right. I set that up," I sheepishly admit.

I can tell by the way he's looking at me he guessed that part.

My smile is tentative. "Lacey is their point person, and I think she has everything under control. All we really have to do is stay out of the way."

He glowers. But after a pause, he pulls a set of keys off a pegboard on the wall, glares at me and says, "Let's go."

Manny stops him. "Oh, hey, the clutch was sticking on the four-seater. I have to take a look at it before anyone rides it."

Liam looks at him like, *are you serious?*

"Only the single's available, gotta ride tandem." I glance at Manny, whose grimace looks more like a smirk. "Sorry."

Liam makes a show of hanging the set of keys back up, grabbing another set, and then he's out the door.

I try to remember what tandem means as I jog to catch up with Liam. When I do, I find him outside, strapping the posters onto the small back part of one of the ATVs.

The ATV only has one seat.

Tandem.

Me behind him, arms wrapped around his waist, chin

propped on his shoulder, inhaling that familiar yet unfamiliar scent I've come to associate with Liam.

"What are these for anyway?" He nods at the signs.

Okay. A simple question. I can answer this.

"They're happy little signs I thought would make people feel welcome," I say, still staring at the single seat. "And help people find their way around. Plus, I made a little scavenger hunt out of all that mistletoe we hung."

He flips through them. "You drew these?"

I shrug. "It's not a big deal."

"Do you ever sleep?" He secures the last of the signs and swings a leg over to sit on the four-wheeler.

"Sure," I say, pausing and not moving.

He's getting situated and looks at me, then looks behind him, at me again, then tilts his head behind him as if to say, *get on.*

Sure. No problem. I'm just going to straddle the seat and cozy right in behind him.

I'm suddenly very warm.

I cautiously slide onto the four-wheeler.

My mouth starts moving while my logic and emotions are duking it out. "But my brain doesn't always settle, and when I can't sleep, I draw. Sometimes it helps, sometimes it doesn't, and with everything I'm doing for the farm lately, I figured why not just stay up and finish a few things, and so I've been drawing to help me relax."

I'm positive none of what I said had any punctuation, but it's hard to think when he's so close.

This is Liam. Don't make it a thing.

I wiggle a bit on the seat and inadvertently slide forward so my chest presses against his back. He straightens for a fraction of a second, then clears his throat. I shift back a little, desperate for even an inch of space between us.

He reaches behind and hands me a helmet.

It's the kind without the visor, which is bad, because I don't want anyone to see how flushed I am right now. I pull the helmet on, then hold my hands in the air, unsure of where to rest them. I settle for my legs, deluding myself into thinking I can stay on this thing once it starts moving by sheer force of will.

"What do you use?" he asks over his shoulder, strapping on his own helmet. "I mean, they're digital, right?"

"Right," I say, trying to focus. "I use Procreate." The second I say it, I hear the innuendo, and my face gets hot again. "Uh, it's an app."

He starts the ATV and revs the engine. I'm not used to the vibration, and I instinctively wrap my arms around him.

He stiffens for a brief second, then relaxes. He turns his head and talks over the engine. "You okay back there?"

Other than the impending heart attack?

"Yeah, I'm good!"

"Okay, hold on tight."

It's like an invitation to a party I'm not allowed to attend.

He gently pulls away from the garage and out of the parking area, and at the movement I squeeze a bit tighter. He doesn't drive nearly as fast as I've seen the other guys drive these things —maybe for my benefit—and it's surprisingly easy to talk over the engine. Probably because our faces are practically touching.

"Would you ever—" He stops.

"What?"

"Do you do any freelance work?" He keeps his eyes steady on the path in front of us.

I scoff. "After my business tanked, I sort of hung up my Apple Pencil."

"Until now?"

I frown. "Right. Until now." This had initially felt like a favor I was doing for Liam's family, but the more I work on the branding and events at the farm, the less it feels like a favor and the more it feels like a future.

"I have a project I'm working on—" He angles the handlebars as I point for him to pull over at a fork in the gravel road. "I could use a little input."

I pull back from him and lean slightly over his left shoulder. "From me?"

"From someone who understands art better than I do," he says. "I'm a programming guy. And I like the storytelling part, but art is, uh, not my strength."

He stops the four-wheeler, and I hop off, grateful for the momentary distance, if only to give my heart a chance to settle. I remove my helmet and set it on the seat, then grab one of the signs that says, *Pine Creek recommends our Holly Jolly Jam, available in the Pine Creek gift shop.* It has an arrow with big eyes, a goofy smile, and hands, one of which is giving a forced perspective thumbs-up.

I walk over to the fork in the road, double-check that the arrow is pointing in the correct direction, and then use my foot to push the metal stakes into the ground. It stands upright and I grin up at Liam, who has removed his helmet and is now watching me.

I'm feeling a bit bold. Maybe from the crisp air. Maybe because of the distance between us now. Or maybe it's my desperation for things to feel normal again.

I narrow my eyes. "So, you need me."

"Not what I said." He stands.

"Interesting." I squint at him. "What I heard was that you need me to swoop in and save your project thingie."

"I just want your help."

I pretend to think for a second. "I've never been someone's knight in shining armor. I like it. Kind of like when I punched Jared Galecki in the second grade because he wouldn't stop picking on you." I let the grin crawl across my face, then I pump my eyebrows and do a weird dance.

He shakes his head and goes back to glaring at the trees in

front of us. I should be offended, but it almost feels normal. Almost.

Before I can say anything else, a tractor pulling a trailer of children appears in a cleared path in the trees. "Oh, look, it's the field trip!"

Liam winces.

The kids are loud, and when they drive by, they hoot and smile and wave. I wave enthusiastically and holler out, "Merry Pine Creek Christmas!"

When I turn back, I see Liam shaking his head at me.

"What?"

"You really are always like this, aren't you?"

"Like what?"

He motions toward me. "Sunny." He says it like it's a swear.

"Well, I'm not—" I motion to him the same way he just did to me— "cranky if that's what you're getting at," I say, pointedly.

He quirks a brow. "Touché."

I look back at the ATV, getting the same feeling you get when your boyfriend walks you to your car, and you anticipate a kiss.

Stop it, I think. He doesn't even think of me like that. Phoebe can speculate all she wants, but Liam has made his disinterest quite clear.

I try to act casual as I get back on the seat. I clap my hands dramatically in the air. "Chop, chop!" I pull the helmet back on.

He rolls his eyes, sticks his helmet on, and slides onto the seat in front of me. This time, though, he gently moves back so my chest is pressed to his back.

"All good?"

I beg my traitor of a heart not to give me away. I'm sure he can feel it racing against his back.

I do my best to act normal as we drive around, mostly in silence, stopping in various spots around the farm to stick signs in the earth. As we do, I run through possible ways to bring up

CHRISTMAS WITH A CRANK

the fact that I was a total jerk about his apology because all the acting cute in the world doesn't absolve me.

The simplest solution, of course, is to apologize.

Say words.

I'm beginning to understand why he doesn't talk.

Which is probably why I start talking without thinking. Just sort of . . . open mouth, say stuff.

I lean over his shoulder and loudly say, "That thing you said before—" I look around, as if there's someone in the woods who can save me from myself.

"That thing?"

"When you were talking about Travis and the thing—"

He slows the ATV down. "When I apologized to you?" He says this so dryly, I can hear his frown.

"Yeah, that."

"What about it?"

"I accept."

He lets the ATV come to a stop and kills the engine. He turns to the side and looks at me, amused. "You accept?"

"Yes."

He nods and shrugs at the same time. "Okay."

There's a pause.

We're just looking at each other. Our bodies are touching. And we're in the woods. Alone.

We stay like that for a beat. It's long. Like a year.

I scrunch my nose because I can't beat him in a game of *who can stay silent longer*.

"I thought I had the right to be mad at you, but . . . I really don't. It wasn't your job to tell me you were friends with a lying cheater." I glance away. "Or that I shouldn't date him. I probably wouldn't have listened to you. I probably would've gotten mad at you." I sigh. "Travis really is a master in the art of gaslighting."

"Truth," he says.

I go quiet, all out of words.

191

He looks out, off the path and into the near distance of the trees. "I always felt bad about it, Liv."

Liv.

He still calls me Liv. And this time, when he does, something clicks into place.

It's dumb to linger on it, but hearing my nickname in his mouth again feels like the start of something new. A mending of sorts.

But it's more than that, isn't it?

I go still, staring at his profile, trying not to let my gaze dip to his lips. "You did?"

He glances slightly toward me. "Yeah. I did."

I pause, wondering if he can hear my heart pounding in my chest. "You're a lot different than you lead people to believe. I mean, you're actually nice."

He grunts as he spins back around and starts the engine back up. He revs it, then tosses me a sideways glance. "Ready?"

I move closer and wrap my arms around his midsection because I have the distinct impression he's done going slow.

"You better hang on."

"Wait. Hang on? What are we—"

He turns, but not before I catch a glimpse of a wicked smirk. A sexy smirk. My admiration is short-lived though because he guns the motor, and we take off like a shot. My grip on him tightens, and I clasp my hands together around him. It's exhilarating and terrifying and I love every second of it.

If the way I feel now is a sign of things to come, then he's right.

I'd better hang on.

CHAPTER 21

OLIVE

*K*ids are loud.

Before we even round the corner, we can hear them over the ATV. The field trip kids, fresh off the hayride, are standing in a small, bundled up clump, listening to a young guy wearing a Pine Creek hoodie under a work coat.

It seems to be Q&A time, but at the sight of the ATV, the staffer loses their attention, and they all start running toward us.

Liam brings the vehicle to a stop just as the kids circle around the four-wheeler. Their excited questions come out rapid-fire:

"Whoa! Why do you need a four-wheeler on a farm?"

"Do you need a license to drive one of these?"

"Can you jump that thing? I bet you could jump that thing."

"Do you ever race them? I bet I could whip you in a race, Hunter!"

"Can we go for a ride?"

Liam removes his helmet and glances up at the staffer, who lifts his hands, helplessly. "This is the most excited they've been since they got here."

The kids' teacher, a young, dark-haired girl who doesn't look much older than a high schooler, rushes around, trying to corral the kids. "I'm so sorry," she says to Liam. "Back up, kids. They're just driving through."

"It's fine," Liam says. I expect him to start the engine up and drive away, but instead, he gets out and walks over to the staffer, who has moved close enough that I see now his coat has the name *Eddie* embroidered on it.

While the kids chatter on, Eddie gives Liam a wide-eyed, *I'm out of my depth here,* kind of look. Liam glances back at the throng of third graders.

He sticks his fingers in his mouth and lets out a loud, ear-piercing whistle. The kids startle, but they go silent, all eyes fixed on Liam. I slowly slip off the ATV, moving to the back of the group as Liam calls out, "Who knows how many Christmas trees are sold every year in the United States?" He barks it, like a drill sergeant.

Nobody responds, but they're all still captivated. I can't blame them. Liam is captivating. Or, at the very least, he's commanding.

He scans the crowd, then says, "Over 25 million trees. And most come from tree farms just like this one."

He walks over to one of the trees. "Does anyone know what kind of tree this is?"

A little boy raises his hand. "Pine tree?"

Liam points at the kid. "Good guess, but this is not a pine tree. Anyone else?"

"Evergreen?" another kid hollers.

"This is actually a blue spruce tree," Liam says. "You can tell by the diamond-shaped patterns in the needles, and if you get really close—"

The kids lean in.

"—they're actually a bit bluish green."

Some of the kids crowd in to get a better look, *ooh's* and *let me see's* smattered throughout.

He picks up a cut branch from the blue spruce and holds it up.

"These are some of the most popular trees on our lot. Every tree comes to us as a sapling, which is a really small tree—"

"I thought they grew from seeds," a little girl calls out.

"Or pinecones!" another kid shouts.

"Or Connor's mom," a blond kid smarts off from the back.

"Austin!" the young teacher snaps. Then, to Liam, "I'm so sorry."

Liam smirks but continues without missing a beat.

"You're exactly right, they do start small, from seeds, but we don't start them as seeds here. Someone else does that, ships them to us, and when we get them, they look like baby trees." He moves down the row, and the kids follow. "This one, you can see, is a lot younger than, say—" he moves toward a taller tree— "this one."

"How old is that one?" one of the kids asks, pointing to the taller tree.

"Probably nine or ten," he says. "I'm guessing about your age?"

"They have to be our age before they get chopped down?"

"Pretty much," Liam says. "Takes a lot of time and patience to get them to grow. Probably how Austin's parents feel."

This gets a huge response from the group, and even Austin laughs, clearly up for the attention.

"Hey, hey, I'm just kidding. Austin, can you do me a solid?" He tosses the ATV keys to him. "Can you watch those for me? I don't want to lose them."

Now the kids turn toward Austin. "What?" "No way!" "Does he get to drive it?"

And with that simple move, Austin is now Liam's biggest fan.

Liam points at a little girl and motions for her to join him near the tree. "What's your name?"

The girl is a redhead with wide eyes and a bright smile. She grins at him, probably as smitten with him as I am right now. "Brynn."

"Okay, Brynn," he says. "Very carefully touch the branch of this tree and tell me what it feels like."

The girl reaches out and taps the needles of the spruce. "Pokey."

"Pokey, right," he says. "What else?"

"Sharp."

"Right," Liam says. "The blue spruce trees have some of the sharpest needles of all the trees out here on the farm, but that makes them *great* for hanging ornaments on."

Liam briefly meets my eyes, holds my gaze for a three-count, and then looks away. It's long enough for me to marvel at this different side of him, the side that knows and understands—and even seems to enjoy—all the unique aspects of this tree farm. The side that can communicate that knowledge in a way that keeps small children engaged.

Liam tells a story about a time he was helping a customer cut down a small tree and it fell the wrong way and landed directly on the man's wife.

They *loved* that story.

He doesn't talk down to them the way a lot of people do—he talks to them like they're people. And they're completely into it.

The young teacher makes her way around the back of the group and stands next to me. "Is he your boyfriend?"

"Oh, no," I say, glancing at her. Her eyes are full of admiration. "We're just friends."

Her expression shifts. "Do you know if he's single?"

I half-laugh. "They say he's *chronically* single."

Her face falls.

"He doesn't live here," I tell her. "He's just home for the holidays."

The teacher leans in. "That's a Christmas fling I wouldn't mind having."

A wave of heat rolls through my body, and I recognize it instantly—jealousy. I force a smile, which I'm sure is awkward, and go back to listening to Liam.

He makes Austin his second in command as they set off to harvest a tree, using a small saw he had stashed in the back of the ATV.

He holds their attention so well, it's like he's cast a spell on them.

They're not the only ones.

I watch as he interacts with these children with remarkable ease, thinking how nice it is that I can see a trace of the Liam Fisher I knew all those years ago. The one who used to geek out about the way things around here work.

By the time he's done, the kids have completely forgotten that they wanted ATV rides and are now excitedly heading back to the main barn to plant their own tiny trees in buckets to take home after school. Before they go, several of the kids thank Liam. One little girl tells him she wants to be a tree farmer when she grows up, and when the boy standing behind her says it's not a girl job, Liam sets him straight with a gentle reminder that girls can do anything boys can do, probably even better.

I smirk at that.

Austin runs up and tosses the ATV keys back to Liam, who gives him a high five and tells him to be nice to Connor.

I'm standing off to the side as the class makes its way back onto the trailer when the teacher walks over to Liam with a bright smile on her face.

I can't hear what she says, but when she reaches out and squeezes his arm, I get a pretty good idea. She walks back toward the kids and hoists herself onto the trailer, and my insides burn.

What is my problem? Why am I so annoyed that she's hitting on him right here in front of thirty-two nine-year-olds?

Liam glances at me, and I pretend not to have noticed any of this, waving at the group as they pull away.

He walks back to the four-wheeler and gets on.

I stand, unmoving, arms crossed over my chest and glare at him.

"Are you getting on?" he asks.

"Not until you tell me what that was."

He frowns. "What?"

"You just taught a whole class of children about the different kinds of trees on the farm," I say.

He only stares.

"You know a *lot* about the trees . . ."

That comment gets me a side-eye.

"You actually seemed . . . happy."

He rolls his eyes. "Eddie was dying a slow death out there. I was just trying to help."

I raise my eyebrows. "Well, I think you made quite an impression. On the kids *and* their teacher."

He looks at me. "Are you getting on or . . .?"

"Did you get her number?" I feign excitement as I slide onto the seat behind him.

"No," he says.

"Why not?" I ask, aware that I'm hoping he'll say something romantic like, "Because I'm hung up on a girl I knew a long time ago," which is totally stupid for so many reasons.

But as he starts up the engine, he says, "Because I'm going back to Indy right after the holidays. Be stupid to get involved with someone who lives here."

"Right."

Right.

CHAPTER 22

LIAM

I wonder if this is the new routine.

It's Saturday morning, and I'm up with the sun, sitting on the back porch with my dad and Hank, drinking coffee.

Hank's not drinking coffee. Hank's currently lying on his back, belly available for free rubs.

It's not a scene I would've ever expected to see, but this whole trip has been full of surprises. Dad's apology, especially, took me off guard.

Dad and I don't talk much out here. It's funny—we don't need to. And it's actually pretty nice to be around someone who doesn't expect conversation to fill in every gap of silence.

I think of Olive. Because sometimes it's also nice to have someone who happily fills in those gaps, whether I reciprocate or not.

We sit in silence, both lost in thought and appreciating the view, which is probably why I don't hear Olive until she's standing in the yard a few feet away. She pauses at the base of the steps and stares at us.

"Morning, Olive," Dad says.

A frown shadows her face, and I can practically see her trying to put together the scene in front of her. Olive doesn't know everything about my relationship with my dad, but she knows enough to be curious.

Also, we're both sitting here in silence, which is probably a foreign concept to her.

After a moment of hesitation, she says, "Sorry to interrupt."

Hank rolls over onto his feet, hops up, moves about five feet closer to Olive, plops back down, rolls back over, and looks at her expectantly.

She smiles. "Ooh, Hank, does this good boy need his belly rubbed?" She does so, and Hank's tail shows his appreciation.

"Do you want some coffee? Jo just made a fresh pot." Dad's different these days, I realize now. Friendlier. Calmer.

Now that I'm older, I can appreciate the rigors of keeping this place going. The physical toll alone could make a person difficult—cranky—but add the stress of making ends meet and supporting a family? It was a lot.

I never thought about it that way before.

Olive says I'm different too, though in my case, I don't think she meant it as a compliment. I was never an outgoing person. But I wasn't rude, and I wasn't unkind.

I wonder how she sees me now . . .and I wonder how I can go back to the way she saw me before.

"Um, no thanks," Olive says, walking up the stairs just as my mom opens the door and steps out onto the porch. She puts an arm around Olive and smiles, then looks at Dad and me. "Have you seen what this girl did yesterday?"

Olive's cheeks turn pink.

"She made the cutest signs, all in that perfect hand lettering she does. Liam, did you see them? They just bring things to life out there in the fields. And the Mistletoe Walk is just *brilliant*. Your creativity never ends."

"Well, thanks, Jo," Olive says. "It was fun to put together. And

I really am loving spending so much time out here." She casts her gaze off to the side of the porch, where the large yard extends back to a tree line that instantly makes this place feel like it's hidden from the rest of the world. "It's so peaceful." She turns back toward my mom. "Thanks again for letting me be a part of it."

"Are you kidding? You are a *gift*." Mom squeezes her. "I heard we have you to thank for the field trip yesterday too. We haven't done field trips in years! But I heard the kids had fun."

"Oh yeah! I set it up," Olive says. "But they had fun because of Li—"

I jump up. "Did you say you wanted coffee?"

Olive smiles sweetly. "No. I was going to tell your parents about your little presentation."

I glare at her. She doesn't budge.

My mom tilts her head. "What presentation?"

I slump back in my seat while Olive tells the story of the way I *saved* Eddie from the throng of third graders and the way they were completely *enamored* with everything I said, hanging on my every word.

She tells this like it was a celebrity encounter for these kids, and I want to go hide in a ditch.

When she's finished, my mom walks over and squeezes my shoulders. "That Pine Creek blood runs thick in your veins, kiddo."

I wait for it to annoy me, the way Pine Creek comments used to. I wait for the twist in my gut, knowing there's a double meaning to the words.

But it doesn't come.

Instead, I glance over at Olive, who's still beaming, and I shake my head. "They really only cared about the four-wheeler."

They all laugh, and I go along with it. I don't know why, but I'm not upset. The pressure of expectation seems to have vanished, maybe because there aren't any expectations.

I wasn't asked to run the tour. I wasn't asked to work trimming the trees—I chose to do those things.

Maybe that's the difference.

Plus, it's almost like my father's apology wiped the slate clean. We're just four adults with a history, sharing a funny story over coffee.

I meet Olive's eyes. "Did you come out here this early just to embarrass me?"

She smiles and points at me. "That *would* be a great reason to get up at the crack of dawn, but no." She makes a pouting face. "I know, it's hard to think you're not the center of the universe."

Mom and Dad both laugh as Olive's smile returns.

"Olive is here to see *me*," Jo says, like she's the favorite. "We have work to do before people start showing up. I've got my wreath-making classes later." Her wince is slightly dramatic. "I'm nervous."

"You're going to be wonderful," my dad says. "Just like always."

Mom moves into the space behind him, wrapping her arms around his neck. "You would say that even if I was a complete disaster."

They start talking in low, hushed tones.

Are they flirting? My parents are flirting. I glance at Olive, who has clearly noticed.

"Get a room, you guys," I say, hoping to alleviate some of the tension.

Mom stands upright. "You should be thrilled you have two parents who are still so in love."

"Gross." Lacey has caught the tail end of this conversation as she walks out of the house. She's wearing jeans, a pair of too-big work boots, and one of my dad's old Carhartt jackets.

Mom looks confused. "Where are you going?"

She barely stops long enough to say, "Going to help Manny!"

My parents exchange a worried glance, but Lacey is already gone. "I really hope she's not holding on too tightly to this place," my mom says. "She should be letting it go, not trying to save it."

"I don't think she's still trying to save it," I say. "We talked the other day."

Olive looks away, most likely because no matter how many times my mom insists she's practically family, I'm guessing these family conversations have to feel a little awkward to her.

"About . . .?" Mom raises a brow.

"Just the farm," I say, not wanting to get into it with them. Lacey reminded me of all the ideas our dad had rejected. Tried to say we could do them now. That it would be great for us to be in charge. I got the impression it was her last cry for help. I felt bad turning her down, but hopefully she's starting to accept the facts.

"Probably just her way of saying goodbye," Dad says.

"What's crazy is that Manny said she was one of his best workers," I say. "Maybe you guys aren't giving her enough credit." I pause. "You didn't ask her if she wanted to take over, did you?"

Mom goes quiet, then says, "It's more complicated than that. Lacey *is* a great worker, but you know her. She gets bored. She likes change. Besides, I don't think she'd enjoy doing this without—" She snaps her jaw shut and looks away.

"Without me," I finish. "It's okay, Mom. I get it."

And she's probably right. This farm has so many moving pieces, and even if Lacey understood every single one, there's no way she could handle it on her own. Plus, it'd be too expensive. It's not like our parents can afford to just hand it over. They need the money from this sale.

"Anyway!" Mom claps her hands together and turns to Olive. "Are you ready to go?"

"Yes!" Olive looks relieved.

As they start down the stairs, I move toward her. "Hey, do you have a second?"

Olive and Mom both turn toward me, Mom doing nothing to hide her obvious surprise and interest in this.

But Olive hitches a thumb in the direction of the driveway. "Actually, no. We have a ton of work to do."

I nod and shove my hands in my pockets.

She clears her throat. "But, uh, I'll be done in a couple of hours. Maybe meet me in Santa's Village around eleven?"

"Yeah. Yeah, that'd be good," I say. The building across from the main barn has housed Santa's Village for years now, but now it'll also be home to workshops and classes, starting with Mom's. It's the perfect space for it, really. Rustic, but with that signature Pine Creek charm.

Olive gives a single, forceful nod, like she's just dismissed an underling and walks off at a pace that would have an Olympic sprinter jogging to keep up.

I turn and find my dad looking at me quizzically. "What?"

He doesn't respond, just shakes his head, pats me once on the shoulder, and walks past me into the house.

CHAPTER 23

LIAM

*T*he next two hours feel like five.

Finally, at a quarter to eleven, I hop in the truck and drive down to the main entrance, expecting to park in the lot right outside the barn, but when I pull through the gate, I discover there are no empty spots. I drive up the hill to the equipment garage and park in the staff lot. I get out and find Manny standing in the doorway of the garage, drinking coffee and looking at something in the distance.

I step into the space beside him and follow his gaze. "Is it always like this?" The place is crawling with people. Families hold Olive's maps leading the way to the pre-cut lots while couples pick up kits for the Mistletoe Walk she dreamed up.

It feels like it used to.

It feels like Christmas.

"It hasn't been like this," he says. "Not in a long time."

In the distance, I see the trailer hitched to the big tractor, and there, in the driver's seat— "Is that Lacey?"

She greets the excited families who settle in for a hayride, the kind our dad used to give.

"It is," Manny says. "She's our best tour guide." He bumps my shoulder with his. "Though I heard you might give her a run for her money."

"That was a one-time thing," I huff.

"Yeah, yeah, pretend you didn't love it, kid. You're not fooling anyone."

I go still as I spot Olive just outside the other building. Several people are walking inside, and she appears to be greeting them.

She looks so pretty. Her smile is bright as she tucks her hair behind her ear, talking with her hands, and her eyes—

I turn and find Manny watching me watching Olive.

He laughs and shakes his head. "You going to do something about that?"

"Absolutely not," I say.

"Ah," he throws a hand in my general direction. "You never were brave when it came to that girl."

I never told Manny how I felt about Olive, but clearly that doesn't mean he didn't know.

Manny takes another drink. "Thanks for all the help these past few days. If I didn't know better, I'd almost think you're enjoying it."

"It's a good change." I shrug.

"Different from what you do, I'm sure."

"That's an understatement."

He takes another drink. "How's it going? With the job and everything?"

I cringe. How do I accurately answer this without getting into all of it?

"Work is . . . a lot."

"But you love it, right?" He leans against the doorjamb, watching me.

In the distance, I hear the excited screams of small children. It feels familiar. I used to resent having to share our home with so many people, but now it feels . . . nice.

"I love the creating part," I say. "Not the bureaucracy."

Manny nods, but I know he doesn't understand. If there's one thing Pine Creek is free from, it's office politics. Vying for position. My parents were intentional about making sure the staff feels like a part of the family.

Now, though, looking at it with fresh eyes, it all makes more sense. I'm starting to understand.

"You don't think about—" Manny waves his hand out in front of him, letting the motion finish his sentence.

"About moving back here and running this place?" I scoff. "The exact thing I swore I would never do? No."

"Huh."

He doesn't say anything else, just takes another drink of his coffee.

I instantly want to explain myself, to defend my choice. Does it feel selfish and thoughtless to him and the others on staff that I'm not jumping in to save this place? They understand, right?

"I went to school for game design. I'm with a top company in my field," I say. "I can't give that up. Even if I wanted to, it would be a bad move."

"Hey, didn't mean to offend," he says, raising one hand in surrender. "I had to ask. Forget I said anything. I know it's a sore spot."

I soften. "It's fine. I wish things were different."

And I realize I mean it.

Olive is still standing at the door of the building across the way, greeting an older woman with her trademark smile, and something clicks into place.

Something that's been off kilter for a long, long time.

Everything I thought I believed, things I was so certain of, things that I swore off—they don't seem so true now.

She sees me.

She lifts a hand and waves at me, then points to her watch

and motions for me to come over for the conversation I requested.

I wave back, and my nerves kick up. Which is stupid. This is work.

"Go get her, kid," Manny says.

"It's a work thing," I say, reminding myself out loud in hopes that I'll believe it.

"Huh."

And he doesn't say anything else.

I've never met a guy who could make one word mean eight different things.

He walks away, and I head off in the direction of the barn, aware that there are several people—all women—also going in that direction. I hold the door open for an older woman who gives me a once-over.

"Well, *thank* you," she says. "It's nice to see a young man with good manners."

I give her a nod and look up to find Olive smirking at me. The woman walks away and Olive shakes her head. "If only she knew the truth."

"Ha ha." I look around the building. I haven't been in here since I've been home. The back side of this barn houses Santa's Village, where kids can get photos with Santa, dress up like an elf, make a Christmas craft.

This part of the building used to be mostly storage, but looking at the way they've set it up, it's the perfect spot for classes like this one.

There are a few rows of wooden tables positioned throughout the space, and several people standing behind them, all facing my mom who is bustling around at the front of the room, looking equal parts excited and nervous.

I glance at Olive. "Are you still working? I can come back. We can talk later—"

"No, here's fine." She runs a hand across one of the long tables. "We can talk while we work."

I frown. "While we work on what?"

"Wreath making," she says. "I thought we could make one for right over—" she points to the door— "there." Her grin is wide. "For the door."

"You want me to help you make a wreath?"

"Actually, I'm going to help you," she says. "It's today's attempt at spreading Christmas cheer."

"You're still on that?" I ask dryly.

"You're still grumpy, so yes." She points to an area off to the side. "Do you want to go pick out some greens?"

"Pick out some greens," I repeat.

She faces me. "Yes. I'll get the other supplies."

I start toward the door. "Let's just talk later."

"I thought you wanted my help," she says.

I freeze and turn around, narrowing my eyes as I meet hers. "I do, but I—"

She scrunches her nose. "This is what works for my schedule, so . . ."

I draw in a breath, aware that the best course of action is to go along with her crazy idea. There is no way she's going to relent.

"Liam!" my mom calls out from the front of the room. "I didn't know you were joining us!"

I glare at Olive. She only grins.

I wave lamely at my mom, then shrug out of my jacket, aware that a few of the women are curiously watching me.

Olive moves into the space behind a table at the back, then hisses at me— "Greens!"

OLIVE

I force Liam to listen to his mom's instructions, then force him to start trimming the greenery he selected from the table.

He loves it. I can tell.

To his credit, what he picked is beautiful, the benefit of understanding the trees, I guess.

I notice a few of the women around us looking at him. A few are way too old for him, and I hope they're eyeing him on behalf of a daughter or granddaughter. A few, though, are exactly the right age. The two women at the table directly in front of us, for instance, seem less interested in Jo's instructions and more interested in her son.

It's rude. For all they know, Liam and I could be a couple.

I get it, ladies. He's good looking. Move along.

And now that he's given in to the fact that I'm not going to talk to him until he indulges me by participating in this class, he's working on our wreath so intently it's adorable.

It's like he wants the teacher to give him an A.

Jo laid everything out for us at the beginning, and now she's walking around the room, helping people create their living masterpieces. I'm working on making a bow out of wired ribbon, and Liam is hot gluing the greenery to what's called a grapevine, the base of the wreath that looks like a brown circle of bendable twigs.

"Okay," I say, confident that it's okay to talk out loud now that Jo's done with her spiel, "Tell me what you want me for."

He gives me a quizzical look.

"Wait. Shoot. I didn't mean it like—" I snap my mouth shut. My face is on fire.

He smirks.

He turns back to the wreath and then says, "Oh."

"What's wrong?"

"Um . . ." He freezes. "I think I glued my finger to the brown thing."

"Seriously?"

He leans in closer, peering at it. "I didn't realize this glue was that strong. I think it's going to take my skin off if I try to pull it off."

I move toward his hand, trying to get a better look while also trying not to giggle because for some reason it strikes me as funny. A crafter he is not.

"Do you want me to go get some soap? Or I could ask the café for, I don't know, some oil or something?" I reach down and touch his stuck finger, carefully pulling the skin away from the glue, inching it back, little by little. "Is this okay?"

"Yeah, that doesn't hurt," he says quietly.

I glance up. "You can probably do this yourself."

He shakes his head. "If I do it, I'm probably not going to have a fingerprint on that finger, so if you don't mind—" He nods toward his hand.

Right. No big deal. I inhale a slow breath and go back to work. Only now I'm keenly aware of his eyes on me, of the proximity of my face to his, of his skin underneath my fingertips.

My heart races, and I can feel beads of sweat gathering above my lip. When I finally free his finger, I take a big step back and dab my face with the sleeve of my sweater. "Eureka!"

I say it so loudly that Liam's two age-appropriate admirers turn and look at me.

He holds up his unstuck finger at them. "She got it."

They turn to each other and say something, then turn back at him and smile.

I want to tell them that he's taken.

By me.

Which he clearly is not.

I try to focus on other things. "I'm used to the occasional art injury." I smile and go back to making my bow, but my hands are hot, like his skin branded them.

He's quiet for a few minutes, and my brain has gone blank. I can't think of anything except the fact that I *liked* being close to him. I *liked* having a reason to take his hand in mine. I *liked* the way he watched me as I worked the glue off his skin.

Oh, crap. I *like* Liam.

"So, uh—" I'm sweating again—"what did you want to talk about?"

Bringing him here to have whatever conversation he wants to have *seemed* like a good idea. With us being occupied, it would be easier to talk, a little trick I learned from my mom when I was young. She'd set me up with all the ingredients to make cookies or my box of markers and a blank sketch pad. Inevitably, while I worked, I'd open up about whatever was bothering me. Somehow it made talking easier.

And I thought Liam might appreciate anything that made talking easier.

"I'm working on a new game," he says, voice low.

I watch him, silently encouraging him to go on and trying not to concentrate on the twitch in his jaw or the sharp green of his eyes.

I also get the sense that he's letting me inside his world, even if it's just for a moment.

"I want it to be different from the last few I've worked on," he says. "I've, uh . . . struggled to find my footing lately."

"Creatively?"

"Yeah, I guess."

"Relatable," I muse. "Go on."

"I've been trying to land on the idea for a while, and then I saw something in one of your notebooks in your garage. A little doodle of a kid? Wearing a propeller hat?"

I stop and look at him. "You saw that?"

"Yeah, it was all over one of your notebooks."

"Really?" I frown, wondering if my subconscious is trying to tell me something.

He eyes me. "Yes . . .?"

"Oh." I make a mental note to check on that because I don't remember doodling him. Not recently anyway. It's been ages since I drew that boy.

Only . . . apparently not.

"You okay?" he asks.

"Yes, of course," I say. "Sorry. Keep going."

"I guess I'm wanting a unique art style," he says.

"Why not something like *Castle Crusade?*" I ask. "I mean, that was a huge hit."

He stiffens at the mention of it, and it's not the first time I've seen him do this.

"I'm looking to do something new," he says. "Something different."

"Fair," I say, considering. "But I've never made art for a video game." I work on making a second bow, certain I've got the hang of it after the first one, which looks like someone sat on it. This one will be better.

"Right now, I just need concept art for the pitch," he says. "And your style, it's sort of, I don't know, quirky? Whimsical? It's cute, I guess, is what I'm trying to say."

"You think my art is cute?" I face him, mock menace, holding wire cutters in one hand.

He shakes his head, eyes wide, but I see amusement playing at the corners of his mouth.

"You think my art is cute." I grin to myself as I go back to my bow.

"Don't let it go to your head." I hear the tease in his voice.

"Oh, it's already there, buddy." My smile holds. "Straight up here." I make an explosion gesture around my forehead.

He makes a point of sighing.

After a pause, I say, "It's odd to me that you like it."

"Why?" he asks. "It's great."

"It doesn't really seem like your style," I say. "I mean, when I hear the name Liam Fisher the first words I think of are not quirky or whimsical."

"What about cute?"

I laugh, and he rewards me with a smile.

And I'm not going to ruin the moment by saying so, but for a second, it's like having the old Liam back.

"Yeah, you're adorable," I say. "Like a cozy teddy bear."

"I'll pretend you mean that," he says.

There's a pause, and I start thinking about the propeller hat boy. A doodle I started drawing when I was young. It's Liam, of course, though he doesn't realize that. A boy who is off on a grand adventure, traveling by way of his magic hat.

"What about the girl?" I ask. "Do you want her too?"

He is holding a branch in place, but he looks up. "What girl?"

"The girl with the jetpack," I say. "She's always trying to catch the boy with the propeller hat because he sometimes goes off on these fun adventures and leaves her behind." I'm suddenly very interested in the ribbon I'm cutting.

"I didn't see the girl with the jetpack," he says.

I try not to find a hidden meaning in that phrase.

I draw in a breath. "What if they go on quests?"

"What do you mean?"

"Well, like the boy's propeller hat sends them off on these adventures, and they work together to solve problems or complete puzzles."

He sits forward in his chair.

"That's exactly what I thought, but it's not just the hat. There are a ton of other pieces of clothing that do crazy things too. Like, springy shoes to jump over walls, cargo pants with unlimited storage space, and if there's a girl too, her dress could be a parachute, her backpack could have the jets on it—"

Oh my word. His idea is *brilliant.* I can already picture what they look like. And all the clothing.

We start talking over one another.

Me: "And what if the boy is the son of a crazy inventor, like Doc Brown from *Back to the Future* or something? And the inventor made this magic hat, the shoes, the coat, the pants—"

Him: "Yes! But the inventor tells the boy to never put those things on, like tries to warn him, but of course, he doesn't listen. So, like, the hat can transport him all over to different parts of the map to face problems he has to solve—"

Me: "—and he can fly and hover and go underwater. The hat becomes like a boat propeller—"

Him: "—and the jetpack girl is totally essential on these quests because she has a completely different set of powers."

This goes on for another few minutes, and we've completely stopped working on our wreath. Once the creative whirlwind dies down, we sit back and look at each other. Then, simultaneously, we say: "We need to write this down."

"You just came up with all of that off the top of your head?" he asks.

I bite my lip, feeling suddenly self-conscious. "I don't play video games, so what I said might be really stupid."

He shakes his head. "No, it's not. Not for the kind of game I'm thinking of creating. It's cooperative. For girls *and* boys. I've never heard of a game like it before."

"Plus," I add, "I think it will appeal to kids."

"*Yes,*" he says. "Younger kids are an untapped market at our company. Developers often target teens and young adults, mostly male, honestly, and they have nothing . . . softer. Or whimsical. Nintendo does, but beyond that? I think it could be the thing I need to get me back—" He clams up and goes back to the wreath.

I frown. Did he just shut down again?

"Get you back to what?"

"Nothing," he says. "I just think it'll impress my bosses."

I don't want him to stop talking.

I don't want him to shut this door.

The Liam I knew had a lot of thoughts and a lot of feelings. When they got to be too much, that's when he'd retreat—and that's when I'd imagine him flying off to some foreign land, solving problems and puzzles. That's when I drew the jetpack girl because I wanted a way to reach him, and I never found one in real life.

"Hey, do you want to go for a walk?" I ask. "I feel like I need to go get my iPad so I can make notes about what you're wanting."

"So, you'll do it?" He sets the wreath down.

"Of course," I say. "And if you want to throw in the crazy inventor idea, it's all yours. I'll just need ten percent off the top."

He smiles, but looks away, almost like he doesn't want me to see it.

We wave to Jo, to let her know we'll be back, and then head outside, both shrugging into our coats. Mine gets twisted and I can't find the sleeve, so Liam steps forward. "Here, let me."

He holds it out so I can put it on, then falls into step beside me. "Where is your iPad?"

"Back at the office," I say. "Jo drove us down here."

"I'm, um . . ." He points in the direction of the staff parking lot, I'd guess where his truck is parked.

"I assume we have you and Lacey to thank for the crowd that's out here today?" he asks as we walk.

I shrug. "All we did was get the word out."

"You gave people reasons to want to come," he says.

"Yeah. We might've." I smile. It's nice to think that all these patrons might be here, in part, because of something I did.

"What happens once you come up with the idea? You pitch it to your boss, and then what?"

He scrubs a hand down his chin, not looking at me. "Then

216

they decide if they want to move on it. If they do, they have the choice of letting me head up the project or not."

I frown. "Wait, so someone else would be in charge of a game that came straight out of your head?"

"Yep."

"That's dumb." It's out before I can censor myself.

He laughs ruefully. "That's the way it goes. Like, they're making a sequel to *Castle Crusade*, and I'm not on the team for that one."

I stop walking. "Wait, what?"

He stops and shrugs, as if it's no big deal. But it has to be a big deal. Right?

"You can't be okay with that," I say. "It's horrible, Liam, that's *your* game."

His smile is sad. "Not anymore."

"I don't understand."

He sighs. "I sold it to them."

It feels like there's a story there, but I don't press. If he wants to tell me, he will.

We walk in silence as I follow him to the staff parking lot where we get into his truck. "Wait. What if you did it yourself? Is that a thing? The way so many musicians can put music on Spotify now."

He starts the engine and pulls out, driving slowly through the main area, carefully avoiding all the people. "It's a thing."

"So, do that."

He laughs. "It's not that easy."

"But you did *Castle Crusade* all on your own, right?"

He presses his lips together and a frown line stretches across his forehead. "I did," he says, thoughtfully. "That *was* all me. Just a fun project I did with an artist buddy of mine."

"And this giant company loved it enough to buy it," I say, switching into cheerleader mode. "But you were the brain behind that game." I look at him. "I would not like someone else dictating what I did with my art. I mean, the art I make for myself. Making art for the tree farm or like, another business is different. But the stuff I make for myself . . . the stuff I *used* to make for myself . . ."

Now I'm looking out the window, thinking about how I've left my creativity on the side of the road. I abandoned that whole side of myself, and now that I'm rediscovering it, it's working overtime. Keeping me awake at night. Giving me ideas about a video game, of all things, which is not something I know a single thing about.

Creativity doesn't care. When it's flowing, it's best just to hold on.

Like Liam and the ATV.

"Are you going to finish that thought?" He parks the truck outside the office.

"No." I get out and start walking toward the building. When he comes up beside me, I say, "Let's go finish brainstorming your game."

CHAPTER 24

TEXT THREAD BETWEEN OLIVE AND LIAM, LATER THAT NIGHT

OLIVE

So how do we feel about Jetpack Girl? I think we put her in a pink space suit with a cute helmet, but leave her pigtails sticking out, like this:

\<Insert image of Jetpack Girl\>

LIAM

Wow. That's perfect.

OLIVE

And I think Propeller Hat Boy needs a name. How about Larry?

LIAM

No

OLIVE

Liam?

LIAM

Absolutely not

OLIVE

Okay, we'll put a pin in that. Do you want to go the inventor route? Because I sketched his laboratory. I thought showing the environment might be good for your pitch. If you are still pitching it.

LIAM

I'm pitching it

OLIVE

<sends drawing of laboratory, followed by drawing of crazy-haired inventor>

Or maybe I need a different take on the inventor. Maybe the Albert Einstein knockoff is too common?

LIAM

I'll send over the ideas I have so far. I have a whole Google doc, just no artwork

OLIVE

You want me to quit throwing ideas at you?

LIAM

Actually, no. I love to hear them, and I love to brainstorm.

Just maybe not at midnight

OLIVE

You're such an old man.

LIAM

Go to sleep

OLIVE

Probably won't.

LIAM

I have to get up early to set things up for Family Day.

OLIVE

That's sweet of you. 🖤

LIAM

I'm a sweet guy

OLIVE

😂😂😂

LIAM

. . .

OLIVE

. . .

LIAM

When did you start drawing the propeller hat guy?

OLIVE

When we were kids

LIAM

Is it supposed to be me?

OLIVE

Cocky, much?

LIAM

. . .

OLIVE

Just kidding. Yeah, it is.

LIAM

What's it mean?

OLIVE

Sometimes you would sort of go off in your own little world, and I wondered what it was like inside your head. I imagined these big, wild adventures you must be on. I guess I made up a way to get you to share them with me.

LIAM

Jetpack Girl.

OLIVE

Dumb, right?

LIAM

Not dumb

OLIVE

But dumb that I still absently draw them. I guess I'm still trying to find a way to get you to let me in.

LIAM

Night, Liv

OLIVE

Night xoxo

. . . but I erase the *xoxo* before I hit send.

CHAPTER 25

OLIVE

"What happened to you?"

Lacey is standing on my front porch, holding up a brown paper bag, but the second she sees me, she lowers her hand and frowns.

I forgot she was coming over this morning to work on the presentation for the city council meeting. Town buy-in is a good thing, and I know this is important, but how much good am I actually going to be on zero sleep?

I push a hand through my wild morning hair. "I didn't sleep well."

"Oh," she says, stepping inside and closing the door behind her. "Are you sick?"

"No, I just have too many ideas," I yawn. "It's like my creativity is on overdrive." Which is a good thing, because if I didn't have something to occupy my mind, I would've been awake all night thinking about Liam—something I'm desperately trying not to do.

"For the farm?" Her eyes brighten.

"The farm, the market, and other stuff . . ." I say, when I realize Liam may not want me talking about his video game.

I plod into the kitchen. I'm still wearing the leggings and oversized sweatshirt I slept in. My hair is in a loose bun, and I can't remember if I put on more deodorant. The creative fury that happened after Liam stopped texting me last night was unlike anything I've experienced in a very long time.

He emailed me his ideas for the game—turns out, there is no wacky inventor. But there are quests and puzzles mapped out for a minimum of five environments. My goal was supposed to be to draw the characters in a few different outfits, and then choose one environment to illustrate.

But once I started, I couldn't stop, and I ended up drawing both main characters in various poses, each with ten different facial expressions—like a cartoon collage. Then I added a lineup of possible secondary characters, along with the specialized clothing that offers different ways of getting around and solving the puzzles.

I also fleshed out three of the environments—a space station, a submarine in the ocean, and a rustic mountain lodge.

I fell asleep with my Apple Pencil in my hand.

"I think you should do it," Lacey says. "It's your idea, and you're great at those things. You'll sell out of everything for sure."

I look at her, only now realizing she's been talking, and I didn't hear a word she said. "What?"

"A booth. At the market," she says. "You should do one."

I shake my head. "Maybe in another lifetime."

"Olive, you're good, the stuff you created is—"

I hold up a hand to stop her. "Super sweet of you to say, but it's a hard pass. But I do think you should let people see the inside of your van. Set up a photo station, get a map with pins of where you've been, looping video of your channel, that sort of thing. People will probably come out just to meet you."

Her face lights up. "That's actually a fun idea."

"What's a fun idea?" Phoebe walks in carrying a tray of Beanery coffee. "I brought the good stuff."

"Thank God," I say, reaching for one of the cups.

She pulls it from my reach. "Whoa. What happened to you?"

"Art hangover," I say.

Her brow quirks, and then her whole face smiles. "You're drawing again."

I snatch the coffee and take a drink, *mm-hmm*-ing while I sip. "I've been drawing. I made all that stuff for the farm."

"But this is different. I can tell."

I don't doubt it. Phoebe has known me through all my art phases. She's one of the few people who can determine where I'm at creatively with a single look.

Phoebe hands a cup to Lacey, and we all gather around the island in my small kitchen. "Are you making more art for the market? Like for your booth?"

I make a face at Lacey, and she shrugs a *told ya*.

"No."

"A new line to debut on your website?"

"I don't have a website." I reach in the bag and pull out a muffin.

"How can you not have a website?" Lacey takes a muffin out and slides it over to Phoebe.

"I shut it down when the store closed." I break the muffin in half and take a bite of the bottom, dropping crumbs on the counter. "I shut everything down when the store closed. I packed up all of the old inventory, put it in my garage, deleted my *Wit and Whimsy* accounts and let the website expire. I still own the domain name—probably time to let that go too." I chew my bite, then take a drink.

I glance up and find them both staring at me.

"Let's see the garage," Lacey says.

"Heck. No." I say firmly. "We're here to brainstorm this

presentation thing. If you want to find people to join this collective, we need to do a good job with this."

"And we will," she says. "The city council meeting is still days away. And we've got time. The important thing right now is what you're hiding in that garage."

I roll my eyes. "It's nothing exciting, I promise."

"False," Phoebe says. "It's a ton of really cool stuff. I helped her pack it away."

"I want to see!" Lacey is way too excited for what's in that garage.

Phoebe rushes over to the hook by my back door and picks up a small keyring. "Lacey, come look!"

Before I can stop them, they're on their way through the door and into my garage. My packed-full-of-junk-that-no-one-wants garage.

I walk into my living room and sit down next to my wonky tree, happy I found the time to decorate her. I don't bother turning on the overhead lights because I like the gleam of the tree and the strands of white lights I hung around the ceiling. Together, they cast a perfect warm glow for someone who isn't exactly awake yet . . . and someone who isn't sure she wants to be.

I open my iPad, looking over all the ideas I dreamed up for Liam's game. I arrange them in a Dropbox folder, along with my notes, then send the link to Liam.

And then I eat and drink and wait for Lacey and Phoebe to finish whatever they're doing. When they return, they're each carrying a bin, each one marked *Christmas*.

"What are you doing?" I ask.

"*Nothing.*" Phoebe walks her bin over to the front door and sets it down.

Lacey does the same.

"Okay," I say. "Do I want to know?"

"I just want to show Jo," Phoebe says. "I think she'd put some of it in the shop."

I think about protesting but choose not to. I have a feeling she's going to do this whether I'm on board or not. I don't hate the idea of having my artwork out there—maybe if I can stay anonymous.

Just in case I fail.

Again.

"We definitely need to get you back on social media," Lacey says.

"I don't have time."

"A lot of full-time jobs knocking down your door, are they?" Phoebe quips.

"Hey. I think that's enough out of you," I laugh, noting her playfulness.

"What's it going to hurt?" Lacey asks.

I take a deep breath. "I don't have the capacity to fulfill orders at the moment."

"So we just tease some ideas," Lacey says. "Tell people something fun is coming. Show them some stuff and get them excited about what you'll be offering. That garage is a gold mine. It's basically found money, just sitting there."

"Olive, there's no risk here," Phoebe says. "Just start with the merchandise you already have. It's not doing you any good packed away in boxes in your garage." She pauses. "Besides, I think it's time you finally realize that failing at something doesn't make you a failure."

I screw up my face. "Pretty sure that's the exact definition of a failure."

"It doesn't make you a failure *forever*," she adds. "Did you jump in too quickly? Maybe. Did it not go according to plan? Yeah. So, learn from it. Don't hide yourself away and stop using your gifts. You don't quit on a dream because it's hard."

Well, that was profound.

And . . . it resonates with me.

I glance down at the iPad, looking over these fun drawings Liam's ideas had brought out in me. I think about all the artwork I'd created for Pine Creek, not because it was my job, but because I was inspired.

Phoebe is right. Per usual.

I realize that nobody else is making me feel like a loser and a failure. I'm doing that all on my own.

Sometimes I wonder why I'm so mean to myself.

I look up and find them both watching me.

"You . . . you really think . . ." A lump forms in my throat, and my eyes cloud over with fresh tears. I try to blink them back, but a couple spill out. I really don't want to get emotional this early in the morning.

"Oh, Olive," Phoebe moves onto the couch beside me and slips her arm around my shoulder. "Hey. I'm sorry. I just think you're so good. I don't want you to let this detour make you think you aren't."

"Thanks, Pheebs," I say, sniffing. "It's just hard because I did try. I poured everything—literally—into that store. *Everything.* And I failed. My art wasn't—" I have to hold back the emotion at this admission— "good enough to keep people coming back for more." I study my hands, folded in my lap. "*I* wasn't good enough."

My artwork is a direct representation of who I am. A vulnerable look into my soul. People looked at it and walked right on by.

"Okay." She faces me. "I'm going to say this with the utmost love and respect."

"Okay." A tear streams down my face, and I swipe it away.

"You suck at business."

I half-laugh, sniffing and wiping more tears from my eyes. "I know."

"But you are *brilliant* at art."

My chin trembles at the compliment.

"These two things don't belong in the same mental box," she says. "If you decide to do this, you can do it smarter."

"And we can help," Lacey says. "I know a lot about social media."

"And I know a lot about numbers." Phoebe squeezes my hand.

"We were never made to spend our lives doing everything alone." Lacey reaches for her coffee and takes a long drink. "And after years of doing exactly that, I've learned that lesson too."

I fleetingly think of Liam. He also does everything alone.

"Speaking of which," Phoebe says. "We need to come up with a plan. How do we get interest in the collective and did you change your mind about telling your parents?"

"No," Lacey says. "But they're both coming to the city council meeting."

"The city council meeting where you pitch the idea of stopping any possible sale in favor of selling the farm to a non-existent group of people?" Phoebe says this, clearly hoping to make a point.

"I know," she says, frowning. "I just . . ."

"What?" I ask. I don't know what it was like to grow up with her parents, but they're reasonable people. I have to believe they'd at least entertain Lacey's desires if she shared them.

"I don't want them to tell me all the reasons this won't work," she says. "Or all the reasons why I'm not the person to make it work. My parents are amazing people, but they never thought of me like they thought about Liam. Even after he switched his major and made it clear he wanted nothing to do with the farm."

"They're just underestimating you," Phoebe says. "People do that to me all the time."

Lacey glances at Phoebe. "Really? But you're so confident."

"Yeah, but do I look like an accountant?" She looks at Lacey. "You better say no."

We all laugh.

"The best thing about being underestimated? You have the perfect chance to prove everyone wrong," Phoebe says with a smile.

Even though she's talking to Lacey, her words are a double-edged sword to me.

I'm pretty sure that's what I did with my store. I was underestimated by everyone, and I jumped in headfirst to prove them all wrong.

The difference, I think, is that I tried to do it all on my own.

I wonder if the only person I needed to prove wrong was myself. Because if Lacey's and Phoebe's and Liam's opinions are any indication, I'm surrounded by people who think I'm good at what I do.

I squeeze my iPad a bit more firmly.

I think it's about time I did too.

CHAPTER 26

OLIVE

*I*t's Family Day at Pine Creek.

For one afternoon only, the family and staff of Pine Creek will switch roles, becoming the patrons of Pine Creek. And this year, for the first time since I was a kid, I'm included.

For years, our family was invited, which is why I shouldn't be surprised when I pull in and see my parents parking their Taurus—but I am. I had no idea they were coming. I park in the spot next to them and see that my brother is in the back seat.

I get out of my car, grinning. "I didn't know you guys were coming today!"

"Oh, we thought you invited us," my mom says.

"No, that was me." We all turn and see Lacey standing there. "I wanted it to feel as much like our best Christmases as possible. I thought we could recreate some of our favorite memories."

"Oh, Lacey, that is so nice of you!" my mom says.

"Are they grilling burgers in the barn?" Dad asks.

"You know it." Lacey grins.

"I'll go see if I can help with anything." He gives me a quick hug. "They might need a taste tester. Catch up in a bit."

Because all the staff is participating in the events they usually oversee, Family Day has an "all hands on deck" kind of feeling. Most of the activities are self-led, with the exception of the carriage rides, which Brant will run, and of course, Manny couldn't be talked out of playing Santa, even for a night.

I look at Benji. "No girlfriend today?"

"No girlfriend." He shifts.

I raise a brow. "You broke up with her already?"

Benji reaches in his pockets and pulls out a pair of gloves. "Eh. She made mouth noises when she chewed."

"You're so weird," I say with a light laugh.

He shrugs and pulls the gloves on.

I look at Lacey. "Benji doesn't do relationships."

My brother rolls his eyes.

"Sounds like my brother," Lacey says.

Heat rushes to my cheeks, because when Lacey says "my brother," I picture Liam's face. His strong jaw and piercing eyes. I clear my throat, wishing my confusing feelings about Liam would calm down already.

"Scavenger Hunt starts in half an hour!" Lacey seems to be unaware that I'm currently battling a forty-five second fever brought on by my overactive imagination.

"The old team's back together." Benji brightens, his mood shifting.

"I think we might be on our own," I say. "There's no way Liam's going to do this."

"He might if *you* ask him." Lacey puts on a knowing grin.

I frown. What's she mean by that?

Lacey turns to Benji. "Are you still in construction?"

"Yeah," he says.

"Can I pick your brain for a sec?"

It would feel like an abrupt and random change of topic, but I know what she's going to talk to him about. This morning, I shared all my expansion ideas with her. She especially loved the idea of cabins in the woods—cozy, open floor plan bungalows tucked back in the unused acreage of the tree farm, each with their own fireplace, each professionally decorated for the seasons. In the winter, and *especially* around Christmas, the cabins could host couples or families looking for more of an unplugged Christmas experience.

It would be a huge undertaking, and it's years down the road, but I know having ballpark numbers behind our expansion ideas will strengthen our presentation at the city council meeting.

People have a tendency to give more when they can see what their money is going toward.

I start off in the direction of the main barn, where we're all meeting for the rundown of activities. Once inside, I'm met with the sound of excited chatter, and I spot Brant and Jo near the front of the large, open space. The café and gift shop share this barn, one of many outbuildings on the property. I smile and say hello to my (now) co-workers and their families, many I've known for years outside of Pine Creek.

But as I make my way around the room and over to my family, I mostly wonder where Liam is.

Then I see him, through the window of the door leading to the kitchen. He's wearing an apron and appears to be working at the counter.

He's wearing an apron.

Who knew aprons were sexy?

As Brant gets everyone's attention, I inch my way around the back and over to the kitchen and slip through the door.

Liam looks up. He's unloading burger patties from a box onto a large tray. "You're not supposed to be back here."

"I know," I say. "But I wanted to see if you looked at my ideas."

He smirks and goes back to unloading. "You're hilarious."

"What?" I move to the opposite side of the counter and start helping with the food. "I'm excited!"

He smiles at me. "You are?"

"Yes! I want to help. The game sounds fun. Like, I know you want to market it to kids, but I'd play it. And I don't even like video games." I stifle a yawn. The lack of sleep is creeping up. "But I like puzzles, and I like to turn my brain off at night."

"If you turned your brain off, you wouldn't draw," he says.

I frown.

"You said you draw to unwind," he says. "I'd hate to deprive the world of your creativity."

I shoot him a look. "You talked to Lacey, didn't you?"

He chuckles. "Well, it was more her talking to me. She showed up with a giant bin of stuff she stole from your garage to put in the shop and said I need to be more encouraging."

I roll my eyes. "You don't. You're exactly the right amount of encouraging."

"Oh?" he asks.

"I mean, yeah." I meet his eyes, all out of burgers to concentrate on. "You asked me to help with this game concept. You told me you like my style and that it's unique. Didn't feel like lip service. It felt, you know, honest."

He slides the tray to the end of the counter. "Well, good. Because I set up a meeting with my boss, Aaron, for next week. I can't promise they'll like it or even that they won't want to hire someone in-house to do the artwork, but if we get the green light, I'm going to lobby to hire you freelance. Either way, I do have a budget to pay you for the work you've already done."

My excitement falters. Not because there's a chance I won't be working on the game, but because I hate that there are so many hoops he has to jump through. The game could turn out completely different than he—and I—imagine it.

It's the nature of creative business, and I get it. I mean book to movie adaptations are a perfect example that the source material isn't always followed. But Liam's ideas are good, really good, and he has a vision for the propeller hat kid that he should be allowed to see through.

"You okay?" he asks.

"Yeah, totally," I say, trying to play it off and unsure how to articulate what I'm really thinking. "I'd love to see the final pitch when it's ready."

"Of course."

"Are you two coming?" It's Lacey, poking her head in the kitchen. "The Scavenger Hunt is starting! Let's go!"

I look at Liam, eyebrows raised in expectation, hopeful he'll actually join in.

"Come on, Grumpy," Lacey says. "Last Pine Creek Christmas. You can't hide out in the kitchen."

He looks at me, then at her.

"Fine. But I'm pretty sure we're not eligible for the trophy anymore."

"The 'trophy' is a homemade wreath this year. What we're going for here is *bragging rights*," Lacey says.

Some of the staffers will go out to the fields to cut their own trees. Some will take carriage rides. Some will do the Mistletoe Walk. Some will take their kids to Manny so they can tell Santa what they want for Christmas. But tonight, after the sun goes down, everyone will come together to eat summer food in the winter, then sit by a huge bonfire and roast marshmallows.

Considering how tired I am, I might not make it that long.

But the Scavenger Hunt? I'm here for it.

I glance to my left.

And I'm also here for Liam Fisher.

Trying to ignore it only makes the feelings more intense.

I like him. A lot.

It makes no logical sense. He's made it clear a relationship isn't what he wants, especially with someone who lives in Pleasant Valley.

I'm not into casual dating, and I have no intention of leaving Pleasant Valley. Which means, we could never work, even if my feelings were reciprocated. Which they aren't.

That little silent reminder helps me refocus.

We make our way up the hill to the precut lot, where Jo is handing out Scavenger Hunt cards. "For old time's sake," she says as she hands them around our little circle. "You all can't win, so I made these special for you. Photo entries only. If you finish, I'll gift you a bottle of merlot."

I glance down and see what looks like a Bingo card, but instead of "Find a blue spruce" or "Locate Chester, the Pine Creek horse," our tasks are more personal.

Go to the place where Olive found the bird with the broken wing.

Locate the spot of Lacey's first kiss.

Find the tire swing and take Benji for a ride.

Where did Liam hide the stray cat we told him not to feed?

As I scan the tasks, a lump forms at the back of my throat. No matter what happens with Lacey and the farm, this really is the last time Pine Creek will be like this. And the weight of that is heavy.

I look up and see my brother, unmoved. "Are we doing this or what? I want the wine."

I sniff and look away.

"Are you crying?" Benji sounds disgusted.

"*No,*" I say, aware that they're all looking at me now. I sniff and look away. "Shut up, Benji."

Benji shakes his head. "Dibs on *not* being with Olive."

I smack him on the arm.

Lacey reaches over and gives me a side hug. "It's okay, you big baby. Let's have fun today. And let's get that wine! Benji and

I will take the ones that have to do with us, and you guys take yours."

"We can't split up," I say, shocked.

"We're going to be here all night if we don't," Lacey says. "There are like twenty-five things on this list. And I really want to be done in time for dinner. I'm starving."

CHAPTER 27

OLIVE

By fate or by design, I'm alone again with Liam.
Being alone with Liam is exactly what I don't need right now.

I'm doing my best not to think about how bright his green eyes look. I'm working hard not to notice that he didn't shave this morning, and I think I like him better with a little stubble. I'm pretending it doesn't matter that I've grown used to his scent, and it might be my favorite fragrance I've ever smelled.

Liam has built a treehouse in my mind, and I am not quite prepared for it.

"Ready?" he asks.

I nod, suddenly aware that my mouth is so dry I might as well be chewing on cotton balls.

"I thought I was going to be locating trees, not walking down memory lane," he says grumpily.

My laugh sounds nervous in my own ears. "Your mom knows how to keep you on your toes."

"All right," he says. "Where was the bird with the broken wing?"

"You don't remember?" I ask. "I cried about that bird for a week after Benji told me it probably wouldn't recover."

We start walking through the rows of trees the way we did when we were kids. It's colder today than it has been all week, but the sun is out, creating a false sense of warmth. After a few minutes of crunching footfalls and unspoken silence, we come upon the little shed where I found the injured bird.

"Here," I say. "It was on the ground, right by this big oak tree." I reach up and touch the rough bark. "I always loved this tree. It's always been my favorite."

"I remember." His voice is quiet. "You always collected the acorns. Remember you turned that into a game to see who could find the most?"

"I always won that game," I say.

"Because you changed the rules in the middle, like usual." He rolls his eyes, laughing quietly to himself. It's a nice laugh. I wish he did it more. He turns away and starts searching the grass for acorns.

I move around to the back of the tree, then bend over to pick up an acorn. On my way back up, something stops me. There, carved into the back of the giant oak, are our initials—L.F + O. W. in the center of a heart.

I reach out and trace the letters with my finger. "Oh my gosh."

Liam turns, and I see the moment he realizes what I've found.

"What is this?" I meet his eyes.

"Oh, man, I forgot that was there," he groans. "You're going to make a thing of this."

"Heck yeah I am!" I laugh. "When did you carve this?" I pull out my phone and snap a photo.

"Don't—" He moves toward me, reaching for my phone, which I hold behind my back.

"What's the matter, afraid someone will discover you have a heart?" I laugh.

He doesn't. He doesn't like to be teased, which of course, makes me want to do it more.

"It's okay, it's okay, I get it," I say. "Silly kid stuff. Should we take a photo over here? I think I found the bird—" I take a few steps away from the tree— "like here?" I turn and face him.

"That's not what this was."

I raise an eyebrow, but don't say anything.

"It wasn't silly kid stuff," he says. "Not for me." He pushes a hand through his hair, keeping his face angled away from me.

I feel like the conversation in his head right now is completely different than the one in mine.

I watch as he turns away, digging at the ground with his foot.

"What are you—"

He holds a hand up. "Let me—just give me a second."

I snap my jaw shut and take a step back because I don't want to get in the way of whatever he's about to say.

"That night—the party—" He meets my eyes and I nod, encouraging him to go on. He shuts his eyes and quickly says, "You were right."

"About . . .?"

"I *was* going to ask you out."

"Oh." I go quiet and try not to trade Liam for Travis in my memories, picturing the differences.

"I have some regrets." Liam faces me. "I've made some mistakes—a *lot* of mistakes. But one that I've been thinking about a lot lately is that I got out of Travis's way, and I wish I hadn't." He studies me, unflinching. "You should've left with my number that night."

"Why?" The question is so quiet, I'm not sure he hears.

He takes a tentative step toward me. "Because I never would've hurt you the way he did." He searches my eyes.

"Because I would've tried to make you understand how lucky I was just to be around you."

The words are just . . . out there, and I feel like I'm processing them in the wrong order. But then, it starts to click. He was going to ask me out. He never would've hurt me. I should've left with him that night.

I look up and find him watching me, angst behind his eyes. My pulse quickens, and I feel flushed, because once the pieces snap together, all the feelings I've been fighting off rush at me with surprisingly intensity.

Without thinking, I close the gap between us, grab his face with my hands and kiss him.

The kiss is point three seconds long before I pull back, eyes wide, hands dropping to his shoulders. "Oh my gosh, I'm sorry."

He looks shocked and a little amused.

"I just sort of went for it, and—" I snap my jaw shut. "That was a lot like our first kiss." I cover my face with my hands, then peek through my fingers. "I can do better."

He chuckles softly, moving closer and brushing a strand of hair away from my face. "Good. Because I've been waiting years to do this again."

I drop my hands and smile at him, and all the reasons this will never work fall straight out of my mind. "Years?"

"Off and on since we were twelve," he says. "Every time I saw you, I thought about it."

"You should've said something."

"Me? Say something?"

I smile.

"Timing was always off," he says. "I don't think we were ready for—" He stops, inhaling, like he needs a second to decide if he wants to go on— "something real."

Something real.

I force myself not to think that the timing is off now too. Because if I do, I might lose my nerve. And, also, because I really, really don't want to think about it. I want to give in to the feelings I've been fighting off. To let myself get lost in the delusion that there's a future for me and Liam. And yeah, to kiss him with the kind of reckless abandon that makes the rest of the world fade away.

I know I could get hurt, but looking at him, listening to him, finally *seeing* him—it feels worth it.

This is real. To me *and* to him.

He brushes a thumb across my cheek, takes my face in his hands, then leans in and kisses me. He keeps his promise, taking his time with a soft, slow kiss that sends a jolt straight down my spine.

My mind starts to spin, and I think about Liam. His gruff exterior overshadowing his true nature. And I want to know all the parts of him I don't know. I want to hear his thoughts and his dreams and his frustrations. I want to know what he's thinking with a single look, to give him space to be quiet, to gain his trust—to earn that rare smile that makes me feel like I've struck gold.

I focus on his lips, pressed to mine with the kind of sweet tenderness that causes my insides to swoop in anticipation. Liam is slow and deliberate, soft lips and a gentle touch.

I wrap my arms around him tighter, pulling him closer, wanting to memorize the moment so I can relive it any time I want to. And I will because from now on, I'm sure that any time I think about the best kiss of my life, this will be the one that comes to mind.

He pulls back for a fraction of a second and looks at me, eyes searching mine with a quiet intensity that I've come to associate with Liam. The quiet intensity that seems to tell a story all on its own.

And then his lips are back on mine, a kind of desperation taking over. The kiss grows deeper, more rushed, and a tingle zips through my body as I completely lose myself. In him.

I thread my hands inside his coat, tracing the muscles in his back with my fingers, giving in to the kiss and everything it means. Because there's no coming back from this. Not when my feelings for him have grown more real every day. I draw in a breath, mostly to try and still my racing pulse, and I feel him smile against my lips.

I open my eyes, and there he is, in all his beautiful glory, grinning down at me. It's the first real, full smile I've seen. "Is that smile because of me?"

He laughs, but looks away, like he has to hide his face in case someone discovers he's not a heartless grinch after all. "Yeah, it's because of you."

Now I smile and shimmy as I sing-song, "Because you like me."

He shakes his head. "Don't make it weird."

"You hid it well," I say. "I thought you couldn't stand me."

"It comes and goes."

I laugh out loud, then go up on my tiptoes and kiss him again. *I'm kissing Liam Fisher.* And I like it. A lot.

My nerves are on high alert as I soak him in, letting myself feel all the things I've been trying not to feel since the Christmas Kick-Off. Letting myself love being the center of his attention.

I pull back and search his eyes. "What happened that night?" I ask, knowing he'll know the one I mean.

He brushes my hair away from my face and holds my gaze. "It doesn't matter."

"It does to me," I say. "We spent that whole time talking—you *actually* were talking. And it was easy conversation, you know?"

He nods. "I remember. You're easy to talk to."

"Well, that's obvious by the hours of conversation we've had since you got back." I pause for a second, waiting for the joke to land, then smirk.

I'm rewarded with a smile, and then he leaves a trail of kisses on my cheek, then moves to my neck. "I don't want to talk about Travis."

"I thought you were his wingman," I say.

Liam pulls back, a flash of anger in his eyes. "You did?"

I nod. "I thought you were, I don't know, teeing me up, I guess. Is that a thing guys do?" I'm embarrassed to admit this, but at the look of concern on his face, that humiliation melts away.

He leans in and forces my gaze. "Olive, I would never do that."

I meet his eyes. "I know. I mean, I should've known." And it's not like this has defined my feelings about Liam. It's not like it was even more than a passing thought. Once I started dating Travis, I didn't dwell on it. Liam and I were friends, and while I saw a flicker of a chance for something more, it was dashed quicker than it appeared.

Still, knowing now that I missed out on that opportunity, knowing how things with Travis turned out, I can't help but feel the sting of regret.

The pained expression is back on his face, as he takes a step away from me. He pushes a hand through his hair. "I told Travis about you. The second I saw you walk in. It felt like a second chance or something. Like the timing was finally right, and we weren't kids anymore." He looks at me.

He draws me close to him, studying my face like he wants to commit it to memory. "Travis always wants whatever someone else wants," Liam says, a hint of anger in his tone.

The clarity of what happened settles on my shoulders. "He did it on purpose."

Liam grits his teeth and nods. "Yep."

And then, as if realizing something, he says, "But I'm the one who got out of the way." He drags a hand down his face, shaking his head. "I don't . . . like to say how I feel."

"This is mind-blowing information," I deadpan, concealing the smile tugging at the corner of my mouth.

He smirks. "I don't want to do that anymore. Back then, I was too young and too dumb and too embarrassed to tell you I had actual feelings for you." I watch his eyes closely. They never move away from mine. "I'm not embarrassed to admit it anymore."

The smile is back, and I feel the warmth of it instantly. There's something to be said for earning a smile from someone who doesn't give them freely. It starts to feel like currency, and I've always been a saver.

"Now, can we stop talking about Travis?" He wraps his arms around me and pulls me close, kissing me like a man who's wanted to kiss me for a very long time.

CHAPTER 28

LIAM

*B*eing out here, thinking about the past, holding Olive in my arms—it all leads to a realization.

Stepping aside, not saying what I think, not going after what I want—these are the things that have led me here. I don't want to do that anymore.

I want to go after the things I want. The trick is figuring out what those things are. Because at the moment, nothing feels clear.

"I don't want to do the scavenger hunt anymore." I take Olive's hand and lead her back in the direction of the main barn. "I don't even really want to stay here, with all these people."

She laughs. "These people are our families."

"Exactly."

She laughs. "I'm the one who suggested Family Day. We can't bail."

"We could bail." I give her hand a tug and pull her into me, wanting to shield her from everything else in the world even though she doesn't need me to. "Can we just—" I kiss her again. Her lips are soft and taste like strawberries, and I'm pretty sure I could spend the rest of my life kissing her, and it still wouldn't be enough.

She pulls back. "What do we tell people?"

"Nothing," I say.

"They're going to ask." She moves closer, as if trying to get warm.

I hold her tighter. "I'm kind of mad you were the one who made the first move."

She laughs, burying her head in my chest. "It was such an awesome move too—can we just pretend it didn't happen?"

"Not a chance," I tease. "You're never living that down."

She gives me a playful shove, but I hold onto her, something I can't believe I have permission to do. All this time keeping my distance has led me here, and I'm not sure I ever want to let her go.

She looks up at me, eyes flickering mischief. "I made the first move because I was tired of waiting for you to do it."

I laugh. "Oh? Have you wanted to kiss me for a while now, or . . .?"

"I mean, at least a few hours." Her tone is playful, but something inside me shifts.

"Remember that play you did in high school? That Shakespeare thing?"

"*A Midsummer Night's Dream*," she says.

"Right." I grimace. "I have no idea what it was about, but I was there."

She nods. "I remember."

"I went for extra credit," I tell her. "I had no idea you were in it, but the second I saw you, I was . . ." I trail off, because how do I even put words to it? I was gone. For me, it was only ever Olive, and no amount of telling myself the opposite made it true.

"I was going to talk to you, ask you to go get ice cream, but before I could even say hi, some guy—"

"Tim Torino," she says on a groan.

"Hate that guy."

She laughs.

"He appeared out of nowhere and made it obvious you weren't available."

Her face falls. "All this time."

I nod.

"And you never said a word," she says.

"I kissed you in the treehouse."

"We were twelve!" She laughs again. "And it felt more like a pity kiss because I couldn't stop crying." A pause. "I was so sad you were moving."

I smile down at her. "I was really nervous."

"It was a good first kiss," she says generously.

I draw in a breath, remembering. "And then life took us in different directions, and we lost touch, but—" I meet her eyes—"It's always been you, Liv."

At that, her expression shifts, a mix of shyness and something else.

"So now . . . here we are."

She reaches up and touches my cheek. "Here we are."

I stare at her, wanting her, wishing circumstances were different. "Our timing is always a little off." I brush my lips over hers. "Even now."

Her face falls. "Can we pretend, just for the rest of the holidays, that there isn't an expiration date on whatever this is?"

I feel my brow furrow. "You're okay with that?"

"I have to be, right?" She looks up at me, her blue eyes wide, a worry line creasing her forehead. "If I only get you for a few weeks, I want to make the most of them."

I lean in and kiss her forehead, then pull her into a tight hug. "We'll figure it out." I say it with more confidence than I feel because honestly, how does this work? I can't ask her to uproot her whole life, leave her friends and family and move to Indi-anapolis. And I know she'd never ask me to stay here.

I feel her nod, and she holds me tighter, obviously making up for all the days of keeping her distance.

After several long moments, both of our phones start buzzing. I pull out mine and see a text from Lacey.

LACEY

Yo! Where are you guys?

We've got all our photos. Tell me we win the wine!

I show the text to Olive, and she groans dramatically. "We are the worst teammates!" She takes my phone and opens the camera. "Should we send them a picture of us kissing?" She giggles, and it's the most adorable thing I've ever seen.

We don't kiss. Instead, we pose, one thumb up and one thumb down, with matching apologetic expressions. I text to let her know they're on their own.

We have other things to do.

I take Olive's hand, and we walk back to the main barn.

"If we're holding hands, we're going public," she says before we get there.

I look at her. "And we don't want to do that . . ."

"We don't want everyone else's input," she says. "I think our moms would lose it if they thought there was actually a chance we were together." She faces me. "It'll break their hearts when it ends."

"Hey, no expiration date," I say.

"Right." She gives me a firm nod.

I shrug. "It could be fun to have a secret."

We're about to come into a clearing, so I pull her behind one of the trees and kiss her again, feeling like a teenager under the bleachers at the homecoming game. She melts into me, and I love the way it feels, arms wrapped around her, close enough to inhale the scent of her—vanilla and cinnamon.

My mind starts thinking about all the times I've wanted this moment to be real, and I drink it all in, knowing that when it comes time for me to go back to Indiana, I'm going to be the one who's broken.

I pull back and find her watching me. "Were your eyes open?"

She grins. "I wanted to see you."

"You're so weird." I kiss her again, with my eyes wide open. She keeps hers open, and crosses them at me mid-kiss. We laugh, lips still on each other's, and then I take a big step back. "Keep your hands off me now, Witherby."

"No promises, Fisher." She pumps her eyebrows, and it takes all my will power not to grab her hand, pull her back, and kiss her again until she forgets her name.

We go back to the barn, where both of our dads are manning the oversized grill. I'm instantly guilty, like they'll know what we've been doing behind the trees just by looking at us.

Olive must sense it because she bumps my shoulder with her own and hisses, "Act normal."

I draw in a breath, inhaling the scent of burgers grilling in the cool winter air. I don't know who started this particular Family Day tradition, but I'm glad they did. Because my mouth is watering.

"I'm starving," I say as we come into the equipment garage. The big door at one end of it is wide open, giving the illusion of warmth while they flip the burgers and drink their beers.

"We've got plenty!" Dad says.

"Olive, are you okay? Your face is all red," her dad says, frowning.

She reaches up and touches her cheeks, and I regret not shaving this morning. "I'm good. Just cold. It's chilly out there!"

Her dad seems to accept this, and when he looks away, she glances at me, pressing her lips together to hide her smile.

"Liam, help us get these inside, would ya?" Dad asks.

Olive hesitates for a minute, then says, "I'm going to go see if they need help getting set up." She rushes off, and I watch her go, already wishing she were back here, next to me.

I'm doomed.

Her dad picks up a tray of cooked burgers and follows her to the café, and my dad glances over at me. "We heard from Travis."

"Oh?"

"He's going to bring the buyer out next week, but it's more of a formality. Sounds like he's very interested, and with any luck, it's going to go through."

"Oh, wow," I say, a mix of emotions racing through me. "That was a lot faster than I thought it would be."

"It could move pretty quickly, depending on how serious he is," Dad says. "But it sounds like it could actually happen."

I watch him for a few seconds, trying to hear what he's not saying. "Do you know what he's going to do with it?"

Dad shakes his head. "I guess we'll find out."

I look up and see Manny and his son Miguel out in the parking lot. Miguel is holding his little girl, and she reaches for Manny's fake Santa beard and pulls it down. He makes a face, and she laughs, and my stomach rolls.

Olive's words flicker through my mind—*The Last, Best Pine Creek Christmas.*

CHAPTER 29

OLIVE

*M*y exhaustion gets the best of me, and I leave Family Day after dinner but before marshmallows.

Liam walks me to my car and proceeds to give me a proper goodbye, and I want to fold into his arms and make a home there. Now that I've opened the floodgates, my feelings for him get a little more intense every time he looks at me. This has been happening for days, but now, I don't try to stop it.

I loved him once—back when we were kids, defined by friendship and fun. But this?

This is something else entirely.

Even though Liam and I decide to keep a low profile, I call Phoebe on my way home from Family Day and gush my way through the entire story.

Because I know her, I know she won't tell me to be careful or remind me that he doesn't live here. I know she won't hint that I could get my heart broken. She does exactly what I expect her to do—completely freaks out.

After an appropriate amount of squealing and, I assume,

kicking her feet, she says, "Olive, I have such a good feeling about this."

"Even though he's so cranky?" I smile thinking about it. I love that he's cranky. I love it because I'm starting to learn how to make him smile, and it feels like winning a prize every time.

"It's hot," she says. "And I see the way he looks at you."

"I never noticed." I'm grinning so wide my cheeks hurt.

"Liam is a good guy too," she says. "He always has been. I knew it the day he sent those movers to come help when you had to pack up the store. I mean, who does that?"

"Wait, what?" I feel the deceleration of the car as I lift my foot off the pedal.

"The day we were moving everything out," she says. "Remember when those movers showed up with a big truck and helped us get all the boxes and bins over into your garage?"

"Yeah." I frown. "I thought my parents sent them."

"Oh, Olive, that was Liam." She pauses. "I thought you knew."

"How do you know this?" A car passes me, and I realize I'm going about twenty under the speed limit. I try to focus on the road as I press on the gas, but my mind is still trying to catch up to what she's saying.

"You were super busy, and I signed the paperwork," she says. "His name was on the invoice."

I'm not sure how to process what she's saying. How is it possible I didn't know he did that? All these years, he's kept tabs on my life, and I had no idea.

I go to sleep thinking about him. Replaying every second of every kiss until my face flushes all over again. Because Liam is a *good* kisser. The kind of kisser that makes me realize everyone else has been doing it wrong.

I think about the way he held me so sweetly and about how anyone who knows him would be surprised to learn he has this gentle side, and I feel honored he's shown it to me. I think about how thoughtful and kind and inherently *good* he is.

Then I think about the day after Christmas.

And I never want it to arrive.

It's the week of the Christmas Market, and everyone is all-go-no-quit. Jo's asked me to gather the staff before we open Monday morning and get everyone on the same page about what this week of set-up will entail, which is why I'm currently standing at one end of a large open space in the office building.

Lacey is at the back of the room filming a few of the staff members, and I scan the space, looking for Liam. When I find him near the back, standing next to Manny, I'm hit with a flash of heat from the inside out.

He glances over and meets my eyes. I feel the smile crawl across my lips. His gaze lingers for a few long seconds, and then Jo walks in, pulling everyone's focus.

She smiles brightly as she greets her staff, moving toward the front of the space. "You look flushed." She presses the back of her hand against my forehead. "Are you okay?"

My eyes dart to Liam, then back to her. I force a smile. "Maybe a little nervous to talk in front of everyone."

I'm such a liar.

"You'll be great." She unwinds her scarf, takes off her coat, then turns and faces the group. She makes a few announcements, then motions for me to take the floor. I follow my notes and go through all the information they need about when to set up, when and how to tear down, how many people to expect, how to ease the flow of traffic, signage, attitude, and every other potential planning point I can think of. It's going to be a lot to try and keep up with our normal activities *and* prepare for the market, so Jo is bringing everyone in instead of splitting shifts.

I think we might actually pull this off.

I avoid looking at Liam the entire time I'm speaking because I know my face will give me away. There's no way I can hide all the deliciously giddy feelings bubbling up when I think about him.

Once I'm done, I turn to Jo. "I think that's everything."

"Wonderful, Olive." She squeezes my shoulder, then turns to the group. "I know Olive is a new-ish addition to our Pine Creek family, but I want to take a minute to publicly brag on her."

I scrunch up my face and shake my head.

"This girl is a creative powerhouse, and we are so, *so* lucky she has gone to such lengths to make this a Pine Creek Christmas to remember." She turns to me, and I see her eyes welling with tears. "You've made things so special and added so many fun details. It truly is shaping up to be, as you said, the last, best Christmas." She pulls me into a tight hug, and it cracks something open inside me.

I bathe in her words, encouraging and uplifting, and I think about what Lacey and Phoebe said, and how Liam knew I failed but he still asked for my help in something as important to him as this new game idea.

None of them think of me as a disaster. Or a failure. All of them think I'm worthy of another chance.

These people have put me back together, and I couldn't even see I needed it.

Jo pulls back and looks me square in the face. "You are a very special, very talented young woman, Olive. Don't forget it."

I didn't expect to be tearing up this morning but here we are. I thank her as the rest of the staff starts applauding. For me.

I scan the room and wave a thank you, when my eyes find Liam's. He's clapping along with everyone else, but the fire burning in his eyes is uniquely his.

The jolt is like someone has just yelled, "Clear," and hit me with defibrillator paddles, and I wonder if he's replayed our kisses as many times as I have. Or if he's just itching, like me, to get out of here so we can do it again.

"All right," Jo hollers over the din. "Have a happy Pine Creek day, everyone!"

I pull my lower lip between my teeth and search for a reason to follow Liam out the door, but I come up empty.

Jo turns to me. "The newspaper is going to do a story about the market. Clark wrote the first blurb to help spread the word that this would be our last year in business, but now he'd like to do a full spread. Something a little more in-depth." Her face is pinched, her smile forced.

I reach over and squeeze her arm. "Are you doing okay?"

Her smile holds. "I am. I know it's all going the way it's supposed to—but it's just getting real now, isn't it? That this is it?"

"Yeah, it is. We're all going to feel it. This place is really special. Because of you."

"Thank you, Olive."

"Thank *you*," I say, "for letting me be a part of it."

She squeezes my arm, and I get the sense she's choked up.

I smile. "I'm going to head out to Christmas Tree Row. I want to double check the measurements and make sure there aren't any branches that need to be cleared away."

"You shouldn't do that yourself," she says.

I quirk a brow and pretend to think for a moment. "Maybe I can con Liam into helping me. He'll love that," I say it in a way that makes it sound like he won't.

She grins. "Good idea! Put him to work."

I pack up my things and head out the door. As I walk outside, an arm reaches for me and pulls me around the corner of the building.

Normally, this would freak me out, but I know it's Liam before I even meet his eyes.

He backs me up against the wall of the barn and steps in close. I expect him to kiss me, but instead, he just looks at me—almost like he can't believe I'm real. Almost like he's admiring me.

It's nice to be admired.

I drop my bag on the ground as I wrap my arms around his neck. He leans down and kisses me, and I have my answer. He's definitely been replaying our kisses as much as I have.

He pulls back and searches my eyes. "Good morning."

"Good morning," I say. "I was just coming to find you."

"You need help?"

"If you're free."

"Hmm. Let me check my schedule." He kisses me again. "Yeah, I think I can work something out."

The door of the office opens, and he pulls away, then we both freeze. "We're going to get caught," I whisper.

He holds up a hand, and we wait. I half expect Jo or one of the staffers to come around the side of the building and find us there, in a place we have absolutely no reason to be.

I'm holding my breath, and I don't let it out until I hear a vehicle start and whoever it is drives off.

We both crumple in laughter, and Liam kisses me one more time before we walk toward his truck and head out to survey the area where the vendors will set up.

If my life were a movie, this would be the point where there would be a montage of several days of happy moments, set to an upbeat, romantic pop song. There would be images of Liam and me, stealing kisses behind buildings, in his truck, outside under the mistletoe. Images of us working together on the market, talking to Clark from the newspaper, taking a late-night carriage ride. Moving pictures of us ice skating on the pond and me falling more than skating. And, of course, there would be a shot of us standing outside, kissing under the light of a full moon, during the first snowfall of the year.

For the next several days, we spend every evening at my house, making dinner or eating takeout, brainstorming about his game and preparing the pitch for his meeting next week, which usually devolves into making out on my couch under the light of my wonky little Christmas tree. When we come up for air, he helps me stuff the vendor packets and swag bags for the Christmas Market, one of several personal touches I hope makes the vendors feel special.

And even though it feels like we're trying to squeeze every second out of the time we have, I do all of this without ever mentioning the ticking clock on the most natural, easy, amazing relationship I've ever had.

Liam's family all comment about how much happier he's been, and while none of them seem suspicious of us, I'm ninety-eight percent certain that Manny knows exactly what's going on.

I can tell by the way he looks at me, almost like, *I'm onto you.*

It's Thursday afternoon, and with all of us so busy with market preparations, Lacey, Phoebe, and I have had to finalize on our presentation for the city council meeting via a shared Google folder.

We're ready.

Lacey will do all the talking, appealing to the council members for their support in this somewhat unorthodox plan. I hope they go for it. Getting the city's support will go a long way.

I'm packing up my things when Liam shows up in the doorway of the office space. His hair is the perfect amount of disheveled and his eyes are a shade lighter than usual. They flicker when he looks at me, and I'd pay a lot of money to know what he's thinking.

I smile at him. "Hey."

"You look pretty."

"Thank you." My smile widens, and I add, "So do you."

"Gee, thanks," he jokes.

He jokes with me now.

He stares at me for several seconds, then asks, "Hey, I know we don't have plans tonight, but are you free later?"

"Not exactly. Why?" I know I'm being a little cagey, but tonight is the city council meeting.

"My parents are going to the city council meeting," he says. "They want to discuss the sale of the property."

I frown. I knew they were going, but I didn't know they had their own reasons for doing so. "Has something changed?"

"I think the buyer wants to move forward," he says. "The guy Travis found."

I nod. "The developer guy."

"Yeah, Travis is bringing him out here next week for a tour, but I think he's looked over the paperwork and photos, and he's very interested. Sounds like something would have to go really wrong for it not to go through."

My stomach rolls. I wonder if Lacey knows they've moved on to the next step. I wish she would've told them about her plan. I have to believe that Brant and Jo would do whatever they could to help her make this happen, but Lacey wanted them to see her presentation along with the members of the city council. Something about needing her family to see her as a professional. And wanting her parents to have the retirement they deserve.

Honestly, I don't blame her. It's hard to be taken seriously when you've screwed up. And Lacey's life, though professionally successful, isn't traditional or easy for people to understand. Her persona is more "free spirit" than "solid investment," and while I understand why her family would hesitate to listen to her plan, I also believe her passion and excitement for Pine Creek will go a long way.

"Do you know what this guy is planning to do?" I ask.

His eyes dart off to the side. "Not sure."

But I can tell he has at least a vague idea, and the fact that he's not telling me is all the answer I need. "He's going to bulldoze it, isn't he? Build vacation homes for an investment firm or something. Liam, he's going to ruin it."

His smile is kind. "Unfortunately, this place can't run on sentimentality."

"I know, but Travis and whoever he finds, is not going to do right by it." I sigh and look away, feeling the weight of all of this. Just because this isn't a topic Liam and I have discussed, that doesn't mean I didn't know this was happening, I just didn't think it would happen so quickly. "And there's really no part of you that wants to—" I meet his eyes, and it feels like a betrayal to finish the sentence. "Never mind."

I want to plead my case with him right here, to tell him the entire plan to look for investors to help shoulder the burden. I want to ask him to be a part of it, to stay here, to give the farm and us a real shot.

But I know it's not fair.

I force myself to smile even though I really don't feel like it. "So, you're going to the city council meeting?"

He nods. "Will you come?"

"Uh, yeah," I say. "I'll be there."

I want to tell him I was already planning on being there. He deserves to know, and I think he'd be on our side. A voice in our corner. Because while he may not want to stay, surely, he'd rather Pine Creek stay in his family.

But I stay quiet because I promised Lacey. She has her reasons—understandable reasons—for wanting this to all go a certain way. I can't betray her trust by sticking my nose in their family affairs.

Hopefully it'll all work out exactly how Lacey wants it to. Her parents will hear her pitch, see how well thought-out it is, and the members of the council will want the town to be an investor. We'll secure private donations from several other wealthy Pine Creek customers, and then Liam will jump on board and he'll see a future with me and Pine Creek.

And we'll all live happily ever after.

While I'm at it, I'd like a million dollars and a pony.

CHAPTER 30

OLIVE

*T*he Pleasant Valley City Council meets in the community center downtown, just a block from my former store, in the opposite direction of my house.

Tonight, I want to walk. Maybe I *need* to walk, to mentally prepare. The cold Christmas air will hopefully lift my spirits, which have been a little low since my conversation with Liam.

I don't like that I'm keeping things from him, especially something as huge as Lacey potentially taking over the farm. As much as I tried not to be, somehow, I've landed smack in the middle of this whole drama—head over heels for one sibling and keeping secrets for the other.

I don't like it.

Most of the trees lining the street have lost their leaves, finally surrendering to a new season. While I have vowed not to think about expiration dates and endings, when things get quiet it's impossible not to.

Yesterday, I found a small jar of acorns on my desk that wasn't there before. Proof that he was thinking of me. Proof that he knows me.

It's nice to be known.

I worry it's too fast to like him this much—that I won't recover when it's time to let him go. And because I know I will have to let him go, everything is heightened. My senses are all on high alert, like I want to cram a year into the short time we have left.

I said I could do this. Why is it so hard?

Because Liam has seeped into every aspect of my mind. I replay our kisses and conversations. I try to memorize the way he makes me feel, the way he looks at me, the way he touches me. I want to bottle it all up, like the acorns, so I have access to these memories and feelings anytime I want.

Dim light falls on the sidewalk from the streetlamps overhead. Even though I'm bundled up in my coat, scarf, gloves and hat, with the waning of the sun, I'm chilled to the bone.

I don't walk downtown often anymore. It's always a little depressing to pass by the old shop space and not see my adorable *Wit and Whimsy* sign above the large front window. Decorating the space for Christmas was one of my favorite things to do. My hand-painted storefront windows accidentally started a new town tradition, and it hurts a little to not have windows to paint anymore.

The wind kicks up, and I swear the temperature has dropped ten degrees in the few minutes I've been outside. I pick up my pace when a shiny, black Escalade slows down beside me. I glance over and see Travis behind the wheel. "You need a ride?"

"I'm fine." I keep my eyes forward. I shouldn't have walked.

"Come on, Olive, we're going to the same place," he calls out. "And you look cold."

I stop. "Why are you going to the city council meeting?"

He looks at me like I should know already, duh. "Because I'm involved in the sale? Brant and Jo are going to talk about it, so I'm going."

"It's not a done deal," I say. "The buyer hasn't even seen it."

"Yeah, but it's good to get community support, especially for something as ingrained and historic as Pine Creek."

I scoff and take a few steps closer to the car. "You think you're going to get community support to bulldoze one of the community's favorite businesses?"

His grin is cocky. "You're cute when you're upset."

"I'm not upset."

"Well then, you're cute all the time," he throws out.

I'm starting to lose my patience.

He doesn't seem to care. "You always were passionate about the things you cared about."

I lean down and put my hands on the door of the car. "You don't know me anymore, Travis."

He reaches across the seat and pushes open the passenger side door. "Truce, Olive. I'm not trying to upset you. I want what everyone wants—for the sale to go through and to make sure Liam's parents have a great retirement."

I draw in a breath, slowly and silently counting to five. I'm really trying to take the high road, but there is a detour sign that I'm having a *really* difficult time ignoring.

"Once again, you have no idea what everyone wants. You know what you want. And that's all that matters to you." I start walking again, thinking that should be enough to shut him up.

"Olive, come on, don't be like this."

Obviously not enough.

Fine. I'm taking the detour.

I rush over to the car and slam the passenger side door shut. "You knew Liam was going to ask me out that night. You knew he liked me, you *knew* he probably wouldn't say anything if you stepped in, but you made your move anyway. You were a crappy friend then and an even crappier boyfriend, so guess what, Travis, I really don't want anything to do with you. *Ever. Again.*"

I storm off and don't look back, and a few seconds later I hear Travis drive off.

I no longer feel the cold.

I stomp up to the community building steps and see Liam's truck pull into the parking lot. If my body was a fist, it would be unclenching as the anger begins to dissipate.

I wait for him on the sidewalk, thinking about all the reasons I could let myself fall in love.

Get it while it lasts, right?

I'm pretty sure I couldn't stop these feelings anyway.

Liam crosses the street and stands a few feet away from me. To any passerby (and there are none), we probably look like two people talking and not like two people who'd much rather be cozied up under a blanket in front of a fire, pretending to watch movies.

The second he sees me, his face falls. "What's wrong?"

Hm. Maybe I don't have a poker face after all. I force a smile. "Lots of emotions."

He gives the area a cursory glance. "I want to hug you, but people might see."

I like our secret, stolen moments, but right now I need to feel his arms around me. "I don't care."

He reaches for me, wrapping his arms around me and pulling my body against his. "I don't like seeing you upset. Can I do anything?"

Stay?

Of course, I don't say that out loud, but the thought reveals that I'm not emotional because of Travis. I'm emotional because losing Liam—now that I know how truly incredible he is—is going to rip my heart out. And knowing that is like an open tab in my browser, running in the background all the time.

"No," I say. "Unless you want to ditch this meeting, go back to my place, get a pizza, and watch *It's a Wonderful Life.*"

"Don't tempt me. Plus, if you're going to insist on Christmas movies, then I suggest *Die Hard.*"

I laugh. "How about *The Polar Express?*"

He shudders. "With the train hobo? Too creepy."

I rest my cheek on his chest, aware of the way his hands hold me firmly to him.

"Uh, hey, guys."

I draw back and see Lacey standing behind Liam with a curious look on her face. "Is this—" she points at him, then at me, then back at him— "a thing?"

Liam looks at me, and I give a little *might as well admit it* shrug.

He starts to respond, but Lacey cuts him off.

"Finally!" Her eyes go wide. "I cannot *believe* you didn't say anything! I approve. I absolutely approve."

He wraps an arm around me and pulls me closer. "I mean, I don't care if you approve or not, but I guess it's good that you do."

She smacks him across the shoulder, then loops her arm in mine and pulls me toward the front door of the building. "You sneak!"

I giggle as she pulls the door open, thankful for the warmth of the community building. It has a distinct smell that only old buildings have, like the woodsy dankness of a small-town church.

Now that the weather has officially decided on winter, I can see myself spending far less time outdoors. Cozy fires, warm sweaters, and my favorite blankets are going to be on constant rotation.

We make our way into the meeting room, and it takes me back to the last city council meeting I attended before closing the shop. When I was a small business owner, being part of the local community was important to me, so I made a point to be involved.

But once the shop failed, I stopped showing my face around town leadership. I felt like I'd let everyone down.

I stop outside the door of the meeting space to gather

myself. I take off my coat and unwind the scarf. Liam reaches for my winter things. I hand them over, and he turns to hang them up, alongside his coat.

It makes me think of the night of the Christmas Kick-Off— how that Olive, the one who stood at the coat check counter blabbing on to a very grouchy Liam, could never have predicted that just a couple weeks later she would feel this strongly about the boy who grew up next door.

It also makes me thankful I'm not in coconuts.

I draw in a breath as Phoebe walks up. "You ready for this?" she asks.

Liam looks over, and I widen my eyes at Phoebe, willing her to be a little more discreet.

"Olive! You didn't tell him?" she asks, voice low.

"No. I promised Lacey," I say in a stage whisper.

"But Olive. It's Liam," she says.

I glance at him, suddenly afraid that keeping Lacey's confidence was the wrong choice. "I didn't feel like it was my place. It's family business and none of mine."

I can tell by the look on Phoebe's face she disagrees, which only makes me worry more.

"You think I should've said something?" I ask quietly, grateful that Liam's parents have shown up, giving me a few minutes alone with Phoebe.

"Yes, I do," she says. "Lacey didn't know you were hooking up with her brother."

"We aren't *hooking up*." I pull her a few steps away, as if that will make a difference. "That makes it sound so cheap." What I feel for Liam is so much bigger than those words capture.

"All the more reason to be honest, don't you think?" she asks.

"Phoebe, you were there," I remind her. "Lacey specifically asked me not to say anything to him. I feel weird, and I want to tell him, but I'm not going to break Lacey's confidence."

Ironically, at that precise moment, Travis pokes his head out the door. I glare at him, but he ignores me and walks over to Liam's parents.

Liam catches my eye but doesn't move. He looks like he's trying to not punch Travis, and a part of me sort of wishes he would. I turn back to Phoebe. "I can't stand that guy."

She frowns. "Are you okay?"

"Yes." I push my hand through my hair. "I just feel jumbled. I'll fill you in later."

"Okay, well, take a breath, say a prayer, and let's go save a farm!" She starts off, and I reach for her arm.

"Do you really think this plan is going to work?" I ask.

She pauses for a second, then says, "Yes. I feel safe betting on us."

CHAPTER 31

LIAM

I don't want to be here.

I don't live here anymore, and if my parents are happy with the sale of their farm, then I really have nothing else to contribute.

But they asked me to be here. It's the least I can do.

Once Travis is finished schmoozing my parents, he follows me into the meeting room. My eyes are instantly drawn to Olive. She's with Phoebe and my sister, all three huddled together like they're gossiping cheerleaders at a Friday night football game.

I'd rather be at her house, on her couch, under the fleece blanket she said her grandma made for her thirteenth birthday.

I take a seat next to my parents, ready to get this over with. Over the last several days, and with Olive's help, I've polished my pitch for Aaron, which is scheduled for next week. I know I could wait until after the holidays, but I want to return to Indy with this worked out.

I'm ready for a new challenge and a new success.

I absently think about the propeller hat kid and the jetpack girl. Maybe I was so drawn to her doodles because a part of me knew it was personal—to her and to me. I think about how much her creativity has sparked my own, how she makes me better. At work, yes, but also as a person.

I actually feel—happy.

I look over at her again.

Part of me doesn't want to give that up.

A short, chubby guy I don't recognize walks up to the front of the room. The meeting room is more rectangular than square, and at this time of year, with snow on the ground outside, it's a great space. Makes me think about the spaces at the farm, how underutilized some of them are.

It's a little out of the way, but I wonder if locals from Pleasant Valley or Loveland would drive for the atmosphere. Office parties, staff retreats, weddings, meetings . . .

"Lacey Fisher."

My sister's name, coming from the man at the podium, catches me off guard. My parents look at me, clearly as confused as I am.

Lacey is dressed more professionally than usual, and I wonder if she had to go out and buy the outfit—a blazer over a pair of navy blue dress pants with a red belt. Her wavy blond hair is pulled back, and her eyes are sparkling. For a second, she looks like a kid playing dress-up, but then something comes over her, and I see her change.

She clears her throat and glances to her left—at Olive and Phoebe, who both smile and nod, as if to encourage her to go ahead.

What is happening?

"Good evening, ladies and gentlemen," she begins. "My name is Lacey Fisher, and you most likely know my parents. They own the Pine Creek Christmas Tree Farm, located about forty miles outside of town, between Pleasant Valley and Loveland. Because of our location, we serve both towns equally, and I do plan to present my ideas to the Loveland city council as well."

She looks up. "But, of course, I had to start here, with the superior of the two towns."

A chuckle moves through the crowd.

"Tonight, I'm grateful for the opportunity to talk to you about my home."

I straighten.

"And I want to talk to you about why we shouldn't let it fall into the wrong hands."

My parents shift. They both look at me, wearing matching frowns.

"What is she doing?" Mom whispers.

I shake my head. "I have no idea."

"Pine Creek has been in our family for generations. It was my great-great-great—" she scrunches her nose— "and maybe a couple more greats in there, grand-parents who started it, and every generation, someone in our family has been its caretaker. But this year, as you might already know," she nods toward our parents, seated in the crowd, "our parents have decided to sell the farm."

The people turn to Mom and Dad, who look a bit embarrassed to be put on the spot, and they give a little wave and smile.

"I'll be honest . . . it was hard to hear that this was the plan. I grew up there. The north lot was my stomping ground. There are things that my brother and I got into that my parents *still* don't know about." She smiles at me, then at them. "Sorry Mom, it was us who broke the fence on the back lot."

Another ripple of laughter as my mom exclaims, "That was *you?*"

Lacey smiles, and continues. "And to think it will no longer be a part of our family?" She pauses, and shakes her head. "I can't imagine it most likely going to a development company that will build houses or vacation homes or something equally as depressing."

Travis leans forward. "What is she doing?"

"I don't know," my mom says.

"Can you stop her?" Travis asks.

He obviously doesn't know my sister.

She looks down at her notes. "My family is amazing at a lot of things. But communication isn't one of them. Which is why my parents don't realize . . ." she looks up at the small group, "that I want to run the farm."

At that, Travis swears under his breath. I lean forward, confused why Lacey is sharing this in a public forum and not over dinner in our parents' kitchen.

Lacey glances at my mom. Something silent passes between them.

"Purchasing property like Pine Creek is, as you can imagine, very expensive. Over the past week, with a lot of help," she nods at Phoebe and Olive, "With the money I've saved, I've managed to tentatively secure a loan for a portion of the cost. That gets me almost fifty percent of the way there."

Whoa. I know the listing price Travis set for the farm, and for Lacey to have that kind of money saved?

I have a feeling everyone—me included—is about to find out there's a lot more to Lacey than any of us give her credit for.

She takes a deep breath. "And that's why I'm here tonight, talking to all of you. I'd like to offer the opportunity for members of the community to become a part of the Pine Creek family by helping to purchase the farm—before it's sold to someone who doesn't appreciate it for what it is." She looks at me. "Our legacy."

Travis gets up, pulls out his phone, and walks out.

Lacey clicks a button and the screen behind her lights up with the Pine Creek logo. She clicks another button to reveal a slide labeled "Benefits of Investing in Pine Creek."

I recognize the hand lettering.

I glance at Olive. Her eyes are fixed on Lacey, and she looks like she's holding her breath.

Lacey outlines plans for expansion.

Events. Weddings. Staff retreats. School outings. Catered corporate dinners.

New outbuildings, new construction, all themed.

I haven't talked to her about any of my ideas, the ones I pitched to Dad that he shot down—but here so many of them are.

Lacey and Olive, it seems, have the same vision I did.

She mentions hot tubs in the woods and private cabins. Then she outlines, in common sense detail, all the ways the farm could stay profitable throughout the year. Her plan is ambitious, even a little idealistic, but she has data and research and charts and graphs to back her up.

The initial investment and upfront costs are high, and the expansion would be done in stages. But Lacey argues it would be a benefit to both of the towns on either side of the farm. She's pitching the idea, asking for investments from businesses, individuals, and the city. If the costs were shared, they would share in the profits, and it would bolster the economy of the town.

Like JFK said, "a rising tide lifts all boats."

Even I can see the potential. But this is a massive gamble. A complicated plan that requires a significant investment. Is anyone really going to go for this?

I can see the hopefulness in Lacey's eyes, and I know where it came from.

I glance at Olive.

She has a way of enhancing possibility in other people. Her personality, her demeanor, even her ideas—it's like yeast in dough or an ignited flame in a hot air balloon.

Your own ideas and hopes get bigger, are lifted higher, and rise.

The problem is combining that hope with my sister.

Lacey has never been one to stick with anything. She's a leaf on the wind, blown around aimlessly and landing whenever the motivation dies down . . . only to be picked up in a completely different direction five seconds later.

Did Olive pump Lacey full of grandiose ideas? Did she fail to stop and ask if my sister might get her heart set on something that is never, ever going to happen, no matter how good of an idea it is? Did she stop to consider Lacey's unique personality and—I hate to say it—her limitations?

There are so many moving pieces to keeping the farm going —even if she finds investors, this is not a solo endeavor. She's going to need real help.

My muscles are tense, and I try to relax them, but I can't. When did they put this all together? And why didn't one of them tell me?

After Lacey finishes, she opens the floor for questions. I have a few, but I'll reserve them for another time.

A woman in the front raises her hand, and when Lacey points at her, she stands.

"If this is a family business, why doesn't your brother want to buy half? Shouldn't he be a part of this venture?"

Lacey looks at me and clears her throat. "I love my brother," she gives a little wave to me which elicits a few smattered *aw's* from the older people in the crowd, "but his passion isn't at the tree farm. He lives and works in Indiana, and he's doing really well there. He has a right to pursue his own passions. I can't ask him to give up that for this."

Yeah. Doing really well. I bite the inside of my cheek.

Once the first question is asked, as often happens at these meetings like this, the floodgates open and people start asking harder questions.

"But if it matters to the community as much as you say it does, shouldn't it also matter to him?" a man asks.

"It's not really about my brother or my family," Lacey says, a bit of panic crawling across her face.

"If your own family isn't supportive, shouldn't we proceed with caution?" the first woman asks.

"Oh, I never said they aren't supportive—"

But they aren't listening. Just firing off questions in rapid succession:

"Are you going to hire someone else to run things?" a man asks.

"Aren't you the one who lives in a van? Like online or something?"

"Are you even qualified to run the farm?"

Lacey straightens. "I am." She looks back at my parents, and I see the moment they realize.

The one to take things over was there all along . . . they simply overlooked her.

"No offense, young lady, but that's a big operation out there, and tree farming is hard work," an older man says. "I'm not sure you've got what it takes to keep it going or to take on this expansion."

At that, Olive stands. "All due respect, John, but Lacey knows how hard the work is because she grew up doing it."

John snaps his jaw shut.

Olive continues. "I can vouch for Lacey. I've spent the last several weeks working with her on the farm. She's a marketing genius with a huge social media following. As we've come up with brand new events and activities to host at Pine Creek this year, Lacey is the one who has gotten the community buy-in we need to get people through the door."

"But that doesn't mean she can harvest trees."

Olive glances back, but it's not me she's looking at. There, standing against the back wall, is Manny.

"She actually can," Manny calls out.

Everyone turns.

He starts down the aisle, pausing only to nod quickly at our row.

"I've worked at Pine Creek all my life, and my father before me for all of his. I've seen workers come and go, ones who could hack it and ones who couldn't."

He looks at Lacey and smiles. "You wouldn't think it to look at her, but she's scrappy. She's what I call a 'tree whisperer,'" he says. "Ever since she was young, she's shown a great interest in taking care of and growing these trees. I have no doubt in my mind that she is strong and capable and knowledgeable enough to take this on. And what she doesn't know, she can learn." He looks at me. "The Fisher kids come by this work naturally. It's in their blood."

I look away. I don't know if the intention is to make me feel guilty, but I do. Why can't everyone acknowledge that it's not what I want to do? Even if it's "in my blood"?

I clench my fists at my sides. This is a terrible idea. The more I think about it, the more I can't see it working. And the more frustrated I am that nobody bothered to loop me in to this plan.

It feels like a mutiny. It's the opposite of what my parents want, and they roped Manny into it?

Lacey answers a few more questions, then Olive stands to hand out flyers with information on how to become an investor. It's all surreal.

I love this woman—I have no doubt about that—but I can't help but feel a little annoyed that she did all this behind my back.

After the meeting ends, people mill around, many of them anxious to talk to Lacey, and a few of them anxious to talk to my parents.

And I'm anxious to leave.

I stand and walk toward the door when a tall, wispy woman steps in my way. "Why aren't you jumping in to help save your family's farm? You know how much that place means to your parents."

I scowl at her and walk out.

I hear footsteps behind me, and I don't have to turn to know it's Olive.

"Liam."

I keep walking.

"Liam, wait!"

I stop moving and inhale a deep breath, hoping it will calm me down. It doesn't work. All I can think is how this messes everything up.

She moves in front of me, and at the sight of her wide, questioning eyes, I almost come undone. I look away. "That was you? Your ideas? Your—"

"What? No." She blows out a breath. "I mean, not all of it."

I close my eyes and sigh. "What is Lacey thinking?" I look at her.

She takes a step back. "She really wants to do this, and—"

"And you encouraged her?" I ask, harsher than I mean to.

She looks hurt, and I instantly want to take it back.

"Yeah. I encouraged her. She's my friend."

I sigh. "Olive, there's a reason my parents never considered her to take over the farm. She's flighty and she never sticks with anything."

She straightens. "Maybe you're underestimating her."

I start to count on my fingers. "One year she was convinced she wanted to be a tattoo artist, the next, she was taking classes to teach English to kids overseas. Then her pottery phase. Then the van life."

"So she took some time to figure out what she wanted to do in life. Is that so bad?"

I'm trying my hardest to be patient. I don't want to have to explain this. Lacey might be a tree whisperer. Heck, she might even be a social media genius. But she's not reliable. I love my sister, but that doesn't mean it's not true.

I draw in another breath, wondering why people claim that calms a person down. It doesn't.

"Yes, Olive," I say. "Pine Creek needs stability. What's going to happen when nobody wants to invest in it with her? Or she loses interest in a month? Or she gets in over her head? She should've been spending the last few weeks letting it go, not trying to force it to happen."

"I disagree," she says, crossing her arms over her chest. "I think if you really want something, you should go for it." She narrows her eyes.

"What is *that* supposed to mean?"

She softens, changing her tone. "No, that's not what I—"

"I said I was sorry for—" my frustration kicks up a notch. "This is so wrong, Olive. Lacey can't handle this on her own, and you shouldn't have made her think she could. Just let my parents sell the stupid place. You've taken a bad situation and made it so much worse."

I regret the words the second they're out of my mouth.

Her face registers the hurt so plainly as she nods and backs up.

"Olive, wait—" I reach for her, but she pulls back, shaking her head.

And then she walks away.

CHAPTER 32

LIAM

"You're going to have to fix that."

I turn around and find my dad standing in the lobby behind me.

My shoulders slump. "You heard that?"

He nods. "Yeah. I did. And it's not Olive's fault," he says. "Your sister is headstrong. Stubborn. You know that about her. I just had no idea she would ever want to do this." He goes still.

I face him. "That's because you never asked her," I say as nicely as I can.

Dad gives me a slight wince. "I have a knack for that."

"In your defense, neither one of us spoke up."

Something about that realization anchors at the back of my mind.

The city council members have started to filter out, and as solid as Lacey's presentation was, based on the chatter, it sounds like people are loving the idea, but no one is stepping forward to get involved.

"Do you think she can do this?" Dad asks.

I pause. The words, *not without me ,*are right there, on the tip of my tongue, but there's no way I'm saying them out loud.

"I don't know. I think she romanticizes things. And she's not the most reliable person." I sigh. "She's going to need a lot of help to pull it off."

"The plan was pretty solid, though," he says.

I think back to Lacey, standing up at the podium, talking in a way I've never heard her talk before. Maybe she had something to prove tonight. Maybe she's tired of everyone making assumptions about her. I can't fault her for that.

"Yeah. Yeah, it was."

"She had some great ideas for expansion."

Several were ideas I'd floated years ago, but yeah, they were great.

"We could give her some time to try and get the money together." Dad seems to be verbally processing their options.

"But if you drag your feet, my buyer will walk." Travis enters the conversation—he apparently made a phone call in the lobby and stuck around to eavesdrop. "He's not a sentimental guy. He's a money guy. So if you're planning to drag this out while Lacey and Olive start some grassroots campaign to save the Christmas tree farm, tell me now so we can move on."

The way he says it irks the crap out of me. So condescending. I can't believe I was ever friends with this guy. Hindsight sucks, showing someone's true colors in vibrant, vivid colors that you didn't see at the time.

"I'll talk to Jo and let you know," my dad says, probably not appreciating Travis's tone either.

"Tomorrow," Travis says. It comes out like an order.

My dad straightens. "Son, we own the farm. You work for us. I said I'll let you know."

Travis's inflated stance gets knocked down a peg, and I have to turn away to hide a smile.

"Great, I'll, uh, be in touch," Travis stutters, backing up.

Dad raises his eyebrows at him, and then nods.

After Travis leaves, Dad looks at me and blows out a breath.

"You were friends with that guy?"

I chuckle. "Yeah, I don't know why."

He makes a face, scratching at his chin. "We're counting on the sale."

"Retirement. I know."

A thought hits me. "Could you sell her a portion and keep a portion?" I ask.

"And walk away?" He gives me an *are you kidding* look, and I get it. He ran this place for years. If he owns half of it and he's worried about Lacey, he's never going to be free of it. He's always going to want to have his hands in the pot. And my mom? Forget it. She's going to find it hard enough to leave.

"Not just that though," Dad says. "I've got real concerns about Lacey taking on something this big all by herself. She'd have employees, but as great as ours are, I can tell you from experience, it's not the same."

I sigh. It's true. Lacey seems capable, smart and stronger than she looks. But even if she doesn't get bored, even if she decides to stick around—she's going to need help. And silent partners aren't going to roll up their sleeves and trim the boughs. Not like this business requires.

I hear footsteps before I see Lacey and my mom. When they reach us, they stop.

Lacey frowns. "Where's Olive?"

Dad shifts, avoiding my eyes. "She left."

"That's weird. She was so pumped before we got here." She pulls out her phone and clicks it open. "Oh, she texted. Migraine."

Dad looks at me, and my muscles tense.

Lacey shoots off what I assume is an *I hope you feel better soon* text and tucks her phone away. "So . . ."

"Let's go to Joe's and get a pizza," Dad says.

I'm supposed to be eating pizza with Olive. I'm supposed to be finding new ways to kiss her and memorizing every curve of her face. But I'm sure I'm the last person she wants to see right now, and besides, what would I say? *I'm sorry* is hardly enough.

Still, I pull out my phone and text her:

LIAM

I'm sorry. I'm an idiot. Can I call you?

Three dots appear, then disappear.

"You ready?" Dad asks.

I sigh, slide my phone into my pocket, and nod. "Yeah."

Once we're seated in a booth at Joe's and have ordered our food, Lacey studies all of us, eyes bouncing from our dad, to our mom, to me and back again. "So, what did you guys think?"

"A little warning would've been nice," I say.

"So you could talk me out of it?" she says. "Not a chance." She raises an eyebrow. "You know you would've."

I don't respond. Because she's right.

She pulls three flyers out of her bag and hands one to each of us.

"Olive's design," Mom says softly, and I wonder if she feels betrayed too. "I should've known you girls would cook up some way to keep Pine Creek." She glances at Lacey, her eyes welling with tears. "Sweetie, I just don't know if it's going to work."

Lacey's expression holds. "I can do this, you guys."

"Only if you get the money," I say.

She pulls a paper from her bag and turns it around so we can see the numbers, the calculations of what she already has and what she still needs to raise.

It's impressive. And staggering.

She's not as flighty as I thought. Not by a long shot.

"You have this much already?" Mom asks.

She nods.

"Who helped you with this?" Dad asks.

"Olive's friend, Phoebe," Lacey says. "It was actually their idea, to form a collective. We were talking one day, and we just sort of landed on it."

"When was that?" I ask.

She shrugs. "I don't know, a week or so ago?" She looks at me, and I see the moment it clicks. She leans closer. "I made her promise not to tell you."

My eyes dart to my parents, who are on the outside of our inside conversation, and I'd like to keep it that way.

Lacey doesn't get the hint. "Liam, she told me to come and talk to you guys. I didn't want to. I wanted you to see the whole presentation so you'd know how serious I am."

She did make me see her in a different light. I'm just not sure she convinced me she can handle a task this big. Not that it matters—I'm not the one selling the farm.

She turns to me. "I was hoping you might be more willing to help if you knew you didn't have to give up everything in order to do this. You could invest in the farm, still do game design, maybe work remotely a little more so you could come check on things?"

I close my eyes and draw in a breath. "That's not how my job works." I look at her. "Look, it took me a really long time to make it clear how I felt about owning the farm. And back then, you were the only one who understood. Now it seems like you're the only one who doesn't."

Her face falls. "Because I see you out there, Liam. I see the look on your face. You're so much happier."

I frown.

She points at me. "See? That face. That has disappeared lately when you're working with Manny."

There's no way she can know that, and yet, there's truth in it that I don't want to consider.

"And if we did this together, you and me, we'd be a great team. We have different strengths."

I scoff and look away. "How did this turn into *another* pitch for me to jump on board?" And was this the plan all along?

Our mom puts a hand on my arm, her way of diffusing things. "Lacey, why didn't you just come talk to us about this? Why go to all the trouble of getting on the city council's agenda and making this whole public presentation?"

My sister takes a few seconds to think on this. "Because, I think . . ." She looks at my parents, who are both quietly waiting for an explanation. Because seriously, what was she thinking?

"I think I needed to show you that I'm not a total screwup," she says.

Our parents start to protest with encouraging words contradicting that thought, but she silences them with an upheld hand.

"I know I jump around a lot. I know my life choices up until this point haven't been the most mainstream." Lacey glances at me, then back to Mom and Dad. "Let's face it, I ride around the country in a van. It's not something you love bragging about to your friends."

My parents shift in their seats, because Lacey is telling them exactly how they feel. And everyone at the table knows it's the truth.

She sits forward a bit. "But what you don't get is that it's not because I don't have any ambition. I do. And I've figured out a way to see the world and make money doing it. It might not be your way, but it works." Her gaze falls to her folded hands on the table, and I can see her trying not to fidget.

A thought hits me. For as many years as I wanted to be out of my parents' spotlight, Lacey has been trying to get into it.

We both dealt with that in different ways. I rebelled, changed my major without telling them, never explained why I didn't want this life. And Lacey, it seems, quietly learned how to plant and harvest and soak up every aspect of the farm. She weeded the plants and learned how to run the shop. She got to know our staff the way our mom always did, so they looked at her like a friend.

And when none of that caught our dad's eye, she left. Went on the road. Made her own way. Carved her own path.

This realization makes me admire the heck out of her, even if I do think living in a van is weird.

I wish I were half as brave as she is. I fell into a job that was supposed to be my dream, and I haven't seriously considered leaving once.

Until now.

"Look, I know I need investors to make a go of this. Yes, I'm your kid, and this could be just a handoff, but that's not fair to you. You've worked too hard and too long to not reap the benefits of what you've put into Pine Creek. I know what the farm is worth, and I'm putting my own money into this."

She looks right at our dad. "I'm serious about this."

And to our mom, "And now that my presentation is done, I'm going to take the idea to social media and see what happens. I don't have a lot of friends, but I have a lot of followers. Someone could be a gazillionaire and want to invest. We have no idea."

"That sounds dangerous," Mom says. "What if it's drug money?"

Lacey rolls her eyes, and I smirk at her. It's such a Mom thing to say.

"We do have a problem, though," my dad says.

I grit my teeth. "Travis."

"Yep. We signed a contract with him. He's got someone coming out to look at the property next week," Dad says. "And he said the buyer isn't going to wait around."

Lacey's gaze drops. She's begging them to believe in her, but they're understandably cautious. "Let me try. Let me at least try." She's so earnest in her pleading, even I'm moved.

"Of course. Of course, we'll let you try," Mom says. "And let us look it over on our end." She looks at my dad. "We need to talk through our options."

Lacey concedes. What choice does she have, really? There is so much to consider here.

The waitress returns with our pizza, something I'm pretty sure none of us wants anymore, and after she sets it down she scans the table and smiles. "Y'all are the tree farm people, right?"

"We are," Mom says. "Pine Creek."

The waitress smiles. "I read about you guys in the paper. 'The Last, Best Christmas.'" She says this wistfully, the way Olive said it when Clark interviewed her. He'd liked her tagline so much he'd used it for the title of his article. "My husband and I bring our kids every year. We just love it." She smiles. "Some of our favorite Christmas memories were made there."

"It's a pretty special place," Mom says.

She smiles. "I hope whoever buys it keeps all of your traditions."

Dad looks at me, and I raise my eyebrows and shrug.

"Enjoy your pizza." She walks off, leaving us sitting there, trying to mentally navigate everything that's happened in the last hour.

And all I can think about is Olive.

CHAPTER 33

OLIVE

*S*aturday. It's here. And I slept through my alarm.

It's the day of the market, and I'm rushing around, trying to get out the door, late for work for the first time since I started at Pine Creek.

Also, for the first time, I don't want to go.

Yesterday, I stayed so busy I managed to avoid any uncomfortable run-ins with Liam, but I hated every second of it. I wasn't purposely avoiding him, but there was so much to do to get ready for the market. I should've found the time because while the market is important to me, not knowing where things stand with Liam is more important, and that's what kept me up all night.

We could just call it good and go our separate ways. We probably should. He's leaving. I'm staying. And it's not like he wasn't up front about it. I just didn't think he would blame me for trying to help. I could be offended enough to let that ruin what we have. Had.

Did we have something long enough to lose it?

Doesn't matter. I'm not going to do that. It's juvenile, and I'm not in the habit of ending relationships, even new ones without labels, because I got my feelings hurt.

But I am going to give him a piece of my mind.

Because I did get my feelings hurt.

I sigh. I just want things to go back to the way they were. I don't like being at odds with Liam. And I already miss kissing him.

As I pull in and park, the wave of excitement knocks the apprehension right out of me. I look around and see dozens of vendors arriving—trucks pulling trailers of everything needed to set up their booths—and I take a second to marvel at the variety of makers and small business owners who agreed to jump in.

One last, best market before Christmas.

Homemade jams and jellies, dog treats, tea and coffee, handcrafted candles, homemade sourdough bread, all kinds of baked goods—it's a good mix, and I'm proud of it.

And not just food, either. Charming jewelry and necklaces, carved wood art, handcrafted charcuterie boards, turned vases . . . the variety is amazing.

Already, the market has made a significant profit, on the cost of the booth fees from the vendors alone. That doesn't include the money that will be collected at the door, or the revenue the shop and café and activities will bring in.

This idea was a good one. It worked.

People are coming, and people coming to the farm is a good thing.

Sitting in that meeting Thursday night, listening to Lacey talk through so many of the ideas we'd come up with, I felt like I was a part of something amazing. I felt like what I contributed to her plans was notable. I felt valued.

I wonder if her presentation made the impression we were hoping for. On the town leaders. On her parents. I left too quickly to get a read on the response beyond how Liam felt about it.

A knot forms in my stomach at the thought. What if Liam was right? What if all I'd done was give Lacey false hope? What if my excitement was only delaying the inevitable?

I shake the thoughts away and get out of the car, grab my bag, and rush off toward the main barn which will serve as our headquarters for the day. I walk in and find Lacey standing behind the counter.

When she sees me, relief washes over her. "Thank God. I didn't see you at all yesterday. Were you here? Was it your migraine? How's your head?"

"Oh, I'm fine." *White lies are still lies*, I think. Something my grandma used to say. But I can't tell Lacey the humiliating truth that I ran home because her brother hurt my feelings and spent all day yesterday avoiding all signs of human life.

Act like a grown-up, Olive.

"Okay, here's your vendor packet and swag bag." Lacey hands me a small gift bag and a large white envelope identical to the ones I've been putting together all week. Inside the bag, there's a Pine Creek keychain, a handwritten note thanking vendors for being a part of our Christmas Market, information on the other vendors, a coupon for twenty percent off lunch at the café, a voucher for an exclusive Pine Creek candle, two Christmas postcards from my stash, and a site map I designed and printed when we finalized the vendors.

"*My* vendor packet? I don't need one, I have the map memorized, and I know where all the vendors are going."

She taps the name on the packet.

It reads *Wit and Whimsy*.

I pull the map out and look at it, noticing that someone has also written *Wit and Whimsy* in a little square at the end of the row of vendors.

"What did you do?" I look up and find her smiling.

"It's time you get back on the horse, Olive," Lacey says. "So, Phoebe and I decided to give you a little push."

My embarrassment and fear kick into overdrive. "Lacey! I appreciate the thought, but I have *way* too much to do. I can't work a booth. Plus, my art. It's way out of date, and I don't know if people are going to like it—if it's what was there before. And the booth, I didn't set one up—my stuff is all stashed in my garage."

She gives me a comical grimace, reaches into her pocket, and pulls out my garage key. "You should really keep track of who has your key if you don't want anyone to go inside."

"Oh my gosh." She pocketed it the day she and Phoebe were over at my house. Phoebe was right. Lacey is a sneaky genius.

"Don't worry," she says, reassuringly. "We've got it. Got everything set up early this morning so it'd be ready to go when you got here. And Phoebe and your mom are manning it, so you don't have to."

I play that whole explanation back in my mind. I start to protest, but can't.

It's different from before. Now I have people in my corner, lifting me up, filling in the gaps, and helping me succeed.

I swallow around the lump at the back of my throat. "I don't know what to say."

"Say you're excited about today!" She's beaming.

"Okay! I am excited!" I match her enthusiasm. "Wait. You seem happy," I say. "Does that mean you got a good response from the meeting?"

The smile falters, and she scrunches her face and shakes her head. "Unfortunately, no. Lots of people are excited about it, but no one has officially come forward to invest, so I guess now we just wait."

I squeeze her arm. "Okay, so we wait. I'm not giving up hope yet." The words *false hope* echo in my mind.

Lacey straightens and puts on a brave face. "Either way, I tried, right? I would've kicked myself if I hadn't, so . . ."

"So?"

She shrugs sadly. "So, I guess you were right. This is actually the last, best Christmas at Pine Creek."

My brain stumbles over the words. I hadn't said last, best Christmas thinking it would actually be true. Somehow, I deluded myself into believing that we'd sort it out. That someone would change their mind. That we wouldn't lose Pine Creek.

In just a few short weeks, this place has come to mean even more to me than it did before . . . and what? I'm just supposed to let it go?

My mind adds, *Like Liam?*

Someone walks up to the counter, pulling Lacey's attention. "Sorry, Olive, I've got to get this. You good?"

I nod.

Her smile is back, and I have a very good feeling she's learned to compartmentalize her feelings a lot better than I have. "The reindeer are here! Did you see them yet?"

I shake my head. The reindeer had been Lacey's idea. She heard about a reindeer farm a couple of hours away and got the owners to agree to bring some of the herd to our market. Manny and his crew set up their pens earlier in the week.

I admit, I'm excited to see them. Real reindeer? My eight-year-old self would be giddy.

I hold up the white envelope. "Hey. Thank you for this."

She nods and smiles. "Go see your booth. It's fabulous!"

I walk out into the chaos of pre-market set-up, and an ache of nostalgia washes over me. Showing at markets was always exhausting, but always fun. I loved meeting other makers, talking about art, and chatting with customers. It became a little community, and as I wave to a few familiar faces, I realize I've missed it.

When my shop failed, I took every single thing I love and put it in a box. I'm starting to see that a critical piece of who I am has been missing—and the people who care about me are the ones who are gently, though not subtly, pointing it out.

I make my way up the hill toward Christmas Tree Row. I hear the familiar chatter of voices before I see the booths and the people and the excitement, but the second they come into view, I stop and watch. I don't know what's going to happen with the farm, but I do know that I've learned so much being here. And that will never feel wasted.

"Olive! It's so good to see you!" Sally from The Honey Hut waves me over. She looks exactly the way I remember her. "How've you been?"

"Really good!" I say, and I realize I mean it.

We catch up for a few minutes when Alicia, the Sourdough Goddess, spots me and rushes into Sally's booth. "I was so happy to get your email, Olive! It's like the whole gang's back together. Wes has got some new artwork over there you've got to see. And Annika has a whole display of vintage Christmas decor."

"And then there's your booth," Sally says, knowingly. "It's beautiful."

I grin in appreciation. "I haven't even seen it yet! I had nothing to do with that, my friend set it up for me. I found out about it this morning."

"Oh, that was sweet of him," Alicia says.

"No, my friend Phoebe," I say.

Alicia frowns. "I didn't see a woman, but there's been a guy over there working on it since I got here."

"A guy? Like my dad?" I ask.

"If your dad is a hot guy about the same age as you, then I guess that could've been him." She laughs. "He hauled in bins and hung your cute banner and unloaded all those sweet things you always had on display, but all the new stuff is next level! Was it your idea?"

"The new stuff?"

"Oh, shoot—" she glances at something in the distance— "I have to run, but let's catch up later!"

A hot guy about my age? I start to feel antsy, suddenly anxious to get over to my booth.

I look at Sally, who hands me a small jar of her famous local honey. It's like nectar for gods, it's so amazing. "My bees made this just for you."

"Thank you, Sally."

She smiles. "Happy Christmas, Olive."

I walk off, greeting and waving to so many old friends, wondering how I could've let go of this wonderful community.

I've judged myself and my failure so harshly, and I falsely assumed everyone else did the same.

That was a mistake. These people don't care that I no longer have a storefront or that I have a pile of debt to work off. They're just happy to be here, to see me here.

I pick up the pace, walking toward the end of Christmas Tree Row, right at the spot where customers will enter the market, because I know from the map that's where Lacey put my booth.

Alicia's comments have lit a fire under me, and I'm anxious to see if the "hot guy" is still there, but when I reach the booth, it's only my mom and Phoebe inside.

And the booth. Wow.

It looks like a cottage, with a false front that mimics the exterior of a house—white planked siding with shutters and windows on either side of a wide opening. On the siding, there are doodles and quotes from my art (did someone trace them?) and above the door hangs the old *Wit and Whimsy* sign from my garage. Inside, shelves that look like built-ins perfectly display my cards and 4x6 notes, and at the center, there's a large wood table that Phoebe and my mom are standing behind, both engrossed in arranging my artwork.

I've done these markets before. I know what it takes to set up a booth, and this clearly took a lot of planning and a *lot* of work.

"Hey," I say to get their attention.

They look up, wearing matching worried expressions, undoubtedly waiting for my reaction to the surprise. My mom seems to be holding her breath.

When my face lights up with a bright smile, they both smile back. "You guys!" I shout at them.

Phoebe grins. "I told you that you needed a booth out here."

"Yeah, but I didn't think you'd just go ahead and make it happen!" I walk over and hug her, then hug my mom. "This is absolutely stunning. She roped you into this too?"

Mom squeezes me. "I'd do anything to see you making art again." She smiles. "The world needs the joy you put in it."

If anyone has a right to think my art is frivolous and expensive, it's my parents, the ones who co-signed on my loan and then gave me a hefty sum when things started to go south at the store. My parents aren't wealthy people, so I know it was a sacrifice. Sometimes thinking about that keeps me up at night.

To think that my mom still sees the value in my art in spite of that heals a part of the wound my failure forged. I can't process it without tearing up.

"If you're okay for a minute, I'm going to go get some coffee," Mom says. "Dottie's Coffee Truck is parked down the hill." She holds up her phone. "Text me your orders!"

I turn back to Phoebe, shaking my head. "This is . . . I can't even. It's amazing."

"Well, we had help," Phoebe says.

Help. There's that word again, doing everything it can to remind me that success isn't found alone.

My eyes meet hers, and understanding passes between us.

"He did everything. Most of it before we even got here. I don't think he slept at all last night." Phoebe points to the beautiful display in the back corner. "Even set all that up."

I go still, looking over the display. "There's no way."

"I mean, I had to, you know, make a few adjustments," she says. "But yeah. He picked up everything this morning before I was even out of bed. Lacey asked if he could just get everything in here so all we had to do was make it pretty, but he did a lot more than that."

"When did he have time to make the frame? He must've been working on it for days." I press my lips together and look around the booth. At the back, the handmade wreath we made together is hanging on the makeshift wall.

I move closer to get a better look.

Behind the wreath, sketched on the faux interior cottage wall is something that most people would totally miss. And even if they saw it, they wouldn't know what it means.

There, tucked away behind the wreath, is a drawing of a little boy in a propeller hat. It's like a signature on a love note, sent in the kindest, most selfless way.

My heart swells.

"Any idea where he is now?"

Phoebe shakes her head.

The sound of a loud bell draws our attention to the front gate where Jo is standing with a bullhorn. "Attention vendors, we are opening the gate in two minutes! Everyone get your game faces on!"

"You go, do what you need to do," Phoebe says.

"You sure?" I ask, feeling guilty for leaving her.

"Yes, we've got this," she says, waving a hand. "You're not allowed to come back until the end of the day!" She beams at me, then takes her red lipstick from her pocket and reapplies it.

"You are *not* putting out vibes at a Christmas Market," I say.

"The only men who come to these things come because their wives or girlfriends force them."

"Seth with the homemade dog bones is here." She pumps her eyebrows. "And that guy who makes soap."

I lift my hand in a wave but make a point of rolling my eyes. "You're insane."

Jo gets on the bullhorn and calls out, "Gates are officially open! Have fun, everybody!"

I turn to go but stop short, because a few yards away, moving straight through the row of vendors, is something that I never expected to see—two very large reindeer with equally large antlers. The bells on their collars jingle as they happily trot in my direction.

They make a sharp turn, most likely spooked by the people, and head into the trees.

Like everyone in the immediate vicinity, I just stare.

Then a man in overalls runs in and wildly shouts, "My reindeer are loose!"

I glance back at Phoebe, whose eyes are wide.

At the same time, a crowd of people rush through the open gate.

Liam appears in the clearing, along with two teenagers who help wrap and load trees on the weekends.

Our eyes meet, and my mind floods with all a million things I want to say, but when I open my mouth, I say the only thing that makes sense.

"The reindeer are loose!"

CHAPTER 34

OLIVE

"Which way?" Liam calls out, and I point in the direction the reindeer ran.

Christmas Tree Row is immediately crowded, something I'm equal parts thrilled about and frustrated by. If we could've had ten extra minutes, we might've been able to take care of this issue before we let people in.

"You guys go up that way." Liam tells the teenagers, pointing in the direction of the trees behind the row of booths. "There's a taller fence that way, maybe we can corner them there. I'll see if I can head them off on the other end!"

The kids start up the hill, and I absently think they are both going to be completely useless in helping corral these reindeer.

They're massive. Like discount moose.

Liam tosses a quick glance in my direction, then turns to go.

"Wait!" I call after him. "I'm coming with you!"

"Are you nuts? These things could knock over a car!"

I don't listen and jog up next to him. He starts to protest again, and I shoot him a look.

He shakes his head, losing the silent argument, and we race into the trees toward the cut-your-own lots. Liam stops abruptly, and I see a downed tree in our path along with a few others splayed to the side. He turns toward me and holds out his hand to help me over it. I stop and look at it, then at him. He doesn't say a word, yet the look on his face communicates plenty.

I slip my hand in his and gingerly step over the fallen tree, then drop his hand and pick up the pace again. In the distance, I see one of the reindeer. The way it runs, it almost looks like it's just happy to be out of its pen and taking its human friends on a little jaunt.

"There!" I point in the direction of the animal, and we follow it.

"Look, Olive," Liam says, still walking fast. "Can we talk?"

"We're catching reindeer."

"I know, but—" He stops moving, grabs my hand, and turns me to face him, then promptly stops talking.

Classic Liam.

"What you said—" I snap my jaw shut, then force myself to go on. "I'm going to make this quick because there are more important things happening right now."

"Yeah."

"What you said really sucked."

"I know."

"It hurt my feelings."

"I know."

"It made me want to throw darts at your picture."

"You have a picture?" He frowns.

"No. But I could find one," I say, chin out, trying to make my point.

"Okay . . ." he says.

My shoulders drop, and he quirks a brow, a silent truce passing between us. It's that moment in an argument where you sense that everything will be okay.

"You're not a cruel person, Liam," I say. "But that was a cruel thing to say."

He takes me by the arms and levels my gaze. "It was. And I'm sorry. But there's a lot going on here that you don't understand."

A huge *crrraaack* followed by a *crash* come from our left, fifty yards away, and we both snap our heads in that direction.

We start moving that way, quickly.

I'm slightly out of breath, but we still need to talk. "Okay, so tell me."

He turns and frowns at me, not slowing down. "Now? You want to do this now?"

Our boots crunch sticks and snow and dead leaves, and there's a guttural *hoot* mixed with a grunt up ahead.

"Yes. We're chasing animals that outweigh us by a few hundred pounds, in a tree farm that's most likely closing, but yeah. Now."

He stops abruptly and holds up a hand, forcing me to stop as well. He silently points up ahead, and I see the head of one of the reindeer, shaking from side to side, setting off the bells.

He brings a finger to his lips, letting me know to keep quiet. He whispers, "I don't like talking, you know that."

"Well, get over it," I whisper-shout back at him.

We crouch and creep a bit closer.

"Fine," he whispers. "What do you want to know?"

We hunker down near a row of trees, and I take him by the shoulders, turning him toward me.

"I want to know everything," I say. "I want to know about your job and your game design and your life and your thoughts and your feelings. I want to know what happened that changed your impression of this place that you used to love so much, and I want to know why you won't fight to keep it." My shoulders drop like someone just unplugged a cork and let the air out. "I want you to feel like you can talk to me."

He shakes his head and blows out a hot breath, steamy in the cold air. "You want to know the truth?" He looks at me. "You want to know about my job and about this place and my life?"

"Yes."

He inhales slowly. "It sucks. All of it."

I go still. I forget the market and the reindeer. I forget everything except this moment right here. This moment feels critical.

He sits on the ground, brushing the pine needles off his jeans, then takes his hat off and rubs his hair.

"I made a game. In college. I didn't think it was going to be anything, I just did it for fun. But it turned out to be really, *really* good. I knew it was. I was sure of it. I felt like I was going to be one of those guys who did the whole thing himself.

"And along came Arcadia. I know you don't know about them, but when it comes to mobile gaming, they're it. They're huge. They have some of the biggest games out there, and people like me would sell their left kidney just to be an intern there.

"They contacted me. I don't know how they heard about it, but they wanted my game. That was more than I could've ever dreamed. They would distribute it, and in return, they'd give me some money and set me up with a job—no matter what. I have job security for the next ten years, developing with them."

My eyes go wide.

"The payout covered all of my student loans, and that game, *Castle Crusade*—" He looks away and laughs, sardonically— "Sounds so stupid to say it out loud. I mean, it's a game."

I frown. "It's not stupid."

He looks back at me. "I was a kid and didn't understand what I was signing."

I wrap my arms around my knees, listening.

"I gave away all ownership and copyright to the game. I don't own it. It's no longer mine."

"Oh my gosh." I want to reach for him, but I hold back. His frown deepens.

"Yeah. It gets better. There was also a clause in my contract that said they also have the exclusive rights to all merchandise. I don't get a dime for T-shirts or Funko Pops or the deal with LEGO. And it's crappy, but they do have the rights to develop any sequels to *Castle Crusade*, whether I'm working on it or not."

I feel horrible for him right now. I had no idea. I'm guessing no one does.

"A sequel's in development. It's my idea. My characters. My storyline. And I'm not working on it." His pained eyes meet mine.

"They can't do that," I say, knowing full well that I have nothing but emotion to back up that claim.

"Turns out they can," he says. "They can't fire me, but they said they needed me on a different game. Didn't ask what I wanted—just moved me."

"Oh, Liam," I say on an exhale.

"Yeah, so, you're not the only one who knows a little something about failing," he says.

I try to think of something, anything I can do or say that will help, but I come up empty.

"I hate my job, Olive," he admits. "I haven't said that out loud to anyone, not even to myself." He goes quiet for a few seconds before going on. "I traded *Castle Crusade* for this job, and I hate it." He shakes his head. "And other people would kill for it. Do you know how hard it is to get a job at Arcadia? At any big video game company?"

The question feels rhetorical, so I don't respond.

"It would be crazy to give that up." He shakes his head.

"Not if you hate it," I say. "If you hate it, it would be crazy not to."

"It's the dream," he says. "My dream come true—" He laughs, unamused— "and I hate it. I don't want it anymore."

I press my lips together. I don't want to be that person who takes someone else's problem and relates it back to myself, but if anyone understands this—it's me. Because my dream blew up in my face. And I'm still paying for it. Literally.

But when our eyes meet, I see that he already knows that, even without me saying a word.

"And the farm?" I ask. "What happened?"

He looks out in the distance. "It's dumb."

"Feelings aren't dumb."

"I don't like feelings," he says.

"This is shocking," I say, feigning surprise.

"The move." He shakes his head so slightly I almost miss it. "It took me away from everything I loved. From my baseball team and my house and my school and my friends—" he looks at me— "and you." He shakes his head. "My dad assumed this would be my future, and he never let up. Everything I did from the time I was thirteen was run through the filter of what the farm needed from me. I was expected to be here, to do this, to take up the family business. I missed out on internships. I missed out on time with my friends. I didn't do anything except work here." He sighs. "I should've been grateful, but I wasn't. I resented it. I don't like having my future dictated to me. Selfish, right?"

"No." I shake my head. "I understand wanting to choose your own life. I mean, you're not Prince William."

He laughs. "Thankfully."

"But aren't they telling you what to do at Arcadia?" I ask carefully. "Isn't your future still being dictated by somebody else?"

He sighs, and it's obvious he hasn't made that connection until now.

"Nobody's telling you what to do about the farm now." I reach for his hand. "This place, it *is* special. It's magical. But our memories don't change even if it goes away. So if they decide to let it go, then aren't we the luckiest to have had such a charmed childhood?"

He nods.

"Maybe . . ." I look away.

"What?"

"Maybe I don't want to let go of Pine Creek because it means letting go of you," I say. "How's that for selfish?" I laugh to myself. "And Lacey's plan, you're right, it was crazy, and I got her hopes up, but—I got my hopes up too. I know it was dumb, but—"

Before I can finish, I feel something wet drip on my cheek.

We both look up, and right over our heads is the oversized, drooling face of a reindeer.

I had forgotten all about it.

I immediately tense up, having an animal this huge this close to me, but it's just calmly chewing, softly grunting, and acting like all of this is completely normal. Almost like it wants in on the conversation.

Liam puts a hand on my knee, holds the other one up in warning, then gently reaches up and takes a hold of the leather strap hanging from the reindeer's bridle.

We slowly stand. The reindeer shakes his head back and forth, standing near us, calmly, like a pet.

I reach out and put a hand on its head, in the space between its enormous antlers, and give it a scratch. It leans into me, liking it, pushing me slightly.

I look at Liam, and he looks back at me and shrugs. "I guess we caught the reindeer."

We head back toward the lot where Manny built the pen, leading the reindeer by the strap, who is more than content to follow.

Maybe, like us, he's had enough of an adventure for the day . . . and it's not even ten in the morning.

"I shouldn't have said what I said," Liam says as we trudge through the rows of trees. "As soon as I said it, I wanted to take it back."

I meet his eyes. "It's okay. I forgive you."

"Good."

"And I'm sorry I didn't tell you about Lacey's plan sooner," I say. "Actually, I'm not sorry about that. She asked me not to, and I didn't want to betray her trust."

He nods. "I get it."

"It doesn't matter anyway," I say. "It doesn't sound like the council wants the city involved, so if she can't find private investors, the plan dies."

He stops, and the reindeer stops behind him. With his free hand, he takes my gloved hand and kisses it. "Can we not fight again?"

The big animal snuffs a breath behind us.

I move closer and press my body against his, wrapping my arms around his back. "If we never fight again, then we never get to make up."

His smile is wicked as he goes in for a kiss, and I surrender to it, because I missed it—and I missed him. Because he said something thoughtless and apologized and I want to put it behind us, not hold onto it and let it ruin something good or wreck me inside.

Mid-kiss he's yanked away from me because he still has his hand in the strap attached to a four-hundred-pound animal, that seems to be getting bored.

He laughs as the reindeer yanks again. "Okay, okay, fine," he says to the reindeer, "I got it. We'll go, it's weird kissing in front of you, anyway."

I smile as we start walking again.

"I didn't have 'catch a loose reindeer' on my to-do list today," I say.

"It's always an adventure with you." He gives the reindeer a tug. "Let's get this guy back."

We fall into step next to each other, tracing our path back

the way we came. Liam takes my free hand in his. "What are you thinking about?"

"You set up my booth," I say. "Thank you."

He nods, then looks at me. "You shouldn't be making coffee. You should be making art."

I glance at him. "I'm starting to think that just because something doesn't go the way you want it to, if you learn from it, it's not really a failure."

"And what if something doesn't go the way you want it to, and you're just not sure you want it anymore?" he asks.

"Also not a failure," I say with a shrug. "Life moves us at the speed its supposed to."

"Do you really believe that?" he asks.

I squeeze his hand. "I really do."

CHAPTER 35

LIAM

I like being here.

I know it's partly because no one told me I had to be. I'm choosing it.

The other part is Olive.

I actually enjoy helping out where I can. I don't even mind the small talk. But I love watching Olive in her element.

Once the reindeer were apprehended, of course.

Knowing Olive had been responsible for pretty much every aspect of the market left me feeling proud and impressed. She had crews of volunteers positioned exactly where help was needed. She had signs hung exactly where people could get confused. She'd rented oversized outdoor heaters and created warming stations, which were critical to the overall enjoyment of the day.

And to hear my mom tell it, she'd made Pine Creek a lot of money.

I spent most of my time helping people get things from booths to vehicles and back, but I made a point to check in with Olive several times throughout the day. I also checked on her booth, and by the end of the afternoon, almost everything I'd set up this morning had sold.

People love her artwork. There was hardly anyone without a *Wit & Whimsy* tote bag on their arm.

Maybe she just got in over her head in that store. Knowing the size of her heart, she most likely had a large, overpaid staff. Hopefully, this whole experience will give her a push to try again.

The thought taunts me. I know she's not the only one who needs to try again.

I think about the new game idea. I think about showing it to Aaron. I think about how much I don't want his input on it. At all. Then I think that only crazy people walk away from opportunities like working for Arcadia.

After Christmas Tree Row has been returned to its natural, less exciting state, I find Olive near the area where her booth had been. A strange sort of nostalgia creeps over me, like the kind you get after leaving the high school gym after Homecoming. A surreal mix of coming off an amazing experience mixed with reconciling the fact that it's over, and you can't repeat it.

For a fleeting moment, I imagine a future here. With her.

I imagine her market becoming an annual event, and her passion for Pine Creek filtering through to everyone who visits. I imagine stealing kisses among the trees and sneaking off behind the barn. I imagine falling asleep with her and waking up with her.

I imagine all the moments that make a life worth living.

Not a life worth just existing.

"Hey!"

I shake away the thoughts and find Olive watching me. "You good?"

"I'm great," I say honestly. "How'd you do?"

"The market? It was bonkers," she says. "I think your mom is really happy. Everything sort of went off without a hitch." She smiles. "Except for the reindeer."

"And this?" I motion toward what's left of her inventory, which isn't much.

"Oh, my booth?" She grins.

"Yeah."

"My booth that you made for me?" She says it with a sly grin.

I roll my eyes, but love her goofy side.

"It went really well." Her lips quirk, like she's holding in a smile. "Phoebe even got a business card from a licensing agent. She was passing through to visit a friend who lives in Loveland, and . . . she's interested in representing my work."

"Wait. Seriously?"

She nods, still holding back a grin even though I know she wants to let it loose.

"That's amazing, Liv," I say. "Congratulations."

"It's not a done deal or anything, but . . . it's bizarre, right?"

I shake my head. "Not really."

She tosses me a look, but her face finally lights up into a bright smile. "It *is* though. I quit on all of this—I just—"

I move toward her and take her in my arms. There are still people milling around, but I don't care. I want to be close to her.

She steps into my hug and rests her cheek on my chest. "I'm so thankful. Like I'm getting a second chance to do it right."

Me too, I think.

She looks up at me, arms wrapped around my waist. "Hey, the day I had to move all my stuff out of the store, this moving truck showed up, like, out of nowhere. There were two guys who basically took over and handled getting everything packed up and then unloaded it into my garage."

I pull back and meet her eyes. "Oh, yeah?"

"Yeah. I was kind of a mess that day, and I don't think I would've gotten it done without them."

My hands are on her arms, her eyes searching mine. I'm trying not to look caught, because I know where this is going.

"Phoebe said you're the one who sent them."

My frown is a little too obvious. "Why'd she say that?"

"She saw your name on the invoice." She pauses, obviously waiting for me to react. When I don't, she softens. "I always assumed it was my parents."

I don't know what to say. I had never wanted her to find this out.

"You and I hadn't talked in years," she goes on. "Why would you do that for me?"

I shrug. "I had to do something."

"You didn't."

"I wanted to," I tell her. "And I couldn't be here to do it myself, so I did the only thing I could think to do." I drop my hands to my sides. "It wasn't a big deal."

"It *was* a big deal," she says. "A huge deal. Losing the store was such a gut-punch." She takes a step toward me. "That was my lowest point, and you were there. I didn't know it, but you were." She pauses, then narrows her eyes. "How did you even find out?"

"Small town," I say. "My mom doesn't like silence on the other end of the phone, remember?"

"So, you've really just been a big softie this whole time."

"The *whole* time? No."

At that, she smiles, and I want to bottle the way it makes me feel and hand it out on the streets. The world would be such a happier place with a dose of Olive.

My life would be happier too. It *is* happier.

"I'm going to kiss you now," she says.

I quirk a brow. "Here?"

"Yep."

"There are people around."

"Don't care."

"Okay."

"It's going to blow your mind." She smirks.

"Prove it."

Her eyes dart around. There are Pine Creek employees and vendors still packing things up. I'm certain she'll lose her nerve, or at least lead me into the woods or something. But then, she grabs two fistfuls of my coat and pulls me to her, stopping for a brief moment to make eye contact before kissing the heck out of me.

And she's right—it blows my mind.

It's something I'll never get tired of, her lips on mine, her body pressed up against me, my hands tangled in her hair, hers pressed against my back.

I've fallen for her. And I'm pretty sure these feelings are going to make the day I leave one of the worst days of my life.

CHAPTER 36

OLIVE

I'm having the best dream. It's the kind of dream where I know it's a dream, but I don't want to wake up. I'm floating on a raft in a big pool, no people in sight, the sunlight pouring down on my face, bathing me in the most glorious, warm glow.

"Olive?"

The smell of pancakes and bacon pulls me from sleep, the feeling of warmth lingering because of the sun hitting my face from the window.

I slowly crack open my eyes to find my bedroom door open and Liam walking in, carrying a tray and looking like something straight out of that dream.

Only he's wearing a shirt.

I frown, and then sit up. "How did you get in here?"

"Side door," he says. "You should really lock that."

My frown deepens. I replay the events of the night before in my mind. Liam helped me unload everything from my booth and pack it back into the garage. It was late, and I was freezing after being outside most of the day, so we came inside and he made a fire. I popped popcorn, and put on my pajamas, and then fell asleep watching *Arthur Christmas*, one of my all-time favorites.

He woke me before he left, and I vaguely remember him telling me he was leaving, but I have no memory of much else. I was totally crashed out from the market.

I pick up my phone and see that it's not even eight yet. "What are you doing up so early? You didn't leave 'til after one." I scoot over and he sits on the edge of my bed.

"The farm has this way of waking people up at dawn," he says. "I guess I'm used to it already. Plus, I wanted to get here before you ate."

He shifts the tray from his lap to mine as I sit up and look at the spread he made for me—pancakes, bacon, coffee, juice, eggs, and a little carafe of maple syrup.

"You made all this?" I look at him. "In my kitchen?" I'm shocked he could even find enough pans.

He turns shy. "I thought you might need a rest day after the market, but I wanted to see you."

I smile. "You're not sick of me yet?"

He shakes his head. "Not even a little."

I smile and pick up the coffee cup and take a drink, letting out a little sigh of appreciation as I realize— "You stopped by The Beanery."

"Yep."

"White chocolate mocha?"

"The kid behind the counter said it's your favorite," he says. "He also wanted to know exactly what my intentions toward you are."

"Jackson." I take a slow, warm sip and grin. "He has a crush on me."

"I don't want you working there anymore." He watches me for a second, then smiles.

The sight of it ignites something inside me, and I have to remind myself not to get used to this.

"What do you want to do today?" he asks.

"Hmmm . . ." I take a huge bite of the pancake, then with my mouth full, I say, "Umm . . . I think I want to hurkle durkle."

His eyebrows shoot up, and he lets out a laugh. "You're just making up words now?"

I take a bite of the bacon and close my eyes, letting out a hum of appreciation. "This is so good." I open my eyes and take another big bite of pancakes. "I promise it's a thing."

He stares.

"You have to go home," I say.

"Oh." He looks a little shocked. "Okay, guess I'll just leave then." He starts to move.

"No!" I'm laughing, but my mouth is full, so I hurry and swallow the food so I can say, "You just can't hurkle durkle in work boots."

"You want me to go home and change my boots?"

"No, go home and get pajamas," I say. "Then, we just, you know, hurkle durkle."

"You keep saying that word like it means something."

"It does."

"I don't own pajamas," he says.

I frown. "Who doesn't own pajamas?"

"Guys don't."

"Then what do you sleep in?"

He just makes a face.

I can't do a thing to stop my brain from filling in the blanks. It alerts every nerve in my body.

He grins. "You're picturing me in my underwear right now, aren't you?"

I totally am.

"No."

His smile doesn't falter, making it clear he knows I'm lying. Mercifully, he doesn't tease me about it, even though I'm struggling to erase the image from my mind.

"I have sweatpants, but you're going to have to explain."

"Explain a hurkle durkle day?" I ask.

He raises his eyebrows by way of a response.

"It's an old Scottish term," I say. "It's like—" I shift around, looking for the right words— "like lounging around when the rest of the world is out there doing things. Staying under covers way longer than you should."

"So, like a rest day," he says, obviously not catching the vision.

"Well, yeah, if we were boring people." I shovel another bite into my mouth. "Oh my heck, this is so good."

"Okay," he says. "So, you want to lay around, and I need different clothes to do that."

I shake my head. "I want to hurkle durkle—" I raise my eyebrows. "It's not the same thing." I chew my bite. After I've swallowed it, I say, "You've gotta say it."

"I'm not saying that."

"Then you don't get to come back." I grin.

He stands. "You are so weird."

He kisses me before he leaves, and I grin while his lips are still on mine. "You like weird."

He pulls back and looks at me, shaking his head. "No, I don't."

He stands to leave, and I call after him, "Yes, you do!"

Walking out of my bedroom, he calls back, "I'm calling the police to have you committed."

Whatever, I think. *He loves it.*

While he's gone, I shower, brush my teeth, and put deodorant on because, while I might want to hurkle durkle, I don't want to stink.

When he returns, he's appropriately dressed in black joggers and a comfy black Nike sweatshirt that I'd like to steal. I take a second to appreciate how good he makes loungewear look. I'm wearing pink and red flannel Christmas pajama pants with a

This is my Christmas movie watching sweatshirt hoodie and big, fuzzy slippers.

We spend the entire day at my house, and we find ways to do nothing. We watch a movie under my big, cozy fleece blanket. We bake and decorate sugar cookies. We come up with a new character for Liam's game—a dog in a helicopter. We make an easy lunch of sandwiches and chips and watch *Die Hard*. We play *Clue,* then take a nap. I beat him at gin rummy, and he beats me at chess.

It's the most natural, normal, wonderful way to spend a day.

And by the time the night ends, there is one thing I know for certain: I am completely, wholly, and one-hundred-percent in love with Liam Fisher.

Even if it's only for a few more days.

CHAPTER 37

LIAM

*T*ime has a certain inevitability about it.

Christmastime doubly so.

Excitement builds and there are so many events to attend, then they happen and then they're over.

Every year.

I'm sitting on the porch a few days later, bundled up in my winter coat under a big blanket, drinking coffee.

It's too cold to be out here, but I can't seem to quiet my mind inside.

In a few days, we'll have our last big event. The Christmas Eve Candlelight Walk.

After that, we'll wind down for the season.

We'll celebrate Christmas, we'll exchange gifts, then we'll close the doors for the last time.

And then I'll go home. Back to reality.

Leaving should make me happy. Four weeks ago, leaving would've.

Today? Today it doesn't make me happy at all.

The door opens, and my dad sits down next to me, also in his coat, also holding a cup of coffee. Our morning ritual.

I'm surprised to realize I'll actually miss it.

"You're up early," he says.

I draw in a breath of cold air, feeling it all the way into my lungs. "Yeah."

"Couldn't sleep?"

I shake my head.

"Me neither."

We sit for a few minutes, watching as the world wakes up around us. The soft, blue, morning hue is only interrupted by the dim light from the Christmas tree in the window and the white twinkle lights strung along the edges of the house.

"You and Olive . . .?" Dad asks.

I smile at the thought of her. "All good."

He nods. "And after you go back?"

I take a drink, the coffee's warmth replacing the chill.

I shrug.

Another nod. "Be a shame to let her go."

I want to be annoyed by the comment. He's stating the obvious, after all. But I can't be, because I think this is just his way of telling me he likes her. That she's good for me. Maybe if I'd learned to read the subtext of what he says a little sooner, our entire relationship would be different.

"I've been thinking," I say, because some things can't remain unsaid.

"Uh-oh," he says. "That can't be good."

I smirk at him.

A bit of silence passes.

"I'm sorry too." I keep my gaze on the trees in front of us, watching as the light from the morning sun finally, finally hits them. "I could've maybe been a little more, you know—communicative."

He lets out a single, hearty laugh and claps a hand on my arm. "The apple doesn't fall far."

"No, it doesn't." I take another drink. It's strange talking to him like this, but I think I could get used to it. "I think I expected you to ask me what I wanted. But I never told you how I felt. That there were other things I wanted to pursue. Instead, I just . . . got mad."

"You were a kid," he says.

"Still," I say. "I'm sorry."

He presses his lips together, thinking, the way I've seen him do so many times before. "It's okay, son." He angles his face in my direction. "Everything worked out the way it was supposed to."

Did it?

I'm not so sure.

A rush of cold air whips across the porch. We should go in—it's too cold to sit out here, watching the morning wake up, but I don't move.

"Do you regret it?" I ask, turning the mug around in my hands.

He glances at me. "Regret what?"

"This—" I motion out in front of us, all the acres of beautiful trees, a whole life built one long, hard, sweaty day at a time. "The farm. The work. Not going after the thing you wanted."

He sucks in a long, slow breath, then shakes his head. "Not for a second." He props his boots up on the porch railing and leans back slightly in the chair. "How can I regret this?"

He doesn't have to explain for me to know what he's talking about. This—the land, the work, the farm, the peace, the joy—that's not a thing to regret.

"I feel like I contributed something valuable to the world, to this community, and to my family," he says. "And this isn't a bad way to spend a life." He glances over. "Your generation is in such a hurry. Everyone is in such a rush. Don't you know that when you die, your inbox is still going to be full?"

I smile. I hadn't thought about it that way.

"When you get a few more years under your belt, you might see a shift in what you think is important."

I already feel that shift. Everything I thought I wanted—even idolized—feels less important now than it used to. The things I used to resent have more value than I thought.

And then, as if he's read my mind, he says, "You never go wrong if you pursue peace, Liam. Peace will never take you down the wrong road."

Peace.

"I haven't had that in a long time," I say quietly.

He nods. "About time you found some, isn't it?"

I hold up my coffee mug to him and he does the same. We nod, and drink at the same time, then laugh a little to ourselves.

"Well, I've got to meet Travis and his buyer." Dad stands. "Do you want to come?"

"Sure."

"One more thing, kid," he says. "If you haven't already, tell that girl how you feel. I know we're not great with flowery words, but straightforward ones will do the trick. Worked on your mom." He starts for the door.

"It's pretty new," I say. "A little early for proclamations."

He barks out a laugh. "New. Like it hasn't been since you were kids."

"That obvious, huh?" I follow him into the kitchen and watch as he rinses out his mug.

"You've been pining after that girl since you were too young for it to be appropriate," he says, chuckling.

The feelings I feel now started when we were young—time has only made them more intense.

Am I actually going to walk away from the woman I've loved my entire life?

I grab a hat and gloves and follow Dad out to his truck. We drive down to the main barn, and I take a moment to appreciate the comfortable silence between us. There's no tension in the air anymore.

It's nice.

"Have you talked to Lacey any more about her ideas?" I ask as we pull into a parking spot in the staff lot.

He shakes his head. "She knows we need to find out what the deal is with this buyer. I know she's still looking for investors too. The plan she came up with is a good one, but finding people willing to invest will be a challenge on a short timeline. If she had another year, no doubt she could do it." He looks at me. "But she's going to be in over her head. She needs someone to shoulder the physical responsibilities of this place, someone to take ownership of it. A co-owner is different than an employee."

I know he's not implying that I'm that person, but that doesn't stop me from thinking it.

Lacey and I have different strengths. Together, along with our employees and Olive, we *could* make a go of this place. Maybe even tackle the expansion in phases and find ways to bring in money year-round.

If that happened, I couldn't keep my job at Arcadia, but I wouldn't have to give up game design all together. I could work on *Whirlybirds* exactly the way Olive said I should—on my own.

My thoughts are interrupted when Travis's Escalade pulls through the gate. We get out of the truck and start walking toward them as he parks. Travis hops out and stands in the parking lot as another man gets out and joins him. He's got dark, slicked back hair, and he's dressed in a suit and shoes that are completely inappropriate for walking around the farm. His coat looks expensive but not warm, and I just stand for a second and shake my head.

Pretty sure I can judge this book by its cover.

It's clear that this guy does not belong here any more than I belong in an opera.

Dad sighs. "This should be fun."

I can tell by his body language that Travis is in sales mode. He turns toward us as we reach them, and plasters on that fake smile. "Morning, Fishers," he says, rubbing his hands together. "How are we this morning?"

"Oh, can't complain," my dad says.

Travis motions toward the man. "This is Warner Sharpe."

My dad extends a hand, and Warner Sharpe shakes it. "Brant Fisher." He looks at me. "This is my son, Liam."

I shake the man's hand, and he barely looks at me. "Quite the business you've got here," he says. "You could be doing so much more with this land."

Travis clears his throat. "Uh, Mr. Sharpe, let's show you around the property."

They start off toward the shop, and Dad glowers in my direction.

"We don't have to be the tour guide," I say, voice low.

"Would you mind showing us around?" Travis calls out, as if on cue. "Show us the best parts of the property."

Warner Sharpe has his phone out, and as he taps around on the screen, I glare at Travis. "You want us to do your job for you?"

He laughs awkwardly. "Of course not. I just think you have a better sense of what someone might be interested in if they were to," he lowers his voice, "you know, fork over the money to buy this place."

I take a few steps toward Warner. "Depends on what that person was interested in doing with the property."

Warner slides his phone into his pocket. "I'm interested in developing the land."

"So, get rid of everything that's here," I say.

"It's the land that's worth the price, not what's on it," he counters.

"Not to us."

Travis's laugh is nervous.

"I get it. You have memories connected to this place," Warner says, looking at me, then at my dad. "I understand the emotional attachment."

I doubt it.

"But my gift is taking places like this and having them actually make money. Turn a profit. Make an impact on the community around it."

I can feel my dad bristle at that last comment.

"It's as simple as that," he continues. "Yeah, it's a little farther out of the way than I thought, but close enough to the city that people looking for some peace and quiet would make the drive on a long weekend or for a week away."

"Vacation homes," Dad says.

"Residential. Investment properties. Long and short term rentals." He turns in a circle. "We already saw the lake at the back end of the property, *huge* selling point. People love a water view with boating and fishing." He nods. "We could do a lot with a plot of land this big."

"But you'll have to bulldoze everything that's here," Dad says.

He looks at my dad like it's obvious. "Well, yeah. No sense in keeping something that only operates a minimum of three months out of the year."

My dad tenses. "There could be ways to expand to make it more of a year-round destination." I know where Dad's going with this, and I want to tell him not to bother.

This isn't the guy to partner with Lacey on her ideas, no matter how deep his pockets are.

"We're counting on it," Warner says. "But we think our plan is a better option."

"So, the employees—"

"Wouldn't need them," Warner cuts in.

"And the trees—"

CHRISTMAS WITH A CRANK

"We'd keep some of them for privacy, but most of those would go too." He looks at Travis. "Do you have those plans?"

"In the car," he says. "Maybe we could go up to the office and look them over."

Dad inhales. "Fine." He turns and walks toward the truck, and before I follow him, Travis shoots me a look as if I'm going to have any control over how my dad reacts to this.

Warner scoffs. "What's his deal?"

I turn and face him. "His *deal* is that you've just insulted his entire life's work. You've just told him *to his face* that this place he's spent years building has no value to you."

"You've seen the books, right?" he asks, as if this whole conversation is a waste of time and, therefore, money. "I'm sure you agree that this *tree farm*—" I note the disdain in his voice— "is a long way from a successful business. That's just a fact."

"There's a lot more than money that makes a business successful," I say.

He laughs. "Not where I come from."

"Well, that sucks for you then." I give him a once-over.

Another scoff. "Either sell it to me or stay underwater. Your choice. But I guarantee no one else is going to come around with an offer like mine."

Just then, everything comes into focus.

I take a step toward him. "I feel sorry for you."

He looks me up and down. "Yeah, I don't need your pity."

"Actually, you kind of do." I fold my arms and tilt my head at him. "See, you'll never understand the value of watching the sun cast a light over the ridge onto the trees in the morning. You would hate how quiet it is out here or the fact that some nights, it's so clear, you can see every single star. How last month, all my parents had to do to see the northern lights was to walk out the back door. You'll never get how special it is that thousands of people start their holiday season right here, and most of them come back year after year because they like what this place does for their family. People crave what Pine Creek gives them. Tradition. Togetherness. Peace."

Peace.

And there it is.

All this time, Olive was trying to get me to see this place through her eyes.

And it took seeing this place through the eyes of someone who just doesn't get it.

I see her vision for all the things we could do here.

I see why Lacey won't let it go. I see what my parents have worked so hard for.

I understand now.

I see the peace.

CHAPTER 38

OLIVE

J'm trying not to look at the calendar or keep track of the days of the week or think about how the holiday season is already coming to an end.

All the warnings in the world weren't enough to stop me from A. falling in love with Liam and B. falling in love with Pine Creek.

I don't want to say goodbye to either one.

My job is wrapping up, but that hasn't stopped the ideas from exploding. It's sad to think I'll never get to implement most of them.

I stop by The Beanery on my way to work, thinking that soon I'll need to ask them to put me back on the schedule. As I wait for my drink, I spot Lacey sitting at the same table where we dreamt up the plan to save the farm, working on her laptop. She glances up and waves at me.

I grab my mocha and walk over to her.

Her smile is sad. "I don't think it worked."

I sit across from her. "The collective?"

She nods. "I'm here because my dad is meeting with the

buyer and your gross ex-boyfriend right now, and I couldn't risk running into them."

I let my disgust show on my face. "Okay, let's call him your parents' gross Realtor and not link me to him. I had to be delusional to ever think he was a decent human being."

She sighs. "The PV council doesn't want to take it on. They love the thought, but don't have room in their budget for what would essentially be a gift, especially to a business that's not a non-profit. The people I've reached out to are sympathetic, but not willing or able to invest. We need money, not thoughts and prayers."

I take a drink, wishing I could wave a magic wand and make this all okay. For everyone. But I can't. "I'm sorry, Lace."

She blows out a huff of emotion. "It's okay. I'll be okay. It's just hitting me, I guess, that it's really, truly happening. I'm really losing Pine Creek."

I want to say, "We all are," but I don't because I know this loss is ten times worse for her than it is for me.

"Oh, I did some work on a social strategy for you." She turns her laptop around.

"What?" I pull her laptop closer and look at the screen. On it, Lacey has outlined ideas for at least three months' worth of content to help me build an audience online.

"I mean, you'll have to get your website back online and updated, but I think we could plan for a specific launch and build excitement for that."

I scroll through her ideas, gobsmacked at how well-planned out it all is. "Lacey, this is amazing." I look up. "But I'm not great on social media."

She waves me off. "That's what I'm here for. I can help you with all of that."

I press my lips together. "So, you're going to stay around? Even without the farm?"

She nods. "Yeah. I want roots, Olive. I need some time off the road. I don't know where my parents are going yet—I don't even think they know—but I know I belong here."

I smile. "I'm so glad. We can do girls' nights and spa days."

"And get you back to making art," she adds.

Heat rushes to my face. "First, I need to dig myself out of debt. My parents aren't charging interest, but I don't feel right launching something else until I pay them back."

"Well, working here with Jackson isn't going to get you there." She levels my gaze. "Olive, use your gift. You're a little older and a lot wiser now. Plus, you have me. A social media genius with zero education and a double dose of grit. And Phoebe, who you know will help with the numbers."

And Liam, for a few days more, I think.

I chew the inside of my mouth. It's not like she's saying anything new, it's just that now, I'm ready to hear it.

"Okay."

Her eyes light up. "Yeah?"

"Let's do it." It's time. Because she's right. This season of my life has felt like a redirection, and it's led me back to myself. "I'll be smarter and more cautious this time, and really, I have nothing to lose."

"Good, because I just emailed you the plans. Also, I want to hire you." Lacey takes a giant bite of her breakfast sandwich, and I'm suddenly starving.

"You don't have any dogs for me to walk."

"Ha. Ha." She rolls her eyes. "I need a logo." She pulls her laptop back to her side of the table.

"A logo for what?" I take a sip of my drink. "And thank you for the plans."

"I'm going to start my own social media consulting firm. Business? Company? What do I call it?" She laughs. "I have a lot of research to do."

Now I laugh. "Well, I can definitely do that, but you're not paying me for it."

"Eh . . . we'll chat," she says.

I nod and push my chair back, excited for the first time in a long time that I might actually get to make art again. As a job. I stand. "I'll probably see you in a little while."

"I'll be back eventually."

"And Lacey, I really am sorry this hasn't gone the way we wanted it to."

Her smile is sad. "We tried, right?"

As I drive out to the farm to check on all the details for the Christmas Eve Candlelight Walk, my mind wanders. I think about the events that have brought me here. Of course, I have regrets, but the mistakes and failures of the past, even ones in my personal life, have helped me get where I am today.

Yes, I took time off to hide myself away and walk dogs and make coffee. And yes, that meant sticking my gifts in a box and burying them in the garage.

But I don't regret that time. I think I needed it to heal. To forgive myself.

That thought stops me as I make the turn into Pine Creek and drive to the office. I didn't think I needed to forgive myself, but maybe I do. Maybe I've been holding a grudge against myself, punishing myself by withholding this thing I love so much simply because I didn't feel like I deserve it.

I don't want to do that anymore.

I'm smarter now, and I'm surrounded by people who want me to succeed. Who are willing to help make sure I do.

I finally, *finally*, feel ready to try again.

I park my car and pull the business card Phoebe gave me out of my pocket. *Marisol Sanchez: Licensing Agent.*

Normally, I would opt for email, but it's a brave, new Olive Witherby.

"Go for Marisol."

I'm taken aback. I didn't realize people answered the phone like that in real life. "Uh, hi, is this Marisol?"

"Marisol is in a meeting. Can I take a message?"

Of course this is an office number, and of course, she has an assistant. "Uh, yes." *Get a grip, Olive. You are a talented, smart, and creative woman.* "Marisol left her card with my, uh . . . assistant this weekend, wanting to discuss possible representation—"

"Please hold."

I snap my jaw shut, confused, as elevator music starts playing in my ear. It's a slowed-down, instrumental version of "Bye Bye Bye" by NSYNC, which is surprisingly catchy.

I look up as Travis and a smarmy-looking dude in a long, black dress coat exit the office. The guy immediately pulls out his phone, and Travis is smiling when he meets my eyes from across the small parking lot.

He lifts a hand in a wave, then trots over to my car.

Ugh. I could *bye, bye, bye* him.

He makes a motion for me to roll down the window.

Begrudgingly, I do.

"So close to closing this deal," he says. "It's a gem of an offer, too."

My stomach rolls. "Bye Bye Bye" plays in my ear.

"You know," he starts.

Before he even can finish, I blurt out, "I'm seeing someone, Travis."

"Oh." His eyebrows shoot up. "Really?"

"Yes," I say. "And even if I wasn't, I'm not sure how much clearer I can make it that I would never, *ever* entertain the idea of wasting time on someone like you."

"Well, okay." It's a woman's voice in my ear, on the phone that I forgot I was holding. "Glad we got that cleared up."

"Oh my gosh, no, Miss Sanchez—" I pull my attention away from Travis— "Mrs. Sanchez? Marisol? I didn't mean you." I wave Travis off and roll my window back up. "I'm sorry, that was just—never mind."

"I like an assertive woman," she says. "I hope you were telling off someone who deserved it and not talking to yourself in the mirror."

I laugh. "Oh, I absolutely was telling off someone who deserved it," I say. "Ex-boyfriend. Will *not* take a hint."

I glance up and see Liam exit the office building with his dad. He looks so handsome in his jeans and that familiar coat that matches the one his dad is wearing. He's wearing a baseball cap, which will do nothing to shield him from the cold, but looks crazy sexy.

"I assume this is Olive," Marisol says. "I've been hoping you'd call."

After my call with Marisol, who wants me to submit my designs to her as a formality (*what?!*) because she's already seen my work and thinks I've got commercial appeal, (*the heck?!*), I walk into the office where I find Jo, sitting alone at her desk in one of the offices near the back of the open space in the building.

I don't have to be a detective to put the pieces together about the morning she's had and how she's feeling about it.

She looks up and smiles. It's a sad smile, though she does seem genuinely happy to see me. "The candles for the walk arrived this morning."

"Oh, good." I sit in the seat across from her. I don't know if she feels like talking to me, but I do hope she's talking to someone. This change is going to be really emotional.

She reaches into the desk drawer and pulls out an envelope, sliding it across the desk in my direction.

I frown. "What's this?"

"Christmas bonus," she says. "Actually, it's more of a market bonus."

I meet her eyes.

"You did so much work to make that happen," she says. "You earned it."

I try not to think about how different my life would be if I'd started working here right out of college. Would being around Jo and the rest of the Pine Creek staff have been enough to take away the need to prove to everyone that my art was good enough? Would her belief in me have seeped down into my core and made me more patient?

I tuck the envelope inside my bag without looking at the check, thinking that whatever she gave me is going straight toward my debt.

"I saw you kissing my son, by the way."

The comment catches me off guard. If I was drinking something, I would've spit it out all over her desk.

"I'm sorry?"

"I'm not sure if it was meant to be a secret, but neither one of you is very good at hiding anything." Her smile isn't sad anymore. "You seem like you really care about him."

Just the thought of Liam is enough to make me smile. "I really, really do. I have . . . for a long time."

"I think you're good for each other," she says. "And I hope you can find a way to make long distance work."

My heart breaks a little.

"I'm rooting for you," she adds.

"I'm rooting for us too."

And with that, my stomach drops. It's almost Christmas, which means he's going to leave. I can't pretend I'm going to be okay to just walk away after the holidays. A thought flits through my mind, something I hadn't considered before.

Am I willing to uproot my whole life for him? Am I willing to move just to be close to him?

The quiet answer reaches my soul before it reaches my head, and I play the word over on a loop in my mind.

Yes.

CHAPTER 39

LIAM

*T*ime to pitch.

I'm sitting at the desk in my dad's home office, looking over my layout, the breakdown, and the sketches for *Whirlybirds* in preparation for my meeting with Aaron.

Olive walks in with a bottle of water for me and a big mug of hot chocolate for her. "Are you sure you want me in here?"

I smile. "Definitely."

She calms me. The part of me that felt knotted up has softened, a result of letting go of so much anger and embracing so much goodness.

She's wearing a red turtleneck sweater, her blond hair pulled up in a messy ponytail, and she's just about the sexiest thing I've ever seen.

Hopefully I can focus on the call.

"Did you see Lacey's latest video? She shows the entire process of trimming a tree out in the field, cutting it down, hauling it to her room, and decorating it—start to finish—in about forty-eight seconds. It's amazing." She takes a sip of her hot chocolate, and some of the whipped cream hangs around on her upper lip. It's absolutely criminal what that does to me.

"You've got a little—" I point at my mouth, then stand and lean across the desk and kiss her, taking time I don't have to make sure I do it properly.

I pull back and meet her eyes.

"I should get whipped cream on my face more often."

"I wish you would." I go still. "If this goes well, it's because of you."

She shakes her head and stands, moving around the desk and drawing me close. "Nah, this one's all yours, chief."

My laptop sounds with the Zoom ringtone. "Okay, ready?"

She gives me a quick peck on my lips, then pumps her fist. "Let's do this!"

I click the button to accept Aaron's call and find him in his office, as expected. "Afternoon, Fisher," he says.

"Thanks for taking this meeting so close to Christmas," I say.

He gives his head a little shake. "Eh, it's just another day to me, you know how it is."

Across from me, Olive's eyes widen, and she pulls a face. I try not to smile, but she doesn't make it easy.

I look at the pitch on my iPad, then back at Aaron.

"What are we talking about?" Aaron asks, because I never gave his assistant a topic for this meeting. "I assume you have issues with your current workload or the deadlines?"

My eyes jump to Olive's then back to the screen.

"No, not that at all, it's something else I wanted—"

Frustration winds itself into a tight ball in my belly. I think back on all the times I wanted to speak up, to say, "no, this isn't okay with me," but didn't.

It hits me—the things my silence has cost me.

He jumps in. "I just want to say, if this is about the sequel to *Castle Crusade*, sorry man, I'm not budging on that one. It needs fresh eyes, and we really need you for other things. Best you get out from the shadow of that one, right? Get our little Boy

Wonder on a project that will make up for the last three tank-ing." He chuckles like he's said something funny.

Olive's eyes practically bug out of her head.

"Yeah, about that—" I start.

He jumps in again, "Look, I'm doing this for you, okay? I don't want you to peak at, what are you, thirty-eight?"

"Thirty-one," I correct.

"Yeah, well, I don't want you to be washed up at thirty-one, that's all I'm saying."

A switch flips in my head. Normally I'd be all balled-up fists and flinging oil filters.

But today? With Olive? I'm not.

"I disagree," I say, voice calm. "I don't think I've even scratched the surface of what I'm capable of. I just don't do well when people put me in a box."

I don't like to be restricted. I like to be free to make my own choices. My own decisions. And if I mess up, then I'll own it because the mistakes are my own. I won't have to take the blame for a failure that doesn't belong to me.

I look down at the images of my game.

Do I really want Aaron to be in control of this?

"Parameters are part of the process, Fisher," he says. "Now, what's up? Why am I here?"

I drag my attention from the screen to the iPad, then over to Olive. "Actually, sir, I wanted to thank you face to face for the opportunity to work for you and learn from you and the rest of the Arcadia team. It's been a truly incredible experience." I pause, aware that Olive has started to lean forward in her chair.

"But it's time for me to move on."

Across from me, Olive gasps.

In front of me, Aaron frowns. "I don't understand."

"I quit," I say. "I'm going to do my own thing for a while."

"You know if you quit, the deal we have in place goes away. We don't have to take you back."

I nod. "I'm aware." People in my field will think I've lost my mind, but Olive is right. There's no reason to hold on to a dream after I've realized I hate it.

For the first time ever, I see panic settle on Aaron's face. He clears his throat. "Maybe we take the holidays to think about this? Not make a hasty decision?" He starts fumbling with papers on his desk.

"No, I've thought about it quite a bit. I'm good."

"I think you're making a mistake," Aaron says into his webcam.

"I don't," I say matter-of-factly. "This just isn't the life I want anymore. Plus, I've got a new idea for a game," I look up at Olive, who looks as though she's about to jump out of her skin. "And I found the perfect person to brainstorm it with." And I'd much rather it have her fingerprints on it than his.

"New, uh, new game?" He leans over and snaps at someone off screen, waving his arm to get their attention.

"Yep."

"Any chance you, uh, you came up with that on company time, using our laptops or equipment?"

I lean in. "Nope."

He fumbles around with a few more things, then mutes his end.

"Hey, Aaron, I'm pretty busy here. What do you say we end things on a good note?"

Aaron taps a button and the mute icon disappears.

His mouth forms a tight line. "How can you walk away from Arcadia?"

I glance at Olive. "Because I've got everything I need right here."

He raises his eyebrows, like he can't believe what he's just heard. He sighs, and I hope that means it's dawning on him what he's losing. "Okay, well, I wish you all the best then."

"Thanks. You too."

I close my laptop to reveal a radiant, teary Olive staring at me.

"What did you just do?" she asks.

"I said what I want," I say. "And what I don't want."

She smiles. She gets it, without having to explain the whole tangle of thoughts wrapped up in this decision.

"I just quit my job." I lean back in my chair and scrub a hand down my face, over my beard.

She jumps up and practically vaults to the other side of the desk. "You can make this game on your own." She lands in my lap and wraps her arms up around my neck. "You can call all the shots and make it exactly what you want. You have such great instincts—it's going to be amazing." She kisses me, her body melting into mine, and all the stress of what's to come disappears.

I kiss her back, pretty sure that if I never got another job, I could sustain myself solely on this right here.

When she pulls back and as I search her eyes, I see a question there. "What is it?"

"This decision wasn't . . . about me, right?" she asks.

I shake my head. "I'd do just about anything for you, Olive, but no. I had to make this decision for myself. I've been unhappy for a while and being back here just showed me I can choose something different than what I originally planned."

At that, she smiles. "It's funny because I'm doing the same thing."

"Oh?"

"I spoke to that licensing agent," she says. "I think she's going to sign me. And Lacey's going to help me get the word out about my brand new *online* store." I watch the smile light up her face, and I get it. This feeling of finally figuring out how to let go of the past and move forward.

"So, what now?" she asks. "Will you go back to Indy?"

"Yeah."

I feel her deflate a little, but she nods.

"I have to clean out my condo to get my stuff back here."

She presses her lips together to try and conceal her smile.

She leans in and right next to my ear she whispers, "I'll hire the movers."

CHAPTER 40

OLIVE

*W*e're about to leave Brant's home office on the main floor of the old farmhouse when Liam says, "Wait, Olive?"

I turn back. "Yeah?"

"Let's not tell anyone about this yet."

I level his gaze. "We aren't very good at keeping secrets. Your mom saw us kissing."

He laughs. "She has eyes everywhere."

I wrap my arms around him. "I won't say anything. It's not my news to share."

"I just—" he sighs— "I don't want to get Lacey's hopes up. This changes things . . .but it doesn't change *everything*."

"Right." I nod. "You've changed your mind about your job, but not about the farm."

He gives me a soft shrug. "There's a lot to consider."

I try to cover my disappointment with one forceful nod.

He kisses my forehead, and I lean into him a little longer than I should. I want to give him my list of reasons he should run Pine Creek with Lacey, but I don't. Because he still has

CHRISTMAS WITH A CRANK

dreams and things he wants to do. The game we worked so hard on to design.

And I'd never ask him to give that up.

He's not going back to Indy, but that doesn't mean he's moving back home. *Remember that, Olive.* Where we're concerned, nothing's changed.

We're still on borrowed time.

We walk into the kitchen and find Jo wrapping Christmas gifts on the counter.

"Oh, should Liam not come in here?" I ask, covering his eyes.

"It's fine," Jo says. "These are for a Pine Creek angel family."

Liam and I each sit in a stool across the counter from her. There's a big box of new toys on the floor next to her, along with some clothes, three shoeboxes, and another box behind her that I can't see inside of.

"You guys still do that?" Liam asks.

"Oh, yes!" She beams. "We haven't missed a year since we took over." She walks over to the built-in desk and pulls a big envelope out of the drawer. She hands it to Liam.

"I haven't heard about this," I say.

"We don't advertise it." Jo walks back to the half-wrapped gift.

Inside the envelope, there are countless handwritten notes and letters and cards. Liam and I flip through the notes, all thanking "Mr. B and Jo."

He explains it to me. "Every year, Mom and Dad quietly put out feelers to find families in need, then supply them with a full Christmas spread—dinner, gifts, a tree, the works."

Jo pulls a piece of tape from the dispenser and sticks it on the box to secure the paper, while my eyes scan the letters—heartfelt, overwhelmed, grateful people—every single one so blessed by something Liam's parents do without anyone knowing.

I take out a small, folded piece of paper with a kid's drawing of a tricycle on the front and the words "Thank You" in large, blocky letters.

"I keep them right here in the kitchen, and whenever things start to feel really hard, I take them out and read them. Partly because it reminds me that no matter how difficult things get, some people would love to have what we have. But also it reminds me that even in our most challenging times, we can find ways to help other people. It's the Pine Creek way." She yanks at the tape and finds herself at the end of the roll. "Well, shoot. I've got more in my room. Be right back."

After she's gone, I look at Liam, who's holding a folded sheet of paper a lot like the one in my hands. "What are you thinking?"

He sets the handmade card back on the pile. "Just that there's no way this Warner guy is going to do right by the people of this community." He sighs. "I'm not sure we can match his offer though."

I fill in the blanks and come to the conclusion that "this Warner guy" is Travis's buyer, a man Liam has told me almost nothing about, but who, I can already tell, is not someone any of us want to associate with.

I cover his hand with mine. "But look at the legacy they're leaving behind. I mean, maybe things are changing, but your parents aren't. I bet they do this for families in Colorado too, or wherever they end up."

He nods. "I know. But it won't feel the same. Or right."

Jo returns with another roll of tape. "Do you guys want to help me wrap?"

I stand. "I'd love to."

She smiles.

Liam doesn't. "I have a few things I need to take care of if it's okay with you, Ma?"

"Of course."

He looks at me. "Catch up later for dinner?"

"I'm having dinner with Lacey and Phoebe." I smile sweetly. "We're going to talk about you the entire time."

"Don't tell me you're becoming friends with my sister." He grumbles, and he reminds me of a grumpy, old man.

"Oh, it's a done deal," I say. "I got her a best friend's necklace for Christmas."

Jo laughs.

Liam shakes his head. He kisses me on the cheek, then starts to go. I follow after him, just out of Jo's earshot, and ask, "You okay?" Because what if he's having second thoughts about quitting his job?

He smiles. "I'm good. But you don't get to be nosy at Christmas."

My eyebrows shoot up. "Are you going shopping?!"

He kisses me. It feels comforting and familiar, but entirely new all at the same time.

"Okay, love you!" I turn around and freeze, realizing too late what I've just said. I cringe so big he can probably tell just by looking at the back of my head. I close my eyes and take a step—hoping we're going to pretend I didn't just say that—but before I can make another move, he says my name. I slowly turn back, the cringe still evident on my face.

I smile. It's awkward. "Sorry—I . . . it just slipped . . ."

"Love you too." His eyes pin me in place, and my pulse quickens.

"You do?" I whisper.

"Always have," he says.

I press my lips together and do a little curtsy, because my embarrassment turned my face into a hot ball of fire, and I don't know how to walk back into the kitchen gracefully.

I resist the urge to kiss him again, instead choosing to plaster on a smile and walk back into the kitchen.

Jo is smiling, but she doesn't look at me. I hold back my own smile, pick up a Barbie doll and start wrapping, thinking that this might be the happiest I've ever been.

The busyness of the season winds down. Liam and I help deliver the angel gifts to a single mom and her four kids. I haul in wrapped presents, many of which are necessities like school supplies and new shoes, while Liam and his dad set up a small Christmas tree in the window.

A young boy watches as Liam pulls presents from the box and puts them under the tree. One gift, clearly a skateboard, catches the kid's eye. Liam looks at the tag on the gift. "Are you Noah?"

The boy nods.

"Looks like Santa did right by you this year." He tucks it under the tree, and the kid jumps up to help with the rest of the gifts. "Is there one for Sadie?"

Liam searches the box as I carry another box over to where they're kneeling. "Looks like there are a few for Sadie." He picks one up and hands it to Noah.

Noah shakes the box, then whispers, "Do you think that's a Barbie?"

Liam glances at me, then back to Noah. "I guess we'll have to wait to find out."

"Sadie!" Noah calls out. "You're getting presents!"

Jo is going over cooking instructions with the young mom, who's bouncing a baby on her hip. The house is small and sparse, and Lacey is filling it with twinkle lights and a few well-placed Christmas decorations.

The mom offers us all a hot cup of wassail, telling us it's a family favorite that she makes every year, which we're all happy to try.

I make a note, because this warm, apple-y, cinnamon-y,

spice-y goodness is *so* tasty. I wish we'd found it sooner—it would've been a great addition to the Christmas menu in the café.

We spend about an hour chatting and hearing her story, and then, when it's time to go, Noah tugs on Liam's sleeve. Liam kneels and Noah whispers something in his ear.

Liam's eyes go wide, and then he presses an index finger over his lips. "Our secret."

Noah winks over-dramatically, and I smile. How someone who initially seems as grumpy as Liam comes across can be this good with kids is a mystery to me.

But everything about my life lately has been a surprise. A surprise I wouldn't trade for anything.

Once we're in the truck headed for my house, I scoot over so my thigh is pressed against Liam's. It's how two high schoolers might ride in a pickup truck on the day he asked her to be his girlfriend, but I don't care.

He drapes his right arm around me, and I rest my head on his shoulder. We drive like this for a few minutes, and then I whisper, "What was the secret?"

I don't have to look at Liam to know he's smiling. "Sadie got her Barbie."

I sit up. "How does he know?"

"He opened the end of the present, then stuck the tape back on." He chuckles to himself. "Good kids."

"Really good." I don't say so, but it was nice not to think about Pine Creek or the sale or our last Christmas or where Liam's going to move or what's going to happen with us for a little while. It was nice to set all my problems aside and bless someone else.

I decide at that moment that even if Pine Creek no longer exists, this tradition can carry on.

I'll make sure of it.

CHAPTER 41

OLIVE

*C*hristmas Eve morning, I wake up to the obnoxious buzzing of my phone on the nightstand.

I pick it up and look at it, bleary-eyed, when I see a photo of Liam on the screen.

I smile. "Hello?"

"Did I wake you?"

"Yes," I say. "And I was having a really good dream too."

"About me?"

"About pizza."

He laughs. "I wondered if you could come for breakfast."

I sit up, stretching and shaking off the sleep. "Oh, I don't want to impose. Last Pine Creek Christmas and everything."

"I want you there," he says. "And I'm in your driveway."

"What?" I throw the covers off and walk over to my bedroom window, which has a clear view of my driveway, where, sure enough, Liam's truck is parked. I laugh. "What are you doing here, creeper?"

"Came to pick you up," he says. "You know, if you're hungry."

"I *did* miss dinner last night," I say. "So I hope there's a lot of food." I walk over to my closet and do a quick scan for an appropriate outfit. "Are you sure it's okay that I come? I mean, I don't want to crash your party."

"It's breakfast," he says. "And my family wants you there."

"Okay, fine. Give me a few minutes to get ready, and I'll be right out."

After I make myself presentable, I pull on my coat, boots and knit stocking cap then trudge out to his truck.

I get in and find him staring at me. "What?"

"Gorgeous."

"Delirious."

He leans across the cab and kisses me. When he pulls back, I frown. "We could just stay here."

He laughs. "No, there are cinnamon rolls waiting for us."

"Oh, I see where I rate."

"Yeah, it's pretty much cinnamon rolls, pie, a good sandwich, those mozzarella sticks from Joe's, and then you." He pauses. "No, wait. Hank, *then* you."

I slug him.

We drive in the most comfortable early morning silence, and I let my mind wander about anything that isn't *what is going to happen to the farm?* Still, I note the twinge of sadness at the possibility of it all coming to an end.

Liam quit his job, yes. But there's still the matter of the future of Pine Creek.

The truck ambles up the gravel driveway and the big, white farmhouse comes into view. I'm filled with an instant pang of nostalgia. I love it here.

"When you showed that Warner guy around, did he see this?" I ask.

"No," Liam says. "He wasn't interested."

I sigh. "He wasn't?"

"Nope."

"Such a shame," I say. "If they do go through with the sale, maybe they'll at least keep the house."

"Hearing this guy talk, I don't think he wants to keep anything," Liam says.

He parks in the driveway behind Lacey's van, and I think about how we're all embarking on new adventures at the same time. Except Phoebe, the most unexpectedly stable one of all my friends.

Inside, we're met with the smell of cinnamon and coffee.

"Olive!" Lacey is wearing pink and green Christmas pajamas and a Santa hat, holding a mug of coffee and eating puppy chow, Chex cereal drenched in melted chocolate and peanut butter, then coated with powdered sugar. A culinary delicacy, in my opinion.

"You're already eating," Liam says.

"Just a light snack." She grins, then looks at me. "Is your Bluetooth on?"

"Uh, I think so?" I pull out my phone as an Airdrop notification shows up on the screen. I accept it and see a video Lacey made showing off my booth at the market. It's her and Phoebe, dancing around with the cards and puzzles and T-shirts and water bottles that used to line the walls of my shop.

"I'll send you the audio, but I thought this would be a fun one for your TikTok account."

"I don't have a TikTok account," I say. "I think I'm actually too old for TikTok."

"You're not," she says. "I mean, you're pushing it, but you've got a few good years left."

I laugh.

"I was bored last night, so I made about six videos for you."

"Are you serious?"

She smiles. "Merry Christmas."

I smile back. "Thanks."

"All right, family," Jo says, pulling a pan of cinnamon rolls from the oven. "Gather round." She looks at me. "Olive, you can take your coat off. Liam, be a gentleman and hang up her coat."

I smile at Liam, then unzip my coat to reveal, once again, the coconuts and threaded chest hair, in all their glory.

Lacey barks out a laugh, which leads to giggles all around. "I heard the story, but now I am so glad I get to see it for myself."

I grin. "I figured it was fitting to celebrate the end of the holiday season the same way I celebrated the beginning."

Liam takes my coat and kisses my cheek, whispering, "I love you, you little weirdo," in my ear before walking away.

Lacey laughs again. "That's seriously the best. I think our family needs its own ugly Christmas sweater tradition every year from now on."

"I'm game," I say, shocked to discover I actually mean it. I was initially so embarrassed to be seen in this hideous sweater, but now, after only a few weeks, I'm so much more comfortable in my skin.

My mother is going to be so proud.

"All right, everyone. Time for family Santa gifts," Jo says.

My eyes go wide. "Wait, what?" I look at Liam. "You didn't say anything about gifts!"

He scrunches his nose and waves me off, as if to say, *don't worry about it,* but I am worried. What kind of impression am I going to make if I'm the only one who has nothing to give?

Lacey pulls a small box from behind the toaster. "I got Dad." She slides it across the counter, and he opens it to reveal a vintage Chevy keychain.

She smirks at him. "The perfect gift for the Ford-lover, don't you think?"

"Oh, I see how it is," he cracks, giving her a rough side hug. He's pretending to be annoyed but does a bad job of hiding his amusement.

"Can I go next?" Liam asks.

His dad nods.

Liam reaches into the pocket of his hoodie and pulls out a small, thick box and hands it to me. "First, Olive."

347

I frown. "I didn't know we were doing gifts," I announce again.

"It's fine," he says. "I didn't want you to have to bring something."

I scan the circle and find all eyes are on me, something that surprisingly doesn't make me uneasy at all. I tear the wrapping paper off and open the box to reveal a small, clear block and in the center of it, a bright green four leaf clover.

I look at Liam.

"You gave it to me when we moved," he says.

"To keep you from forgetting me," I say.

He shrugs. "I guess it worked."

My breath catches in my throat. "Is this the same one?"

He nods.

"You kept it this whole time?"

Another nod.

"Oh my gosh." I look at his parents. "Is it okay if I kiss him in front of you?"

Everyone laughs as I throw my arms around Liam's neck and kiss him through tears that I can't keep from falling. "Thank you."

He smiles and kisses me again.

"Ew," Lacey says. "That's so weird."

"I have something for you too." He looks at his sister, and her eyes go wide.

"I thought Mom had my name," she says.

"So did I." Mom frowns.

"Think of this as a bonus." Liam moves across the kitchen and pulls another wrapped gift out of the cookie jar and hands it to Lacey.

Lacey's face lights up. "Are you making a video game based on my hashtag van life?"

He chuckles. "Not quite."

I reach over and slip my hand in his as he watches Lacey

with the look of someone who is anticipating a huge reaction to the perfect gift.

I look at his mom, then his dad, and it's unclear if they know what's inside this present, and now I wish he'd clued me in.

Lacey gets the wrapping off of the box, then pulls out a small stack of folded papers.

She opens them and as her eyes scan the pages, she gasps. Her hand covers her mouth, and tears spill down her cheeks. "Liam . . . what?"

I frown. "What is it?"

"Is this for real?" She asks. "Like, for *real*?!"

His parents are both smiling, and it's obvious that I'm the only one who has no idea what was inside that box.

Lacey looks at me. "Did you know about this?" Her eyes are bright with a mix of shock and excitement.

"I still don't know about it," I say. "What is it?"

She holds it out to me with trembling hands.

At the top it reads "Transfer of Ownership," and at the bottom are Liam's and his parents' signatures.

There's a blank spot for Lacey to sign, too.

"It's a transfer of ownership deed," Liam says.

Tears spring to my eyes. "What?"

"I couldn't tell you before because I needed to work it out with my parents, but—" he holds his hands out in front of him— "I decided to stay. We're going to be partners." He looks at Lacey. "If you still want to."

She rushes around the counter and hugs him so forcefully he loses his footing for a second.

"You're staying?" I ask, registering the shock in my own voice.

"Yes," he says. "I wanted it to be a surprise."

I cover my face with my hands and Liam pulls me into the hug.

"How?" I ask. "I mean—how?"

"I promise, you'll get the full story," he says, still being squeezed by Lacey.

"And we're going to keep a share," his mom says. She looks at Brant. "Silent partners."

He grumbles comically, then crosses his arms over his chest.

"He's got the silent part down." She pats his shoulder.

Lacey wipes her cheeks dry. "I should be offended that you wouldn't do this until Liam got on board."

"You could," Jo says, "but one third of the total amount is very different from one half."

"Besides, I'm the muscle," Liam says.

"Except I'm way better in the fields," Lacey says. "Ask Manny."

"You each bring different things to the table, and the way we see it, it's a perfect pairing." Jo is beaming. It's the best possible outcome.

I look at Liam. "What made you change your mind?"

He smiles back at me. "This crazy girl who wouldn't quit until she showed me the last, best Pine Creek Christmas."

My cheeks flush. "No. Way."

"Partly," he says. "That and I wasn't about to let that tool Travis brought out here bulldoze our home."

Brant laughs. "I second that."

Liam looks at me. "I finally realized what's been missing from my life."

"Reindeer?" I quip.

He smirks, shaking his head. "You."

I cover my mouth with my hands, still finding it hard to let myself believe it.

"I mean, also peace, but mostly you." He grins.

"I can't believe it." I shake my head. "You're going to stay. You actually *want* to stay."

He takes a step toward me, leading me away from the others,

who dutifully start chatting with each other to give us the illusion of privacy. "I actually want to stay."

"This is a big deal," I say. "What about your game?"

"I want to do it on my own. Same way I made *Castle Crusade*. I did that one between classes in a dorm room." He smiles. "Imagine what I can accomplish here."

"I would've moved to Indianapolis for you," I say, meaning it. "You know that, right?"

"Now you don't have to." He pulls me into his arms and studies my face. "We're going to need you. Are you up for it?"

"Absolutely," I say. "I can't think of a better ending to the last, best Christmas than finding out it's not the last anything after all."

He smiles.

I smile.

"Cinnamon rolls are getting cold," Jo calls out.

Liam smirks down at me, and without looking away, he says, "We'll be right back."

He pulls me around the corner, into the living room, where we're out of sight of his family. He takes my face in his hands and kisses me so sweetly, I melt, right there in his arms. My arms tighten around him as I pull him closer, the kiss leaving me breathless and undone.

"I think I'm gonna kiss you for the rest of my life," he says, forehead pressed to mine.

"And I think I'm gonna let you."

THE END

ABOUT THE AUTHOR

Courtney Walsh is the Carol award-winning author of twenty-five novels and two novellas. Her debut novel, *A Sweethaven Summer*, was a *New York Times* and *USA Today* e-book best-seller and a Carol Award finalist in the debut author category. In addition, she has written two craft books and several full-length musicals. Courtney lives with her husband and three children in Illinois, where she co-owns a performing arts studio and youth theatre with her business partner and best friend—her husband.

Visit her online at www.courtneywalshwrites.com

ACKNOWLEDGMENTS

Special Thanks to Alexa Zurcher of Pippi Post for the creation of the Pine Creek logo and map. I've long admired Alexa's work, and it largely inspired Olive's profession.

To Sophie Riley, a rising literary star and brilliant artist. Thank you for your work on this cover.

Thank you, Adam, for everything, always. And to my kids for becoming my friends.

To Becky Wade, Katie Ganshert and Melissa Tagg for your friendship. I am so thankful.

A LOVE LETTER

FROM THE AUTHOR

If there's one thing I know for sure, it's that the world needs happy things. For years, I felt a little like Olive, like I needed to write a certain way to be legitimate. It's like that sometimes for creative people—and many of us believe the lie that art needs to be dark, serious, heavy or emotional to mean something.

That's not my goal. Not with any aspect of my life. Do I love a good drama? Yes. But I also love providing happy, little escapes for readers.

I love being able to share stories that make my heart swoon, to create characters I can relate to, and to provide the happiest endings so when you need a little pick-me-up, you can find it in these pages.

The fact that you are here, reading my book, is something of a wonder to me. I still have to pinch myself every time I think that this is what I get to do for a living. What a gift!

And you make that possible.

I know you have so many choices when it comes to what you pick up to read, and I'm absolutely thrilled you've chosen to give this book a try. I hope you loved the story as much as I loved writing it.

If you did, I'd be honored if you'd share it, review it, tell your reader friends about it, and I genuinely hope it brought you Christmas joy this holiday season.

As always, please don't hesitate to reach out. I love to hear from my readers and love to make new book-loving friends!

Have a happy holiday & may your days be merry, bright & bookish!

With gratitude & love,

Courtney

Made in the USA
Columbia, SC
29 November 2024

47820496R00219